**Praise for James Deegan:**

'Brilliant.'
*Jeffrey Archer*

'Inevitably Deegan will be compared to Andy McNab and Chris Ryan, but he adds his own brand of contemporary authenticity. Carr is a hero for our times.'
*Daily Mail*

'As close as it gets to the real thing.'
*Mark 'Billy' Billingham MBE, former SAS Warrant Officer and star of TV's* SAS Who Dares Wins

'James Deegan writes with masterful authority and unsurpassed experience.'
*Chantelle Taylor, Combat Medic and author of* Battleworn

'Authentic detail and heart stopping narrative grips you from the outset bringing the shadowy world of today's special forces bursting in to life in a v … 't hope for

*Major Chris H … d* Extreme

'Exposes the … h intensity

*Bob She … author*



'Move over Andy McNab and Chris Ryan, there's a new SAS veteran writing thrillers and he's good. Very good.'
*Stephen Leather*

'An impressive debut, that rates up there with Gerald Seymour and Fredrick Forsyth; blending a realistic vernacular of special forces soldiering to make a cracking read with page turning pace from start to finish.'
*Stuart Tootal*

JAMES DEEGAN MC spent five years in the Parachute Regiment, and seventeen years in the SAS.

He served for most of that time in a Sabre Squadron, from Trooper to Squadron Sergeant Major, and saw almost continuous service on operations in Northern Ireland, the Balkans, Africa, Iraq, Afghanistan, and elsewhere. He fought in both Gulf Wars, and was on both occasions amongst the first Coalition soldiers to cross the border into Iraq. He was twice decorated for gallantry and, on his retirement from the Special Air Service, as a Regimental Sergeant Major, he was described by his commanding officer as 'one of the most operationally experienced SAS men of his era'.

He now works in the security industry, in some of the world's most hostile and challenging environments. His first John Carr novel, *Once a Pilgrim*, was published in January 2018.

# The Angry Sea

James Deegan

ONE PLACE. MANY STORIES

This novel is entirely a work of fiction. The names, characters and incidents portrayed in it are the work of the author's imagination. Any resemblance to actual persons, living or dead, events or localities is entirely coincidental.

HQ
An imprint of HarperCollins*Publishers* Ltd
1 London Bridge Street
London SE1 9GF

This paperback edition 2019

1

First published in Great Britain by
HQ, an imprint of HarperCollins*Publishers* Ltd 2019



James Deegan asserts the moral right to be identified as the author of this work.
A catalogue record for this book is available from the British Library.

ISBN: 978-0-00-822956-6

This book is produced from independently certified FSC™ paper to ensure responsible forest management.

For more information visit: www.harpercollins.co.uk/green

Printed and bound in Great Britain by
CPI Group, Croydon, CR0 4YY

TO ALL THE BRAVE MEN I HAVE KNOWN WHO WILL NOT SEE OLD AGE. THEY ACCEPTED THE RISKS, THEY STEPPED INTO THE BREACH, AND PAID THE ULTIMATE PRICE.

*UTRINQUE PARATUS*
*WHO DARES WINS*

## AUTHOR'S NOTE:

THIS IS A WORK OF FICTION.
NONE OF THE EVENTS DESCRIBED HAPPENED,
AND NONE OF THE CHARACTERS CONTAINED IN
THE NARRATIVE ARE BASED ON ANY PERSONS,
LIVING OR DEAD, UNLESS EXPRESSLY STATED.

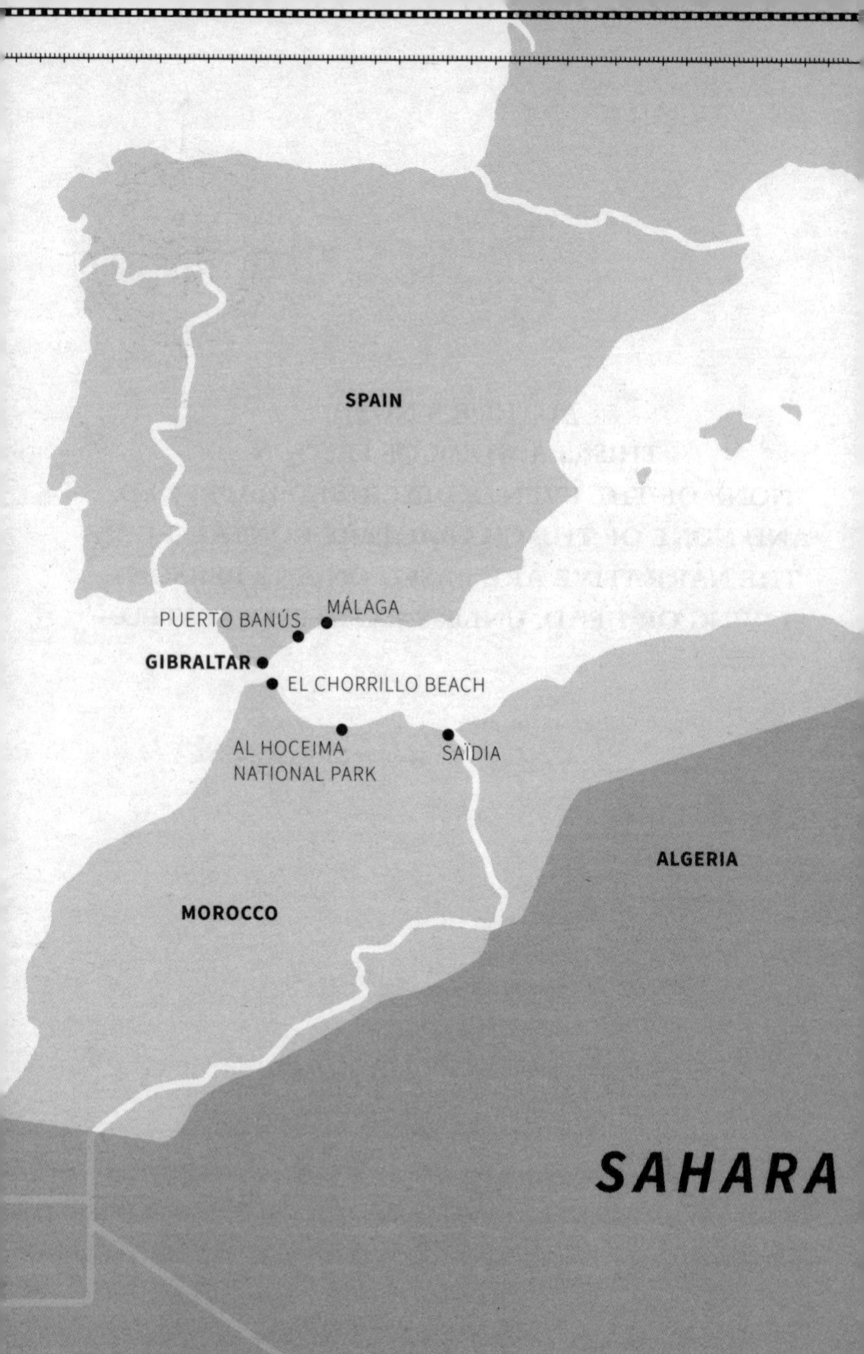

SPAIN
MÁLAGA
PUERTO BANÚS
GIBRALTAR
EL CHORRILLO BEACH
AL HOCEIMA
NATIONAL PARK
SAÏDIA
ALGERIA
MOROCCO
SAHARA

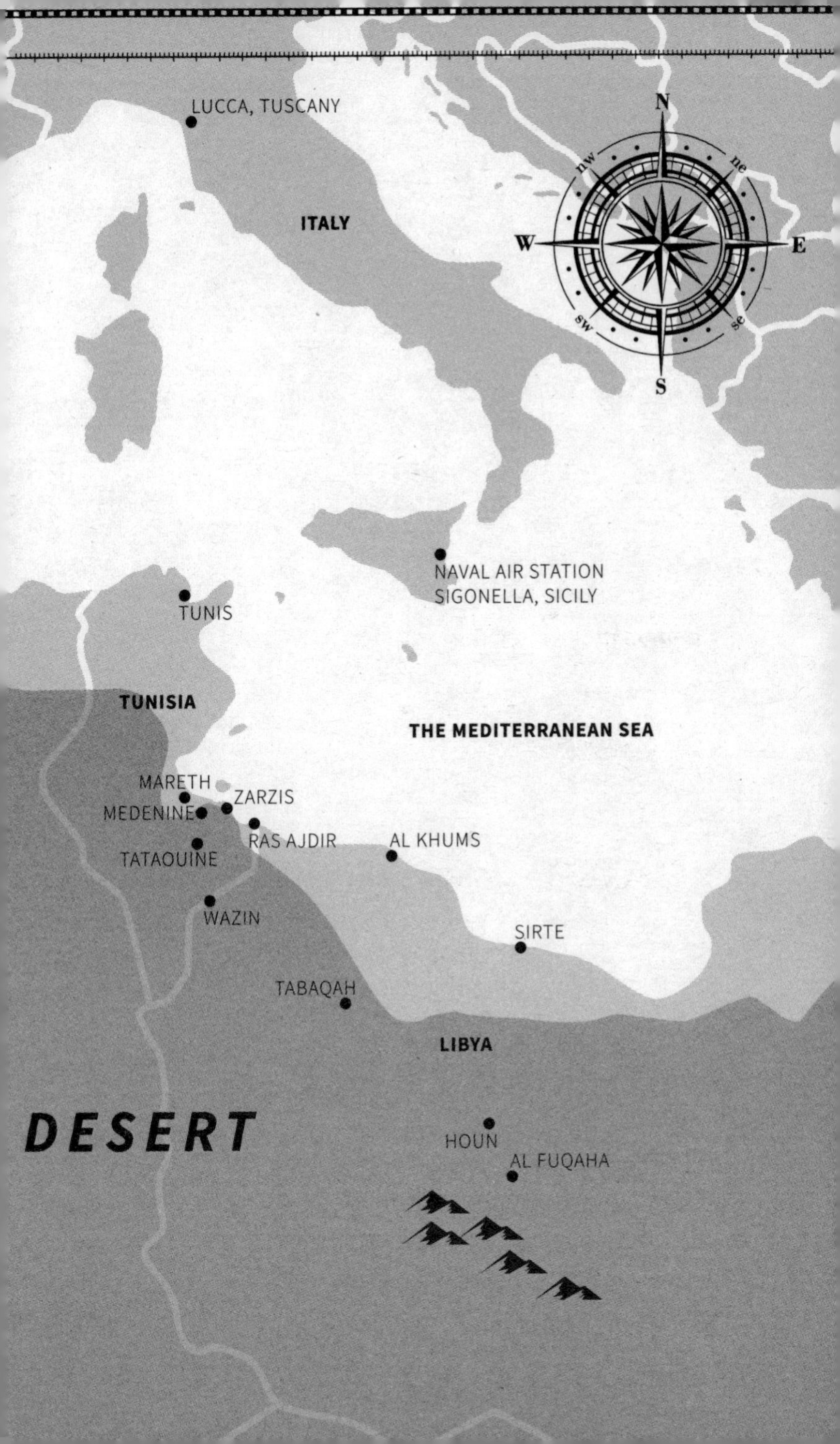
LUCCA, TUSCANY
N
nw
ne
W
E
sw
se
S
ITALY
NAVAL AIR STATION
SIGONELLA, SICILY
TUNIS
TUNISIA
THE MEDITERRANEAN SEA
MARETH
MEDENINE
ZARZIS
RAS AJDIR
AL KHUMS
TATAOUINE
WAZIN
SIRTE
TABAQAH
LIBYA
DESERT
HOUN
AL FUQAHA

*O turn your eyes to where your children stand*

From *The Story of Hassan of Baghdad and How He Came to Make the Golden Journey to Samarkand* (1913)
JAMES ELROY FLECKER (1884–1915)

# PROLOGUE

THE TWO MEN knew each other of old, having fought as brothers-in-arms in various places over many years, but they had not seen each other in person for a long time.

Life for men like them had become a good deal more challenging and dangerous since September 11, 2001, so their contact was restricted to darknet chatrooms, snatched conversations on encoded VOIP systems, and, once in a blue moon, cryptic notes passed via trusted intermediaries.

Their secret conversations through these unorthodox channels were often surprisingly banal. One would grumble about the filthy weather in the grubby little town in which he was currently hiding, and the other would counter with complaints about the terrible food in his present, miserable location.

On the rare occasions when the mood was lighter, they talked of happier times, and of their families. Each had a wife and children back home, but neither expected ever again to kiss his wife nor hold his children; the path they walked was a path of shadows and sorrow, and it led in one direction only.

Their lives were full of uncertainty, and privation, and fear, and precious few comforts and the wise man cut his ties, of friendship and of blood, permanently.

Death stalked them daily, and, being only human, they

sometimes wondered how it was that they, who had given so much, had ended up living like rats, while others, who had given so little, lived like kings.

Why were *their* days all stone and no fruit, all grit and no pearl?

Of course, each tried hard to cast this unworthy thought from his mind; it was dangerous to harbour such ideas – and not merely in the spiritual sense.

That had been the way of their lives for so long that they had almost – almost – forgotten what it was like to live normally.

And then, one day, the younger of the two men contacted his older friend via a mobile telephony app with secure, end-to-end encryption.

After the usual small talk, the younger man – a giant Chechen called Khasmohmad Kadyrov, who was presently living in a cramped room in a safe house in Cairo – made a tentative suggestion.

*Very tentative.*

What, he asked, if there were a way in which they might *both* strike the enemy *and* – and he tried hard not to be vulgar about this – achieve a more… *earthly* reward for themselves?

At first, the older man – a Yemeni called Saeed al-Shafra – was sceptical, and even hostile.

But this was something of an act.

Al-Shafra was nearly sixty, now, and he had grown tired, and listless, and, as he looked around the spartan room, in his modest, baked-mud home, in the compound on the edge of the dusty village in the dreary Balochi outpost of Nushki, it occurred to him that he was perhaps even a little bitter about the turns his life had taken.

'Go on,' he said.

'I have a friend,' said Kadyrov, hesitantly. 'A good friend, from the old days. I mean, a *long* way back – he's from Vedeno, fought with the 055 at Mazar-e Sharif.'

'I missed that party,' said the Yemeni. 'So many men, slaughtered like goats.'

'Indeed,' said Kadyrov. 'But my friend was lucky. He got injured, some shrapnel took a chunk out of his right calf, so he got taken away before the massacre.'

'In that sense,' said the older man, 'he *was* fortunate.'

'I saw him last in Now Zad,' said the Chechen. 'Or perhaps the Korengal. I can't remember, exactly. He's a fighter, but lucky again, because the *Americans*' – he almost spat the word – 'they don't know him. This is the beauty of it. Two years ago, he's in Islamabad, he flies to Turkey, then travels to Germany. Nobody says a word to him, nobody even looks at him. For the last year, he is in England, in London. There he has made a very good contact, with someone who has a very interesting situation. Very interesting indeed. But we need funding and I know that you can find money for us.'

Khasmohmad Kadyrov talked some more, and the Yemeni called al-Shafra listened, and he smiled.

And the more he listened, the more he smiled.

And when Kadyrov had finished talking, Saeed al-Shafra looked out of his window, across the empty, sun-baked Balochi desert, which lay between his humble home and Afghanistan's distant Helmand River, and he chuckled.

'Oh, Khasmohmad,' he said. 'Khasmohmad, *Khasmohmad*. Truly, this is a gift from Allah.'

# PART ONE

# I.

AT SEVEN-THIRTY, half an hour before unlocking, the prison came banging and rattling and echoing to life.

But Zeff Mahsoud and his cellmate had been up since well before sunrise, in order to perform their *fajr*.

Now they sat facing each other, Mahsoud on a tubular chair pushed hard against the cream-painted wall, the other man on his steel-framed bed.

'I have a good feeling about today, brother,' said the cellmate. 'I think it will be good news.'

'*Inshallah*, Hamid,' said Mahsoud. 'Time will tell.'

'Be confident. Tonight you will be in your wife's arms. Tomorrow…' Hamid paused, and lowered his voice. HMP Belmarsh was not a place which rewarded the incautious. 'Tomorrow, who knows?'

Mahsoud smiled. 'Who knows indeed?' he said.

Lazily, he got up and walked to the cell door, bending down to pick up the breakfast tray which had been handed over the previous night.

A plastic bowl of own-brand cornflakes, a carton of UHT milk, and a bread roll: he curled up his lip.

'You'll visit my friend?' said Hamid. 'Like I said?'

'If I am released…'

'You will be.'

'*If* I am released, then yes, I will visit your friend.'

'He will be most interested to meet you. I think he will have very interesting proposals for you.'

'I hope so.'

'I *know* so. He has big plans. *Dramatic* plans.'

Zeff Mahsoud smiled.

Cornflakes in hand, he walked over to the small window, and looked up at the clear blue skies over south-east London.

Seven or eight miles away, over Bromley, a passenger jet was climbing away through 6,000ft.

Mahsoud watched it go.

Three hundred souls and a hundred tonnes of aviation fuel, in a thin aluminium tube.

So thin.

So vulnerable.

'I have plans of my own, brother,' he said.

*But I'm afraid I cannot share them with you,* he thought.

# 2.

SEVERAL MILES NORTH, on the other side of the river, Paul Spicer – senior partner at the human rights law firm Spicer, McGraw and Hill, and long a thorn in the side of the government – was already at his table in the Booking Office restaurant at the St. Pancras Renaissance Hotel.

He was eating a much grander breakfast, his plate piled high with crispy bacon and waffles, drizzled with maple syrup in the American style.

He ate methodically, his chin wobbling as he chewed, pausing only to drink from his cup of strong black coffee.

Around him buzzed smart waitresses, eager waiters.

On his left, the morning *maître d'* showed another small group of businessmen to their seats, smiling unctuously.

At 7.45 a.m., Emily Souster joined Spicer.

Slim and elegant in her grey trouser suit.

Roedean and Cambridge.

Blonde.

Stunningly pretty.

At one time, Spicer had half-hoped... But she'd made it quite clear that there was no chance of that.

Emily sat down and looked at him, eyebrows raised.

Said, in her cut-crystal Queen's English, 'How on *earth* can you eat that?'

'Easy,' he said, in his broad Leeds. 'Open your gob, shove it in, and chew.'

She shuddered. 'I'm a bag of nerves,' she said.

A waitress came over.

Took her room number and her order – no food, just a fresh pot of coffee and a glass of orange juice.

Spicer said, 'What's there to be nervous about?'

'Aren't you?' she said.

'No. I'm ninety per cent certain we're going to win. And even if we don't...'

*Even if we don't, we bank our money and move on.*

He left it unsaid.

Shot her a glance.

The junior solicitor sitting across the breakfast table from him was a true believer: a passionate human rights lawyer, a righter of wrongs, a romantic burner of midnight oils in pursuit of every cause she could find.

Why was it so often like that?

Emily had known every advantage in life – an ambassador father, the best education money could buy, a trust fund to fall back on... If you grew up like that, it allowed you the space to spend what felt like half the year working *pro bono*, seconded to crew aid convoys, and going on marches and demonstrations.

Whereas, if you grew up like *he* had – born to a single mum in Harehills, eating chip butties for tea, sharing bathwater with three brothers...

Make no mistake about it, he loved the challenge, loved picking holes in the government's cases, but if you came up like that then you knew the value of a quid.

'There's no *even if we don't*, Paul,' said Emily. 'We *have* to win. We can't let him rot in there for the next fifteen years.'

Spicer smiled absently.

'I'll say one thing, Emily,' he said, forking half a waffle into his mouth. 'It won't be for want of trying.'

# 3.

AS HE SAID that, Charlotte Morgan was getting out of the shower of her flat in Pimlico, and wrapping a towel around her dripping body.

She opened the door and leaned out.

'What time is it?' she shouted, wrapping another towel around her wet hair.

'Quarter to eight,' came the reply from the bedroom. 'You'll be fine.'

'Bloody alarm,' said Charlotte, half to herself.

Eddie appeared in the doorway of their bedroom, in his boxers and a white T-shirt.

'You'll be *fine*,' he said, again. 'It's only twenty minutes. I'll make you a cup of tea and some toast.'

'Half an hour, if the traffic's bad,' said Charlotte. 'I need to be there by nine. And my hair's still soaking.'

'You just crack on,' he said. 'I'll check the cab's booked.'

He passed her, and they kissed, before he disappeared downstairs, and she walked through to the bedroom to begin drying her hair.

Clicked on the *Today* programme.

'…in the case of Zeff Mahsoud.'

The voice of the BBC Radio 4 presenter drifted from the speaker.

'Mr Mahsoud, a charity worker from Yorkshire, you'll remember, was arrested after arriving home to the UK on a flight from North Africa. He maintained that he'd been on a humanitarian mission to Libya, but six months ago he was given a lengthy jail sentence for terrorism-related offences. He has always protested his innocence, and an increasingly noisy campaign for his release has led us to the Court of Appeal where, later today, his case will be re-considered. Whatever their lordships decide, the appeal has thrown into sharp relief a number of questions about the operations of both MI5 and MI6, and…'

She clicked the clock radio off.

She most definitely *didn't* need that.

# 4.

AT JUST BEFORE 8 a.m., Zeff Mahsoud was taken from his cell to the holding area.

There he was handcuffed to a prison officer, who led him through three sets of steel doors to the cold air outside.

He breathed in deeply, despite the diesel fumes which were filling the vehicle yard.

Overhead, the blue sky was slowly clouding over, but still he felt an overwhelming sense of release.

No matter who you were, and what you were doing there, prison was prison, and Belmarsh was worse than most.

Several police officers, wearing body armour and carrying MP4s fitted with suppressors, watched with undisguised contempt as he was loaded into the back of a prison transport vehicle.

There was a short delay as they waited for an armed robber whose appeal was to be heard on the same day, and then the truck fired up and lurched out of the prison gates, sandwiched between two Met Range Rovers and assisted by a pair of motorcycle outriders.

It's an hour dead from Belmarsh in Woolwich to the Royal Courts of Justice on the Strand – for ordinary vehicles.

With their sirens and blue lights, and the motorcyclists zipping ahead to hold up crossing traffic, they made it in forty minutes.

On arrival in the secure parking area, Mahsoud was debussed and led into a cell in the bowels of the court.

Paul Spicer and Emily Souster were waiting nearby, and were shown to the cell a few moments later.

Spicer and Mahsoud shook hands – Emily knew better than to offer hers – and Spicer cleared his throat.

'I'm pretty confident, Zeff,' he said. 'As discussed, we've a strong case and you'll not find a better pair to put it across than Jim Caville and Charlotte Morgan. But nothing in life is guaranteed, as I've said, and there's always the risk that the judges won't see it our way.'

Zeff nodded.

'It wouldn't necessarily be the end,' said Emily Souster. 'Even if they find against us, there are other avenues. The Supreme Court, the European Courts…'

Mahsoud held up his hand. 'Please,' he said. 'Don't worry. I have every confidence.'

For a moment, he looked almost preternaturally calm.

Then, as though he'd been in something of a daze, he shook his head slightly.

'But, of course,' he said, 'if we fail we will fight on.'

# 5.

THREE HOURS LATER, five people stood on the Strand in London, in the shadow of the Royal Courts of Justice, and waited for the hubbub to die down.

On the left were James Monroe Caville QC and his junior, Charlotte Morgan, in black gowns, barristers' wigs in hand, smiling.

Then Emily Souster, carrying a leather case across her middle.

Next to her was Zeff Mahsoud, in a dark, ill-fitting suit, a serious, even angry, expression on his face.

And next to Mahsoud was Paul Spicer – pink and plump, and wearing collar-length hair and a suit which fit him very nicely indeed. Three thousand pounds, bespoke, from Gieves & Hawkes, so it should.

Spicer held up a hand. 'Ladies and gentlemen, please,' he said, raising his voice over the traffic noise. 'I have a statement to read on behalf of my client, Mr Mahsoud.'

The hubbub slowly died down.

Spicer cleared his throat and looked down at the sheet of A4 paper in his hand.

'Today is a great day for British justice and the British people, and a terrible day for the repressive agents of the British State,' he read. 'Two years ago, on my return to this country from a fact-finding and aid expedition to Libya, I was detained by the border authorities at Gatwick Airport. I was held on remand for six months, and astonishingly, although I was wholly innocent, I was eventually convicted of several terrorism offences and given a substantial prison sentence. I have since served a further six months of that sentence. Today the Court of Appeal found that my convictions were unsafe.'

Paul Spicer paused for a moment, and looked at the assembled journalists. Then he continued to read.

'I am grateful to their Lordships for their decision, but the story does not end here. It is no exaggeration to say that this whole experience has been a waking nightmare for me and my family, and I have asked my legal team to explore ways in which I can take action against the authorities for their disgraceful actions.'

Spicer paused again, and shot another glance at the reporters.

'My release today would not have been possible without the tireless work of that legal team, especially Paul Spicer and Emily Souster of Spicer, McGraw and Hill, and my barristers, James Monroe Caville QC and his junior, Charlotte Morgan. I intend to spend the next period of time with my family, especially my young daughter, before considering that legal action, and exploring once again ways in which I can help the people of Libya, whose plight remains my main focus.'

Spicer folded the A4 sheet and slipped it into an inside pocket.

Then he looked up once again. 'The last year or so has been very trying and stressful for Mr Mahsoud, as I'm sure you can imagine,' he said. 'I would request very strongly that you allow him and his family time and space to decompress and recover from this ordeal. He will take no questions today. That is all. Thank you.'

With that, the five turned and walked back into the Royal Courts.

Once they had re-cleared security, they made their way to the consultation room which had been booked for the duration of the appeal hearing.

Three days, they had expected.

'What the hell happened in there then, James?' said Spicer, as he closed the door. He shook his head in something that looked like amused wonder. 'I mean, we had a good shout, anyway, but once they withdrew the sources…'

'Just give thanks, Paul,' said the QC, unbuttoning his starched collar. 'It's a lot easier when the other side makes your argument for you.' He chuckled. 'I'll have a chat with Bernard later, but I suppose they just saw the writing on the wall. Charlotte should take a lot of the credit for that.'

Charlotte Morgan blushed. 'I don't think I did very much,' she said. 'I'd say it was Emily, more than me.'

'I always thought there was a chance they'd fold if we could put them on the spot over their covert sources,' said Emily Souster, her eyes almost ablaze. 'But even I didn't expect it to be as easy as that.'

Coffee was poured, and drunk, and there was the usual small talk which follows the end of a major case.

After twenty minutes or so, James Monroe Caville looked at his watch, stood up, and reached for his collar and wig and black leather box briefcase.

'Well,' he said. 'There's no rest for the wicked. My clerk has managed to squeeze in a con in Chambers at two, so I must bid you *adieu*. Best of luck, Mr Mahsoud.'

'Thank you,' said Zeff Mahsoud with a nod and a distant smile.

'I'll see you to the door,' said Spicer. 'While we have you, there's another little matter that we need to run by you. Emily, do you mind…?'

He indicated that Souster should accompany them.

'I'll be back in a few minutes,' she said, before following the two men.

Once they had left, Zeff Mahsoud turned to Charlotte Morgan.

'I'd like to thank you for your assistance also, Miss Morgan,' he said, in an accent that hovered somewhere between Bradford and the tribal badlands of southern Waziristan. 'I was worried that we might not succeed.'

'You can never be certain,' she said. 'But once they withdrew the evidence from those sources it was really only going to go one way.'

'It has been a very difficult time for me.'

'I'm sure it has. But it's over now.'

'Yes,' said Mahsoud. 'Well, as I say, I am grateful.'

He paused for a moment.

Then he said, 'I suppose you're very busy also?'

'Rushed off my feet,' she said, with a laugh. 'But it's better than the alternative.'

'I expect you are looking forward to your holiday,' he said, with a smile. 'Spain, I think you said?'

'Oh, goodness, yes,' she said. 'I'm shattered. Yes, my boyfriend and I are going with some friends at the beginning of August. Emily, too.' She nodded at the door through which Souster had left. 'Can't wait.'

'I had the greatest holiday ever in Barcelona,' said Zeff Mahsoud, sitting forward in his seat. He paused. Then he added, with a twinkle in his eye, 'And, of course, Spain was a muslim territory from 717.'

'Bit before my time,' said Charlotte Morgan, with a laugh.

'Wonderful galleries and architecture,' said Mahsoud.

'In Barcelona?' said Charlotte. She began gathering up her papers, and stood up. She smiled. 'So I believe. But too much culture never did a girl any good. It's Marbella for me, I'm afraid. I'm all about the sun, sea and sand.'

# 6.

LATE THAT EVENING, after he had travelled north from Euston, and been reunited with his wife and their daughter, Zeff Mahsoud slipped out of the family home.

He had an important call to make, to a keeper of secrets.

It was the first of many.

# PART TWO

# 7.

THREE MONTHS LATER

JOHN CARR LAY on a white towel in the hot sand, propped up on his elbows, staring out at the tranquil Mediterranean Sea.

Gentle waves – no more than ripples – broke, soft and frothy, on the beach.

Close to the shore, the Med was striped in dazzling turquoise shades, decorated with playful flashes from the noonday sun; further out, the waters turned a dark and mysterious blue, flat calm but hiding myriad untold secrets in their timeless depths.

It was very beautiful, Carr had to admit.

But despite that he was as restless as ever.

There were things John Carr liked about beaches, and things he didn't.

The things he liked were good-looking young women in bikinis – who often liked him right back.

The things he didn't like were sand, heat, flies, screaming kids, lying around doing nothing, and being caught looking at good-looking young women in bikinis by his teenaged daughter.

There was plenty of eye candy in the vicinity, but Alice was immediately to his left.

Stretched out on her towel, wearing mirror shades.

He *thought* she was asleep, but he couldn't be sure, because he couldn't see her eyeballs, because of the mirror shades.

So he kept his own eyes front.

John Carr had retired from 22 SAS as a Squadron Sergeant Major, having fought his way across every theatre of operations from the first Gulf War onwards in a long and distinguished career.

He'd twice been decorated for gallantry – not for nothing had he been known as 'Mad John' – and he had taken no shit from anyone in a very long time indeed.

But Alice, seventeen years old, and sixty-two kilos wringing wet, could bring him to heel with one withering look and a few choice words.

He wasn't sure what they were filling her head with at Cheltenham Ladies' College, for his thirty-five grand a year, but a lot of it seemed to revolve around the patriarchy, feminism, and the objectification of women.

It mystified Carr, who'd grown up in the 1980s on the streets of the rough Edinburgh suburb of Niddrie: he respected birds, right enough, but since when had it become a sin to fucking *look* at them?

Still, better safe than sorry.

He rubbed the livid, inverted-crescent scar on his chin, and stared dead ahead.

They were twenty metres from the sea.

It really was beautiful.

Shame about those screaming kids.

One of them was really wailing now – he'd dropped his ice cream in the water, snot was bubbling from his nose, and his fat, orange, German dad was trying to calm him down.

Shame about the kids, and a shame about the sand in Carr's shorts, too.

And in the crack of his arse, and between his toes, and gritty in his mouth.

He sighed, and looked to his right.

His son George – seven years older than Alice – was eyeing up a couple of pretty Spanish girls, his own girlfriend face-down on her towel and oblivious.

Beyond George, a couple of older blokes casually ogled Alice as they trudged by.

Carr stared at them, hard, and once they caught his eye, and clocked his menacing physique, they looked quickly away and moved on.

He glanced down between his legs and flicked at a piece of dried seaweed with a grey driftwood twig.

Funny how life turns out.

You grow up in a council tenement block, surrounded by concrete, broken glass and graffiti, you don't expect to find yourself rubbing shoulders with Europe's filthy rich on a beach at Puerto Banús.

Back home in the UK, Carr's day job was as head of London security for the Russian oligarch Konstantin Avilov. Earlier in the year Carr had taken out a Ukrainian hitman who had tried to kill his boss on the streets of London, as part of the ongoing, low-level power struggle which increasingly stretched out from Moscow in every direction around the globe.

As a thank you, his boss had given him a big payrise, and a Porsche Cayenne – bit tacky, for Carr's taste, so he'd quickly swapped it for a classy 5.0L V8 Supercharged Range Rover, in Spectral British Racing Green.

Avilov had insisted, too, that he take a couple of weeks at his Marbella villa, a ten-bedroomed, chrome-and-white monument to vulgarity, in a gated community five minutes away at Vega del Colorado.

*Take the family, Johnny. It's a thank you for everything what you done for me.*

*Including saving my life*, he hadn't said.

But both men knew.

A woman in her early thirties came into his eyeline, canvas bag in hand and diaphanous sarong hugging her hips, and gave him a long look through her Dior shades as she passed by.

Carr grinned at her, and then she was gone.

He looked at his watch.

One o'clock.

God, he was bored.

Sitting here, slowly chargrilling himself to death, in the heat of a Spanish midday in early August.

Christ, the heat.

Unlike many Scots, he was dark-haired and he tanned easily. Added to which, he'd spent enough time in hot, sandy places – carrying a rifle, 100lbs of kit and ammo in his webbing and bergen, *and* wearing a lot more than a pair of shorts – to have got used to it.

But somehow Afghan heat, Iraqi heat, African heat, didn't feel so bad.

He grinned to himself: maybe it was the rounds cracking off past your swede. That had a funny way of putting things like the ambient temperature into context.

The two pretty Spanish girls got up and wiggled and jiggled off down to the water, giggling as they went.

Carr risked a quick glance.

Caught George's eye.

'You sad bastard,' said his son, with a grin and a shake of his head. 'You sad, *sad* bastard.'

# 8.

SIXTY KILOMETRES NORTH-EAST, the MS *Windsor Castle* sat at anchor on Pier 1 of Málaga's Eastern dock.

On the bridge, the captain – an Italian, Carlo Abandonato – sipped his coffee and studied the latest weather reports.

In a few hours, they would be underway again, heading up and through the Strait of Gibraltar, three days out from Southampton on the final leg of the cruise.

The Strait could be a tricky little stretch, even for a ship such as the *Windsor Castle*, which – while not in the front rank of such vessels – was relatively modern and well-equipped.

The convergence of the roiling Atlantic with the almost tideless Mediterranean, in that narrow channel where Africa stared down Europe, created strange and unpredictable currents, and local weather conditions could make that much worse.

The cold Mistral, blowing down from the Rhone Alps, could quickly turn a warm summer's day such as this a bitter, wintry grey, and when the Levanter blew across from the Balearics it often brought with it a sudden summer fog.

Worst of all was the Sirocco, which whipped up heavy seas and hurled sand from the distant Sahara at you in a blinding fury.

But today the water was duckpond flat, the wind no more than a warm breath, and the radar was set fair for the next few days.

Good news for Captain Abandonato, good news for the crew, and good news for the five hundred passengers who were currently drinking, eating, and sunbathing on the six decks behind and beneath him, or enjoying lunch ashore in one of Málaga's many excellent restaurants.

He was looking forward to getting to Southampton; from there he would head up to Heathrow to fly home on leave to Civitavecchia.

His wife was expecting their second child – a son, the doctors had said – and was due to give birth the day after he arrived home.

Abandonato had booked a whole month off to spend time with Maria and their children.

He was looking forward to it so much it hurt.

It was always a wrench to leave, but at least it paid the bills: Maria was under an excellent but cripplingly expensive obstetrician, they were looking to move to a bigger house inland, near the lake at Bracciano, and their daughter was down for one of Roma's best private nursery schools.

Such things did not come cheap.

He finished his coffee and looked at his watch.

Shortly after 13:00hrs.

He turned to his Norwegian staff captain, the second-in-command and the man who really drove the boat.

'I'm going to freshen up and then have a walk round and see how the passengers are, Nils,' he said. 'Let's have dinner together later?'

'Sure,' said Nils.

Abandonato pulled on his cap, straightened the epaulettes on his crisp, white shirt, and left the bridge.

# 9.

A GUY WITH dark eyes came out of nowhere and walked in front of John Carr.

There he stopped, temporarily blocking Carr's view of the sea.

Flip-flops in hand, white three-quarter length linen trousers, billowing ivory shirt.

Flashy gold watch, which stood out on his tanned wrist.

*Another Eurotrash millionaire*, thought Carr.

The place was crawling with them.

Carr thought at first that the guy was staring at *him*, and Carr didn't like being stared at, but then he realised that the man's eyes had swept on, and that he was looking *past* him at another bunch of people.

Five seconds he stared, and then he carried on walking.

At which point Carr looked closer, his eye drawn by the guy's odd, limping gait, and the deep scar on his right calf, where something had taken a big bite out of the muscle.

It looked to Carr like shrapnel damage, something he'd seen plenty of.

As the guy moved away, almost unconsciously, from force of habit, Carr stored his image in the vast filing cabinet in his head.

Longish black hair, wavy and greasy, held back by a pair of Oakleys pushed up on his forehead.

Dark eyes.

Kind of a cruel mouth.

Lopsided walk.

And that big, pink hole in his right leg.

Once inside Carr's head it would never leave. He had an uncanny knack for remembering stuff like this – the skill had been honed during his near-two decades in the Special Air Service, and it had often proved invaluable on ops.

He looked over his right shoulder at the group the guy had been eyeballing.

Four young couples were in the process of laying out their towels, paperbacks, and iPads.

Their pale skin, Boden and Crew kit and beach cricket gear, would have marked them out as members of the British middle class, even if their accents had not confirmed it.

'For goodness' sake, Jemima,' one of the young men was saying, 'I thought *you* were bringing the Kindle.'

'Oh piss off, Thomas,' said Jemima. 'You're really getting on my nerves today.'

'Yeah, Tom,' said one of the others, good-naturedly. 'Take a day off, why don't you? What are you reading, anyway? *Fifty Shades of Grey*?' There was a ripple of mocking laughter and jeers. 'Right, who's coming in?'

The second speaker pulled off his T-shirt and headed for the water, followed by three of the girls.

*Very tidy,* thought Carr. *Especially the tall brunette, and the blonde girl in the shocking pink bikini.*

He could see why the guy with the gammy leg had been gawping at them.

But it wasn't worth the aggro, not with Alice by his side and George running his gob, so he turned his head and looked conspicuously in the opposite direction.

Way off at the top of the beach, unnoticed by Carr or anyone else, a young man in cut-off denim shorts and a Manchester United replica shirt hung around under a palm tree, and made a phone call.

As he did so, he watched the new arrivals keenly – though he took care not to show it.

The call was answered a hundred metres away, by the man with the dark eyes and the cruel mouth.

He was by now standing on the deck of a powerful white yacht, moored up in the marina at the extreme western edge of the Puerto Banús beach, at the end of Calle Ribera.

The open sea a matter of metres away.

'Yes,' said Dark Eyes. 'Keep watching them, and await further instructions.'

He killed the call, stood up, pulled his Oakleys down from his forehead, and stuck a Marlboro Light in his mouth.

The dark-eyed man did indeed look like a member of the wealthy, leisured Eurotrash, who idled their summers away sailing around the Med, their winters in Klosters and Courchevel 1850, and the rest of the year drinking pink champagne at 38,000 feet.

But the flashy gold Rolex was fake, and the linen trousers stolen, and John Carr was quite correct about the damage to his leg – it had been caused by a piece of red-hot Hazara shrapnel at Mazar-e Sharif, Afghanistan, in 1997.

He was actually a Chechen, called Argun Shishani, and he was not the owner of the boat, the Mistral 55 class *Lucky Lady*.

He was merely borrowing it from someone – someone who, admittedly, would never need it again.

He had chosen this particular boat because its twin 7,400hp Codag engines made it capable of more than fifty knots – 52kts, to be precise, or 96kph, or a shade under 60mph.

And because it had a mooring ticket at Puerto Banús.

Argun Shishani threw his half-smoked cigarette into the water.

Watched in amusement for a moment or two as a dozen silver sardines flashed in and fought over it.

Then looked up at the endless blue sky, smiled, and went below to make the final preparations.

# 10.

CARLO ABANDONATO HAD taken time to walk around the sun deck, and all looked in order.

About half of the *Windsor Castle*'s passengers had gone ashore, and those who had remained were sipping cocktails, splashing in the pool, or slowly giving themselves skin cancer in the roasting sun.

It was a mid-range boat, so they were mostly families and a few pensioners – the bulk of them British with a few Americans, Canadians and Europeans thrown in.

A young woman waylaid him as he walked by, and Abandonato stopped to crouch down by her sun lounger.

She was a Londoner, he thought, and not unattractive, and she was flirting furiously; her husband was taken up with their toddler, and either didn't notice or was used to it.

'So how do I go about getting an invitation for dinner at the Captain's table?' the young woman was saying, looking at him over her sunglasses.

'It's a big mystery,' said Abandonato, smiling. He was a handsome man, and he knew it, but he seemed to exert a particularly hypnotic effect on English women which he had never really understood. 'The *maître d'* has his ways, but I'm afraid I leave it to him.'

'Well, tell him Becky in 414 on deck four would like to come,' she said, with a conspiratorial grin. 'Just me, my husband will be busy with our daughter.'

'Oi, oi,' said the husband, distractedly.

'I'll see what I can do,' said Abandonato, standing up. 'Everything else is okay for you?'

'Wonderful,' said Becky, looking him up and down. 'The view especially.'

Carlo Abandonato chuckled and walked on, heading to the elevator.

He'd travel a deck down, to two of the ship's three restaurants, to make sure the lunch service was going well.

After that, he'd book himself off for an hour, go back to his cabin, and call his wife via the sat-link.

Then back to the bridge, go through the departure checks ready for 17:00hrs, when they were due to weigh anchor and be on their way.

He smiled to himself as the elevator doors closed and he started sinking.

There were worse jobs in the world.

# II.

EIGHTY FEET BENEATH him, below the waterline, in the belly of the *Windsor Castle*, Farouk Ebrahim stood in the humming, throbbing engine room of the huge ship, looked at the wall clock, and spoke to the first engineer.

'Excuse me, boss,' he said, wiping his hands on a rag. 'Is okay if I go toilet?'

The first engineer – an experienced ex-Royal Navy man called Phil Clarke – glanced at Ebrahim over his clipboard.

'*Again*, Farouk?' he said. 'That must be the fifth time today.'

'Sorry, boss,' said the young Filipino motorman, putting the rag into the pocket of his red overalls. 'I have a problem in my stomach.'

Clarke scratched his head. There wasn't much doing – the engines were only running to generate power – and Farouk seemed like a good kid.

Not long on the crew, but eager to learn, and well aware of his place in the scheme of things.

'Okay,' said Clarke. 'But don't take all day, yeah?'

Ebrahim nodded and hurried from the engine room, and up and out to the tender station on deck three.

He squeezed himself out of sight in between two of the boats and leaned on the rail, breathing deep in the sea air.

He still couldn't believe how easy it had been to get hired, and how lax was the security. His interview for the *Windsor Castle* – a ship carrying five hundred Westerners, each paying a king's ransom to float around half-naked, eating, and drowning themselves in alcohol – had taken no more than half an hour, and only five per cent of bags were screened coming aboard.

You could get *anything* on.

Especially if you knew the guy doing the screening.

Perhaps it was not surprising that half the crew were alternately getting high on cocaine, or mellowing out on hashish.

Or that he and a few fellow travellers had managed to slip through the net.

He looked out at the Mediterranean, shimmering in the heat haze.

He was from a long line of Mindanao fishermen, and the chances were that, at this exact moment, seven or eight thousand miles away, his father was chugging back towards the twinkling early evening lights of the harbour at General Santos City to offload his day's catch.

Saltwater ran through Farouk Ebrahim's veins, and the sea looked particularly beautiful today – so beautiful that he could have cried.

And, in fact, he did.

The tears came with a rush, as a sudden melancholia broke over him.

But they'd warned him to expect this, and as quickly as the tears had come they were gone.

He wiped his cheeks dry with the backs of his greasy hands and pulled himself together.

In another life, he would perhaps have joined his father and his uncle in their little wooden, three-man pump boat – would have spent his days pottering around the Sarangani Bay looking for mackerel and anchovies, and maybe a few bigeye scad, to sell at the bustling market.

He'd have got married, raised a family, lived as his ancestors had lived for generations, more or less.

But Allah had had other plans for him, and if He called then you answered.

Still, the calm, electric-blue sea… he could almost taste its fresh salt, feel its ancient and mystical powers cleansing his body and soul.

For a fleeting moment, he actually thought about jumping overboard.

But then, in his mind's eye, he saw the pride on his father's face, and it lent steel to his spine.

He would not let anyone down.

# 12.

SIXTY KILOMETRES BACK down the coast, in the luxurious, cream leather lounge on the lower deck of the *Lucky Lady*, Argun Shishani had his mobile phone to his ear once again.

He made two calls.

The first was to a Yemeni security guard on the MS *Windsor Castle*, who quickly passed on the message to a pair of Moroccan waiters.

The second was to a young Mindanaoan in greasy red overalls on the same ship.

When Farouk Ebrahim finished taking that second call, he looked down at the phone in his hand and thought for a moment.

*Perhaps a quick call, to his mother, to tell her that he loved her, and was thinking of her?*

But he quickly cast the notion from his mind – he did not want to cloud his mind with unnecessary emotions, and, more importantly, he did not want what he was about to do to come back to his family.

His trainers had warned him repeatedly of the fearsome reach and expertise of the Western intelligence agencies, and he knew that, in the coming days, every call made to and from the *Windsor Castle* on this voyage would be followed up and analysed.

So, instead, he took a final, longing look at the sea – was it his imagination, or were the waves getting up a little? – and whispered a quick prayer before throwing the mobile overboard into the eternal depths.

His last connection with the material world – the world of men, the world he despised – was gone: now there could be no turning back.

Ebrahim squeezed back out from between the lifeboats and hurried back inside.

First he went to the cabin he shared with an Indonesian oiler.

After a few minutes, he left the cabin and walked back down to the engine room of the *Windsor Castle.*

First engineer Phil Clarke was standing looking up at the various monitors and LCD panels, clipboard still in hand.

Off to the side, the third engineer was talking an engine cadet through a minor issue they'd had with one of the oil pressure gauges.

No-one paid the young Filipino any notice.

Until he walked up behind Clarke and, without warning, plunged a kitchen knife into his upper back.

The blade slid off the edge of Clarke's right scapula, bending under the force of the blow, and plunged through his right lung, clipping the edge of his heart, and burying itself in the cartilage where his ribcage met his sternum.

The first engineer fell forward and hit the floor, gasping and dying, blood flowering on his shirt and spurting onto the steel deck.

The motorman calmly looked down at him and then turned round.

The two other men were staring at him in horror.

The third engineer, torque wrench hanging slack in his hand, took a step forwards.

'What…?' he said.

But he got no further.

Ebrahim, his mind and body fizzing with adrenalin and hope, raised his arms above his head, as his instructor had shown him, to arm the built-in mercury tilt-switch attached to the suicide vest that he was now wearing underneath his red overalls.

In the event that anyone tried to take him down, that switch would initiate the eight one-kilogram blocks of military-grade C4 plastic explosive, each taped up with approximately two hundred steel ball-bearings, which were sitting in the pouches of the hand-made canvas waistcoat.

Unbeknownst to Ebrahim, the vest contained a further switch, which meant that the device would detonate if he tried to remove it once it was clipped on.

This was designed to deal with any change of heart on the part of the young martyr.

But he had no such change of heart.

'Allahu akbar!' he shouted, staring at the two men in front of him. 'Allahu akbar!'

At the same time, he closed his fist around the button in his hand, which was attached by two feet of copper wire to the electrical detonator on his vest. The wires met, and the contact sent a pulse to the detonator, the resultant explosion in turn initiating the detonation cord linking the blocks of C4. The det cord exploded at 8,000 metres per second, igniting the C4 and spreading 1,600 ball bearings out through 360 degrees with the destructive force of a thousand shotguns.

The explosive energy turned Farouk Ebrahim into a pink mist where he stood.

A millisecond later the molten shrapnel destroyed all of the computers and levers and LCD screens and gauges in that end of the engine room, threw the four Converteam/Rolls-Royce engines instantly offline, and shredded the other men.

They did not even register the flash of the explosion which obliterated them.

# 13.

UP ON THE BRIDGE of the MS *Windsor Castle*, the power surged and died, and then the emergency batteries came on line.

A second later, a red light began flashing, and a horn started sounding.

Fire in the engine room.

The staff captain wasn't unduly disturbed – on a vessel of this sophistication, it was far more likely that this was a false alarm, linked to whatever had caused the engines to shut down, than that there was an actual fire.

But still.

He knew that the ship's duty fire control party would have received the alarm on their personal radios, but he called the head of the party anyway and made sure he was *en route*.

He had a quick look at the fire suppression system – it was showing deployed, which meant a fine drizzle was already descending in the compartment; if it was not cancelled it would be followed shortly by a mixture of argon, nitrogen, and carbon dioxide.

Still not overly troubled – this was an automatic response to an alarm, false or otherwise – he keyed in the command to close the fire doors in that zone of the ship, before glancing up at the overhead CCTV panel.

It was divided up into many dozens of small images; he called up a new screen showing the six views of the engine room.

All were blank.

He grunted in surprise.

Okay, now that *was* concerning.

He immediately put an intercom call out to the men down there.

No reply.

Tried first engineer Phil Clarke on his personal radio, with the same result.

*Well, Houston*, he thought to himself, *perhaps we* do *have a problem*.

He checked the ambient temperature sensors – they were elevated.

He clicked his own radio again.

'Captain to the bridge, please,' he said. 'Quickly.'

Then he called the second deck officer, whom he knew was in his cabin not far from the engines.

The man picked up quickly.

'Jerry, it's Nils,' said the staff captain. 'Can you do me a favour? The engines have gone offline, there's a fire alarm down there, and I can't raise Phil Clarke or anyone else. Fire control are on their way, but would you mind just going along and telling me what's going on?'

'Sure,' said Jerry.

The staff captain ran through some checks on his bridge systems, and then made another attempt to contact the engine room on the comms.

Same result.

His radio crackled.

It was Jerry.

'Nils,' he said, 'it's me. It's… it's a bit weird down here. I can definitely smell burning, but the door's locked somehow. And one of the junior engineers reckons he heard a loud bang from inside about a minute ago.'

'*Shit.* Are fire control there?'

'Yes, we're forcing it. We'll be inside in thirty seconds.'

'Okay,' said Nils. 'Keep me in the loop. I'll need to know whether it's a general evacuation situation in…' He looked at his watch. 'In one minute. If I don't hear from you, I'm calling it.'

'Roger that. We're nearly through.'

# 14.

FAR ABOVE, CAPTAIN Carlo Abandonato had known that the engines had stopped – he'd felt the slight change in vibration, and had seen the momentary dimming of the lights – but he was not terribly concerned.

They were not scheduled to shut down, but things cropped up now and then.

He assumed that Phil Clarke and his team had noticed something – almost certainly nothing major, the damned things had under 6,000 hours in them since a complete rebuild – and had taken them off for a short while to sort it out.

Clarke had done twenty-two years in destroyers in the British navy, and was fresh from a three-day manufacturer's refresher course at Rolls-Royce Marine; it couldn't be anything that he couldn't fix.

Still, Abandonato had been keen to get back up to the bridge, and his unease had doubled or trebled with the radio message from the staff captain.

So now – careful to look smooth and unflustered – he took his leave of the tables full of family diners and walked out of the burger restaurant.

It was as he was starting upwards in the elevator that he heard the first shots.

And then the human sounds of fear and horror.

Outside, unseen by the captain, the Yemeni security guard, called by Argun Shishani from the yacht along the coast at Marbella, was standing on the sun deck with an AK47, taking aimed shots at the sunbathers and swimmers in and around the pool.

Several people were already floating in red-tinted water, and others were scrambling to get away.

The Yemeni had been chosen for this operation precisely because he was battle-hardened; he had cut his teeth on the US Marines in the Second Battle of Fallujah, during the insurgency in Iraq, and had travelled the Middle East and Africa throughout the years that followed, fighting the kuffar in the name of Allah.

He'd spent most of the recent past fighting the Pesh and the al-Hashd al-Shaabi in Iraq, and the YPG and others in Syria.

He was remorseless and dedicated: he accepted that death would embrace him today, and he welcomed the fact.

He thought of his friends, men who had gone before him and died in the same glorious cause, and he smiled.

This was for them: he would see them soon.

He had ten magazines of thirty rounds each on his chest rig, and he intended to make as many of those rounds count as possible.

He took aim at a young child, standing by a gangplank on the deck below, screaming in frozen fear next to its dead mother, and heard the click as the hammer of his weapon struck an empty chamber.

His magazine empty, he allowed it to hang free on its sling, and took a grenade – a Swiss-manufactured L109A1, liberated from a British Army stores in Germany, on a four-second fuse – from his bag.

Leaned against the guard rail.

Pulled the pin.

Almost casually, he threw the grenade over the side at the child, and the panicking stream of humanity – if you could use that term to describe the dogs who were running like cowards down the nearest gangplank.

The grenade detonated with a dull crump, killing the child and two others outright and wounding many more.

Smiling, he reloaded the AK, fired a dozen rounds into the survivors and then turned and walked in the direction of the cabins in search of more victims.

It was a good day to die, here in the land of the infidel, bringing terror to the enemy, and his womenfolk, and his young.

# 15.

BY NOW, CARLO Abandonato had reached the bridge deck, his blood running alternately cold and hot.

He found the bridge empty, the staff captain and the navigator having leaped overboard into the warm embrace of the Med when the shooting began.

'Merda!' spat Abandonato. 'Bastardi codardi!'

He activated the *Windsor Castle*'s distress beacon, picking up the ship-to-shore telephone – as though the authorities were not already aware of what was happening.

He pressed the click-to-talk.

And then he saw movement outside.

A young man.

Abandonato recognised him.

An assistant purser?

No, a waiter.

Either way, it didn't matter – he was here, and he could help.

'You,' said Abandonato, in English. 'You need to get below and get as many passengers as possible off this damned ship. Boats, gangways, tell them to jump overboard… anything.'

In response, the man said nothing, but raised his arm.

Something in his hand.

Abandonato ducked instinctively as the man fired, and the

shot passed two feet over his head and spidered the bridge windscreen.

Deafened, the captain scrabbled left, hidden from view by the centre console.

His mind was scrambled.

He could hear the man's feet slapping on the deck as he walked across to get another shot at him.

Abandonato looked wildly around.

The main door was ten feet away.

There was no way he could make it.

He felt a terrible sense of despair, and of resignation – but luck was on his side.

Fleetingly.

The shooter had suffered a stoppage – the empty cartridge, which should have been cleanly ejected, had stuck in the breech and jammed the pistol. He'd gone through the clearance drill a thousand times, but the shock of the moment had fried his brain and turned his fingers to thumbs, and he was fumbling with the slide.

It gave Abandonato the moment he needed.

His eye lit upon the drawer above his head.

The Very pistol.

Keeping low, he pulled open the drawer and groped for the pistol.

His hand closed around the grip.

Felt for a flare.

Found one.

Hands trembling, he loaded the gun.

As he snapped it shut, he saw the shooter's legs appear at the edge of the console.

Heard the sound as the man racked the top slide to load another round into the breech, ready to finish the job.

Abandonato crossed himself, offered a prayer to his own God, and launched himself at the guy with the gun, yelling 'Segaiolo!'

The shooter rocked back on his heels in surprise at the sight of the captain coming for him, tripped on his own feet, and fell onto his arse.

If Abandonato had pressed home his attack in the second, second-and-a-half, that his enemy was disoriented, he might have prevailed.

But instead he hesitated.

And now the attacker raised his pistol and fired from eight or nine feet away.

The round hit the skipper in the right side of his groin and knocked him backwards like he'd been kicked by a mule. There was remarkably little pain – his left brain noted this fact with no little surprise, even as his right brain was overwhelmed with shock and alarm – but the bullet had severed his femoral artery and his life was now measured in seconds.

Still prone, the attacker pulled the trigger again, but the top slide was back and jammed again – the curse of cheap ammunition – and the weapon didn't respond.

He pulled the trigger again – frantically – and then smashed the thing on the deck, in a futile attempt to clear it.

And then looked up at the captain.

Saw the Very pistol.

The boot suddenly on the other foot, his bottle went.

'No,' he screamed, holding up a hand. 'No!'

Staggering forward, pumping blood, Abandonato raised the pistol and fired the flare into the other man's face from a distance of three feet.

Fifty grams of potassium perchlorate, dextrin, and strontium nitrate entered the terrorist's right eye at 330 feet per second, and came to a stop two inches inside his skull.

Burning at 2,000 degrees centigrade.

The bridge was filled with an unearthly screaming and banging as the man howled and clawed at his face, but Abandonato was past caring.

Suddenly weary, breathing laboured, he slumped to the floor in a puddle of his own blood.

Pressed his hand to the front of his trousers.

Looked at his palm.

Bright, shiny red.

He didn't know how he knew it, but he knew that he was dying.

He didn't feel frightened, only sad.

As the room started to go dim, a tear formed in his eye.

He wanted to speak to his wife, and his daughter, but he hadn't the strength to stand and reach for the sat-link.

His last conscious thought was that he would never see his unborn son.

Never smell him.

Never hear or hold him.

As that realisation formed, he slipped into oblivion and was gone.

# 16.

THE SPANISH SECURITY complex had been dreading – and preparing for – a nightmarish attack like this ever since the Madrid train bombings way back in 2004.

Cruise liners and tourists were just too big and soft and tempting a target.

So within three minutes of the first shots, *Guardia Civil* officers were on scene at Málaga's Eastern dock, and dead and wounded people were being carried away at a crouching run.

Within six minutes, two mini-buses carrying locally based *Grupo Especial de Operaciones* teams – the *Policia Nacional* SWAT men – screamed on to Pier 1.

The shooter, or shooters, had by now disappeared inside the vessel, so the *GEO* inspector-jefe sent three snipers to take up the best positions they could find, stuck another couple of men on the cordon as liaison, and then led the rest of his blokes charging up an empty gangway to get aboard.

Forty kilometres out into the Med, aboard the amphibious assault ship SPS *Juan Carlos I*, the twin rotors on a giant, black Boeing CH-47 Chinook helicopter were almost up to take-off speed.

In the rear of the aircraft were sixteen special forces marines from the *Fuerza de Guerra Naval Especial.*

Flight time to Málaga, a little under eight minutes.

And the final response came from down the coast at Marbella, where that town's on-duty six-man detachment of *Grupo Especiales de Operaciones* special ops soldiers boarded their Eurocopter AS532 Cougar helicopter and lifted off, heading west.

Absolutely flat out, their aircraft was capable of around 140 knots. That gave them a flight time of around fourteen minutes, which disappointed the soldiers – they knew the *Juan Carlos I* had been patrolling through the Med not far from Málaga, and that its SF marines were already inbound.

Chances were the whole party would be over before they even got there.

But they pressed on regardless.

# 17.

JOHN CARR WAS not a patient man at the best of times, and now – just as those special forces troops from Marbella arrived over Málaga, sixty kilometres to the north-east – he finally cracked.

'Hey, George,' he said, leaning over on an elbow. 'D'you fancy a pint? I've had enough of this.'

George Carr turned to look at his father, eyebrows raised, mocking grin on his face.

The expression said, very clearly, *How can you have had enough of* this?

'Nah,' he said. 'I'm good, thanks.'

'What about me?' said Alice, pushing those mirror shades off her eyes and squinting up at her father.

'I'd love to take you, sweetheart,' said Carr, with his best attempt at sincerity. 'But you're under age. We can't break the law, can we? Your mum'd kill me.' He turned back to George. 'I said, *Do you fancy a pint?*' he said, with meaning. 'The correct answer is, *Yes, I do.*' He stood up. 'Come on, I havenae brought my wallet.'

George chuckled. 'There's a fucking surprise,' he said.

He stood, brushing sand off his back and elbows, and off his Union Jack swimming shorts.

'Watch your language in front of your sister,' said Carr. He looked at George's shorts and shook his head in disdain. 'No class whatsoever,' he said. Then, innocently, 'And have you put a bit of weight on, by the way? 3 Para must have softened up since my day.'

'Fuck off,' said George, good-naturedly.

A slightly taller, slightly skinnier version of his old man, he was in the kind of shape you'd expect of a twenty-four-year-old Para Reg full-screw who was scheduled to undergo Selection later that year.

This holiday being his last blow-out before he got down to training proper, ahead of his journey to Hereford, Pen-y-Fan, and the jungle.

He looked down, and nudged his girlfriend with his toe.

'We're off up into town for a bit, Chloe,' he said. 'The old bastard's shit drills have left him dehydrated. You coming?'

She groaned. It had been a heavy night the night before.

'No,' she said, sitting up. 'I think I'll go for a swim instead.'

'Suit yourself,' said George. Then he looked at his dad. 'Come on, then,' he said. 'I'm in the chair. Again.'

'Too right,' said Carr, with a grin, poking his son in the ribs. 'Tips on passing Selection don't come cheap, fatty.'

'Fuck me,' said George, shaking his head. 'Don't you ever give it a rest?'

'No way,' said Carr. 'Being this irritating takes a lot of practice.'

He laughed and looked at his boy, and felt an enormous surge of pride – a feeling that he knew was mutual.

The two men turned and started trudging up the beach.

# 18.

A LITTLE OVER ONE hundred metres away, in the calfskin and mohair interior of the gleaming white *Lucky Lady*, four men sat in silence.

Tense, but focused.

One or two knees bouncing up and down on the deep-pile beige carpet with nervous energy.

They were all dressed like everyone else nearby, in shorts and T-shirts or vests, though they were wearing trainers rather than flip-flops.

The better for movement.

Each had at his feet a beach bag, and each bag contained an AKS-74U 'Krinkov', a lightweight, shortened version of the AK47, with a folding skeleton stock.

Each Krinkov had a magazine in place, and each man had five spare mags – a total of 720 rounds of 5.45mm-short death and destruction.

The dark-eyed Chechen called Argun Shishani sat on the steps to the upper deck.

He had a phone to his left ear, and a police radio, stolen three nights earlier, in his right hand.

He was talking to the young man in the cut-off denim shorts and the Manchester United shirt, who had moved down the beach a way but still had a good view.

'I don't care if two have left as long as the main target is still there,' said Shishani. 'She is? Good. Right, sixty seconds.'

He ended the call and looked at the four men. 'Okay, boys,' he said. 'It's on.'

He refreshed an iPad, on which was a single image – a woman, wearing a bikini, on the beach outside.

He tapped the tablet, and the four men took a final long look at the photograph.

'You have seven minutes,' said Shishani, 'and no longer. Kill as many as you can, and bring me back my prize. And may Allah go with you.'

As they left, he followed them up and stood on the deck.

He watched the four men melt into the crowd, and briefly turned to look behind himself.

From his vantage point he could see clear out to sea.

It was a thin ribbon of serenity between the decadence of Europe and the very different lands of North Africa, lurking just over the blue horizon, with their violence, and turmoil, and poverty.

At least, that was how it appeared to the Westerners.

Argun Shishani's lip curled in disgust.

These trivial, shallow people, splashing and playing in the shallows, and drinking themselves insensible in the nearby bars – they thought that that narrow, tranquil strip of water protected them from the rage.

But today it was an angry sea, and it had brought God's wrath to these shores, and after the wrath was spent the sea would carry away His servants to safety.

Shishani smiled, and waited.

# 19.

THE FOUR MEN left the *Lucky Lady*, beach bags over shoulders or in hands.

Walked onto the road leading from the marina to the beach, laughing and joking.

People passing the other way – lucky people, as it turned out – didn't give them a second's thought.

The four walked to the top of the beach, where they linked up with Mr Manchester United, who was standing on the other side of a parked car, a pistol jammed down the front of his cut-off shorts.

One of the men – a tall, slender individual in a faded *Hooters New York City* T-shirt – looked about himself casually, and then said something.

Hooters was carrying two bags, and now he handed one of them to Man U.

Then – with final nods and smiles – they split into two groups.

Three of them stayed where they were, to act as a cut-off team – their job was to intercept any police officers who might try to get to the beach, and to cut down holidaymakers fleeing the main assault.

Which was to be carried out by Man U and a short, stocky man called Khaled.

The two of them now hopped over the low stone wall which separated the road from the heavy, dry sand, and slogged forwards.

When they reached the pre-arranged point, Man U looked at his accomplice and raised his eyebrows.

*Ready?*

Khaled nodded.

Both men reached into the bags at their feet and took out their loaded Krinkov AKs, locking the stocks in place.

Ten metres to their left, a middle-aged woman in a blue bathing suit and a floppy straw hat saw them do it and froze, hand to her mouth, unable even to scream.

Back at the top of the beach, Hooters NYC and the other two casually picked up their own weapons and slipped off the safety catches.

Twenty feet away from them stood a group of ten or twelve Spaniards in their late teens or early twenties, who were arguing, in a good-natured way, about where to go for lunch.

Hooters bent down and retrieved a hand grenade and pulled the pin.

Whispering a final prayer, he lobbed it into the middle of the group and ducked back below the stone wall as he did so.

The safety lever flew off and armed the weapon as it landed at the feet of a young man, looking for all the world like a ball thrown by a child.

Reflexively, he bent to pick it up, ready to send it back to its owner.

But it was surprisingly heavy.

'What's that?' said one of his friends.

'Mierda!' said the man. 'I think it's…'

The grenade detonated, killing him and one other man instantly, and wounding every other person in that group.

It was the signal for the shooting to begin.

The panic was instantaneous and total.

Some dived to the ground.

Others stood and stared at the gunmen, their minds temporarily unable to make their legs move.

Still others ran – only to find that they were running towards the other shooters.

The fat German man was one of the first to die, along with his snotty-nosed son – whom he had scooped up into his arms. His wife went down, too, though their five-year-old daughter survived.

The two pretty young Spanish girls whom Carr had been eyeing up – one of them was shot through the temple, and killed outright, the other through the arm and thigh.

She would bleed to death before help arrived.

The cut-off team were making hay with those who were trying to get off the beach.

Men, women, children.

Flip-flops and shorts and bikinis.

Screaming, shouting.

All the time, the remorseless crack-crack of the weapons.

The first police response came within seconds – a marked *Guardia Civil* Nissan Patrol had by chance been driving down towards the beach.

Three officers – two men and a woman – debussed, drew their pistols, and started moving towards the sand.

They were immediately spotted and engaged by three men some twenty-five metres to their left.

The female officer advanced gamely towards the three, and managed – with one lucky shot – to take out a tall man in a *Hooters New York City* T-shirt, before a skinny kid in an Adidas vest put her down with three AK rounds in the neck and shoulder.

The two male cops skidded to a halt. One slipped over in his panic, but in a flash he was up and turning and running, and following his partner, who was already five yards ahead of him, head down, weaving.

Dealing with drunken tourists and shoplifters was one thing: this was quite something else.

They were neither physically nor mentally prepared for it.

# 20.

A FEW MINUTES' walk along from the beach, John and George Carr were standing outside a bar, halfway down their first pints of San Miguel.

The place was as tacky as it got and it stank of stale cooking oil.

The street was busy with holidaymakers and loud with thumping bass from a nearby sound system, and the heat was still oppressive despite the overhead parasol.

John Carr was not impressed. He shook his head and took another deep, frothy swallow of lager – at least that was cold – as a group of fat, drunken Brits swayed towards them.

'Fuck's sake,' he said as they turned for the entrance to the bar.

One of them – a big guy with a skinhead, a Millwall FC tattoo and a beer belly – clipped Carr as he passed.

'Hey, watch yourself, pal,' said Carr.

'Or what?' said the guy, stopping and staring at the Scotsman.

But when he saw the glint in Carr's eyes, his tune changed.

'Sorry, mate,' he said, before slinking away inside the bar.

Carr watched him go, shaking his head in disgust.

'Jesus,' he said, under his breath. 'You come here to get away from dickheads like that.'

'Chill out,' said George, grinning and holding up his beer.

'You're on holiday, for fuck's sake. You need to get on it. Five or six of these and everything'll look a lot better.'

'Aye,' said Carr, lifting his own pint. 'Well, you'd better enjoy it because you'll no be drinking once you're in training.'

'True,' said George. He rolled his eyes. 'Of course, Selection was much harder in your day.'

Carr chuckled. 'I actually *pity* you, son,' he said. 'You havnae got a *clue* what you're gonnae…'

But then he paused, glass in hand, and cocked his head.

Somewhere to their rear, a bang and then a rapid series of shorter, sharper reports.

'What the fuck's that?' said George, his mind unable for a moment to assimilate the sounds of war with this environment.

But John Carr was already on the balls of his feet, his neck hair on end, pint glass thrown and gone, lager splashed on the dusty cobbles.

The detonation from the grenade was unmistakable, as was the crack and thump of the small arms.

'That's AK, George,' he said. 'A *lot* of fucking AK.'

AK, and screaming.

The hundred billion neurons in John Carr's brain were pulsating with one almost overwhelming electrical impulse: *Get down there, and get Alice.*

But after taking two steps, he stopped.

Even when judged alongside other special forces soldiers, Carr had stood out for his singular ability to stay calm and to think clearly under extreme pressure.

He'd been in some very sticky spots indeed, but in the middle of the biggest firefights, often hundreds of klicks behind enemy lines, outnumbered, overrun, fighting for his very life, his pulse rate had barely ticked up from its customary 60bpm.

And he had never panicked.

It was just logical.

Panicking got you killed.

So he didn't panic.

Not thinking got you killed, too.

So, although he was being tested now as never before, he stopped, and he stood, and he thought.

He could hear several weapons firing, perhaps as many as half a dozen.

People were already running past him, babbling, crying, freaking out.

Some of them wounded.

One guy holding his guts in, stumbling and dragging his bare feet, supported by two of his mates, his mouth slack, minutes from bleeding out.

Carr knew that he couldn't just sprint onto the sand, because that would get him killed, and if he was killed he couldn't help Alice.

But he needed to get eyes-on in order to formulate a plan.

To his left, George was staring at him, his own eyes wide with shock.

He'd joined the Parachute Regiment just after the Afghan draw-down.

He was fit and strong, and no doubt he was brave and well-trained, too.

But he was not tested, not hardened and tempered by battle.

And you never know how you'll react in a contact until it happens.

For an instant, Carr saw him not as the young man he was, but as the child he'd been.

He was on the verge of telling his son to run and hide, to stay safe, when – as if reading his old man's mind – George spoke.

'Wherever you're going,' he said, 'I'm coming with you.'

In that moment, Carr saw a soldier in front of him.

He knew he stood a better chance with some help.

'Okay, son,' he said. 'But you listen to everything I say, understand? No rushing off. You stick by me.'

George nodded.

Then two police officers came into view, running, heads down, terrified, away from the shooting.

Father looked at son.

'Those two,' he said. 'If they're not going to use their weapons, we will.'

# 21.

THEY STOOD IN THE street, against the flow of fleeing holidaymakers, and clotheslined the two cops as they sprinted by.

'Lo siento, señor,' said Carr. 'But I need your pistol.'

The man just stared up at him and said nothing.

It was a look that Carr had seen many times before – notably in Bosnia, when the line was broken around Goražde and the men of the BIH were scrambling for the safety of the town, with only one thought in their minds: *Please let me survive another day, and I'll worry about tomorrow… tomorrow.*

Carr stood up. Next to him stood George, pistol in hand, an unconscious policeman at his feet, his jaw broken.

Carr looked at the weapon.

Heckler & Koch USP.

Made himself take another moment.

No point charging onto the sand with an empty pistol, either.

Dropped the mag out.

Pushed on the top round.

It moved downward only slightly, indicating that the magazine was full.

Hadn't even been fired.

Carr replaced the magazine, pulled the topslide back slightly, to double-check that a round was in the breech, and tapped the slide forward to rehouse the round.

Ready to go.

He looked at George, who had copied him.

'Used one of these before?' he said.

'No, we're on the Glock 17.'

'Same principle. Safety's *here*. How many rounds have you got?'

'Full clip.'

'Take the spare mags, too. Fifteen rounds of nine millimetre in each one. Make sure you count your shots. And get as close as you can.'

George nodded.

Flinched at the rate of fire coming from the beach.

Looked down at the peashooter in his hand.

Hesitated.

'Now, son,' said Carr, clapping his boy on the shoulder, and flashing him a savage grin. 'Come with me, and I'll show you where the Iron Crosses grow.'

In spite of himself, George grinned, and felt his fear melting away at his father's certainty. And then John Carr was off and running towards the sound of the shooting, against the thinning tide of people, past dozens of white, multi-million dollar yachts bobbing at anchor, seagulls whirling overhead, oblivious, as though this was a day like any other.

In a matter of moments, the two men had reached the low wall in front of the sands.

They crouched behind it.

'Safety off,' said Carr.

'Safety off.'

They peered over.

Beyond was a scene of almost unimaginable carnage.

Dozens of people lay dead or dying on the beach.

Two pairs of killers.

One pair, thirty metres away to their left.

Slowly edging backwards on to the sand, covering approach routes from the town.

As the Carrs watched, one of them leaned over a teenaged boy who was trying to crawl away.

Shot him in the head.

The second pair, forty metres to their right.

Levelling their weapons at four people.

Four of the Brits from earlier, Carr realised.

Not far from where he and Alice had been sitting.

But none of them was Alice.

And now, with a three-round burst into the chest, one of them killed the only male of the group.

The other grabbed the middle girl – the tall blonde in the shocking pink bikini – by the scruff of her neck, and started half-dragging, half-pulling her off the beach.

His mate got behind the other women and pushed them after him.

Shouting, *Yallah imshi! Yallah imshi!*

*Hurry the fuck up!*

Carr looked at George. 'Can you see Alice and Chloe?' he said.

'No.'

'Please God,' breathed Carr.

He was not a religious man, and he didn't see the inside of a church from one funeral to the next, but plenty of men find time to say a quick prayer when the rounds start flying.

*Every* man says a prayer when they're flying around his baby girl.

'What do we do?' said George.

Carr thought for a second or two.

His lengthy secondment to the Det in Northern Ireland had left him an outstanding pistol shot, that being the primary weapon of the surveillance operator, but if he engaged the further pair to his right at this range… The best shot in the world would be just as likely to kill the three women.

Whereas the closer pair, to the left, were actually edging his way.

Plus which, they were focused on the streets, not on what was behind them.

No-brainer.

'Those two first,' he said. 'Then we get after the others.' He turned to his son, and winked. 'Hold your fire until they get as close as possible, and if it all goes to shit I'll see you in Valhalla.'

'Bollocks to that,' said George. 'One of these days it's *got* to be your round, and I'm not missing that for anything.'

# 22.

THE TWO MEN were within fifteen metres when they began to turn around.

'Now,' said John Carr.

Both Carrs stood up and levelled their weapons.

The terrorists stopped in the sand, mouths open, startled eyes, and started to raise their AKs.

They never stood a chance.

Cumulatively, John Carr had spent months of his life double-tapping targets in various ranges and shooting galleries in Hereford and elsewhere around the world, and he'd done it for real enough times, too.

At the peak of his skills, he'd have got off four aimed shots in under a second, easy.

He was a little rusty, so it took him just *over* a second – though they were still fired so quickly that it was hard to distinguish between each round.

*Tap-tap.*

*Tap-tap.*

The Grim Reaper reached out from the muzzle of Carr's pistol and took both of the jihadis away to hell, a fifth shot – from George – extinguishing the last vestiges of movement in the twitching fingers of one of them.

Carr looked at his son, eyebrows raised.

George looked back at him, sheepishly. 'Fucked if I'm going back to Battalion and telling them bastards that you did all the shooting,' he said.

'I'll give you that one,' said Carr. 'Now grab that AK, and let's get going.'

He reached down and pulled the Krinkov from the nearest dead man's grasp, turning at the same moment to engage the remaining shooters.

But they were now out of sight at the bottom end of the beach.

George Carr had picked up the other carbine, and frisked his guy for spare magazines, and now he hopped onto the low wall and looked in the direction of the marina.

'No sign,' he said, and hopped off onto the Calle Ribera on the other side.

He started walking down the line of the wall towards the sea, AK at the ready.

John Carr followed him, keeping good spacing, turning often to cover their rear, finger over the trigger, the weapon in synch with his eyes.

Ready to engage instantly.

'Anything?' he said, after fifteen metres.

'No.'

And then they heard the sound of powerful marine engines – twin 7,400hp Codag gas turbines, to be precise – and a white yacht powered out of the marina.

Both men watched the boat go.

It was really shifting.

Carr raised his AK, but it was already out into the open sea and heading due south.

# 23.

'WAS THAT THEM?' said Carr.

'Fuck knows,' said George.

They continued down the line of the wall until Calle Ribera turned right and they were into the marina.

'Go firm,' said Carr.

They both took a knee and listened and looked, covering their arcs as they did so.

Nothing.

At least, nothing but the sound of shouting and groaning from the beach behind them, and a distant wail of sirens.

Carr looked at his watch.

Three minutes since they'd clicked off the pistol safeties.

'Must have been them,' said Carr. 'Let's find your sister and Chloe.'

He jogged in the direction of the patch of sand that Alice had been occupying.

Jogged past the corpses of young children, elderly people, girls in bikinis, young men in dayglo shorts.

Past a man on his back staring sightlessly at the sky, a John Grisham novel still in his hand, the yellow sand dark with red blood.

Another slumped over a cool box, shot in the act of getting himself another beer.

'Fucking hell,' he whispered to himself.

He reached the spot.

Their towels were there, but there was no sign of either of the girls.

A wave of something like panic swept over him – a fear he didn't recognise, because he'd never experienced it before.

And then a police vehicle drove onto the beach, and Carr thought he'd better drop the AK and put his hands up.

'George,' he shouted, over his shoulder. 'Game over, son. Let them see you're unarmed.'

# 24.

IT HAD BEEN a quiet day at the Vauxhall HQ of the Secret Intelligence Service.

Although the threat level across Europe had been high for some years now, there was nothing to suggest any imminent attack, and the duty officer on the Spain desk had spent the morning wading through intelligence related to a revival of Basque separatism in the north.

All that changed with a call from a GCHQ liaison officer, with intercepts of frantic communications between Spanish police and special forces on the Costa del Sol.

The duty officer's blood ran cold, and her hands actually shook for a moment or two.

Then she picked up her phone and called her boss, Director of Operations Justin Nicholls, third-in-command of MI6 and widely tipped to be a future leader of the service.

Within the hour, the world knew that terrorists had launched a massive and deadly attack on two towns on Spain's Mediterranean coast.

By then, Nicholls was just starting an emergency meeting of the MI6 senior management team, chaired by 'C' – the Chief of the SIS.

'What do we know?' said C, his voice brusque.

'Estimates are fifty dead on the ship, and thirty or more on the beach,' said Nicholls. 'Will go higher, I'm afraid. It looks very much as though Puerto Banús was the main target. They hit Málaga first, and then went onto the beach when the first responders were out of the way.'

'Why? What were they looking for at Marbella?'

'That's not yet clear.'

'How did we not know about this?' said C.

'We can't know about everything,' said Nicholls.

'A complex, two-pronged attack, on this bloody scale, and we had no idea? They must have been planning it for months.'

'We're already going back through everything remotely linked to the Costa for the last two years, just in case it was there and we missed it. But at this stage, no, we had no idea.'

'The Spanish?'

Spain's CNI, the *Centro Nacional de Inteligencia*, was not quite at the level of its counterparts in British or American intelligence, but it had improved dramatically since the Madrid train outrage of 2004, and was more than willing to share information and co-operate in the global fight against terrorism.

'I can only assume that they were as much in the dark as we were.'

'This isn't going to go down well at No. 10, Justin,' said C, shaking his head.

'Tell me about it.'

'You know the PM,' said C. 'I'll leave you to brief her.'

Justin Nicholls and the Rt Hon Penelope Morgan MP had dated each other for a couple of years in their student days, and had stayed close ever since.

Nicholls nodded.

On the wall to his right was a bank of screens – some showing news channels, others live feeds from Spanish intelligence cameras. One delivered the confidential feed, the updated intelligence picture available to the SIS.

A status update for the MS *Windsor Castle* said that the incident at Málaga was now over, with four attackers confirmed killed. At Marbella, two attackers had been shot dead on the Puerto Banús beach, and two other men had just been taken into custody.

And then a new line appeared on the feed.

*Spanish police helicopter chasing high speed boat across Med towards Moroccan coast. SPS Juan Carlos I also launching marines. Royal Moroccan Navy alerted.*

'That's them,' said Nicholls.

# 25.

THE BOAT CARRYING Argun 'Dark Eyes' Shishani, the man in the Manchester United shirt, and the shooter called Khaled, and their three female hostages, had had a big head start.

In all the confusion, it was well over forty kilometres from the Spanish coast by the time the *Grupo Especial de Operaciones* Eurocopter EC120 Colibri lifted off in pursuit.

But the two pilots put the aircraft nose down and flew flat out, the single Turbomeca engine straining to throw out its 504 shaft-horsepower, and they had the speeding *Lucky Lady* in sight on their on-board camera well inside twenty minutes, and in visual contact not long afterward.

Two kilometres out, the two *GEO* snipers aboard leaned out of the helicopter on harnesses and trained the scopes of their AMP DSR-1 .338 rifles on the streamlined yacht.

The officer on the left hand side, an *oficial de policía*, had the clearest view.

'I can see two armed men on the rear deck,' he shouted, into his collar microphone. 'Three women are standing in front of them, hands on their heads.'

'Roger that,' said his colleague, a subinspector. 'I'll take the right, you take the left.' Half a minute later, and a kilometre closer, he said, 'Do you have a shot?'

He already knew the answer.

Both men were highly skilled, and their rifles, chambered for the Lapua Magnum cartridge, were effective out to 1,500 metres.

In theory.

At this distance, in a speeding helicopter caught in the up and down thermals of the Mediterranean, with the targets contained on a small rear deck, under an overhanging roof, on a boat crashing through waves, with civilians in the foreground…

'No way.'

The second sniper leaned forward and tapped the pilot on the shoulder. 'We need to get a lot closer,' he shouted. 'We can't take any kind of shot at this range.'

The pilot nodded and pressed on.

Six hundred metres out, one of the men on the deck lifted his AK47 and started shooting.

It was nothing more than a gesture – an AK is useless at that range – but it made the pilot think again.

He slowed the helicopter to fifty knots, so that it was simply keeping pace with the yacht.

'Go on!' shouted the sniper on the left hand side. 'They can't hit us from here. I need to get closer.'

Again, the pilot nodded and tilted the helicopter forwards.

Both snipers were now leaning well out of the aircraft, trying to get their sights on the centre mass of their targets.

The left-hand marksman shook his head in frustration and hauled himself back inside.

'This is no good,' he shouted, to his colleague. 'I can't maintain the target in the scope. I'm going to try with the 41.'

He stowed his AMP, unclipped his Heckler & Koch G41 assault rifle, and leaned back out.

Way outside the effective range of the weapon, but he could at least keep the iron sights on the group and maintain better situational awareness.

'Closer!' he said.

In response, the pilot dipped the chopper slightly, to gain on the terrorists.

At which point, one of them vanished inside the boat.

'One of them just went below,' said the co-pilot.

'Seen,' said the pilot.

'Keep going!' shouted the left-hand sniper.

What happened next happened very quickly.

The *Lucky Lady* suddenly slowed, meaning that the helicopter shot forwards relative to the boat.

Both snipers temporarily lost her, as the controlling pilot throttled back, lifting the nose to avoid getting within 7.62mm range.

At the same moment, the terrorist who had gone below now reappeared, carrying something long and black in his right hand.

In one smooth motion, he hefted it onto his shoulder, braced his feet, and looked up.

'Oh, shit,' said the pilot, instinctively breaking right, away from the contact.

Unfortunately, the manoeuvre simply made the roaring engine – and its heat signature – more visible to the missile's infra-red sensors.

Below him, out of the pilot's eyeline, there was a flash, and the Russian-made 9K38 Igla MANPAD released its projectile.

The pilot had pushed the Eurocopter hard right and down, desperately trying to throw the SAM off, but, with no countermeasure capability on the aircraft, they were dead and he knew it.

The missile detonated a little over a second after being fired, igniting the 280 litres of avgas still in the tanks and turning the front of the aircraft into an inferno.

As the disintegrating helicopter started to spin and descend, the snipers could hear the pilots screaming over their headsets.

The left-hand man unbuckled himself and leaped out, breaking his legs and back when he hit the water two hundred feet below, and knocking himself out.

He drowned shortly afterwards.

The other three men lived only until the aircraft itself smacked into the surface and exploded.

By which time, the *Lucky Lady* was already back up to top speed, and powering south through the choppy Mediterranean Sea.

# 26.

THE LOSS OF THE *Cuerpo Nacional de Policía* helicopter was not immediately confirmed, but there is only one obvious reason why such an aircraft might have both suddenly dropped below the radar horizon *and* lost radio contact, and the controllers in Seville were immediately alarmed.

They made contact with the amphibious assault ship SPS *Juan Carlos I*, which had a section of marines aboard a long-range NH Industries NH90 some twenty minutes away and closing in on the *Lucky Lady*, and asked for a local SITREP.

In London, Justin Nicholls and the rest of the MI6 leadership watched the situation develop.

The *Policía* chopper had disappeared at 14:24hrs BST, and repeated radio messages had gone unanswered.

At 14:40hrs, the *Juan Carlos* aircraft arrived at its last known location and reported debris and at least one body in the sea.

It then departed in pursuit of the yacht, which was by now some thirty-five kilometres off the coast of Morocco.

The Royal Navy of Morocco, meanwhile, had a French-built VCSM fast boat and a Floréal-class frigate, the *Hassan II*, out on exercise to the east. After liaising with the Spanish, those craft were now steaming west to try to intercept the terrorists. The *Hassan* had had its Panther helicopter up, but the ship's captain now recalled it, understandably wary of letting it get within shooting distance of the yacht, which was heading at maximum speed towards Morocco's northern coast.

'What's their game?' murmured C. 'They must know they're going to be caught.'

'They don't care, do they?' said the head of the Spanish desk. 'They're hoping to ram something and go out in a blaze of glory.'

'So why go to the trouble of taking hostages?' said Justin Nicholls. 'Why not just kill them on the beach?'

# 27.

AT THE VERY moment Nicholls said that, the *Lucky Lady* slowed temporarily to thirty knots, and Argun Shishani and the man in the Manchester United shirt pushed the three women – all roped together and wearing flotation jackets – into the water, and jumped off after them.

All five of them got ears and noses full of water, and surfaced, winded and choking, to see the white boat powering off into the distance.

In the open water behind it, a small green RIB – a rigid inflatable, its shape picked out by a rubber buoyancy tube – had been bobbing in the gentle swell, a sea anchor holding it on station.

Low profile, invisible to radar.

The single man aboard it pushed the throttle forward, spooling up the big outboard Yamaha motor, and made his way over.

Shishani hauled himself aboard, and then leaned out to pull the first of the women in after him.

She struggled, at first, but when he punched her in the face she gave in. The others obeyed, meekly.

As the other man clambered into the dinghy, Shishani turned to the women.

'Lie down!' he said.

They did as they were told, huddling together in the bottom

of the small boat. Shishani bent down, unfolded a dark tarpaulin, and spread it over the women.

Then he crawled under and lay down alongside them, the other terrorist following him.

Anyone looking from above would now see a small boat with – apparently – one person aboard.

The guy at the helm turned the inflatable and headed south-east.

Under the tarp, Argun Shishani smiled to himself.

One of the women started crying.

# 28.

TEN MINUTES LATER, the NH90 from the *Juan Carlos* finally caught up with the *Lucky Lady*.

Aware that another aircraft had gone down in the vicinity of the yacht, its crew were wary. Being military, they were at least trained to deal with MANPADs, and their helicopter was better-equipped with counter-measures, but still they stood off some 500 metres, the sensor operator observing the vessel's progress on his screen.

After a few moments, he said, 'No sign of the hostages on the rear deck. Take me to the side.'

The NH90 had a hundred knots on the boat, so it took a matter of moments for the pilots to get alongside.

The operator took his time, zooming in close on the yacht's narrow, darkened windows.

'Nothing,' said the operator. 'Front.'

The helicopter pulled ahead, the underslung camera swivelling to keep the speeding white craft in sight.

'Nothing. Other side… Nothing. They must have taken them below.'

The pilot keyed his microphone to talk to the *capitán* commanding the marines in the back, who had been listening in.

'You heard all that, Ramos,' said the pilot. 'What do you want to do?'

Capitán Ramon Ramos thought for a moment.

Fact was, he wasn't *sure* what to do.

His orders were to recover the three women and take the terrorists alive, if possible.

But Ramon Ramos knew that there was no way these guys were coming quietly – he'd known from the moment he climbed aboard the aircraft that this was going to end in tears for someone.

His best hope had always been that his blokes could see and take out the bad guys.

But if everyone was below deck…

'Ramos?'

'Get back alongside, close enough so I can see the fucking thing.'

The pilot did as requested.

Ramos tugged on his harness and edged closer to the open door of the chopper.

Below him, the gleaming white yacht smashed and bounced its way inexorably through the shining sea.

He turned to the man next to him, Cabo Primero Jorge Fernández, who was sitting with his legs dangling in thin air, his Accuracy International .50 cal rifle cradled in his lap.

'What do you reckon, Jorge?' shouted Ramos, nodding at the rifle. 'Can we stop him with that?'

Fernández shrugged. 'How the fuck should I know, boss?' he shouted back. 'If I hit the engine, yeah. But just firing blind into the damned thing – who's to say I won't hit the fuel lines and barbecue the lot of them?'

Ramos keyed his mike, and got on the net to León, the HQ call sign.

Quickly, he updated them, and listened to the response.

Then he said, 'We can take the entire back off it if you want, sir, but the hostages could be in living quarters directly underneath the rear deck for all we know. Meanwhile, the target will be inside Moroccan territorial waters in five minutes, I say again *five minutes*. Please advise whether we are free to pursue into Moroccan airspace. If not, please advise course of action, over.'

Again, he listened.

Then he turned to Jorge Fernández.

'Fucking hell, Jorge,' he shouted. 'What a balls-up. The Moroccans have pulled back their ships and HQ can't get any sense out of Rabat – it looks like they're swerving it, they don't want the blood of the hostages on their hands. And now HQ are swerving it, too. We're cleared into Moroccan airspace, but the decision as to what to do is ours. Wankers.'

As Fernandez shook his head and smiled wearily, the captain keyed his mike again.

'León, we are…' he said.

But that was as far as he got.

'*What the…?*' he said. 'Stand by, please.'

The helicopter had banked violently right, and out of the open door Ramos could see why.

Below them, the *Lucky Lady* had turned sharply inland.

The pilot came on the net. 'Looks like he's heading towards Ceuta,' he said. 'What do we do?'

Ramos, toying with the St Christopher's medallion round his neck, thought for ten seconds – a long time to think, at times like this.

Then he said, 'In the next few minutes, they're going to have to make a decision about where they go ashore. We're going to follow until they disembark. Maybe we can get a clear shot then. Any reason why that's a shit plan, Jorge?'

'No. I mean, it's not a *great* plan, boss, but we are where we are.'

'Do we put down?' said the pilot, over the radio.

'Not unless I say. Get us within range, but watch out for fucking MANPADs, for Christ's sake.'

'Oh, I will, don't you fucking worry about that.'

Below them, the yacht ploughed on.

Capitán Ramon Ramos looked ahead.

The boat was heading directly for El Chorillo beach.

Crowded with sunbathers.

It was still doing close to fifty knots, and showing no sign of slowing

And Ramos suddenly realised what was happening.

'Oh, fuck,' he shouted. '*Fuck!*'

# 29.

THE FIRST TWO to die were swimmers who were run over and dismembered when the final terrorist – a short, stocky Moroccan called Khaled Benchakroun – deliberately ploughed through a bunch of people in the water.

The next two were a pair of teenaged girls, who were smeared like strawberry jam on the sand as he drove the 190-tonne boat ashore and straight over the top of them.

Six more people were killed when Benchakroun jumped from the stranded, heeling yacht and shot indiscriminately at horrified holidaymakers on the very beach on which he had spent his teenaged summers, selling T-shirts and trinkets to identical tourists.

The eleventh person to die was Benchakroun himself, his head blown half off by Jorge Fernández from the hovering helicopter three hundred metres offshore.

Under Ramos' instructions, the helicopter then landed a hundred metres from the *Lucky Lady*.

Half of his men were sent to clear away those few people who had not run off the beach, and the other half began to approach the yacht, to engage the remaining terrorists, whom they had every reason to believe were still aboard, and to free the hostages.

But as they got within ten metres of the boat, a twenty-kilogram ball of Semtex was ignited by a timed detonator, initiated by Benchakroun in his last act before leaving the vessel, and five marines were killed, Jorge Fernández and Ramon Ramos among them.

# 30.

BY NOW, JUSTIN Nicholls was alone in his office, on the fifth floor of the SIS HQ at Vauxhall, digesting the news from the explosion on the beach at Ceuta and casting his eye over casualty reports.

The numbers would change – they always did – but the best current estimate was eighty-nine Britons killed aboard the MS *Windsor Castle*, out of a total of 104 dead, and seventeen dead on the beach, out of a total of seventy-one.

It could have been worse, he supposed – but then, if you lost more than a hundred of your own and still found yourself looking on the bright side, that was a very bad day.

His phone buzzed, quietly.

It was his assistant, Hugo.

'Alec Palmer from the Spanish desk, sir,' he said.

'Thanks, Hugo,' said Nicholls.

He heard a click and said, 'Alec?'

Palmer sounded breathless.

'The three female hostages taken from Marbella, Justin?' he said. 'We're pretty sure that one of them is the Prime Minister's oldest daughter, Charlotte.'

Justin Nicholls was a very intelligent man, with a double first in mathematics from Cambridge and over two decades in the SIS behind him; it was rare that he was lost for words.

This was one of those times.

He and his wife were family friends of the PM, Penelope Morgan, and he'd seen Charlotte Morgan grow up from a shy teenager to a confident young woman in the early stages of what was sure to be a glittering career at the Bar.

He shuddered at the thought of her being taken by those evil people, and blown apart on some foreign shore…

'Justin?' said Alec Palmer.

'Yes. Sorry. Christ. *Charlotte*? When did you hear this? How?'

'We've just put it together. She was on holiday with a group of friends. One couple had a row and went back to their hotel – luckily for them, as it turns out. That couple contacted the consulate an hour or so ago to say that their friends hadn't returned, and that they couldn't raise them on their phones. They've just identified the other three males in the temporary morgue in Marbella, but there's no sign of the three females. We've had a look at their phones. Nothing since about 1 p.m., which was roughly when they went onto the beach. So we're assuming…'

'Shit,' breathed Nicholls. '*Shit*. Did she not have RaSP with her?'

RaSP was Royalty and Specialist Protection, the Met Police element charged with protecting the Prime Minister and her family, among others.

'She'd turned them down, apparently. Said she wanted to "live her life".'

Nicholls was silent for a moment.

Then he said, 'They must have targeted her. The whole thing, this was what the Málaga distraction was all about. It was aimed at seizing her.'

'It certainly looks that way,' said Palmer.

'Her boyfriend's dead?'

'Yes.'

'Does Downing Street know?'

'It hasn't broken with the media yet. But…'

'But she'll have known Charlie was out there,' said Nicholls. 'So she'll have tried to get in touch with her. And…'

'That was what I was thinking,' said Palmer.

Nicholls was silent for a moment.

Then he said, 'I'll have to break it to the PM. Can you get me the latest from Ceuta? Last thing I saw, the boat was spread over a couple of acres and they were looking for bodies.'

'Will do.'

'Do you have someone getting alongside the surviving couple? We want whatever they have ASAP.'

'The Málaga officer's on his way.'

'Good. Thanks, Alec.'

Nicholls ended the call and dialled his assistant.

'I'm just going to see the chief, Hugo,' he said. 'Can you get me a car, please? When I'm finished upstairs I'll need to go over to Downing Street.'

# 31.

THE MI6 INTELLIGENCE officer arrived at the Puente Romano hotel, on the Bulevar Príncipe Alfonso von Hohenlohe, just as Justin Nicholls climbed into the car to take him to Downing Street.

He was a nondescript Welshman in his early thirties, who went by the name of 'Liam', and who worked – officially – in a back office notarial role in the Málaga consulate.

In reality, his job was to mooch around the place finding out what he could about serious organised crime that might lead back to the UK and assessing and updating the regional terrorism picture.

Thomas Carter answered his knock.

He looked shell-shocked.

'My name's Liam Smith, sir,' said the MI6 officer. 'From the consulate. May I come in?'

'It's not a good time,' said Carter. 'We…'

'I'm afraid I do just need to come in,' said Liam, firmly.

He stepped in, past Tom Carter's weak protests.

It was cool inside. Jemima Craig was lying on the blue-and-gold brocade counterpane, her eyes puffy and red, a tissue in her left hand.

'She's in no fit state to talk,' said Carter.

The MI6 man turned to face him.

'I'm here on the instructions of the Prime Minister herself, sir,' he said, very firmly. 'I need to talk to you about your missing friends.'

'Let him speak, Tom,' said Jemima, from the bed.

Tom Carter's shoulders relaxed. He sat down next to his girlfriend and looked up at Liam, his eyes strained and unbelieving.

'What do you want to know?' he said.

'I need as much information about what happened today as possible.'

The couple both said nothing.

'I know it's tough,' said Liam. 'I'll be as quick as I can.' He pulled out a notebook. 'You've been here for four days, yes?'

'Yes.'

'Did anyone know where you were staying?'

'My mum,' said Jemima Craig. 'But that was it.'

'Could the others have told people?'

'Yes. But I have no idea if they did. Why?'

'Did you tell anyone that Charlotte Morgan was going to be coming with you?'

They looked at each other, blankly.

'No,' said Jemima. 'Why would we?'

'Prime Minister's daughter,' said Liam. 'People might have been interested.'

'It's not a big deal to us. She's just our friend.'

Liam nodded. 'Did you go to the beach at Puerto Banús every day?' he said.

'No,' said Tom Carter. 'Today was the first time. We went to Bounty Beach on the first day. Elvira the next. Yesterday we did the Old Town.'

The MI6 man made a note. 'Who took the decision to go down there today?' he said.

Tom Carter looked at his girlfriend. 'Charlotte, wasn't it?'

'No, it was Emily,' said Jemima.

'That's right, Emily.'

Liam nodded. 'Did you notice anyone watching you? Following you?'

'Today?'

'Any day. But today especially.'

'No.'

'I did,' said Jemima. 'I told you I had.'

Liam sat up straighter and looked over at the young brunette, who had raised herself onto her elbows.

'Go on,' he said.

'There was a guy at the airport in Málaga,' she said. 'He was sort of loitering at arrivals. We'd ordered a minibus to bring us here, and it was ten or fifteen minutes late. The whole time, this guy was watching us. He tried to make out that he wasn't, but he was. Charlotte saw it too, but… Anyway, at the time, I thought… well, Charlotte's really pretty, and her friend Emily, she could be a model, so you kind of expect it. It was a bit creepy, but I didn't think much of it. But then I saw him today, when Tom and I walked off the beach.'

'What was he doing?'

'Just kind of loitering by the palm trees up there.'

'Can you describe him, Jemima?'

'About my height, maybe a bit taller. Indian-looking. Mid-twenties. At the airport he was wearing jeans and a red football shirt. Manchester United, I think. Today he was wearing the same T-shirt, but a pair of shorts.'

'If we could get some CCTV images, would you be happy to have a look at them for us?'

'Of course.'

Liam took a moment. Then he said, 'We're working on the assumption that the three women have been taken somewhere, probably for ransom. What can you tell me about them? Starting with Charlotte.'

Jemima had been friends with Charlotte Morgan since their schooldays, so she was able to talk in great detail about her.

'Tell me about Martha Percival?' said Liam.

'Lovely girl,' said Tom Carter. 'Her husband is… He was a good friend of mine. I've known her for six or seven years. Gregarious, funny, very bright. Lovely.'

Liam made a note. 'And Emily Souster?' he said.

'She and Charlotte know each other from work,' said Jemima. 'She's a solicitor, I think. Mostly human rights-type stuff. They're kind of friends, but *work* friends, if you know what I mean?'

'What's she like?'

Jemima and Thomas looked at each other.

'We don't really know her,' said Jemima. 'First time we met her was at Stansted.'

'I'm sensing something,' said Liam.

'To be brutally honest,' said Tom, 'she's a bit of a pain in the arse. She's a very attractive girl, but massively high maintenance. No sense of humour. Started bad and got worse, to the point where she hardly said a word to anyone today. She was just in a foul mood, I guess. I thought time of the month, maybe.'

'Tom!' hissed Jemima.

'I'm trying to be fair to her,' he said, defensively. 'If she had PMT, fair enough. If not… Anyway, we tried to ignore it. All week she'd been giving her boyfriend a hard time.'

'How do you mean, a hard time?'

'I don't know. She was just very *cold* to him, I thought. What did you think, Jem?'

Jemima nodded. 'Yes, cold's the right word. They hadn't been going out very long, and it was like she had to bring someone, so she brought Nick? He was pretty fed up with her, I think. I don't think they were going to continue seeing each other after… after…'

She started crying again, apologising through her sobs.

'Don't worry,' said Liam. 'It's fine.'

'Boyfriend seemed a decent bloke,' said Tom Carter. 'She's a teetotaller, so she'd go to bed early every night, and he'd stay up boozing with us.'

'You said she was high maintenance?' said Liam.

'Yeah,' said Carter. 'Like, we had a massive drama yesterday because she suddenly realised she hadn't packed her favourite bikini. Sunday and Monday, a green bikini's fine. Then suddenly it has to be her shocking pink one. So we spent half the morning yesterday trawling round the shops in the Old Town trying to get a shocking pink bikini in her size. In the end, the rest of us left her to it. She eventually turned up with the damned thing at about three o'clock. Don't get me wrong, it looked pretty good on her, but…'

He tailed off.

'I don't know what more we can tell you,' he said, eventually. 'It's just a terrible, terrible thing.'

# 32.

AT ABOUT THAT time, Justin Nicholls' car arrived at the gate to No. 10 Downing Street.

He walked to the front door, nodded and smiled to the uniformed copper on duty outside, and stepped in.

As he did so, his mobile rang, with an MI6 identifier.

'Nicholls,' he said.

It was Alec Palmer.

'The Spanish say the boat was empty when it blew up,' said Palmer.

'*Empty*?'

'Yes. There was a guy driving it, but he jumped off and started shooting people, and it exploded a few seconds after that. The human debris field starts a few metres from the vessel itself – there were some Spanish marines nearby who copped the whole thing. But there's no sign of any human remains from the inside.'

'Could they be mistaken?'

'No.'

'If I'm going to tell the PM, I need to be sure.'

'I've spoken to them myself,' said Palmer. 'They're a hundred per cent certain. Meat is meat. No meat, no bodies.'

*Meat is meat.*

Justin Nicholls winced, Charlotte Morgan's face entering his mind.

'How did they get off?'

'The Spanish are working on that,' said Palmer. 'The target boat might have slowed for a few seconds and…'

'A sea transfer?'

'Looks that way.'

Nicholls nodded. 'Okay. Let me know immediately if there's any developments, Alec.'

'Of course.'

Nicholls ended the call.

'Mr Nicholls?' said a waiting aide. 'If you'd like to follow me?'

She took him down through the back of the house and outside to the garden.

On the other side of the large, bowling green lawn, on a wooden bench pressed against the tall, brick wall, and under the shade of a large buddleia alive with butterflies, sat the Prime Minister, Penelope Morgan.

She was ashen-faced but holding it together.

She always had been a tough cookie, Nicholls thought.

Next to her was Sir Peter Smith, the grey-haired Cabinet Secretary.

Smith stood up and pulled a garden chair out and round in front of the bench.

The two men shook hands, Justin leaned down and kissed Penelope on the cheek, and then he and Smith sat down.

'Is she dead, Justin?' said Penelope.

'No,' said Nicholls.

'How do you know? The boat… On the beach at Ceuta… '

'I've just had word. The Spanish say there was only one terrorist left on board when it went ashore, and he got off just before it went up.'

'How can they be sure?'

'Trust me,' said Nicholls. 'They're sure.'

'It was all about her, wasn't it?' said the Prime Minister.

'It does look that way,' said Nicholls, gravely. 'The cruise liner at Málaga seems to have been a diversion. The main target was the beach at Puerto Banús.'

'You mean *Charlie* was the main target?'

'Yes,' said Nicholls. 'She and two of her friends were taken aboard a yacht – some sort of super-fast, millionaire's plaything which had been stolen and the owner killed. The Spanish eventually got a chopper next to it and followed it all the way to Ceuta, where, as you know...'

Sir Peter Smith cleared his throat. 'So if Charlotte and her friends were on the boat when it left Marbella, but not on the boat when it exploded, how did they get off?'

'They must have had another boat waiting somewhere. You slow down, push them off into the water, and then haul them into the new boat... Not pleasant, but perfectly survivable. Clever, really.'

'So where is she now?' said Penelope Morgan.

Nicholls shrugged apologetically. 'I assume they landed somewhere on the North African coast. We're working on it.'

'No word from the... from the men who took her?'

'Not yet. But that's the one thing to hold on to. Look, Penny, there's no point in kidnapping the daughter of the British Prime Minister just to kill her.'

'What happened to Eddie?' said Penelope Morgan.

'Her boyfriend? I'm afraid...'

Morgan looked down, her hands clasped together tightly.

'He was a lovely young man,' she said. 'Paddy and I had high hopes of him. I must speak to his parents. They lost another son two years ago on a motorbike. How awful.'

'I'm sorry.'

There was another, heavier silence.

Nicholls looked up at the mortar fence protruding six feet above the weathered brick wall.

He felt a pang of nostalgia for the old days, when the worst threat they had faced was a few angry Irishmen and their home-made fertiliser bombs. That had been bad, but manageable. He wasn't sure the new enemy was going to be so easy to contain, much less defeat, unless the playing field changed dramatically – and the rules with it.

Penelope Morgan cleared her throat. 'Why didn't we know about this?' she said.

Justin Nicholls was silent.

'It's a major failure of intelligence, Justin.'

Nicholls looked down at his feet for a moment.

The scale and nature of the threat they faced meant that it was impossible to stop every attack, but he knew that she was right.

'Yes,' he said. 'There will have to be a full enquiry. But, for now, let's worry about finding her and getting her back alive.'

The Prime Minister winced.

Sir Peter Smith stood up. 'I have a couple of things to do ahead of the COBRA meeting. Will you be attending, Justin?'

'No. C will be there, though.'

Smith nodded, said his goodbyes, and walked off into No. 10.

Penelope Morgan watched him go, and then looked up at the early evening sky above; it was a perfect blue, with a single fluffy cloud hanging overhead.

'Gorgeous,' she said, absently. 'I remember my mother telling me that I was going to be Prime Minister one day. You know what she was like.'

Justin nodded and smiled, despite the situation.

'We were down by the stables,' said Penelope. 'She said to me, "You'll be the Prime Minister one day. Ten years at the Bar, then fifteen years of politics, then you mark my words, my girl, you'll be the head honcho!" And here I am. I achieved her dream. Would have made her proud.' She sniffed, fighting her emotions. 'But I wish to God I'd married Dicky Coates and become a bloody farmer's wife. When was the last time anyone kidnapped a farmer's daughter?'

Nicholls said nothing.

The air was filled with late evening birdsong, and the muted sounds of London traffic.

Somewhere inside No. 10, a phone was ringing off the hook.

He said, 'Have you told Paddy and the other kids yet?'

'Paddy's in the States on business,' said Penelope Morgan. 'He's cutting it short and flying back tonight. Sophie was at her boyfriend's house and is on her way up to town. Joff's upstairs in the flat. He's in a terrible state. It's his big sister.'

She looked at Nicholls.

'One thing does occur to me, Justin,' she said. 'How did they know where Charlotte was?'

'Yes, that has occurred to us, too,' he said, drily. 'It's something else we don't yet know. We'll look at the airlines and the hotel and all that, but someone probably told someone they shouldn't have. It's usually loose lips.'

Morgan nodded.

She thought for a moment.

Then she said, 'I'll stop at nothing to get them back, Justin. Whatever it takes. She comes home. They *all* come home. Is that clear?'

'Well, we'll...'

'I'm serious. Never mind the courts. Those girls are in this position because I am who I am. And there's no point being who I am if you can't use what little power you have.'

Nicholls nodded.

Perhaps the rules *had* changed.

# 33.

FIFTEEN HUNDRED MILES south, at 20:00hrs local time, John Carr was sitting in an interview room in the main *Policía Nacional* station in Marbella.

He was nursing a few bumps and bruises, and a split lip, and looking across a grey melamine table at a pair of Spanish detectives.

They'd just come back to the room after a while spent checking out his story.

Now the older of the two pushed a sweaty, Clingfilm-wrapped cheese-and-tomato roll across the table, along with a Styrofoam cup of weak Lipton's tea, the yellow tag showing that the bag was still in it.

'I'm formally telling you now that you are no longer a suspect,' said the younger man, Inspector-Jefe Javier de Padilla. He spoke in Spanish, since Carr was fluent – he'd spent a lot of time in South America on Regimental operations targeted against the coke barons of Colombia and Mexico.

'I hope you can see why we were not sure. Everyone else had run away, except for you and your son…'

He tailed off.

'Yeah,' said Carr. 'Don't worry about it.'

He'd had plenty of experience of terrorist situations, and he knew the deal: everyone's hostile until proven otherwise.

In fact, he'd been surprised at the professionalism of the guys who had arrested him and George.

They'd got them face down in the sand, hands on heads, and then he'd felt the muzzle of his No1's weapon pressed hard into the back of his skull, no room for ambiguity, while the No. 2 conducted a good search.

True, once he'd been cuffed they'd stuck a few punches and kicks in – a lawyer wouldn't like it, but lawyers operated in quiet, air-conditioned rooms, not with the air filled with gunsmoke and the groans of dying, blood-spattered children.

As far as Carr was concerned, they'd shown good drills.

'If you feel the treatment was too rough…'

'Nah,' he said, with a slight grin. 'I've had worse off my ex-wife. Like I said, don't worry about it. All I'm interested in is any news on my daughter.'

'I have good news, there, Mr Carr,' said de Padilla. 'I just heard from the officers we sent to your villa. Both she and the other member of your party are safe and well, and at the villa.'

'I need to go,' said Carr, pushing back his chair. 'She'll be worried to death.'

'Please, Mr Carr,' said the policeman, holding up a hand. 'I told my officers to stay with her, and to tell her that both you and your son are fine, and are helping us.'

Carr sat back in his chair.

'One hour,' he said. 'Then I have to go.'

'I understand.' De Padilla picked up a pen. 'So, I would like to take a statement. Is this okay?'

'Sure.'

'Do you want a lawyer?'

'Do I need one?'

'As I say, you're not a suspect. We have broadly the same laws of self-defence as in the UK.' He smiled. 'To me, the only question is which of our civilian gallantry awards you and your son will receive.'

Carr thought for a moment. 'What about the two police officers and their pistols?'

The officer shrugged. 'You did what you had to do. I am more concerned that you don't tell people that our guys were running away. They'll finish their careers in a small town somewhere far away, believe me.'

'My lips are sealed.'

'Sorry?'

'I won't tell anyone.'

'Okay,' said de Padilla. 'So, I really want to see if you can help us identify any members of the gang.'

'Sounds like a plan,' said Carr.

'So, we start from the beginning. You went to the beach with your son and the two ladies at what time?'

'Before we get into that,' said Carr. 'I think I saw one of them.'

'One of the terrorists?' said de Padilla. 'I don't understand.'

Carr sipped his tea.

It was hot and weak.

'You know my background,' he said. 'I've done a lot of surveillance work. There was a guy on the beach. Dark hair, dark eyes, white clothing. Carrying flip-flops in his hand. He was trying to act like a normal tourist – playing the grey man, we call it – but he didn't quite pull it off. There was a group of young Brits, including four girls. Twenties, good-looking. One in a shocking pink bikini, one in a black bikini. A couple of others. I just thought he was scoping them out. I didn't blame him, to be fair. But given that the girls he was looking at were later taken away… He obviously had other things on his mind.'

'Did he see you?'

'No. He was so busy trying to disassociate himself from his target that he forgot about third-party. Most basic mistake in surveillance.'

'What's *third party*?'

'Me. The watcher watching the watcher. He thought it was just him, the target, and a bunch of random civilians. But I'm a paranoid motherfucker, and he stood right in front of me, so I paid attention. He stuck in my mind. He had a big chunk out of his right calf – probably a round, or a bit of shrapnel. It gave him a weird, rolling gait.' Carr finished off his tea. 'That's another mistake. Should have given that job to someone less distinctive.'

'Would you recognise him again?' said de Padilla.

'Aye. At night, in a jungle, blindfolded.'

'I don't understand, Mr Carr. Why *at night, in a jungle, blindfolded*?'

'Sorry,' said Carr. 'Sense of humour trying to kick in. Basically, yes, I would. I'd recognise him anywhere.'

# 34.

AT AROUND THAT moment, the little green RIB finally came ashore, guided by a Garmin GPS device to a rocky beach on the western end of the Al Hoceima National Park, a remote and empty swathe of northern Morocco which was forested with thuja cypresses, and criss-crossed by dirt tracks.

His dark eyes flashing, Argun Shishani and the surviving shooter – Abdullah el Haloui, in his Manchester United shirt – hustled the three women onto the shallow beach and up into the cover of the trees.

'Lie down!' snapped Shishani. 'Face the ground.'

'No, please,' said one of them, but when el Haloui raised his shortened AK they meekly complied.

'Now be quiet,' snapped the Chechen.

He cocked his head on one side, listening.

Nothing but crickets, and the rustling of the trees overhead.

He nodded, satisfied. 'Wait here,' he said, to his comrade. He nodded toward the water. 'I have to speak to him.'

With his strange, lopsided walk, Shishani hurried back down to the inflatable, where the boatman, his face weathered by sixty years of sun and salt spray, was in the process of refuelling the engine from a jerry can.

'Malik, my friend,' said Shishani. 'I have a gift for you.'

'It's not necessary, *saheb*,' said Malik, with an open smile. 'I am just happy to do my duty.'

'But it *is* necessary,' said Shishani, and as he walked towards the other man he reached into the bag over his shoulder.

When he was six feet away, he pulled out a pistol – an FNP, loaded with .45 ACP subsonic rounds – and an angular Osprey suppressor.

Malik's eyes widened as he saw the weapon. 'What are you doing?' he said, nervously.

'I'm putting this suppressor on this pistol,' said Shishani.

'But *why*?'

Shishani didn't answer for a couple of seconds, but continued screwing the suppressor onto the FNP.

Then he said, 'Because although Al Hoceima is a desolate place I cannot discount the possibility that there may be someone nearby, and I don't want them to hear this.'

And, with that, he raised the weapon and shot the boatman twice in the chest.

Suppressors do not 'silence' gunfire, but the right equipment does greatly reduce the report, and subsonic rounds have none of the *crack* caused by a faster bullet as it breaks the sound barrier: the noise of the shots, and the brittle, metallic sound of the moving parts in action, was lost in the humid breeze.

Malik fell backwards into the shallows with a splash and there he lay, eyes and mouth open, his breathing laboured, the water lapping over him, a red cloud forming on either side.

His pupils tracked Shishani as he stepped forward into the water.

The dying man tried to speak, but produced only guttural sounds.

'Hush, my friend,' whispered the Chechen, putting the pistol to Malik's forehead. 'I give you the gift of paradise.'

The single report from the pistol sent the old man on his way into eternity.

Shishani took a knife and stabbed the inflated rubber panels of the boat in several places. As the air hissed out, he pushed the foundering RIB out into the Mediterranean.

Then he walked back up the beach.

Abdullah el Haloui met him halfway, a sardonic smile playing on his lips.

'Did you have to do that, *zaeim*?' he said, his hands relaxing on the AK, which was slung from his neck across his chest.

'I'm afraid so,' said the Chechen. 'I couldn't risk him talking. And he is a martyr now. He should be grateful.'

'I guess so,' said the young Moroccan, with a chuckle. 'But how do you know *I* won't talk?'

'I don't,' said Shishani, raising the FNP to other man's chest.

The smile dropped off el Haloui's lips in an instant.

He went for the pistol grip of his AK, but it was a futile move and the last thing he would ever consciously do.

Shishani fired two rounds, point-blank, into him.

The first clipped the top of his heart, and took his legs away. The second hit him in the throat as he dropped, smashing through his larynx and exiting the back of his neck, taking a chunk of his spinal cord with it.

The body hit the ground with a dead thud; this time, there was no need for any *coup de grâce*.

It was a moment or two before the Chechen could bring himself to look down at the fallen man.

Abdullah had played an invaluable role in the operation, from the moment when he had tailed the Morgan girl and her friends from the airport at Málaga to their hotel, to his glorious actions on the Spanish beach earlier this very day.

But this was no time for sentiment. If they were to succeed, then their mission had to be sealed off from the outside world.

Hermetically.

Not to mention, Abdullah was a true believer, utterly pure in spirit, and might well have caused trouble later.

'I am sorry, brother,' said Shishani, with genuine regret. 'But I cannot bury you.'

He glanced up into the trees.

All three women were still lying face down, not daring to look around.

He bent down, pulled el Haloui's weapon from his dead grasp, and walked back up the slope, looking at his watch.

Soon, soon.

'Get up,' he said. 'We must walk. And if any of you does not do as I say she will die here and now.'

The three women stood up and walked into the forest along a sandy path, the heady scent of cypress filling their nostrils.

# 35.

AS THE MOROCCAN night darkened, the headlights appeared.

Five minutes later, two Toyota Land Cruisers rolled and swayed along the undulating dirt road, and stopped.

A man got out – a giant, dressed in a grubby, blue *gandora* thobe and sandals, with a bushy, greying beard.

He beamed at Shishani, and the two men embraced and kissed each other on both cheeks.

'Oh, it's good to see you, Argun!' said Khasmohmad Kadyrov, in Chechen. 'When was it last, brother? Now Zad?'

'Khan Neshin,' said Argun Shishani. 'I believe.'

'So it was,' said Kadyrov. 'So it was. And today you have done a wonderful thing. Let me see her.'

'Surely,' said Shishani, and he led the other Chechen ten or fifteen yards into the trees where the three women still lay, face down, petrified.

At the sight of their bikini-clad bodies, Kadyrov's face grew dark.

'They're dressed like whores,' he spat. 'What is this insult?'

Shishani raised his palms in placation. 'I'm sorry, brother,' he said. 'We had clothes for them but they were left on the boat by mistake.'

'Which one is she?' said Kadyrov.

'The middle one.'

'Wait here.'

Kadyrov returned to his Land Cruiser. In his left hand were a couple of black sheets; in his right, a digital video camera.

He dropped the sheets and handed the camera to Shishani.

'The middle one, yes?' he said.

'Yes, she…' said Shishani.

'Give me that,' said Kadyrov, pointing to the still-silenced pistol in Shishani's waistband.

Shishani handed it over. Kadyrov stepped over to the women.

'Get up!' he said.

They stood, fearfully, not daring to meet his eye.

'You,' he said, pointing at the woman on the left. 'Name?'

'What?' she said.

'What is your name?'

'Martha.'

'*Martha*,' he repeated, rolling it around his mouth. He nodded. Then he looked at the woman on the right. 'And you?'

'Emily.'

He chuckled softly.

'Well, well,' he said, and looked at Shishani, eyebrows raised.

Shishani nodded.

'Thank you, ladies,' said Kadyrov. 'Everyone stand up, come with me.'

He grabbed Emily Souster roughly by the shoulder, turned her around, and pushed her forwards. The other women followed as he walked them back twenty, twenty-five metres, to the overhanging branches of the trees.

'Kneel!' he snapped.

'Please,' said Emily. 'What are you…?'

He raised the pistol, placed it against her forehead, and said, quietly, 'Kneel.'

She did as instructed.

'You two kneel either side of her,' he said.

'Emily...' said Charlotte Morgan.

Kadyrov slapped her in the face. 'Be quiet, woman,' he said, 'and kneel.'

The three women knelt in the sand, Charlotte and Martha held in position by masked men.

Kadyrov pulled on a black balaclava and stood behind Emily Souster.

'Turn it on,' he said.

There was an electronic beep as Shishani clicked the video camera.

'Begin filming,' said Kadyrov.

Shishani nodded.

The harsh glare of the light from the camera illuminating him, Khasmohmad Kadyrov looked into the lens and spoke, in heavily-accented English. 'Oh, Britain!' he said. 'This is a warning from us, the Warriors of Jihad. A taste of what is to come.'

He placed the pistol to the back of Emily Souster's neck, and she started and looked up at Shishani.

'What's he doing?' she said. 'I didn't...'

'Silence,' said Kadyrov, sharply. He looked into the camera. 'We have the daughter of the British Prime Minister. You can see her here. Now you will see that we are men of action.'

Somewhere overhead, an owl cried out.

The huge, masked Chechen pulled the trigger of the pistol.

The shot was aimed slightly to the right of Emily Souster's spinal column, and was designed not to kill her immediately, but to cause pain and suffering, and to increase the horror of the footage.

The round exited her throat underneath her chin and sent her sprawling forward, her eyes wide with shock as her body tried to draw in air through the ruptured airway. The noise of her dying gasps filled the otherwise silent air, as her lungs filled with blood.

From somewhere, Charlotte Morgan heard a high-pitched scream; she only realised that the scream was her own when the man holding her punched her in the back of the head, sending her face forwards into the sand.

Shishani kept rolling as Kadyrov leaned over the dying Emily and casually dispatched her with another shot to the head, as a hunter might destroy an injured rabbit.

The giant Chechen turned back to the camera.

'We will be in touch with your government very soon,' he said, placing the pistol back in its holster.

'Perfect, Khasmohmad,' breathed Shishani, before clicking the camera off.

Kadyrov pulled off his balaclava.

'You will transmit that to our friends in the Ivory Coast, for them to disseminate?' he said. 'Along with our message?'

'I will upload it as we drive,' said Shishani.

'And we're a hundred per cent sure it's secure? They won't trace our location?'

'We've been using these systems for long enough now, Khasmohmad. The encryption is superb.'

'Designed by American nerds and made available for free to the world,' said Kadyrov, shaking his head and chuckling. 'It must drive the CIA crazy.'

He tapped Charlotte Morgan and Martha Percival on the heads and said, 'To the vehicles.'

They stayed stock still, so the men who were holding them dragged them to their feet.

They were pushed roughly back towards the waiting Land Cruisers, where Kadyrov threw black sheets at them both.

'Make yourselves decent,' he said.

Charlotte slowly wrapped the sheet around herself, but Martha Percival simply stared vacantly at the ground, until one of the men threw the cloth over her.

Another man produced flatbreads, dates and a bottle of water.
'Eat,' said Kadyrov. 'And drink.'

Martha Percival stared at her feet and said nothing.

Charlotte Morgan looked up at him.

'No,' she said. 'You can kill me if you like.'

'All in good time, my dear,' said Kadyrov, with a smile. 'What is your expression? Good things come to those who wait. I won't force you to eat, but it has been some hours since you were taken, and I cannot allow you to die of thirst. So...'

He nodded at the man, who grabbed Charlotte's face, forced her mouth open, and thrust the bottle into it.

She choked and spluttered, but a good half-litre of water found its way into her stomach.

When the bottle was removed, Charlotte looked at Kadyrov, defiance blazing from her eyes.

'Very well,' he said. He turned back to the other men and said, almost benevolently, 'Now tape them. This one first.'

Two of the men approached and seized Charlotte by the arms and legs, and a third began winding white duct tape around her ankles. He worked quickly and methodically, and by the time he was finished, her entire body was taped solid; a fourth covered her head, so that the only visible parts were her feet, her mouth and the top of her hair. She looked like a mummy.

During the entire time, Charlotte Morgan said and did nothing. She knew that resistance was futile, and, while her mind was reeling in panic and fear, she was determined not to show it; she would not give them that satisfaction.

When both women were taped, Kadyrov leaned forwards and spoke to Charlotte.

'Welcome to our lands, my dear,' he said. 'We do things differently here, as you will learn. We are going to travel now on a journey, about three hours, to Saïdia. It's a beautiful place, but ruined by your people. At Saïdia we will catch a boat and go back to the sea.' He chuckled. 'Your intelligence people, we think they will be expecting us to stay on land,' he said. 'But they are not so clever.'

He turned and gestured towards the Land Cruisers.

'Now,' he said, 'you must be placed in the back of one of these vehicles. We have made a special place, under the seats. Because we do not wish you to perish from heat exhaustion, we have fed the cold air through it. But it will be uncomfortable. You must be careful to make no noise. If we are stopped by any authorities, you say nothing. It will not help you, anyway – even if they hear you, some of the police are on our side, some are very stupid, and the others we can either bribe or intimidate. But still, remember this: *you say nothing.* If you disobey, you will die.'

He looked at the men standing nearby and nodded.

They lifted Charlotte Morgan's stiffened, mummified form and carried her to the rear of the nearest 4x4.

It had, indeed, been modified, so that a narrow channel led from under the rear compartment's floor to the passenger seat.

They pushed her into it, head-first, bodily.

Snapped it shut.

She heard them replace the carpeted floor.

Load some bags on top.

Then nothing for quite some time.

Outside, in the warm moonlight, Kadyrov turned to Argun Shishani and sighed, contentedly. 'I can't believe how well things are going, brother,' he said. 'Ride with me.'

They climbed into the rear of the first 4x4, and a few moments later the two vehicles set off in a slow convoy.

Beneath and behind them, in the lurching claustrophobia of the Land Cruiser's secret compartment, Charlotte Morgan was fighting an inhuman terror which was total and absolute and almost all-consuming.

It was like being in a coffin: her body touched the sides of the compartment, and her head was pressed against the end. Her nose was inches from its roof.

After a minute or two the heat was already almost unbearable, despite the air-conditioning.

She wanted to call out, and scream, and beg, and plead, but she knew that it would not help.

She told herself to stay calm.

Breathe.

Started whispering a mantra: 'You're going to be alright, Charlotte, you're going to be alright.'

Somehow, she had to get through this – one second, one minute, one hour, one day at a time.

What was to come she did not know. All she did know was that she was alive, and her friends were dead.

She gritted her teeth, closed her eyes, and concentrated on how she might kill these evil bastards.

And, strangely, she felt her pulse slow a fraction, and her strength return.

Revenge is a powerful incentive.

# 36.

A LITTLE WHILE earlier, the police had finished with John Carr.

The main development was that they had been able to locate a shot of the man with the dark eyes, taken from a CCTV camera at the marina, for Carr to identify.

It wasn't very clear – the best angle was a three-quarter face, shot from above – but it was a start, and it was now being flashed to every friendly security service and police force in the world, to see what came back.

Inspector-Jefe Javier de Padilla had arranged for Carr and his son to be dropped back at the villa.

As soon as she saw her father, Alice flew at him, throwing her arms around his neck and burying her face in his shoulder, sobbing.

It took a while to calm her down, but eventually she settled.

'What happened?' said Carr, to Chloe.

'When you and George went, we went for a swim,' she said. 'We'd only got in up to our waists when they started shooting. It was… There were bullets everywhere. A little boy was killed just in front of us. We just swam further out and came back in up in the town.'

'It was horrible, Dad,' said Alice, wiping away tears. 'He was a toddler. There was so much blood. He screamed and then he went quiet. I wanted to help him, but I was too scared.'

'You couldn't have done anything, sweetheart,' said Carr, stroking her forehead.

As he spoke, he felt a cold rage building in his soul.

Carr had no qualms about killing those who truly deserved it. Throughout his long career in the Regiment, he had come up against plenty of men who *had* deserved it, and he had killed them without emotion, and had walked away without a backward glance.

The battlefield had allowed him that space; the civilian world, a world he was still getting used to, was different. It was a world of prevarication and second-guessing, and judgment by men who had never picked up a weapon and stood firm in their lives, and could not and did not know what it meant to look death in the eye and prevail by sheer force of will.

He lived now by the rules of the civilian world, so he forced his rage back down into the dark depths, and hid it from his little girl.

They talked for a while longer, but eventually the two young women started to flag as the adrenalin died away.

He put his daughter to bed, reassured her that he wasn't going anywhere, and then padded out onto the veranda, into the muggy Mediterranean air, and dialled a number.

Fifteen hundred miles north, at her home in County Down, his ex-wife picked up the phone.

'How are they?' said Stella, the anxiety palpable in her voice.

'Physically fine,' said Carr. 'Alice saw things she shouldn't have seen, but she's unhurt. George did well.'

'How do you mean?'

Carr quickly recounted the events.

'Oh my God, John,' said Stella. 'Oh my God.'

'He grew up today, Stell,' said Carr. 'Never took a backward step.'

They chatted a little more – Carr reassuring his ex-wife that he would be cutting short his holiday and flying Alice home the following day – and then ended the call.

A few moments later, George appeared, still in his Union Jack shorts, carrying a couple of cold San Miguels.

Three large candles were burning on a big wooden table, and the two of them sat there in silence for a while, drinking their beer in the cooling humidity, listening to the crickets and mosquitoes, and watching kamikaze moths fly into the flames.

A big white gecko scuttled up a wall.

Overhead, the stars drifted slowly by, oblivious to the momentous events of the day.

In the town below, the lights of emergency vehicles lit up various streets.

Carr sent George in for more beers, and when he came back he saluted him with a bottle.

'You did well today, son,' he said.

George felt a warm pride suffusing his body: his old man wasn't big on unearned praise, and he knew what he was talking about.

'What now?' he said.

Carr took a deep swig and felt the cold lager fizzing in his throat.

'We get shitfaced, I reckon,' he said. 'I'm taking your sister back home tomorrow. You stay out if you want. Lightning won't strike twice.'

'I didn't mean that.'

'What did you mean?'

'How are we going to get our hands on the bastards who got away?'

Carr looked out and down to the sea, a mile or so distant, and the lights of Marbella twinkling merrily and incongruously in the black water, from which death had emerged so suddenly, and into which it had retreated just as quickly.

'Not our problem.'

George finished his beer and went to fetch two more.

'Maybe I'll get a chance if I pass Selection,' he said, when he came back.

'Maybe,' said Carr. 'But that's a big *if*.'

George turned away, looking dejected.

'Hey, son,' said Carr, reaching over and punching him on the shoulder. 'Nothing against you, you're as good a candidate as any I've seen. But it's tough, and shit happens. I've seen good guys go down with injuries, or lose it in the jungle, or on combat survival, or just purely can't hack it. There's no guarantees.'

George Carr nodded.

'Remember what I said when you told me you were trying for the Paras?' said Carr.

George looked at him, grinning slightly. 'Not to come home if I failed, because no son of yours was failing.'

Carr threw back his head and laughed. 'That's right,' he said. 'Go and join the Foreign Legion. But I knew you'd pass. And I know you've got what it takes to pass Selection, too.'

A smile spread across George's face.

'But if you do fucking fail,' said Carr, finishing his beer, 'you can go and join the fucking Foreign Legion.'

# 37.

LIAM HAD INPUTTED the information he'd gleaned from the surviving couple, and Justin Nicholls picked it up on MI6's confidential feed just after midnight UK time.

There was varying levels of background on each of the eight members of the party.

All under thirty years of age.

A *Times* journalist – Charlotte Morgan's boyfriend, Edward Hanson.

Two lawyers, Charlie herself and a trustafarian solicitor called Emily Souster.

An investment banker called Nick Chandler who had travelled with Souster.

Jeremy Percival, who was a director at Percival Wareham, the London estate agency, and his wife, Martha.

Finally, the two lucky ones: financial adviser Thomas, and his nursery teacher girlfriend, Jemima.

Much of the focus would be on the three women who had been taken, but there was a decent new lead – the young guy in the Manchester United shirt who had followed them from Málaga arrivals, and then been seen on the beach. Some decent CCTV imagery of him had been found, and was being distributed.

And then there were the two who'd been shot dead; the results of DNA tests and fingerprint lifts from those bodies would be available soon.

If any or all of the men could be identified in some way, this would be a major start in working out where they were from and, most importantly, where they had gone.

It was early days, but they had a thread to pick at.

On the muted TV in the corner, tuned to the rolling twenty-four-hour Sky News channel, they were showing pictures of grieving family members starting to arrive at Málaga airport.

It was alternating with looped footage from Whitehall, showing people climbing into cars after the Civil Contingencies Committee meeting in the Cabinet Office Briefing Room.

Truth was, that wasn't much more than theatre: the media loved COBRA, but the real work was being done elsewhere.

He looked at his watch.

Nicholls had developed the ability to work for long stretches without sleep, but he was also long past any macho need to prove himself by staying longer, working harder, sticking at it.

There would be days ahead when he needed to pull longer hours, and he had to save his strength for those.

He switched his work station off, pulled on his jacket, and left the office.

# 38.

JOHN CARR WOKE with a start in the cool morning light, feeling damp and gritty-eyed.

It took him a moment to realise that he'd fallen asleep outside, on one of Konstantin's sun loungers.

He looked at his watch.

05:45 hrs.

He rubbed his eyes, stood up from the lounger, and padded into the villa through the open glass doors.

A security guy was asleep on the sofa.

Carr walked past him into the kitchen.

Made himself a cup of tea, and walked back out to the poolside with that in one hand and a stale chocolate brioche in the other.

Thought for a second, went back inside and prodded the security guard with his foot.

The man awoke with a start and a gasp.

'Morning, pal,' said Carr, cheerily. 'What's your name?'

'Yuri,' said the guard, rubbing his eyes and sitting up in shock. 'I…'

'You report to Oleg, right?'

Oleg Kovalev was Konstantin Avilov's head of security, a former Russian Foreign Intelligence Service spook and a good friend to Carr.

'Yes.'

Carr bit into the brioche, started chewing.

He wiped a smear of chocolate from the corner of his mouth with his thumb, and looked down at the Russian.

Early fifties, he guessed, and thickset, with that hard, Eastern European look about him.

'Spetznaz?' he said.

'No,' said Yuri. 'VDV.'

'Airborne,' said Carr, with an appreciative nod. 'Me too. Afghanistan?'

'Yes, for two year,' said Yuri, proudly. 'Also, First Chechen War.'

'That's some bad ju-ju,' said Carr, with a grin.

He took another bite of the brioche.

The Russian security man relaxed, and smiled back at him.

'You know my wee daughter's asleep upstairs?' said Carr.

The smile faded slightly, shading into confusion.

'So answer me this, Yuri,' said Carr. 'When you were on stag – you know, sentry duty – in Afghanistan, or Chechnya, did you fall asleep?'

Now the smile well and truly fell from the Russian's face. 'No,' he said.

'No,' said Carr. 'I bet you didn't. Because the Muj didn't fuck about, did they?'

Yuri said nothing, but Carr knew he'd understood. On more than a few occasions, Soviet sentries had dozed off, and had awoken to find their camp overrun, and themselves and their muckers about to be skinned alive by gleeful mujahideen.

Carr finished off the sweet bread, and washed it down with a mouthful of too-hot tea.

He paused.

Trying to decide whether to bollock the fucker, or punch him.

The look of contrition in the Russian's face softened Carr a little.

'Listen, Yuri,' he said, 'I'm going to let it go this time, but if you let me down again you and me are away round the back of the block, and then Oleg's going to have a go, and then when you get out of hospital you're looking for another fucking job. Do I make myself clear?'

'Yes,' said Yuri. 'I am sorry.'

'Good man,' said Carr. 'Don't worry about it. But it doesn't happen again, understood?'

The Russian nodded.

'Go and make yourself a strong black coffee, splash some water on your face, and keep alert.'

Carr took his tea outside and drank it while watching the sun rise over the hills to the east.

Felt the humid air warm a degree or two.

Another day in paradise, for some.

He finished the tea, threw the dregs into a flowerbed, and went back inside.

Had a piss, and a quick shower, and then padded along the cold tiles to the study.

He booked a pair of lunchtime flights back to Heathrow for himself and Alice, and then went to pack his kit.

# 39.

JOHN CARR HAD just loaded Alice's suitcase into the boot of the villa's Range Rover, when his mobile rang.

Number withheld.

He tended not to answer unknown callers, but under the circumstances this could be a friend or a relative.

He clicked green, climbed into the driver's seat, and turned the engine on to get the AC kicked in.

'Yes?' he said, looking at his daughter.

The expression on her face, he'd seen it many times: it was the vacant look of a young squaddie who's just gone through his first real firefight.

He couldn't help smiling, slightly.

'John, it's Justin Nicholls,' said the voice on the other end of the line.

Carr said nothing.

'We met at your flat a while back?' said Nicholls. 'You, me, and Guy de Vere.'

A mental image of Justin Nicholls appeared in Carr's head: nicely cut pin-stripe suit, expensive shirt, pinkie ring, discreet silver watch.

Black shoes with a mirror shine.

Sitting, uncomfortably, in Carr's place in Primrose Hill.

With Guy de Vere, Carr's old platoon commander from 3 Para, turned 22 SAS CO, then DSF, and now Commander Field Army.

A meeting to offer Carr a role in a new outfit being set up, strictly on the QT, by certain people at MI6, in the British Army, and various other interested parties.

For various unspecified tasks.

'Aye,' said Carr. 'I remember you.'

'I understand you're in Marbella,' said Nicholls. 'I'm sorry to hear that your daughter got caught up in it.'

Carr didn't even bother asking how he knew.

'She's fine,' he said.

'And I've been reading with interest of your exploits.'

'Oh, aye?'

'Yes. First thing I saw this morning. We have pretty good sources in the Spanish police. Mind you, we're not the only ones with sources in the Spanish police.'

'Meaning?'

'You're all over the *Daily Mail* this morning.'

'Is that so?'

'Yes. With a photo.'

'Aye?'

They must have taken it as he left the cop shop – the place had still been crawling with media.

'Yes,' said Nicholls. 'Not a very good one.'

'Hard to take a bad photo of me, Justin.'

'Low light,' said Nicholls. 'Taken from the side. You wouldn't know it was you.'

'What does the story say?'

'"Hero Brit on beach of hell",' said Nicholls. 'That's the headline. You can look it up online.'

'What does it say about *me*?'

'It names you, and says you're in your forties, and believed to be a former soldier.'

'Does it mention the Regiment?'

'No. It says you live in Hereford. I suppose people will work it out.'

'Does it mention George?'

'Who?'

'My son. He was with me.'

'No.'

'Good.'

'Anyway, I understand you may have seen one of the attackers?'

Carr chuckled – it amused him, the way the English upper classes tap-danced around things, using euphemisms and hints and never getting to the fucking point.

'Justin, you know I saw him. I'm sure you've already read my statement to that effect. Why else would you be calling me?'

'Ha,' said Nicholls. 'I haven't yet seen the statement actually. Though I expect I will fairly shortly. Would you mind giving me a heads-up?'

'Not much to tell. I saw a guy staring at the girls. Just thought he was a dirty old man at first. They pulled a picture of him off of the CCTV. Mean-looking fucker.'

'Speaking of the girls, do you know the identities of the women who were taken?'

'No. Should I?'

'It's all over social media.'

'I don't use social media.'

'One of them was the daughter of the Prime Minister.'

It took a lot to shock John Carr, but that certainly knocked him back.

'I see,' he said, after a few moments.

'Yes,' said Nicholls. 'I understand you're booked on the one o'clock into Heathrow.'

Carr said nothing.

'Anyway, I wondered... If anything occurs to you, if you

remember something you didn't tell the Spanish police, would you mind giving me a bell?'

'Sure.'

'You've got my number?'

'In my head,' said Carr.

He smiled to himself: it was actually stored in his phone under 'James Bond', but he wasn't going to tell Nicholls that.

'Great. Thanks. Look, I'd better get off. It's chaos here, as I'm sure you can imagine.'

Carr certainly could imagine: he had a vision of the MI6 HQ teeming with headless chickens.

Chinless, clueless, headless chickens, at that.

But he just said, 'Aye.'

The call ended and Carr turned to Alice.

'Buckle up,' he said.

'Who was that?' she said.

'Your granny,' he said.

'For fuck's sake, Dad,' said Alice, shaking her head. 'Why's everything got to be secret squirrel with you?'

He chuckled.

'I'm a leopard, sweetheart,' he said. 'I cannae change my spots.'

# 40.

CHARLOTTE MORGAN, MARTHA Percival and their captors had arrived at a compound on the outskirts of Saïdia not long after midnight.

There the first part of the two women's ordeal had ended, with their removal from the stinking, sweating hiding places under the floors of the two Land Cruisers.

They were half-carried, half-dragged quickly in through the open door of a stone house.

There they were split up, Martha being taken through a further door on the left, Charlotte through a door on the right.

The two men carrying her stood her upright, and then a third – and the man with the dark eyes and the livid red hole in his leg, the man who had filmed the murder of Emily Souster – began the process of stripping off the duct tape.

She was dripping with sweat, and it came easily enough off her wet skin, but it pulled strands of her hair out where it was wrapped around her head.

She did not cry out, and when it was finally all ripped away, she stood there defiantly: she was damned if she was going to show these men her fear.

Almost four hours she had spent in the 4x4, being bounced around the cramped interior on the rough roads, and fighting to keep her sanity. Several times she had almost lost control, her mind and heart racing, the panic rising as she imagined she was suffocating, dying in this tiny, claustrophobic box.

If she could survive that, she could survive this.

Dark Eyes looked her up and down, and grinned lasciviously, a bucket of brackish water in one hand.

'You are a filthy whore,' he said, in gutturally-accented English. 'You must be cleansed.'

He stepped forward and tipped the bucket over her head.

Charlotte stood stock still, looking him defiantly in the eye, until he looked away.

A small victory.

He left the room, and returned a few moments with a sheet, which he threw at her. She wrapped it around her dripping body, and then followed his pointing finger to a shabby Persian carpet against the far wall on the dirt floor.

She sat cross-legged on the rug, and looked around her. The rough-plastered room was lit only by a single, bare, low-wattage bulb in an inspection lamp on the floor in one corner, but it smelt curiously pleasant, of bread and coffee.

Sure enough, a moment or two later, the man disappeared, and then he limped back in, holding a flat bread and a steaming glass.

'Eat,' he said. 'And drink.'

Charlotte took the bread and the glass, which was so hot it hurt her fingers.

Slowly, deliberately, and staring into the depths of his black eyes, she tipped the coffee onto the floor beside herself.

Then she spat on the flatbread, and held it out to him.

'Piss off,' she said.

He leaned forward, smiling.

'Maybe I fuck you later,' he whispered.

Then he turned on his heel and left.

Charlotte hurled the bread after him, and immediately realised that she'd made a mistake. She needed to eat and drink; without that, her strength would fail, and her ability to prepare mentally and remain focused would be inhibited, and she would never get beyond this ordeal.

Against the far wall, the two men who had carried her inside now sat, unsmiling and silent, AK47s across their laps. They stared at her unwaveringly, but appeared completely detached from her situation, as if having an Englishwoman seated on the floor in the dirt in this place was the most natural thing in the world.

Charlotte stared back at them for a while, and then decided to find a better use for her time.

She closed her eyes and conjured up a mental image of the face of the man who had killed Emily Souster, and she worked to slow her breathing and imagine his death.

She was not a violent person, but something within her had changed.

Before this she had never hated anyone; now she truly knew the meaning of hatred.

# 41.

ABOUT AN HOUR later, she heard the rumble of a truck's engine outside, and urgent shouts in Arabic.

She opened her eyes and tensed.

A minute or two later, Dark Eyes came limping into the room.

He was all business, now.

'Get up,' he snapped. 'Hold out your hands.'

Charlotte ignored him, so he gestured to the two AK men.

Slinging the weapons behind their backs, they hurried over and pulled her to her feet. One of them held her wrists roughly, and the other deftly lashed them together with a black cable tie.

They did the same with her ankles, and then they gagged and hooded her.

She heard Dark Eyes say something, and then felt herself being grabbed under the arms and half-lifted, half-dragged out of the room.

A moment later she was outside – the smell a strange, damp combination of sea salt, blossom, and sewage – and then she was being hoisted up and dropped in the back of the truck.

Her head hit the bed of the truck with a bang which sent stars flying across her covered eyes.

She lay there for a few moments, winded and disorientated, and then she felt another body land beside her.

Martha.

Then something like a tarpaulin was dragged over the top of them, and all was quiet and still for a few moments.

Somewhere a few feet from the truck, there was a sound of talking. She strained to hear, and suddenly several of the voices grew louder. She heard one man cry out in what sounded like surprise, there was a muffled groan, and then all was silent.

Charlotte moved her bound hands towards Martha and touched her face: the warmth of the other woman's skin, and the knowledge that they were together, gave her some feeling of comfort. Martha began to sob gently, and Charlotte stroked her forehead with the back of her hand, to try to reassure her.

Nothing she could do would take away the image of Martha's husband being executed before her very eyes just a few hours earlier, but that didn't mean she wouldn't try.

The silence lasted for quite some time, and then the vehicle bounced slightly as a man jumped into the back alongside the two women. At the same time there was the sound of the doors to the cab slamming.

The engine started.

The truck began to move, swaying and bouncing on the rough ground.

# 42.

CHARLOTTE MORGAN SAT on her haunches on a metal bench in the hold of the vessel, trying to ignore the foul mix of rotten fish guts and slimy, oily water which washed from side to side with the gentle roll.

She had a single cable tie clipped tight on her left wrist, and was held by that to a cargo loop on the side of the steel hull.

The boat was old, and creaking, and clearly it was not watertight.

Her mind kept telling her that it might strike a rock, or be turned over by a storm, and that she would drown inside its blackness.

Every time these thoughts surfaced she pushed them back down, but they were persistent.

She almost preferred the Land Cruiser – until she recalled the pure, claustrophobic terror of that ordeal.

She was trying to work out what she knew.

She guessed that she and Martha had been brought aboard the boat at around 1 a.m., and she estimated that it was now somewhere around noon: some hours earlier, just before dawn, she had heard her captors perform their *salat al-fajr* prayers and had then watched as the hatch above her head was gradually revealed by a thin square of daylight.

She knew that the boat was moving – the rhythmic chugging of the engine and that gentle roll told her as much.

She did not know which way they were going, but common sense told her that it wasn't west to the Atlantic, or back north to Spain; that meant they were almost certainly following the continental coastline, across the top of Morocco and over into Algerian waters.

She also didn't know how far they'd gone. Her best guess was that they'd set out a dozen or so hours ago. She knew that a ship's speed was measured in knots, but she had no idea what a knot was. So she tried to guess their speed in miles-per-hour. She came up with 12mph – another good guess.

Twelve hours and 12mph meant 144 miles.

She was only a little out. In fact, they were some thirty miles further on, just past the northern Algerian town of Mostaganem, fifteen miles off the coast and just outside that country's territorial waters.

To her right, in the stinking gloom, she could see Martha, slumped on another steel chair, also cuffed, head down between her knees.

She hadn't said a word for hours, and Charlotte was worried about her mental state.

But for now she put it behind her – she needed to conserve all her mental energy for herself.

In the dim light, she saw a loose nail sticking out of a wooden crate to her left.

She looked at the rusty steel hull behind her, and then back at the nail.

A thought had occurred to her.

She began trying to work the nail loose.

Fifteen feet above her head, Khasmohmad Kadyrov and Argun Shishani were sitting, under cover, in the wheelhouse – with the West's satellites and spy planes, it was too risky for either man to show himself on deck in daylight unless absolutely necessary – and looking out at the wide blue Mediterranean.

It was another beautiful day.

'So far, so good, brother,' said Shishani.

'It's almost too easy,' said Kadyrov. 'But I don't like being on this boat. Too slow. The sooner we get off it…'

'How long to Tabarka?'

'We'll be there late tomorrow night, or early the next day. The British and the Americans will assume we are travelling by land, and will be watching the roads in Morocco. The Moroccans will have been alerted – they are in the pay of the West. So the sea is our friend.'

They were silent for a few moments.

Then Kadyrov said, 'We must make her eat and drink.'

'She's wilful.'

'She is. But we will break her.'

# 43.

AT JUST AFTER 5 P.M., Justin Nicholls' phone went.

It was Alec Palmer on the Spanish desk.

'It'll be on the feed in a minute,' said Palmer, 'but I thought I'd let you know first. We've got a lead on one of the shooters.'

Nicholls put down his coffee and sat up. 'Go on,' he said.

'Those CCTV shots of the guy in the Manchester United shirt? The DST have come back to say he's one of theirs.'

DST – the Direction Générale de la Surveillance du Territoire, or – in the local tongue – the Mudīriyyat Murāqabat al-Turāb al-Waṭaniy.

Morocco's domestic intelligence agency, based in Rabat.

'He's Abdullah el Haloui,' went on Palmer. 'Former Royal Moroccan Army soldier, kicked out for petty theft, then believed to have joined AQ in the Maghreb. He's been wanted since 2011 for involvement in the Marrakesh café bombing.'

'Recent movements?'

'He'd dropped off the radar, unfortunately. The Spanish are now liaising with Rabat, obviously trying to find out where Mr el Haloui's been, where he might be going, and who he's been talking to recently.'

'Nothing back on the other guy, yet?' said Nicholls. 'The pictures taken in the marina?'

'Not so far. They're not great shots, and the Spanish haven't found anything else yet. However he got to Spain, it wasn't via an airport. He's been very careful.'

'Let me know, if and when?'

'Of course.'

# 44.

AT ABOUT THAT moment, an encrypted Thuraya satellite phone rang on the floor of a filthy cabin in a boat in the Med.

It awoke Khasmohmad Kadyrov from the light sleep into which he had been lulled by a hearty feed and the throbbing of the diesel engines pushing the vessel steadily onwards through the light seas.

He answered it, and listened intently for a few moments.

Then he ended the call, wrapped a dirty green *shemagh* around his head and face, and went in search of Shishani.

The dark-eyed Chechen was sitting in the wheelhouse, drinking *masala chai* with the skipper.

Kadyrov sat down next to him.

'Rig the wheel and leave us for a few minutes,' he said to the sailor.

Obediently, the man tied the wheel, so that the ship would continue on its course, and left.

'I just took a phone call,' said Kadyrov.

'Oh?' said Shishani.

'Don't worry, brother, it's secure, as you said. And we were careful, anyway.'

'So… what was it about?' said Shishani.

'It was about my friend in Balochistan,' said Kadyrov, pulling at his beard. 'Saeed al-Shafra? The Yemeni who gave me his blessing, and arranged our funding?'

'Yes,' said Shishani.

'He has been detained by the authorities.'

Fear flashed across Shishani's face.

'ISI?' he said.

Pakistan's ruthless and dreaded Inter-Services Intelligence agency.

'Army.'

'When?'

'Not sure. A day or two past. My contact couldn't telephone before now.'

'Are they on to us?' said Shishani. 'The timing…'

'I think not,' said Kadyrov. 'As far as my contact can tell it was coincidental. They were on another of their operations to round up Balochi separatists, and unfortunately he was caught up in the net. As long as it's just the Army, they won't know who they have. Once they realise he is not involved in any of that independence nonsense I would think they'll give him a beating and then just let him go. But ISI are bound to be sniffing around, too, and if *they* come across him…' Kadyrov pulled a face. 'If that happens, he's finished. He's on their systems for Karachi.' He sighed. 'Such is life. He knew the risks. It's the path we follow.'

The path of shadows and sorrow.

They sat in silence for a few moments.

Argun Shishani looked out of the window at the late afternoon sea, now golden with the slowly sinking sun.

'Forgive me, Khasmohmad,' he said. 'I mean this respectfully, but what does this al-Shafra know? In case the worst happens?'

'He knows who I am,' said the older man, with a shrug. 'But the Americans, the British, the French, the Germans… They all want me anyway. I'll take my chances. He doesn't know who you are, and he doesn't know how we knew that the girl would be on the beach. He doesn't know we're on this boat. So we're safe for now.'

'Does he know we're going back onto land at Tunisia?'

Kadyrov nodded, regretfully.

'He arranged to pay off the Tunisian colonel,' he said. 'The one who's due to meet us at Tabarka, and take us across to the Libyan border at Bir Zar in military vehicles.'

It was Shishani's turn to pull a face.

'And he knows our destination is Sirte, also?' he said.

'Yes, that too,' said Kadyrov. 'In fact, he suggested it. He doesn't know the exact location – for obvious reasons, I arranged that myself with a fellow in Sirte called Shaladi. But al-Shafra arranged the money for it, and for the men who are waiting there.'

He cursed, and punched the palm of his own hand with a giant fist.

'So we may be compromised?' said Shishani.

'It's possible. I suppose we should work on that basis.'

'Then we must change our plans.'

'I think so.'

Both men sat there, saying nothing, feeling the gentle roll of the boat.

Eventually, Khasmohmad Kadyrov cleared his throat.

'So,' he said, stroking his huge beard. 'We must assume that Tabarka is blown, yes? So is Sirte. So, really, it's simple – we must land somewhere else, and we must end up somewhere else. The question is where? So let's think logically. We have arranged a safe house in Libya. We have men waiting in Libya, too. And transport.' He stared at his hands, idly picking dirt from under his fingernails. 'What is the logic, Argun?' he said. 'The logic is that we just need a new safe house in Libya. The transport and the men we can move.'

'Moving the men presents a security risk,' said Shishani. 'It took weeks for them to filter into Sirte. If they all leave at once, people will talk, and they will talk wherever we move them to. You can't have thirty fighters arrive in some remote village without someone noticing.'

'So what other suggestions do you have?' said Kadyrov, sharply.

The giant Chechen's eyes flashed with a sudden anger as he spoke, and Argun Shishani felt a momentary frisson of fear.

For the first time, he wondered if Khasmohmad Kadyrov planned to eliminate him as he had dealt with the men on the beach and at the staging house in Saïdia, to ensure the trail stayed as cold as the grave.

It was almost as though Kadyrov read his mind.

'Do not worry, brother,' he said, softly. 'When all this is over, you and I shall be far away, and we shall live in comfort, in the knowledge that we struck a great blow. And it is a good point that you make. Thirty men, it's too many. But if we move Ayub and ten of his best men…? In two or three vehicles?'

'Perhaps we could do that quietly,' said Shishani.

'I have a friend way down in Sinawin,' said Kadyrov. 'I can speak to him. He will send us another ten or a dozen north. That will be enough.'

Shishani nodded. 'So you contact your man Shaladi in Sirte…'

'I tell him we need a new location,' said Kadyrov. 'Somewhere a few hundred kilometres away. The dog will want more money, of course, but it is what it is. We land, we move after dark, we keep a low profile.'

'That might work.'

'So we just need to work out roughly where to land. Pass me the map of Libya.'

# 45.

HALF AN HOUR later, Argun Shishani stuck his head out of the wheelhouse and yelled at the nearest seaman to fetch the skipper.

He appeared a few moments later, a small, stooped man, with a face creased and lined like an old walnut by the sun and the salt of the sea.

'Come in and sit down, captain,' said Shishani. 'The emir wants to speak to you.'

He did as he was told.

'There's been a change of plan,' said Kadyrov.

'Oh, yes?' said the skipper. He was terrified of the giant Chechen, and his dark-eyed companion, but he tried hard not to show it. 'May I ask why?'

'No, you may not,' said Kadyrov. 'We were going to Tabarka in Tunisia, yes?'

'Yes.'

'Now we're not going to Tabarka. We're going to Al Khums, instead.'

'In *Libya*?'

'Yes, in Libya.'

The skipper pulled off his cap, scratching his head as he did so. 'But it's not safe.'

'I will personally guarantee your safe passage,' said Kadyrov. 'You know my reputation.'

'Yes. But...'

'But what?'

The skipper said nothing, but looked at his feet.

'How much longer is the journey?' said Kadyrov.

'I will need to look at my charts.'

'So look at your charts,' said Kadyrov. He turned to Shishani, and rolled his eyes.

The skipper bent his head over the table in the tiny bridge.

'To Tabarka, from where we are now, is approximately three hundred nautical miles,' he said.

Kadyrov waved his hand, dismissively. 'I don't know this measurement,' he said. 'Tell me in kilometres.'

The skipper closed his eyes as he did the mental arithmetic. 'About five hundred and fifty kilometres,' he said.

'And to Al Khums?'

'Three times the distance.'

'At your boat's top speed, how long to get there?'

'I could push it a little. We're currently doing between ten and eleven knots. I can make fourteen. Fourteen knots makes it...' He closed his eyes again. 'Three days. Two-and-a-half at best.'

Kadyrov looked at him. 'You have the fuel?'

'Yes.'

'And food?'

'Enough.'

'So what is the problem?'

'Well, the crew.'

'It is not enough for them that they are engaged in striking the biggest blow against the West since Osama hit New York?' said Kadyrov, jovially.

'Well, I...'

'Listen, brother,' said the Chechen. 'I will pay you one thousand

US dollars per man, for six extra days. Three days there with us, and three days back to here without us. You and your three men – that makes twenty-four thousand dollars. In fact, I will round it up to twenty-five thousand.'

The skipper's demeanour brightened considerably.

His men were on three hundred dollars each for the entire month, and would do as he told them.

So that extra money would go into his own pocket, and stay there.

'I think we can do it,' he said.

'Good man,' said Kadyrov, with a wolfish grin. He leaned over and ruffled the skipper's hair. 'If you had refused I was going to gut you and throw you overboard.'

'To sleep with the fishes,' said Shishani.

'Yes,' said Kadyrov, with a deep laugh. 'To sleep with the fishes.'

The skipper almost burst into tears in his fright.

'Go and make us some chai, and then come back and unrig the wheel,' said the bearded giant.

The skipper managed a nod before scurrying off.

'Not all men are made as we are, brother,' said Shishani, as he watched him go.

'Indeed not,' said Kadyrov, pulling at his beard. 'God made the lamb as He made the lion.'

'It's a shame that he and his crew must die, also.'

'It is a shame. But we must roll up the carpet behind us. Any thread we leave will be unpicked by the Americans and the British.'

Shishani nodded.

'It's good,' he said. 'This new plan. I like it.'

'Yes. We still run them in on an inflatable – once again, the sea will be our friend. Bin Salah can identify the precise new landing spot and collect us offshore.'

# 46.

A COUPLE OF HOURS later, an encrypted telephone rang on a desk in the Pakistan Section in the headquarters of the Secret Intelligence Service in London.

A woman picked it up.

'Ruth Hall,' she said.

'Hi, Ruth,' said the voice on the other end. 'Luke in Islamabad.'

'Luke, hi,' said Hall. 'What's occurring?'

'I've got something for you,' said Luke. 'Just heard from a source in the ISI. The Pakistani Army were out and about on the Afghan border a few days ago. Usual thing, they were rounding up Balochi separatists and cracking a few heads. Anyway, the ISI were called up to Samungli to do a routine interrogation of one or two of the more recalcitrant types, and while they were there they came across an elderly chap going by the name of Walid Shah. Turns out Mr Shah is actually a Yemeni called Saeed al-Shafra. He was up to no good, and my guy thought we might like to know.'

'Very good of him,' said Hall.

'Isn't it?' said Luke. 'This al-Shafra bloke was involved in some bombings down in Karachi, way back in 2002. He'd got away from there, and gone quiet up near Nushki, and got caught up in this recent trawl quite by chance. The Pak military didn't know what they had, and had just duffed him up a bit and then released him. As luck would have it, a member of my ISI guy's team literally bumped into the bastard at the gates and recognised him. My guy's interest was obviously the 2002 bombings, but when they searched al-Shafra's home and had a chat with him they found various indications that he was involved in something more current. Exactly what is not entirely clear, unfortunately, but it seems to be some sort of big attack on UK interests.'

Ruth Hall studied her fingernails. 'Another one?' she said, stifling a yawn. 'Can we get more?'

'Not from Mr al-Shafra, I'm afraid,' said Luke. 'The ISI can be rather enthusiastic in their interrogations, as you'll be aware. Apparently, he died with a truncheon so far up his arse that they could have knocked his teeth out from the inside, if they hadn't already knocked them in from the outside.'

'Shame,' said Hall.

'Indeed.'

'Is that it?'

'Not quite,' said Luke. 'He appears to have arranged for a third party in Saudi to wire a substantial amount of money to another chap in northern Egypt, a mid-level commander in the Sons of the Sacred Desert.'

'The AQ-linked group?'

'The very same.'

'How much?'

'A million dollars,' said Luke. 'A lot of money for a chap living in a mud hut, with a view of more mud. Don't know what happened to most of the cash, but we have established that a hundred grand of it was forwarded on to another guy who lives in Sirte, on the Libyan Med coast.'

That certainly got Ruth's attention. She sat up in her chair. 'Name?'

'We don't have it, sorry.'

'Will the ISI get any more from this al-Shafra guy's close contacts?'

'Wasn't in his interests to show his face locally, so he kept himself to himself,' said Luke. 'Hardly even left his little compound. They've pulled his wife in, but she seems genuinely in the dark.'

'How about his IT?'

'He was quite assiduous at deleting content, but they've harvested a partial list of people he's been in contact with in the last year or so. I'll send it over. Fifty-odd names. Mostly *noms de guerre*, obviously, but the ISI think they can identify a few Saudis and Yemenis. Couple of Pakistanis. A Chechen. Might be an American in there.'

'Great,' said Ruth Hall. 'Send it over, but don't mention the source. We need to muddy the waters. A lot.'

Why those waters required muddying she left unspoken: she didn't want to end up in court explaining how the SIS had used intelligence derived from a man who had been tortured to death by the Pakistani intelligence agency.

'Understood,' said Luke.

Ruth ended the call and immediately messaged the heads of the Egypt and Libya desks, to let them know that men in those countries might be involved in some attack on UK interests, with more information to follow.

Threats like this were ten a penny, and it was probably nothing, but when there was evidence that they were well-funded it paid to take them seriously.

# 47.

TWO FLOORS ABOVE her, Justin Nicholls was about to call the Prime Minister with an update – slight though it was – when there was a knock at his door.

It was a senior analyst who specialised in liaison with Five Eyes – the intelligence alliance between the UK and its partners in Australia, Canada, New Zealand, and the United States.

'Just a quick heads-up, Justin,' he said. 'I've just got off the phone with the NRO, and they have something. It'll be over on the feed in a moment or two.'

The NRO – the National Reconnaissance Office – was one of the US government's senior intelligence agencies, and the one most closely responsible for managing that country's satellite reconnaissance programme on behalf of the CIA, the Department of Defense, and other interested parties.

'Thanks,' said Nicholls.

He keyed in his ID number to enter the confidential feed and drummed his fingers on the desk as he waited for it to update.

A minute went by, and then a message appeared from an American inputter.

'*Non-tasked NSO SAT in LEO believed identified MARBELLA attackers' second escape vessel in MTN,*' it said. '*First SAT pass believed shows changeover from Vessel 1 to Vessel 2. Subsequent tasked pass shows activity at HOCEIMA, inc Vessel 2. CIA REAPER subsequently tasked to overfly. Images attached.'*

The first file showed a large and seemingly empty stretch of the Mediterranean Sea. A white orientation square with a scale along one side had been overlaid in the southern half of the image. The detail of that square showed several small objects at its centre.

Nicholls looked closer.

It was a grey boat, its frothy wake stretching out in the blue waters behind it, suggesting it was travelling at some speed.

And near it… something.

In the top right hand corner of *that* image was a further enlarged detail.

It was blurred, the product of a low earth orbit satellite sitting in the thermosphere, anywhere from a couple of hundred to a thousand kilometres above the earth's surface, rotating around the globe at eight kilometres per second, recording everything beneath it on a loop.

He peered at the screen.

It would need further confirmation, but he'd bet his house that the grey boat was the *Lucky Lady*.

And he'd further bet that the blurred something nearby was a small rigid inflatable.

*They must have had another boat waiting somewhere,* he'd told Penelope Morgan. *You slow down, push them off into the water, and then haul them into the new boat.*

'You bastards,' he breathed.

He opened the next file.

Taken towards the end of the day, it showed a patch of the Moroccan coast, where the sea met the rocky shore, and the shore gave way to an area of forest.

There was another enlargement in the top right hand corner.

Again, it wasn't pin-sharp – contrary to popular belief, satellites are not capable of reading the fabled headlines on a newspaper's front page, for that you need cameras mounted on an aircraft or drone – but it was clear enough.

It showed the RIB, a few metres offshore, and what looked like two bodies – one lying in the water, and other a few metres up on the land.

It was after that second image had been seen that the CIA had stepped in and had sent a Reaper across the Med from Morón Air Base, south-east of Seville, to take a closer look.

Nicholls turned to the third file, which contained a short video shot from the Reaper, timestamped three hours earlier.

The drone's operator, sitting in his little air-conditioned room in a closed-off part of the base at Morón, had flown as low and long as he dared – Morocco was nominally a friendly country, and the CIA was not in the habit of advertising its spy flights overhead friendly countries – so once again the clarity was not exceptional.

But it was pretty good.

The important bits were concentrated in a thirty-second section of film.

In the rough centre of the frame, some six metres from the shore, was the dinghy.

It looked damaged and deflated, and was half-submerged in the sea.

Two metres from the shore was a body, on its back and spread-eagled in a few inches of water.

Anxiously, Nicholls paused the video, and zoomed in on it.

He exhaled slowly with relief; although indistinct, it was clearly the body of a man, in some sort of brown or black robe, and, from the skin colour, probably of North African descent.

Nicholls zoomed back out and ran the film on.

Paused and zoomed in on the second body – another man, blurred but clearly wearing Western clothing – which lay on the beach, a few metres from the trees. He was framed by a black stain in the rocky sand.

He cropped off both men and saved them in a file.

Then he ran the footage on.

And his heart sank.

# 48.

THE PRIME MINISTER was in her study, reading through papers on energy security, trying to take her mind off her missing daughter – and failing, it might as well have been written in Sanskrit – when the phone rang.

Her secretary, putting Nicholls through.

'Justin?'

'Penelope,' he said. 'We have some news. The Americans have managed to locate the point where they went ashore in Morocco. It's a remote national park on the northern…'

'Is there any sign of Charlotte?'

He hesitated.

'Justin?'

'There is what looks like the body of a female there.'

'Oh my God.'

'I'm sorry, Penny. The imagery isn't very clear, and it's on the edge of a wooded area so most of it is hidden by foliage. It may not be her. Three were taken. As I said yesterday, Charlotte is the one they'd most want to keep alive.'

In her study across London, Penelope Morgan's eyes suddenly welled up, and she said nothing.

She fought a guilty urge to pray that this dead girl was someone else's daughter.

'There are two other bodies there,' said Nicholls. 'But I've seen them myself and I'm ninety-nine per cent sure that they're both local males. Whether they disturbed the terrorists as they arrived, or what, we don't yet know.'

'Where did they go from there?' said Penelope Morgan.

'We don't know. We're checking all the available imagery of the area, but it was getting close to nightfall when they landed. If we'd known earlier we could have tasked a satellite but...'

'What are you doing about the... the body?'

There was a pause.

Then Nicholls said, 'I was going to ask you about that. We need to get it back for a formal identification, obviously, but it may also help us forensically. Given the location of the body, in the summer Moroccan heat and so on, it's very unlikely that we'll recover any of the perpetrator's DNA from it. But it's not impossible, and the longer we leave it...'

'What are you saying?'

'We can go through the proper channels, via the Moroccan authorities. But that could take a long time, and there's the issue of contamination. Or...'

'Or?'

'The Royal Navy has an asset not very far away, with a troop of SBS on board. I'm pretty confident they'd be able to retrieve the body without anyone knowing.'

'Tell me the plan,' said Morgan.

He laid it out to her.

She paused for a few moments. Then she said, 'Make sure DSF is in the loop, copy the SBS in at Poole, and get on with it. And no-one gets caught.'

'No-one ever plans on getting caught, Penny,' he said.

# 49.

FIVE MINUTES LATER, the skipper of HMS *Westminster* – which was some twenty miles off the Moroccan coast, and steaming home in the dusk after taking part in a joint NATO exercise with the Turkish Navy – was summoned to the bridge to take an urgent call from London.

After a brief conversation, he put the receiver down, walked to the teleprinter and waited as a document came through. It was marked 'TOP SECRET', and prefaced with the special handling instruction 'NATSEN/UK EYES ONLY'.

It was a dozen or so lines long.

He read it, and then handed it to his No. 2, the ship's first lieutenant.

'Gary,' he said. 'I need the Wildcat pilots and the SBS troop commander and staff sergeant in the wardroom, ASAP. A little job for them. It's all in there. Strictly your eyes only. Then securely dispose, please.'

A few days earlier, the *Westminster* had embarked a small SBS team from Malta, where they had been temporarily based for amphibious training. Since then, they'd mostly been working on maintaining and tanning their cartoonish biceps; that would pay off in the nightclubs of Bournemouth when they got back to base, but the captain suspected that they'd jump at the interruption to the boredom.

He left the bridge and headed down to the officers' mess, which was empty, and waited for the others to arrive.

It didn't take long.

A soft knock at the door, and the two helicopter flightdeck crew appeared.

A minute later, and a pair of hulking soldiers joined them, led to the wardroom by a timid rating over whom they towered.

'Thanks for joining me, gents,' said the captain, when the door was closed. 'A task has come in from London. A little trip to Morocco.'

The four men leaned forward, suddenly very interested, and listened intently as the detail of the mission was outlined.

When he had finished, he said, 'So, what do you think? Doable?'

The Troop boss, a young captain, immediately looked at the staff sergeant, Dave Cummins, hoping he'd be allowed to go along but knowing he probably wouldn't.

Officially, the captain was the ranking soldier; in reality, he deferred to Cummins, a fifteen-year veteran of the Special Boat Service, who would choose the best and most experienced three blokes to accompany him. He would want guys who had been battle-proven in the heat and dust of Afghanistan: this was not going to be a trip for passengers and FNGs, but for reliable hands who would do what was required, and who would not hesitate if it all ended up live-or-die time in a firefight.

Cummins snapped shut his notebook, and grinned widely.

'Piece of piss,' he said. 'Nice evening for a ride in a chopper.' He looked at his watch. 'What time's dark?'

'Fully dark at 22:44,' said the captain. He looked at his watch. 'An hour from now.'

'Let me get the blokes sorted and we'll meet back here for my briefing in fifteen minutes.'

A quarter of an hour later, Cummins stood across a map, facing the helicopter crew and the chosen three – they didn't include the young captain, though he stood to one side, listening in, with a face like a smacked arse.

Quickly, Cummins briefed them, being careful to stress to the pilots that this was his mission, and that they needed to do as they were told. He was used to flying with SF-trained aircrew, and, while he had no doubt that these were good blokes and excellent pilots, they'd not done much of this kind of work before.

'The key thing, fellas,' he said, in his broad Halifax accent, 'is not to start thinking too much. Do as I say, and we'll all be cock-on.'

The other SBS men chuckled; the pilots nodded, perhaps a little anxiously.

They left to get kitted up and inspect their aircraft, and the soldiers disappeared to collect their equipment. Each would carry a Diemaco C7 5.56mm assault rifle – an M4 variant fitted with a heavier-duty barrel, an Elcan night-sight, and a flash suppressor – and full fighting order, body armour, and sidearms. *Don't get caught* was an absolutely redundant instruction: Cummins had no intention whatsoever of letting that happen, even if it meant shooting their way out.

Better to be judged by twelve than carried by six: it might have been an old cliché, but he and his men lived by it.

At 22:40hrs, the same nervous rating led the four men up to the helideck, where the rotors on the AgustaWestland Wildcat were already turning at close to take-off speed, and they hopped smoothly aboard.

Cummins leaned forward in the darkened cockpit, tapped the lead pilot's shoulder, and gave him the thumbs-up by the low red light.

A few moments later, the heli started to lift. As soon as it was clear of the ship, it dipped out of sight of onshore radar to 30ft above the waves – a task requiring extreme skill, at night, over the vast, dark, unfathomable sea, at not far shy of 200mph – and pointed its nose south-west.

Time to target, twenty minutes.

The four men in the back stayed focused but relaxed, gaming the likely events ahead of them, thinking through the plan, mentally going over the images which had been supplied by London, and which showed the locations of the three bodies at the target beach.

Ten minutes out from the Al Hoceima grid reference, the pilot keyed his mike and passed this information on to Dave Cummins, who alone was plugged into the aircraft's comms system.

In turn, the big staff sergeant nudged his men and held up both hands, fingers spread, to show all ten digits.

Each member of the team responded with a thumbs-up.

At five minutes, Cummins showed one hand, and the doors on each side of the helicopter were opened as the run-in to target began.

A blast of warm, damp Mediterranean air filled the back of the helicopter, and raised the noise level inside the speeding aircraft.

Each man was now utterly focused; they would be at their most vulnerable at the moment their boots met the ground.

The pilot confirmed the beach was clear on his forward-looking infra-red optics, and sixty seconds later he flared to a stop, and landed-on.

The team stepped off, two on each side, and knelt on the stony shore – each man taking up a firing position covering his arcs, and scanning the area through his rifle's night-sight for any sign of trouble, while being blasted by sand and gravel thrown up by the helicopter's downdraft.

Behind them, the Wildcat lifted off and moved away, low and fast, into the deep purple sky, to its air holding area over the water, where the pilot would remain until the call to come back in to extract the team.

The SBS men listened to the roar of its twin LHTEC T800 engines, and the *wacka-wacka* of its rotors, dying away.

Silence came remarkably quickly, but still they waited.

It was a lonely spot – the nearest settlement of any size, the small town of Rouadi, was approximately ten kilometres away – but there were isolated hamlets and buildings closer in, and the possibility of passing fishermen or goatherds making their way over to find out what a helicopter had been doing so close in could not be discounted.

Even worse – local police.

Even worse again – Moroccan military of some sort.

So they knelt in place, scanning right to left, looking for movement, and listening, heads cocked on one side.

Not that Dave Cummins could hear anything other than a slight ringing in his ears, thanks to his severe tinnitus – an occupational hazard, caused by putting a hundred thousand rounds through various rifles and machine guns and pistols, not to mention lobbing hundreds of grenades and flash-bangs, and spending what sometimes felt like the rest of his operational life danger-close to artillery, missile strikes, A10 cannon fire, and the like.

But he could see nothing, and clearly the younger guys could hear nothing, so, after a minute or two, he signalled two of the team to move left and right and forward, up to the treeline.

They did so, taking up positions which would provide both protection and early warning, should anyone approach the area.

'Boat first, Trigger,' said Cummins, quietly, to the fourth man.

Sergeant Paul 'Trigger' Stevens – one of Cummins' closest mates, and so-named not because he was quick on the draw but because he looked and sounded exactly like the character from *Only Fools and Horses* – nodded.

With Cummins giving cover back towards the area of threat, Trigger moved off to the gentle waves, and paddled out to the half-sunken RIB, which lay in knee-deep water a dozen or so metres offshore.

He conducted a quick search, took a dozen snaps with a

waterproof camera with an infra-red flash, and splashed back to his staff sergeant.

'Fuck all there, Dave,' he whispered.

They moved towards the nearest body, that of a man in his fifties who was lying on his back, a few metres away in six inches of water.

He had gunshot wounds to his chest and forehead, and his eyes had been pecked out by gulls.

'Say cheese, *sadiqi*,' said Trigger, chuckling to himself as he took several photographs of the man's face and body.

'I dunno about *say* cheese,' said Cummins. 'He *smells* like fucking gorgonzola.'

Trigger put the camera in his pocket and pulled a large, serrated-edged knife from a sheath on his chest rig.

He knelt down in the water beside the body, took its right hand and swiftly separated it from the wrist at the joint.

In an ideal world they'd have taken the bodies for identification, but there wasn't the room on the heli, so hands would have to do.

They'd provide DNA, Cummins supposed, and maybe fingerprints, though he'd done a double-take and confirmed twice if that was the order.

And now he looked away: shooting a man is easy enough, but cutting bits off bloated corpses… that required a certain kind of constitution.

Which Trigger possessed in spades.

In the treeline, through his night-sight, Cummins thought he saw movement.

He keyed his throat mike, but then held off speaking.

Just the wind moving branches.

He needed to…

He felt a tap on his shoulder.

Half-turned.

Almost jumped out of his skin – later, Trigger would enjoy

telling people that he'd squealed like a little girl – at the sight of the dead man's hand being waved in his face by the other soldier.

'For fuck's sake, you stupid bastard,' spat Cummins, when he'd recovered. 'Stop pissing around and put it in the fucking bag, will you.'

Chuckling malevolently, Trigger put the hand in a plastic evidence bag and placed that bag in a pouch on his equipment carrier.

'Check his pockets,' said Cummins, tersely, wiping the sweat from his forehead.

Trigger did as he was told.

'Owt on him?' said Cummins, after a moment or two.

Trigger held up a small leather wallet. 'Four hundred dirhams,' he said, placing it in another evidence bag. 'Drinks are on him.'

'Right, come on.'

They moved to the second body and went through the same process – finding nothing of interest – and then Cummins put in a quick radio check to the two men on point.

'DNA and phots taken, moving to find the girl now.'

Both men acknowledged the call.

Cummins looked up into the trees. 'Right,' he said. 'Come on, Trig.'

It didn't take long.

Emily Souster was lying face down where she had died.

'Nice arse,' said Trigger, pensively. 'What a fucking waste.'

Cummins looked sideways at him. 'Jesus,' he hissed. 'Are you for real?'

'Just saying.'

Cummins turned back to the body, sinking to his knees to take a closer look.

Whoever had left this poor lass here had almost certainly not envisaged her being recovered by British troops, but it wouldn't have been the first time they had booby-trapped a corpse.

Quickly, but carefully, he looked for any sign of wires or pressure plates.

There was none.

'Safe?' he said to Trigger.

'I reckon.'

Cummins sat back on his heels for a moment, almost reverentially, and looked at the insects crawling around in the bloodied sand.

'Poor kid,' he said softly. 'She's nobbut a year or two older than our Kelly. Cowards, these people.'

'No other word for it,' said Trigger.

'Cunts,' said Cummins. 'That's another word for 'em. Evil fuckers. That's another.'

'That's two words,' said Trigger.

'Fuck off,' said Cummins. 'You and your fucking GCSE.'

Trigger chuckled, and took his daysack from his shoulders.

He pulled out a black body bag, stretched it out by the side of Emily's body and unzipped it.

Got down low and carefully brushed some of the sand and dust from around the outline of the corpse, as a final check.

Finally, satisfied that no IEDs were present, he said, 'Ready?'

'Aye.'

They rolled the body onto its back.

Her bikini top had ridden up, exposing a breast, and Cummins carefully and respectfully adjusted it back into position to preserve her modesty.

Trigger took out his camera, took a shot of Emily's ruined face, stowed the camera, and said, 'Okay, then.'

Both men were veterans of Iraq and Afghanistan, and unfortunately well-practised at placing bodies into bags.

In a matter of seconds they were back on their feet.

'Better get them,' said Trigger

Cummins looked down.

Two spent brass casings lay a metre or so behind the spot where Emily Souster had lain.

'Aye,' he said. He picked up the casings carefully and put them in another plastic bag. 'Well-spotted.'

The final task was to ensure that no other bodies were in the immediate area.

Both men quickly conducted a swift area search, extending out a hundred metres or so, and found nothing of interest.

Back at the body bag, Cummins looked down at it.

'Come on then, love,' he said. 'Let's tek yer 'ome.'

Trigger bent down, picked the body up and threw it over his broad left shoulder with one easy motion.

Keeping his right hand on the pistol grip of his weapon, and the weapon itself horizontal and ready to fire if required, he nodded at Cummins and then followed him at a quick jog back towards the area where they had been dropped off fifteen minutes earlier.

Cummins called the other team members in, and now they were close together, kneeling in a straight line, each man covering his arc, with the body bag containing Emily on the ground behind them.

He pressed the talk button on his radio. 'Viper, this is Zero Bravo,' he said. 'Ready for pick-up.'

A momentary hiss.

Then, 'Zero Bravo, this is Viper inbound, sixty seconds to pick-up.'

'Viper, roger, on my mark.'

Cummins switched on an infra-red strobe on the top of his helmet, so that the pilot could identify the exact location of the four-man patrol.

Out at sea, and closing in fast, Viper quickly picked up the flashing light on his night vision equipment and headed straight for it.

A few seconds later, Cummins heard the thump of the Wildcat as it raced across the open water.

Then he saw its silhouette, black against the inky blue horizon, and suddenly the sand and pebbles were being whipped up in a furious roar as the pilot put the machine down away to their right.

He looked at the cockpit of the heli with his night-sight.

The co-pilot flashed an infra-red torch to signal safe to come in.

'Let's go, guys,' said Cummins, and the four of them ran, crouching, to the aircraft, Trigger again carrying Emily's body.

No more than twenty minutes after they had first landed, the helicopter lifted off from the beach, with the team on board, and began charging back to HMS *Westminster.*

Some fifteen minutes later, the Wildcat landed back on the frigate, and the SBS men were met by the ship's first lieutenant and a rating with a coolbox packed with ice.

The severed hands were transferred to the box – to prevent further deterioration – and the shell casings and wallet placed in another box.

Both were then taken back aboard the helicopter by the two youngest SBS men, who would ride shotgun with the body of Emily Souster as it was flown to Spain.

As an avgas refuelling hose was attached to the Wildcat, SSgt Dave Cummins went with the first lieutenant to the bridge, where the Westminster's skipper was waiting to take possession of the digital camera, so that the photographs taken by Trigger Stevens could be sent to London via the secure sat-link, as per his orders.

Back outside, the pilots did a quick torchlight walk-around of their refuelled aircraft in the humid night air. Satisfied, they took off again at a little after midnight, and made straight for Morón Air Base, some 300km north and a little over an hour's flying time away.

There a giant USAF Boeing C-17 Globemaster would take over,

transporting Emily Souster's remains and the forensic evidence the 1,650km to RAF Brize Norton in Oxfordshire.

In London, the Metropolitan Police's Evidence Recovery Unit – among the world's foremost experts in DNA recovery, and sundry other tricks of their trade – were already standing by to begin work.

Their first task would be to match Emily Souster's DNA with that of her heartbroken father to confirm what they already knew.

# 50.

NOT LONG AFTER the helicopter lifted off, a liaison officer at Navy Command HQ on Whale Island telephoned Justin Nicholls at MI6 to confirm the success of the mission, and to say that a full file would be sent across shortly.

As he replaced the receiver, Nicholls allowed himself a fleeting smile. The knowledge that he'd been able to have some small practical input into an investigation which now involved hundreds of police officers, spooks and military personnel in a dozen countries was satisfying.

The smile vanished a moment later, when his secure line buzzed for the hundredth time that day.

It was a senior officer called Kate Carver.

'We have something for you, Justin,' she said.

'Fire away,' said Nicholls, suppressing a yawn, and looking at his watch. It was well past midnight, UK time, and he'd been in the office since 6 a.m.

'A video was released on various online platforms fifteen minutes or so ago. Originated in the Ivory Coast, and now being shared across multiple accounts. It shows the three women kneeling at gunpoint, and then the murder of one of them.'

The hair on the back of Nicholls' neck stood up, and his body buzzed.

'Emily Souster?' he said.

'Yes,' said Kate Carver. 'She gets shot in the back of the neck by a man wearing a balaclava. He waits a few seconds, then he shoots her again to finish her off.'

'Any statement?'

'The usual theatrical nonsense,' said Carver. 'A warning to Britain. They call themselves Warriors of Jihad.'

'How original.'

'Quite.'

'Is it on the TV news yet?' said Nicholls. 'I'll need to tell the PM.'

'Not yet. But you'd assume it will be on the twenty-four-hour channels very soon.'

'Anything on what they want? Any demands?'

'Not in the video. They say they'll be in touch soon. But they aren't as clever as they think they are.'

'Oh?'

'We can tell that the shooter's a Chechen from his accent. So far, so standard. But the man with the camera has given away his name.'

Justin Nicholls sat up, suddenly alert. 'Oh?'

'Yes. Just before he switches it off the guy says under his breath, "Perfect, Khasmohmad". You can barely hear it, but when the techs enhanced the audio…'

Nicholls offered up a silent prayer of thanks: it sometimes felt like the only thing keeping the security services in the game was the incompetence of their opponents.

'Do we know any Khasmohmads?' he said

'Several. Plus, we can narrow it down further. Going on the known size of the kneeling women, we're putting him at around 130kg and 1.9m to 2m tall.'

'What's that in English?'

'Around twenty stone and six foot five, six foot six. He's a big bastard.'

'So do we know any Khasmohmads of that size?'

'We're checking. The audio might help there. The linguists have it and they think they might be able to narrow it down. In fact, here's one of them now. Can you hold on one second…?'

'Sure,' said Nicholls.

In the background, he could hear a man speaking to Kate Carver.

'*…very hard to tell, based on the little we have, but the consensus from the accent is it's one of the Laamaroy dialects, probably Chebarloish. He's certainly a Southerner, from one of the mountain tribes.*'

Carver said, 'That's great, thanks.' Then, to Nicholls, 'Did you get all that?'

'Yes. When will we have his full name?'

'Depends if he's in our system, or the Americans.' I'll know in half an hour, tops.'

Suddenly wide awake, all thoughts of home banished, Nicholls stood.

He went into the ante-room to his office to get another coffee, and sat drinking it, willing Carver to get back to him.

Half an hour came and went, and he resisted the temptation to chase her – she'd be doing all she could.

His phone finally went again forty-five minutes later.

'Kate?' he said. 'What have you got?'

'We may have hit a bit of a jackpot, Justin,' said Kate Carver. 'I'll put his file on the feed in a few minutes. His name's Khasmohmad Kadyrov. Born in internal exile in Kazakhstan, now aged around fifty to fifty-five. Originally part of the Vedensky set-up, down in the south-east. Small role in the First Chechen War, but he first came to the attention of the Russians when fighting in Grozny in 1996. Heavily involved in the Second Chechen War, he fought alongside Shamil Basayev and the 055 at Mazar-e Sharif, and then turned international jihadi around the time of Basayev's death. In Afghanistan between 2008 and 2011, and in Iraq before that.

Last heard of in Libya with ISIS, and then he disappeared. He was presumed KIA, though Amaq never said anything to that effect. Now we see why.'

'Yes,' said Nicholls.

'That's not all,' said Carver. 'Did you see the update from Luke Walsh and Ruth Hall on the Pakistan desk earlier on this evening?'

'Not yet,' said Nicholls.

'Non-specific warning of threats against UK interests,' said Carver. 'So far, so standard.'

Nicholls nodded. Such threats came in thick and fast, and were rarely drawn to his attention.

'Go on,' he said.

'Apparently, the ISI recently came across a new jihadi source up in Balochistan,' said Carver. 'This source provided the ISI with computers with a whole bunch of names on them. Mostly Yemenis, Saudis, a few locals, an American. But here's the thing: Kadyrov's name was among them.'

'That's interesting,' said Nicholls.

'It's more than interesting,' said Carver. 'The same source links a million dollars from Saudi, channelled to a middleman in Egypt. The middleman then transfers a hundred thousand dollars on to another man in Sirte, northern Libya. And listen to this: the guy in Sirte has supposedly been involved in planning what the source described as a major attack on a UK target.'

'Charlotte Morgan.'

'You'd have to assume so.'

'Who's the guy in Sirte?'

'We don't know that, unfortunately.'

'But we're working with the ISI on it?'

'I just spoke to Ruth on the Pakistan desk,' said Kate Carver. She paused, choosing her words carefully. 'Unfortunately, the ISI are unwilling or unable to go back to their source to get any more.'

'Bugger,' said Nicholls.

'We'll keep working on it.'

Nicholls was silent for a moment, as his mind raced to process this information. The whole of Libya was crawling with clans and warlords involved in everything from people trafficking and smuggling to facilitating terrorism, and Sirte was a particular hotbed.

It was a lawless, dangerous place, scene of some of the most brutal fighting in the Libyan civil war, and currently off limits even to what passed for the authorities in that country.

And that made it the perfect place to hide a couple of kidnapped Westerners.

'Kate,' he said, 'this is our number one priority. They must be taking her to Sirte. That's where their safe house is.'

'Understood, sir.'

'For now, that's our focus. Let me know what comes in, any time, day or night. And good work.'

Nicholls put down the phone and sat back in his chair.

He pulled up a map of North Africa.

Form their beach landing spot in Al Hoceima to Sirte was some 1,600 miles, all the way through Algeria and Tunisia, but the roads were good, and there was no way of knowing what vehicles they were in.

They could be there well inside two days, and there would be limited opportunities to identify and interdict them.

He needed to start the ball rolling with friendlies in those countries.

But first...

He looked at his watch.

Close to 1.30 a.m., but she was barely sleeping anyway.

He picked up his phone and called the Prime Minister.

# 51.

SOME TWO HUNDRED miles north, in a darkened terraced house in the Bradford suburb of Little Horton, a mobile telephone rang on a bedside table.

After three rings, Zeff Mahsoud emerged from under a thin duvet, muttering to himself, and switched on his bedside light.

Picked up the phone.

Rubbed his eyes and squinted at the screen.

Pressed the green button.

Said, 'Yes, who's this?'

The voice on the other end of the line said, 'Brother, it's me. Have you heard the news? The attack in Spain? They got the Prime Minister's daughter. It's just been on the news.'

Mahsoud was suddenly wide awake, and propped up on his elbows. 'Really?' he said.

'Yes, brother. They took her and some other women. What a blow they struck!'

'Alhamdulillah!' said Mahsoud, allowing a note of excitement to enter his voice. 'But you should be careful what you say on the phone. Don't call me about things like this.'

'Sorry, brother. I was just… I thought you'd want to know.'

Mahsoud tried to sound more sympathetic. 'Don't worry,' he

said. 'It's marvellous news. But we have to be very careful what we discuss. They can listen in.'

'Sorry,' said the man, again.

'Okay. Thank you. Goodnight.'

Mahsoud clicked the phone off, and replaced it on the bedside table.

Then he lay back on his pillow, arms folded behind his head.

Thinking about his next move.

Heart beating a machine-gun rhythm.

The familiar acid burn rising from his throat to his stomach, a legacy of years spent watching his back, second-guessing everything, planning in secret.

Waiting to be exposed and captured.

His mind conjured up an image of Charlotte Morgan, in her robes at the High Court in London.

*It's Marbella for me, I'm afraid. I'm all about the sun, sea and sand.*

He reached into the drawer of his bedside table, took out a packet of Rennies and a strip of omaprezole.

Next to him, his wife stirred and opened her beautiful brown eyes.

'Are you alright?' she said, in Pashto.

'My stomach,' he said. 'Usual thing.'

'Who was that on the phone?'

'Just one of the usual idiots,' he said.

'What did he want at this time of night?'

'He wanted to tell me that they managed to take Charlotte Morgan in that big attack in Marbella.'

'Charlotte Morgan?'

'The Prime Minister's daughter. My barrister, from the appeal. With two others.'

Now it was his wife's turn to prop herself up on her elbows, her eyes wider still. 'My God,' she said. 'Really?'

'Really.'

Farzana Mahsoud sat up. 'That's incredible.'

'It is.'

'Does it mean what I think it means?'

Zeff Mahsoud said nothing, but lay there, staring at the ceiling.

Then he rolled over and got out of bed, in a single fluid motion – he was in good shape, for a man in his mid-forties – and picked up his trousers.

'You should think nothing, my love,' he said. 'I'll be back in a little while.'

He got dressed, leaned over, kissed his wife's forehead, switched off the bedside light, and padded out of the room.

He crept downstairs in the glow of the orange nightlight he had bought for their daughter, picked up his keys and left the house.

A few moments later, he was steering the little grey Citroën out of his drive and off to the north.

Twenty minutes after that, he parked up in the run-down Windhill estate, got out and jogged down several streets and alleyways until he reached a pub, the New Inn. Wrinkling his nose as he walked past, he entered a BT phone box – which bore a giant Malibu ad proclaiming *Free Pina Colada for Everyone!* – was there anything these people thought of other than alcohol? – and dialled a number he knew by heart.

Pound coins at the ready.

He looked around.

*Empty streets.*

A couple of rings, and then someone spoke.

'It's Ahmed Khan,' said Zeff Mahsoud.

'What did you eat for supper?'

'Pigeon pie and lime sorbet.'

'Did you enjoy it?'

'I liked the pigeon, but the lime was too sour.'

The voice on the other end of the phone grunted in satisfaction.

'The operation in Spain,' said Mahsoud.

'Yes,' said the voice. 'They succeeded beyond their wildest dreams. She's in Morocco already, and they're on their way to Sirte.'

A police car drove slowly by the phone box, the passenger's eyes fixed on Mahsoud; he watched it until it disappeared.

'You still there?' said the voice.

'Yes,' said Mahsoud. 'Just thinking.'

'What are you thinking?'

'I was wondering where my passport is.'

There was a pause.

Then the voice said, 'Be very careful, Ahmed. There are eyes and ears everywhere.'

'I am always careful.'

'If they find you they will make a terrible example of you.'

'I'm well aware of that,' said Mahsoud.

'Good luck, then.'

With that, the line clicked dead.

Zeff Mahsoud held the receiver in his hand for quite some time, staring at it, before he replaced it.

Then he dialled a number for a local taxi firm, and hung up when they answered.

He didn't think anyone suspected him of anything, but it was better to be safe than sorry: now any nosey person who happened to press the 'redial' button for the last number called would get 247 Cars.

Half an hour later, he was back at home and letting himself in as quietly as he could.

But Farzana had got up and was sitting at the little kitchen table, nursing a cup of tea.

'You didn't answer my question,' she said.

'What was your question?'

'Does this mean what I think it means?'

'If what you think it means is that I have interesting times ahead of me, my sweet, then I suspect that it means what you think it means.'

Farzana Mahsoud sighed, heavily. 'I just lost you for a year, Zeff,' she said. 'I don't…'

'Under the circumstances, there was not much I could do about that.'

'I know. But does your family never come before this? What if we lose you for good? What about Aalia?'

'This is the path we have chosen, my darling,' said Zeff Mahsoud, tenderly. He reached over and brushed a few strands of hair away from his wife's face. 'Or the path that has been chosen for us.'

He clicked the kettle on, took down a mug and threw a tea bag into it.

Stood staring at his own reflection in the black kitchen window.

He had many calls to make, and a flight to book.

# 52.

AT 2.30 A.M. BST, two men on a battered old Honda CG125 pulled up outside the British Embassy in Abidjan, Ivory Coast.

The pillion passenger dismounted, his friend keeping the engine ticking over, and walked carefully towards the gendarmes guarding the main gate, in the shadow of the high blast walls.

They watched his approach with little more than idle curiosity – the Grand-Bassam shootings in 2016 had shown the threat to Westerners, and the embassy was certainly a juicy target, but this skinny little fellow was wearing a grubby white T-shirt, flip-flops, and a pair of ragged jeans, and was obviously unarmed.

When he was a few feet away, the man stopped and held out his hand. 'I have a letter for the ambassador,' he said, in the local *dyula*. 'It concerns a matter of great interest to the British government.'

'Oh yes?' said one of the policemen, with a deep chuckle. 'Delivered by *you*?'

'Yes.'

'Go on, get out of here. Piss off.'

'It's important,' said the man. 'I think the guy who gave it to me is from Al Qaeda.'

In fact, the man who had passed on the note was a member of The Movement for Oneness and Jihad in West Africa, but it amounted to the same thing. He was doing a favour for a friend of a friend of a friend, and the two men on the motorcycle were the final link in the chain, delivering a message they couldn't read, on behalf of people they didn't know, for ten US dollars apiece.

'Which guy?' said the policeman, but as he spoke the man dropped the letter in the dust and hurried back to the Honda.

Ordinarily, a letter handed in to an embassy in the dead of night by some anonymous no-mark would go nowhere, but the mention of Al Qaeda was enough for the senior officer at the gate to radio his superior, and before long the letter was in the hands of a bleary-eyed junior staffer, and five minutes after that it was in the hands of the bleary-eyed ambassador.

An hour later, a senior Downing Street staffer woke the Prime Minister and showed her an image of the note.

It said:

*You have seen what we can do. We will release Charlotte Morgan and Martha Percival unharmed in return for $25 million US.*

*We will require $5 million US equivalent to be delivered to us by hand in cash as a good faith gesture, in mixed currencies of used, non-sequential, middle-denomination notes, to include Yen, Sterling, Euro, Australian dollar, US dollar, Canadian dollar and Swiss francs.*

*The remaining $20 million US is to be wire-transferred to a bank account of our nomination.*

*If you comply, we will release the hostages and guarantee them safe passage to the British embassy in a city of our choosing.*

*If you do not comply, they will be slaughtered like goats.*

*Further communications will be made via social media.*

*Warriors of Jihad.*

Penelope Morgan folded the note carefully and looked at the staffer.

'Thanks, Georgie,' she said. 'Not a word about this note to anyone. Please make sure they understand that in the Ivory Coast, too. Then please call the Cabinet Secretary, my Chief of Staff, the

Deputy Prime Minister, and the press secretary. I'd like them all here within the hour.'

After the staffer had left, Morgan went back into the bedroom at No. 10 which she shared with her husband.

He was sitting on the bed in his dressing gown, looking a lot greyer and older than his fifty-six years.

'A note from the kidnappers,' said the Prime Minister, handing it over. 'They want twenty-five million dollars.'

# 53.

IT WAS ALREADY a warm morning, with a bright sun rising overhead in a clear blue sky, when Penelope Morgan stepped out of No. 10 Downing Street to face the world's media.

Her press secretary spoke first, to confirm that the Prime Minister would be making a brief statement, and that she would take no questions.

Then she stepped to the microphone.

'As you'll now be aware,' she said, her voice strong and clear, 'my daughter Charlotte was one of three women kidnapped from the beach at Puerto Banús on Wednesday, in the wicked attack in which so many innocent people were killed. You will also be aware that one of the three, Charlotte's dear friend Emily Souster, was later murdered in Morocco. You may have seen the images, which were released yesterday via the internet. I urge people not to share those images. The grief which Emily's friends and family are feeling at this terrible news is almost indescribable, and our hearts and prayers go out to them all.'

She cleared her throat and looked at the huge throng of TV cameras, blinking in their lights.

'Yesterday evening, Emily's body was recovered from Morocco's Mediterranean coast, and we are grateful to the King and his Prime Minister for allowing us to mount that operation. Their country has been for many years a key ally of the United Kingdom, and their assistance is, as ever, invaluable.'

This would be news to the King Mohammed and his PM – the Moroccan ambassador to London had only just been woken to be informed of the SBS mission to Al Hoceima – but His Majesty and the politicians had more to lose than most at the hands of the insurgent groups in the region, and Penelope Morgan was confident that it would give them the face-saving space they needed.

And if it didn't – well, that was just tough shit.

'We still have two British citizens outstanding. We will do whatever we can to recover them both alive, and we are working with intelligence agencies around the world to bring to justice the men responsible for this heinous crime. Thank you.'

She turned away, the air filled with clamouring shouts from a hundred or more journalists.

One stood out above the rest: 'Are we going to pay a ransom, Prime Minister?'

Penelope Morgan turned back. 'I know my press secretary said I'd take no questions,' she said, 'but I will just deal with this one. We have as yet had no ransom demands from the kidnappers, but you'll all be aware of the British government's longstanding policy on hostages and ransoms. We won't bend any rules, just because my daughter is involved.'

She almost felt herself blush as she turned back to the doorway.

# 54.

LATER THAT MORNING, Justin Nicholls left his office at Vauxhall Cross, walked out onto Kennington Lane, and flagged down a black cab.

The traffic was unusually light, but it still took twenty minutes to cover the five miles to Putney High Street.

After the taxi dropped him, it was a ten-minute walk to the grace-and-favour London home of the Director Special Forces, Mark Topham.

Topham greeted him at the door with a warm handshake – the two men's paths had crossed many times over the years, starting when Topham had been 22 SAS CO – and they made their way through to the kitchen.

'House to ourselves?' said Nicholls.

'Yeah,' said Topham. 'Everyone else is up in Herefordshire.'

Nicholls nodded. 'Thanks for hosting us,' he said. 'I thought it was probably best to be somewhere less… formal.'

'Brew?' said Topham, but just then there was a firm knock at the front door.

It was a thick-set, stern-faced officer from Scotland Yard's Royalty and Specialist Protection team.

Behind him, and quickly ushered inside, was the Prime Minister, Penelope Morgan.

A few minutes later, the three of them were sitting around Topham's kitchen table.

The curtains were drawn, and Topham had placed mugs of tea in front of all of them.

Morgan, looking tired but determined, didn't waste any time.

She looked at Mark Topham.

'You read the briefing notes, Mark?' she said.

'I did, Prime Minister,' he said.

'Can we go in?'

Topham paused for a moment. 'Do we have the capability to launch an assault into a foreign country to resolve the situation?' he said. 'Yes, we do, ma'am. As you know, a naval asset left Devonport for the Med two days ago, as a contingency movement. She'll be in Gibraltar later today. I could embark the Counter Terrorist Squadron at Gib, and steam them on into the Med from there. They'd be fifty kilometres off Sirte in three days' time, ready to launch by Chinook when the moment was right. But there are many unknowns.'

'Such as?' said Morgan.

'Firstly, where are the hostages?' he said. 'Justin's putting them in or around Sirte, but that's a huge area. I need a lot better than that.'

He looked at Justin Nicholls, eyebrows raised.

'I'm confident we'll get there,' said Nicholls.

'When?' said Morgan.

'That I can't say, Penny. We're moving assets around, and we have some excellent sources in-country – guys our people have worked with for decades, some of them grade A.'

Grade A sources were proven, reliable people, with a track record of providing accurate, independently verified intelligence.

'They're good men, are they?' asked Morgan.

'I wouldn't go that far,' said Nicholls, gravely. 'Some of them are very bad men. But they'll give us what we need, if they have it, and if the price is right.'

'I understand. Go on, Mark.'

Mark Topham fiddled with his signet ring. 'Let's say Justin's sources believe they've identified the building. I still need to have my own eyes-on before we launch the main assault, which means inserting a Recce Team first. Grade A or no, I wouldn't risk my men's lives without that, ma'am.'

'I'm not a soldier, Mark,' she said, apologetically. 'Can you elaborate, please? And, please – it's Penelope.'

Topham nodded. 'With the best will in the world, Penelope,' he said, 'intelligence can be flawed. People lie, they make mistakes, they betray you. We don't go in until I have men from Hereford physically verifying the precise location of the hostages – I mean which room, in which building. I also need to know the enemy's strength, his capability, his weapons systems and dispositions. I want forming-up points identified. I want individual assault positions located. I want the route-to-target from the helicopter landing site proven.' He paused. 'I could go on, but I'm sure you get the picture.'

'How many men?' said Morgan.

'The initial Recce Team would be a four-man patrol.'

'Only four men?' said Morgan, a look of alarm passing over her face. 'For how long?'

'Impossible to say, but potentially several days.'

'On their own? That sounds very dangerous.'

'Everything we do is dangerous,' said Topham, with a smile. 'That's kind of the point.'

'Yes, I suppose so,' said Morgan. 'But what if they get caught?'

'We'd need to have the Counter Terrorist Squadron nearby to support them if they were compromised – I wouldn't advocate any plan which didn't give them the best chance of survivability. But, even so, if it all really goes south you're tossing a coin.'

'How do you mean?'

'Heads the CT guys get there in time. Tails they don't.'

'And if they don't?'

'Four dead men.'

Morgan blanched slightly, and Topham smiled again.

'It's the nature of the beast, Penelope,' he said.

'I see. And these four men – they'd call in the rescue?'

'Yes. We'd launch from sea in helicopters and put down at an HLS, well away from the target. The main assault force would walk in from there.'

Penelope Morgan sat back and looked at him. 'How many soldiers?'

'Sixty, in three Chinooks.'

'Casualties? From the main assault?'

Topham shrugged. 'There's a possibility that we would lose men, yes,' he said. 'Perhaps even a strong possibility. It's a multi-factional country, Penelope. Everyone has weapons, they're all vying for a piece of the pie, and you can't tell the bad guys from the good.'

'Could we lose an entire helicopter?' said Penelope Morgan.

'We might,' said Topham, carefully. An airborne assault, flying into territory awash with MANPADs and other ground-to-air weapons systems, always presents significant challenges. We saw what happened to the Spanish heli, and that was over the Med. Now, Chinooks are exceptional aircraft – they're quick and surprisingly agile, they have a good defensive suite, and forward-looking infra-red, and the pilots are the best in the RAF, maybe the world. But they're big, and they're noisy, and they'll wake all sorts of people up. There's no getting around that.'

'So we could lose one?'

'Yes, we could,' said Topham. 'Worst case.'

'Twenty men?'

'Plus aircrew.'

Mark Topham took a sip of his tea.

'Look, Penelope,' he said. 'Don't worry about the blokes. This is what we do. If a plan's good, they'll happily go and execute it, or die trying. They all start out knowing their names might end up on the clock tower.'

'The clock tower?' said Morgan.

Topham replaced the mug on the pine kitchen table.

'One day I'll show you,' he said.

Penelope Morgan breathed deeply and rubbed her forehead. 'Likelihood of success? Of getting the hostages out?' She swallowed hard, and looked away for a moment. 'Alive?'

Topham looked at her, conscious that he was dealing with a mother, and not just the Prime Minister. But he could see no point in sugaring the pill.

'No guarantees,' he said. 'There's no-one better in the world at this than my guys, and, believe me, we'd have every tiny detail nailed. Who's going through which window, which door, who's blowing what hole in which wall, who's killing each guard.' He shrugged. 'But fate has a habit of getting in the way. Someone connected to the bad guys hears the helis land, or a dog barks, or a guard stumbles into the team by accident, and we're forced to execute in haste. The plan goes awry, and your daughter is sitting with a suicide vest on, and there's a man next to her whose sole job is to detonate it if a rescue is attempted...'

He left the rest unspoken, and watched her wrestle with a fear he could only imagine.

'And how big is that risk, Mark?' she said, eventually.

'Unquantifiable,' he said, softly. 'I'm not in the business of speculating. I work on intelligence, and facts, and until I have a Recce Team on the ground we don't have much of either.' He paused. 'Even for us, things sometimes go wrong. We'd only have a very small window to get it right.'

Penelope Morgan tried not to think about that small window.

'Those are the major practical problems?' she said.

'They're a flavour of them,' said Mark Topham. 'But, with respect, I think you have a much bigger problem to overcome first.'

'Which is?'

'The authority under which we go in,' said Topham.

'Of course,' said Morgan, immediately feeling stupid. She'd been so focused on the details of mounting a rescue operation that she'd forgotten the context.

'We can't just operate with impunity in Libya's back yard, without a Memorandum of Understanding allowing us to conduct the operation,' said Topham. 'Without that, if we go in and kill people – and we might well kill a lot of people…' He paused. 'It strikes me that that's a serious international incident. Depending on what developed, it could range from embarrassing to much worse than embarrassing.'

'Yes,' said Morgan. 'I understand.'

'Currently, the area around Sirte is in nominal control of the North Libyan Transitional Authority, which has limited UN recognition. They're the people to ask. Would they play ball?'

Penelope Morgan wrestled with the urge to say, *Yes, they would – of course they would.*

But she knew in her heart of hearts that the truth was very different.

'Unlikely,' she said, eventually. 'They're on a knife edge. The last thing they want to be seen to be doing is collaborating with Western military forces.'

'Well, there's your answer,' said Topham. 'It's one thing landing four blokes on a beach for fifteen minutes to recover a body from a friendly country, with a government which is amenable to reason. It's quite another to conduct an unapproved direct action against a defended location in a place like Libya.'

Penelope Morgan looked at him, trying to fight a feeling of desperation.

The frustration – of being in control of the world's premier military Special Forces unit, of knowing her daughter's location to within a few hundred square kilometres, and yet being at the same time utterly impotent to help her – was enormous.

For just a moment, she allowed her mind to toy with the idea of telling Major-General Mark Topham to do his damned job – to move the boys to Gibraltar, and get on with it.

But she knew that playing with the lives of other mothers' sons, moving them like chess pieces for the sake of her own little girl, was morally wrong.

Topham *was* doing his job – his job was to assess the risk-reward ratio, and choose and execute the best option.

'Is there another…' she said, and then lapsed back into silence.

Eventually, she spoke again.

'You're talking about sending in a whole Squadron,' she said. 'Could your smaller unit… the Recce Team? Could they not get them out? Surely they'd be a lot more stealthy? No-one would have to know.'

Mark Topham rubbed his chin. 'Using a small team presents issues of its own,' he said. 'Yes, there's more chance of getting in and out without anyone noticing. But if you get bumped you don't have the firepower to shoot your way out. If that happens, either the CT Squadron get there in time, and the noise they make alerts the whole world, or they get there too late, and, as I say, my Recce Team are being paraded, dead or alive, on TV.'

'There are no lawyers here,' said Penelope Morgan, 'so, just between us, what would you say if I told you I wanted to do it anyway, one way or another, and sod the illegality?'

Topham looked at her, weighing the strength of her gaze. He'd met Morgan once or twice since her election, but this was his first look at her close-up, and the first serious discussion he'd had with her. And he liked what he saw: it was refreshing for a senior politician to discuss acting in a way that reflected the world as it was, rather than as she *wished* it was.

This was a strong woman, he was sure, with whom he could work well in the future.

'Ours is not to reason why,' said Topham, with that gentle smile again. 'If I'm happy that the plan is militarily sound, and you tell me to go, we go. The politics, the international fall-out, the UN… that doesn't concern me.'

Penelope Morgan nodded. She closed her eyes, and tried to remove Charlotte from the picture and think.

After half a minute, perhaps more, she opened her eyes and looked at Mark Topham.

'I'm sure we shall have a long and fruitful relationship when all this is over, Mark,' she said.

'I hope so, Penelope.'

'But that doesn't help me right now. We can make overtures to the NLTA, see if we can get the Memorandum, but I can tell you now that it would take months to get anywhere. And I don't think we have months.' She turned to Justin Nicholls. 'Do you have any suggestions, Justin?' she said.

'As a matter of fact,' he said, 'I do.'

# 55.

'JUST HEAR ME out, Mark,' said Justin Nicholls, with a wary glance at Topham. He looked at the Prime Minister. 'If we can't go in officially, what about going in *un*officially?'

'Unofficially?' said Penelope Morgan. 'What do you mean?'

Topham was shaking his head, but Nicholls pressed on.

'Let's say a small group of British nationals made their way to Egypt on holiday,' said Nicholls. 'Sharm, perhaps. Beach holiday. The Red Sea's beautiful at this time of year, if a little warm.'

'Deniable ops?' said Topham, a note of incredulity entering his voice.

'It's some distance to Sirte from Sharm,' said Nicholls, 'but it would be doable, for the right men. And with the right assistance.'

'What do you mean by "deniable ops", Mark?' said Prime Minister Morgan, leaning forwards.

'The sort of thing you see in films,' said Topham. 'You send people in, they do your dirty work, and if it all goes wrong then you cut them loose and you've never heard of them. It's not something we do, and for very good reason.'

'What very good reason?'

'What happens if it *does* go wrong? A bunch of Britons, all ex-soldiers, all armed to the teeth, killed or captured in Libya?

How deniable is that? Are people really going to believe that they were tourists? The media would have a field day.'

'Let me worry about the media,' said Morgan, her mind racing. 'If the worst that came out was that my husband and I had privately funded contractors... It might be the end of my political career, but I couldn't care less about that. The important thing is that it couldn't come back to the UK government.'

Topham, a sceptical look on his face, said, 'I suppose. But finding guys who have the right skill sets to do this sort of thing, and are prepared to do it, would be hard. Going into a place like Libya, with little or no back-up, no support... It would take a special kind of man to put his hand up.'

'But you know plenty of them,' said Nicholls. 'Look at the formation of your own regiment.'

'The Regiment was formed by volunteers from recognised military units,' said Topham. 'Serving soldiers, operating within the rules of war.'

'That's as may be,' said Nicholls. 'But if David Stirling and Paddy Mayne were sitting here now, and we asked them if they fancied having a crack at these people, what would they say? They'd be raring to go. They did what they did because they loved it.'

Topham thought about that for a moment; he had to admit there was some truth to it.

'Back in 1942, out there in the North African desert,' said Nicholls, pressing the point, 'they couldn't call in A10s or Apaches if things got dicey. They didn't have any casevac choppers, or night vision, or much else besides a lot of balls.'

Mark Topham said nothing, a thoughtful look crossing his face.

'And it may not be our thing, but the Americans take a very different view,' said Nicholls. 'They do this sort of stuff all the time. You know that.'

Topham had to nod at that, too: the US military and their

cousins in intelligence did operate in a much more relaxed environment.

'Give me reasons *not* to do it,' said Penelope Morgan. 'Worst case?'

'As Mark says, four men go in, they get captured, tortured and killed,' said Nicholls. 'And you still don't get Charlie back. But what are the alternatives? We've just discussed the reasons for not acting officially. That leaves only two choices – try to negotiate, or do something unofficial. And we can't negotiate under the G8 accord and the UN security council resolution which followed it.'

'The French always pay,' said Penelope Morgan, bitterly. 'And the Italians, and the Germans. They all do.'

'But we don't.' Nicholls hesitated. 'I know you haven't had to deal with anything like this since you took office,' he said. 'But could you in all conscience rewrite the rules for your own daughter? When the government has let others die in the past?'

Morgan got up and walked to the French dresser.

There was a picture of Mark Topham with two teenaged boys on a skiing trip somewhere, smiling at the camera.

'Your sons, Mark?' she said, over her shoulder.

'Yes,' he said. 'Les Carroz.'

The Prime Minister turned back to the two men.

'What would you want me to do for them?' she said.

Topham looked at her. 'Anything and everything,' he said.

She nodded. 'I'm not paying those bastards a penny,' she said. 'But I am going to do whatever I can to get those two girls back. I'm going to push it to the absolute limit. I'd do it for your sons, Mark, and I'd do it for anyone else.'

She leaned on the table, fists against the wood, and looked first at Mark Topham.

'I want the CT Squadron in the Med, ready to go, just in case we can get that Memorandum of Understanding.'

She turned to look at Justin Nicholls.

'But I'm working on the basis that that will not be possible, Justin. You can have whatever you need – my private funds. If it ever does come back to us, I take full responsibility. You can have that in writing if you wish.'

Nicholls exhaled slowly.

'It will take some time to pull together,' he said. 'We can give ourselves a little breathing space by demanding proof of life.'

He saw her wince.

'It's standard stuff, Penny,' he said. 'They'll be expecting us to request it. And it will take them a while to get it to us safely and securely.'

She nodded and picked up her handbag.

'Draw up a plan,' she said.

# 56.

NEITHER MAN SPOKE until Penelope Morgan had left.

Then Mark Topham turned to Justin Nicholls.

'Christ,' he said, disbelievingly. 'Did we just agree what I think we agreed?'

'*We?*' said Nicholls, with a faint smile. 'So you're on board?'

'Unless the PM can square the political side I imagine there will be limits to our involvement,' said Topham, 'but I'll give you what assistance I can. I can hardly drop you in the shit, can I? I assume you have someone in mind?'

Nicholls nodded. 'John Carr,' he said.

Mark Topham said nothing for a few seconds.

Instead, he got up, collected the teacups, walked to the Belfast sink, and rinsed them.

'John Carr?' he said, turning and drying his hands on a teacloth. 'I was the Hereford CO when he left. We tried to keep him, but he was adamant. How do you know him? I wouldn't have thought you and he moved in the same circles. He's not a fan of spooks.'

'I was introduced to him a few months ago by Guy de Vere,' said Nicholls. 'Guy and I were at school together.'

'And do I want to ask why you and Guy de Vere were meeting John Carr?'

'Probably not,' said Nicholls.

'I thought he was working for some Russian these days?' said Topham. 'Doing very well for himself?'

'It won't just be about money,' said Nicholls. 'He has a personal interest. He was on the beach at Marbella, with his kids. Got a good look at one of the ringleaders.'

'Uh huh,' said Topham. 'I heard about that.'

'But more than anything I think he'll want to do it for the sheer hell of it. Strikes me as a man who misses combat.'

Topham nodded. 'We all do,' he said. He rubbed his eyes. 'But for most of us there are limits.'

He looked at Nicholls again.

'You know that he was known as "Mad John" in the Regiment?'

'Mad?' said Nicholls.

'He was always prepared to go that little bit further,' said Topham, with a smile, 'always doing something that ought to have got him killed. Someone called him a fucking mad bastard after one incident, and the nickname stuck with the blokes. He absolutely hated it.'

'Should I worry about that?'

'John was always prepared to take chances, and push the envelope,' said Topham. 'But he's not reckless. The risks he took were always calculated, and he's always been quite happy to stand his ground and tell the boss that a given plan is stupid, too – he's done it to me more than once.'

'You rate him?' said Nicholls.

'He was an exceptionally competent soldier, one of the best I've known – and I've known a few. Brave, intelligent, honest. I'd trust him with my life. I *have* trusted him with my life.'

He narrowed his eyes.

'So what's your plan?'

'I don't have one yet,' said Nicholls. He stood up and extended a hand. 'I'd better be off.'

'Well,' said Topham, shaking hands. 'It will take some work, I can tell you that. Whatever you come up with, run it by me. This is going to be hellishly difficult, but if you can get John Carr on board it's a step in the right direction.'

'I'll be in touch,' said Nicholls.

'He's handy with his fists, too,' said Topham, with a big grin. 'So careful with the "Mad John" thing. There aren't many blokes he lets get away with using it, and they tend to be those who know how it was earned.'

# 57.

JOHN CARR WAS in his flat at Primrose Hill, about to step into the shower after a two-hour training session at his martial arts club, when his mobile buzzed.

He read the WhatsApp message and shook his head in irritation.

It was already half-six, and he had a seven o'clock table booked for two at Odette's, just round the corner.

He didn't want to miss it: the girl he was taking, Daisy from the flat below, was very fit and had recently dumped her boyfriend, James.

And Odette's did a cracking fillet of Welsh beef.

A moment later, Carr's mobile rang.

'Yes?' he said. 'I'm busy.'

'Sorry to bother you, John,' said Justin Nicholls. 'I wondered if you could spare me half an hour?'

'What for?'

'I'd rather talk in person.'

Carr sighed.

'When?' he said. 'Where?'

'Two minutes,' said Nicholls. 'That's me ringing your buzzer now.'

Carr pulled his training bottoms and top back on and opened the front door to his flat, looking down at the faint mark on the wooden floor where the IRA assassin Dessie Callaghan's lifeblood had pissed through his carpet a few months earlier.

He had planned to replace the ruined carpet, but in the end he'd decided to stick with the wooden floorboards underneath. He'd had the blood cleaned away, but rather than sanding the last vestiges of the stain out of the boards he'd had it varnished over: seeing it sharpened his wits, and was a nice reminder to take nothing for granted.

'Ten minutes,' he said, when Nicholls poked his head inside. 'I need a shower, and then I'm going out.'

Nicholls followed him through to the living room, and sat on the sofa Carr indicated.

'Thanks, John,' Nicholls began. 'I must say, it's…'

'What do you want, Justin?' said Carr.

The MI6 man hesitated.

'John,' he said. 'You're no longer serving, so… I need to be careful, here.'

'I understand,' said Carr. 'You know where the door is.'

Nicholls hesitated again.

Then he said, 'Fair enough. The Prime Minister's daughter and her friend are being taken to Sirte, in Libya. A very dangerous place, as you know.'

Carr nodded.

He knew that stretch of north Libya well.

His mind's eye was showing him pictures of the main Tripoli-to-Tobruk highway on the outskirts of the city.

To the north, the Mediterranean Sea – that barrier between the familiar comforts of Europe and the savage, untamed wildness of North Africa.

To the south, stony desert, irrigated farmland.

Kids playing football. Women in burqas. Men with suspicious eyes.

The usual donkey-carts pulling water bowsers, or laden with date fronds.

That sulphurous, background stench from the stagnant saltwater lagoons in the marshland to the north, blending with thin, acrid smoke from oil-barrel rubbish fires outside every other home.

Gaddafi had gone to school in Sirte, and had long dreamed of turning it into the capital of a future United States of Africa, with landscaped gardens, wide boulevards and impressive buildings. Those grandiose dreams had died with him, when rebels had caught him hiding in a sewage pipe during the civil war of 2011. By then, the place had been bombed to fuck and it was still in the slow process of rebuilding.

'Who's in charge?' said Carr.

'Nominally, the North Libyan Transitional Authority,' said Nicholls. 'In reality, it's in possession of a loose collection of local tribal groupings, and militias. Precisely who the boss is, if there even is one, we don't know.'

'How do you know that's where the two birds are headed?'

'Intelligence.'

Carr raised his eyebrows.

'That, I really *can't* discuss,' said Nicholls. 'You know that. Trust me, that's where they're going.'

'But you don't know precisely where.'

'Not yet. We're watching overhead, but they know that, so they're being very careful.'

'Who are they?'

'Chechens.'

Carr winced. 'Nasty bastards,' he said.

'Yes,' said Nicholls. 'Their nom de guerre is The Warriors of Jihad.'

'What a surprise,' said Carr. 'I'd have gone for Jihadis R Us.'

Nicholls smiled. 'It is a bit off-the-shelf.'

'But they're not fucking idiots,' said Carr. 'This was a serious operation. Money, weapons, safe houses, vehicles…'

Nicholls nodded. 'You're right,' he said. 'We know quite a bit about one of them. They released a short film of the third girl being executed, not long after they arrived back in Morocco. You may have seen it? Edited versions have been on the news.'

'Yeah,' said Carr. 'I saw it.'

'The shooter was a chap called Khasmohmad Kadyrov. Massive guy, early fifties, a Chechen mountain-man of the old school. He's been everywhere, done everything. Last seen in Lybia with ISIS. Now this.'

'Obviously he wasn't alone.'

'No. We think your chap with the dark eyes from the beach was also involved at a leadership level. They were well-funded – as you say, a safe house somewhere in Marbella and another in Málaga, two teams of men, weapons, a boatman. Reception committee and vehicles in Morocco. Some means of transferring the two women to Libya, and a safe house there, too. Various people paid off here and there, presumably. They're also whacking their own as they outlive their usefulness, to make it harder for us.'

'Ruthless,' said Carr, rubbing the large, crescent moon scar on his chin. 'I like that.'

'They obviously had inside information,' said Nicholls. 'It wasn't a coincidence that they hit the beach at Puerto Banús at the moment they did. They had a fair bit of luck, too, but this would have taken time to plan.'

John Carr nodded.

'The kidnappers have been in touch,' said the MI6 man. 'Between you and me, they're offering to release Charlotte Morgan and the other girl in return for a ransom.'

'Cash?' said Carr, surprised.

'Yes. Unusual, but you know that these people have funding needs the same as anyone else.'

'How much?'

'Twenty-five million US. Five million hand-delivered in used, non-sequential notes, various currencies, as readies. The balance by wire transfer. Once that's confirmed, they're released.'

Carr raised his eyebrows.

'Have they got that kind of money?' he said.

'The Prime Minister's husband heads up a multi-billion-dollar investment fund. I won't say he wouldn't notice it, but he could pull it together.'

'So they're thinking of paying?'

'The Prime Minister's exact words were, "I'm not paying those bastards a penny",' said Nicholls. 'But it allows us to open a comms channel with them, play for time, that kind of thing.'

Carr looked at him with expressionless eyes, and a deadpan face. Then, after a few moments, he smiled.

'So, Justin,' he said, looking at his watch. 'I'm supposed to be out eating steak with a very tidy bird in ten minutes. I need a shower because I smell like a dog from spending the last two hours kicking the shit out of Albanian doormen, and I don't like being late. Do you want to cut the bullshit, and tell me why you're really here?'

# 58.

JUSTIN NICHOLLS SIGHED.

'We're going to find out where she is,' he said. 'But going in officially presents… problems.'

'Let me guess,' said Carr. 'International law? You cannae go in all guns blazing, because the Libyans won't play ball?'

'Correct. Look, I'm not going to give you all that black ops, plausible deniability bullshit, but someone's going to have to bring the two women home.'

Carr chuckled. 'Like we talked about in my flat, after the IRA thing?' he said, a mocking smile playing at his lips. 'You're sounding a tiny bit like the CIA. Which is not a bad thing, by the way.'

'As I said, things may be changing. And what's the harm in me and you looking at some options, and you giving me your professional opinion?'

'No harm at all,' said Carr.

'Before I go any further, are you in? Hypothetically speaking.'

'If you're asking me if I'd like to flat-pack the cunts who shot up that beach and scared my little girl, that's a no-brainer,' said Carr. 'Sort of thing I used to do for my day job, and I fucking loved my day job. If I rescued those two birds into the bargain, so much the better. But I'm not suicidal, or stupid, Justin. It would all depend.'

'On what?'

'On the plan. And the financial reward. I'm not a charity.'

'We can deal with the financial side in a moment,' said Nicholls. 'Let's talk about how we might do it.'

'No,' said Carr. 'Time's marching on. If you want me to miss out on my steak, we'll deal with the financial side first. You cross that hurdle, you can stick around.'

Nicholls hesitated.

'Dinnae get me wrong, Justin,' said Carr. 'I am extremely sorry for the Prime Minister and her daughter. If I was still in the Mob I'd be champing at the bit.' He looked around his flat. 'But I've got a nice life, and a daughter of my own who needs me, and I'm not gonnae put all that at risk just because it'd be the right thing to do.'

Nicholls looked at him.

What had Penelope said?

*You can have whatever you need – my private funds.*

'Your fee would be two per cent of the ransom demand,' he said. 'Five per cent if we get her back alive. Cash.'

Carr didn't bat an eyelid.

'Wait one,' he said.

He dialled a number on his mobile.

'Daisy?' he said. 'It's John, upstairs. Listen, I'm sorry, sweetheart, but something's come up. I can't make Odette's. Another time. But if you want to come up in an hour I'll chuck a pizza in the oven?'

He chuckled.

'I'll see you then,' he said.

He ended the call and looked at Nicholls.

'Two per cent and five per cent?' he said. 'Nah. Three, and six.'

'Three and six it is,' said Nicholls.

'Did I say three and six?' said Carr. 'I meant four and seven.'

Nicholls looked at him. 'Seven per cent of twenty-five million dollars is one-and-three-quarter million,' he said.

'You obviously got a maths GCSE,' said Carr, with a smile.

'It's a lot of money.'

'Aye. And how much would it cost for you to put *your* balls on the line and go out there to get her back?'

Nicholls sat forward.

'Any chance of a cup of tea?' he said. 'Or perhaps something stronger?'

Carr stood up and padded out of the living room – surprisingly light on his feet, for a man of more than 210lbs in weight and six feet two inches in height.

He was back with two tumblers of scotch in a few moments, a single ice cube in each.

Nicholls took a sip and nodded appreciatively.

'Macallan Estate Reserve,' said Carr, placing the bottle and an ice caddy on the coffee table between them. 'Accept no substitute.'

'Okay,' said Nicholls. 'Four and seven per cent it is.'

'That's just me,' said Carr. 'You'd also need to sort out my team – a hundred-and-fifty grand apiece for going, double if we succeed. And a million for death-in-service. Agreed?'

'Agreed,' said Nicholls.

'This is starting to sound interesting,' said Carr. 'So what's your plan?'

'There's the thing,' said Nicholls, with an awkward smile. 'I haven't got one yet. All I've got so far is a few thoughts.'

'I've never known anyone from Six have more than a few thoughts,' said Carr, with a wide grin. 'Tell me what they are.'

'It seemed to me,' said Nicholls, suddenly feeling hesitant, 'that we might be able to insert a small team, people with the necessary skills and familiarity with the area.'

Carr nodded. 'Insert them how?' he said.

'My idea was to fly them into Egypt,' said Nicholls. 'Obviously with a suitable cover story – I thought just four mates, over for a beach holiday in Sharm El Sheikh.'

Carr picked at his teeth.

'Nah,' he said, with a finality in his voice. 'Four's the right number – any more and you attract too much attention. But the rest of that is shite. For starters, Sharm's fucking miles from Sirte. Way south of Cairo, and Suez is in the way. If you were going through Egypt, the launch point would have to be Cairo.'

'Okay,' said Nicholls. 'Go on?'

'But Egypt's a no-no all round,' said Carr. 'I've worked out there before – a long time ago, with Mubarak's secret police. Never mind the regime change, and the Arab Spring, and all that bollocks, those guys are born survivors. You can bet they're still around, and they were good. Okay, they might not put two-and-two together, so you get out of Cairo. But you still have the problem of crossing the border. For obvious reasons, that border is very well patrolled by the Egyptians. They're mostly looking for people coming the other way, because almost no fucker is stupid enough to try to get *into* Libya, but they have military and police patrols, overflights, intelligence operatives... The risk of compromise before we start is too high. So Egypt's a non-starter.'

'A boat, then?' said Nicholls. 'A mothership – a trawler, with back-up on board – twenty kilometres off the Libyan coast? A couple of rigid inflatables, get onto the beach somewhere west of Sirte and...'

'Jesus,' said Carr, draining his scotch. 'I thought the "I" in MI6 stood for intelligence?'

'This is why I'm here,' said Nicholls, with a wry smile.

Carr laughed. 'Fair one,' he said. 'No, you're still way off. At least you're not suggesting we parachute in. Unless that's option three?'

Nicholls shook his head.

There was no point in rubbing it in, Carr thought. He was no fan of spooks, but this one came recommended by Guy de Vere. Maybe he ought to go easy on him.

'Look, the boat option's no good,' he said. 'Like you say, you'd have to have a mothership offshore to launch from. Okay, you can probably arrange that. But we're not going to coxswain ourselves up onto the beach, are we? That means bringing more guys in to hide and guard the boats, and more guys attracts more attention. That shore's well-patrolled by various people. Big risk of compromise. Locals might be able to talk their way out of it, but a bunch of white blokes? Not to mention, more people also expands the circle of knowledge.'

He let that sink in for a moment.

Then he said, 'Even if we get ashore unseen, you're now on foot and – what? Tabbing inland? I can tell you now that you do not want to be tabbing about the place out there.'

He dropped another ice cube into his tumbler, poured himself another Macallan, and showed Nicholls the bottle.

Nicholls shook his head.

'Your first plan was on the right track,' said Carr. 'Cross-border vehicle infiltration is the way. Just not from Egypt. From Tunisia.'

'Okay,' said Nicholls. 'So – what? You fly into Tunis, I assume? How far from there to Sirte?'

'Fuck me,' said Carr, with a chuckle. 'I'm good, Justin, but I'm not that good.' He pointed to a leather document wallet on the sofa next to Nicholls. 'I bet you've got an iPad or something in your man-bag there, eh?'

'Yes,' said the MI6 man.

'Get it out,' said Carr, 'and fire up Google maps while I go for a piss.'

When he returned, Nicholls had called up a map of the area. He slid the tablet across the table.

Carr looked down at the iPad and switched it to the satellite view, studying it closely.

Then he tapped in two waypoints – one on the Tunisia-Libya border, at a place called Wazin, and the other at a point where two tracks intersected in the middle of the desert, roughly forty-five kilometres south of Sirte.

The distance came up as 550km.

He turned it to face Justin Nicholls.

'There you go,' he said. 'So we land in Tunis, cover story is we're tourists, and we get a lift down south, near the border, here.' Carr pointed to a spot. 'Five klicks in, something like that. We collect our vehicles, and all the kit – which you will have pre-arranged – and just drive across. From there...'

'What sort of kit?' said Nicholls.

'I'll have a big shopping list,' said Carr. 'Personal arms, machine guns, anti-tank weapons, ammunition, grenades, explosives, comms kit, body armour, helmet-mounted night optics, med kit...'

Nicholls held up a hand, apologetically.

'I get the picture,' he said. 'But this is a worry. The whole reason for getting you involved is to minimise political embarrassment. What if you were compromised on the Tunisian side of the border? Four Brits, with enough guns and bombs to start a small war? I... I'm sorry, but I can't see that being possible.'

Carr nodded. 'Okay,' he said, scratching his scarred chin. 'I think you're worrying unduly – the Tunisians are fucking useless compared to the Egyptians – but I take your point. So we RV on the Tunisian side and collect personal weapons, body armour and night vision only. Not going anywhere without those, but there's lots of little wadis and caves and shit in that area, so we're unlikely to get compromised on foot. We just tab across the border and collect our vehicles on the Libyan side.'

'How do the vehicles get into Libya?' said Nicholls.

Carr laughed. 'That's your problem, isn't it?' he said. 'I would suggest you get all the weapons systems into Tunisia in diplomatic bags, separate out our personal kit, and just get local drivers to ferry everything down and across. If they're operating a couple of hours in advance of us, they won't have to wait too long. It's a fucking empty stretch of land there, they should be fine, but if someone compromises them at least it's not Britons, eh?'

Nicholls frowned. Then he said, 'Yes, that sounds doable.'

'So we collect the vehicles, and off we go,' said Carr. 'Forty-eight hours to be in position, eyes-on target, all being well. Worst case, seventy-two hours. Then we proceed accordingly.'

'As easy as that?'

'You taking the piss?' said Carr. 'I am not saying it's easy. It's very fucking difficult. You're talking a lot of planning, the right vehicles, the right equipment, the right team. But deep penetration, cross-border, behind-enemy-lines mobility was my speciality, and I've done it plenty of times. Iraq springs to mind, in '91 and '03, and back then there were half a million Iraqi soldiers looking for me each time. And I've navigated across much worse terrain than the Libyan desert. It's difficult, but it can be done, that's all I'm saying.'

Nicholls' mind went back to Mark Topham's words to Penelope Morgan: *Using a small team presents issues of its own… You get bumped, you don't have the firepower…*

It was followed by an image: four men, stripped, bloodied and mutilated, being dragged across the world's TV screens.

'What about…' he hesitated.

He felt guilty asking the next question, but he had a duty to protect his friend, the Prime Minister, and the country.

'What if you're caught?'

'That whole deniability piece?' said Carr. 'Listen, we both know that's bollocks. But if we commit to this, it's all or nothing. Getting captured is not an option, and we wouldn't let ourselves get into that position. I assure you that, if I go, I'll be coming back. But if it does all go wrong somehow…' He shrugged. 'I wouldn't be taken alive, let's leave it at that. And I understand that you'd need nice clean corpses, to give yourselves as much breathing space as possible. I'd make sure we were sanitised before leaving the UK – no driving licences, credit cards, pictures of girlfriends or boyfriends *et cetera*. You'd need someone to take our passports from us in Tunis.'

Nicholls said nothing.

'I take it you'd support us?' said Carr.

'Whatever you need.'

'I'd want the normal stuff – which areas are active and which are quiet, who controls what. Hopefully, your intelligence will allow us to move around main concentrations of militia groups, military, blah blah. If we get a chance encounter, then we'll just have to deal with it as it appears in front of us.'

'Whatever we have, it's yours.'

'And then there's the kit.' Carr looked at him. 'Who's funding this?'

'The PM's family.'

'Because *if* I get involved – and it's still a big if – this is going to fucking sting.'

'I appreciate that.'

Carr nodded.

'Okay,' he said, downing his scotch. 'I'm happy with the fee. Next thing is I need to see if I can find three fuckers who are crazy enough to tag along. Give me twenty-four hours.'

# 59.

AS SOON AS Justin Nicholls had left, Carr poured himself another scotch and sat down with a notepad and pen.

It didn't take long to draw up a shortlist of a dozen or so ex-SAS men he knew from his nineteen years in the Regiment who might be interested in doing the job and who fit his bill.

He wanted guys he'd worked with before – fit, resourceful blokes, with a good selection of patrol skills, whom he knew he could trust with his life. That went without saying. Beyond that, he needed at least one who was good with engines. The temperatures and terrain in the Sahara were going to put major strains on their vehicles, and a proper mechanic was vital.

Eventually, he put down his pen, picked up his mobile and dialled the first name he'd written down.

Dave 'Geordie' Skelton was his closest and oldest mate from the Regiment. They had passed Selection together and had fought side-by-side across Northern Ireland, the Middle East, Africa, the Balkans, and in other places where the SAS's involvement went unrecorded.

More than once, he'd saved John Carr's life, and Carr had been able to return the favour more than once, too.

He was one of a small number of men with whom Carr would gladly have stepped through the gates of hell. The feeling, he knew, was mutual.

After what seemed like forever, the big Tynesider picked up his phone.

'Geordie,' said Carr. 'It's JC. Listen, how do you fancy a week or two in the sun? And don't worry, you tight bastard, it's on me, all expenses paid.'

'What sort of work, man?' said Skelton.

'Right up your street.'

'Will I get to kill any bad bastards?'

'Yes, my friend, you certainly will.'

A few moments later, Carr had ticked the big northerner's name off on his shortlist, confirmed that the team would RV at his house in Herefordshire as soon as they were on board, and was making his second call.

Halfway through, Daisy from downstairs knocked on his door.

# 60.

GEORDIE SKELTON LIVED in a stone-built Georgian mansion near Longtown, right on the edge of the Brecon Beacons where Herefordshire met Wales.

It always made Carr chuckle to see this giant, rough-arsed son of a Newcastle foundryman standing on the steps to his beautiful country pile like a member of the landed gentry, but he'd earned the money to buy it the hard way.

As their Squadron's Quartermaster Sergeant, Geordie had been in line to take over from Carr as Squadron Sergeant Major when he finally knocked the Army on the head and left to earn some real money.

But on the final operation of Carr's final tour, Skelton had taken a round to his femur while clearing a house alongside Carr in Baghdad.

It was a horrendous injury, and he'd been left with a slight limp despite three operations.

That had put paid to his hopes of leading a Sabre Squadron, and while he could have stayed in – the SAS never discharges a man for injury – desk jobs were not the big northerner's style.

He'd left Hereford shortly afterwards.

And in one sense it had been the luckiest round anyone ever took – as soon as he was out, Skelton had started up a private security firm, just as the Americans were looking for civilian operators to take over key positions in Iraq and Afghanistan.

Within a year he was rich; within three he was ludicrously rich.

He'd recently sold the business to an international outfit run by a bunch of ex-SEALs and based on the east coast of the USA, and was now keeping himself occupied fighting his ex-wife in the courts, and finding clever ways to hide his cash from her.

Carr had known that it was driving him mad, and would have bet good money that he'd jump at the chance to hear more about the job in hand.

And he'd been right.

Carr had firmed up the other members of the team the previous night, and then got his head down.

He'd left London at 05:30hrs to beat the traffic, and it was just after 08:30hrs when he turned into the long private road which led up to Skelton's pad.

A quarter-mile later, he drove through a pair of stone gateposts in his Range Rover and on into a sweeping, semi-circular gravel driveway.

Skelton was standing on the steps, grinning.

Carr crunched to a stop on the gravel and got out.

Skelton took his hand in a giant paw and shook it firmly, before pulling him into a bear-hug.

'Good to see you, man,' he said. He looked Carr up and down. 'Still spending your life in the fucking gym, are yous?'

'Superior genetics,' said Carr.

Skelton laughed. 'Good trip?' he said.

'Boring fucking motorway,' said Carr.

'You should move out here, man,' said Skelton. 'Clean air, green fields…'

'Aye, and cow shit, and you,' said Carr. 'No, ta.'

'What time are the boys here?'

'Kev reckons they'll be here about eleven,' said Carr. 'Fred's down in Brighton seeing some bird. Kev was going to wait for him to get up to London on the first train this morning.'

Skelton nodded, and took Carr's overnight bag. 'Let's get you squared away and get a bacon sarnie inside you.'

After that and a brew, Skelton said, 'I've just bought some more land. Let me show yous.'

They walked out of his house and up the hill at the back. From the top, they could see into Brecon, and the Beacons where they'd spent so many filthy, wet, lung-busting days in training.

Skelton pointed to a distant line of trees.

'From there,' he said, with a long sweep of his hand, 'to that farmhouse over there.'

'Jesus,' said Carr. 'How much?'

'Just under one-point-three mill,' said Skelton.

'*Jesus*,' said Carr, again. 'How did they get a tight bastard like you to pay that?'

'It's an investment, mucker,' said Skelton, with a grin. 'Hundred and eighty acres, and they're not making it any more. I had the final stage payment from selling the firm, and eighteen grand a hectare's a good price. Plus it's all rented out to the local yokels, so I'm making coin that way, too. Bought it in trust via my sister, so Karen's not getting her hands on it.'

'You sure that's legal?' said Carr.

'Solicitor says it's sound as a pound.'

The two men sat down on a giant block of old red sandstone which marked the top of the hill, and looked out over the lush green countryside below, enjoying the golden heat of the morning sun.

In the distance, Carr could see a blue combine harvester slowly working its way through one of Geordie's fields, sending up a cloud of yellow dust behind it.

'You sure you want in on this?' he said, eventually. 'It's not like you need the money.'

He waved away a wasp.

'Not that that'd stop you *wanting* it, mind you,' he said. 'Your house is built out of fifty pound notes, and you still wear Primark pants.'

Which was true, basically. In his nearly twenty years in the SAS, Skelton had never knowingly bought the first round, nor the last, and his wallet was no more than a rumour to many of the soldiers he'd served with.

Geordie chuckled. 'You're a fucking sweaty sock, man,' he said, taking off his black beanie and rubbing his close-cropped hair. 'I knew you'd have negotiated hard. Go on, then.'

'Hundred and fifty grand. Cash, obviously.'

'Contingent on success?'

'No,' said Carr. 'Three hundred grand if we're successful.'

'That's what we're all on, is it?' said Skelton, with a sly look.

'Is it fuck,' said Carr. 'You three, aye. But I'm setting the job up, so my deal's my deal.'

Skelton laughed. 'Why does that not fucking surprise me?' he said. 'Still, three hundred large, tax-free, for a bit of work we used to do for four grand a month?' He stuck a long stalk of grass in his mouth, a contented smile on his face. 'I'm not turning that down.'

'It won't be like it was when we were in the Mob,' said Carr. 'We won't have the back-up we used to get. It's going to be risky as fuck.'

Geordie turned to him with a grin. 'Bollocks,' he said. 'What risk? This is me you're talking to.'

'I'm serious, mate. We might have the CT boys on standby, I don't know yet, but even if we do they'll be two hours' flying time away. This is modern-day Libya we're talking.'

Skelton chuckled. 'D'ye think I'm daft, man? What was it Pete Squire used to say? *We're just shadows and dust, here for a blink in eternity*. Mystical fucker, but he was right, wasn't he?'

Carr looked back at the Beacons. The memory of Squire – killed by a Taliban sniper's lucky shot in the dusty foothills of Afghanistan – was as fresh as if his friend was lying there at his feet at that very moment.

'Of course I'm sure I want in on it, you daft bastard, man,' said Geordie. '*I'd* fucking pay *you*. I don't know how many nights I've laid awake in that fucking luxurious bastard mansion down there, wishing I was in me maggot in some shithole, or stacked up outside a door waiting to make entry and bring vengeance down upon some fuckers.'

He stared out through the grey-blue haze to the distant Welsh hills.

'Nah, man,' he said. 'Right now it's not the dying I'm fucking worried about, it's the not-fucking-living.'

The smile had gone from Geordie Skelton's face now, and his eyes were wide and bright, and they held a look as old as time itself.

'I *need* it, John,' he said, quietly. 'I need to fucking live, need to get my heart beating, feel that thump in my chest, that taste in my mouth.'

Carr laughed. 'Talk about mystical, you big twat,' he said.

But he understood exactly what Geordie was talking about, and he felt it himself.

That moment before the shooting starts… getting focused, getting ready to kill or be killed, everyone thinking, *Is this it for me?*

And then you're into it.

Contact.

The noise from the weapons, the crack and thump from rounds coming past you, the smells, the screaming, the organised chaos of men, desperate to live.

You, and the bad guys.

The cards in the air, slowly falling as fate dictates.

No doubt about it: combat was a drug, and he was a recovering addict.

They both were.

'Don't get me wrong, I want the wedge,' said Skelton, his face relaxing back into its customary grin. 'I'm just saying that's not what it's about.'

Carr nodded. That just about described his own position. The money was important – his old man could have worked a hundred years as a welder and never seen that much cash – but what he really wanted was the fight, and the chance to find that fucker with the dark eyes.

'Of course, there's the question of what happens if we *don't* get back,' said Geordie.

'A million, after tax, chopped up any way you choose,' said Carr. 'All mortgages and other loans paid off, and twenty K a year to widows in perpetuity, and children until they reach eighteen.'

'I'd better take out a fucking mortgage, then,' said Skelton, with a big grin. 'No missus, no kids, but my brother and sister could do with a hand.'

'Same thought occurred to me,' said Carr, with a grin of his own. 'But the loans have to predate the day of the offer.'

'Stingy fuckers.'

Both men laughed.

Geordie threw away the piece of grass he'd been chewing.

'Fucking hell, man,' he said. 'Bring it on. I cannat wait.'

# 61.

THE OTHER TWO men arrived just before 11:00hrs.

Kevin McMullen and Paul 'Fred' West had both soldiered under Carr and Skelton in the same squadron, and had left the Regiment in the last eighteen months.

McMullen, a stocky, bearded, ball of energy and attitude, and a former Mobility Troop Staff Sergeant, had been the first name on Carr's list after Skelton, and the only married man on it.

Ideally, for obvious reasons, Carr had wanted single guys, and the Londoner was a devoted father-of-four, still married to the childhood sweetheart he'd first met at junior school in Hackney. He'd written down and scrubbed out McMullen's name several times, before finally deciding that the only selection criteria that really mattered was quality, and to rule out a man of Kevin McMullen's sheer ability, guts, and drive would be a mistake. Added to which, to think that way was to acknowledge – even subconsciously – the risk of failure.

In Carr's experience, men who thought about failing often failed.

So McMullen had got the call, and had jumped at it.

Truth was, unlike Carr and Skelton and West, he actually *did* need the money.

Things hadn't gone so well for him since he'd left the Regiment.

He'd gone on the spur of the moment, after thirteen years at Hereford and three years shy of his full twenty-two in the Army, after being passed over for selection as SQMS. That meant that he could never go on to become a Sabre Squadron Sergeant Major, and he'd taken this as a personal slight on his professional ability.

That was crazy, as Carr had told him repeatedly, during several late night attempts to change McMullen's mind. No-one doubted his soldiering, it was just that there were four troop staff sergeants in a squadron and only one SQMS: simple maths said that three quality men were bound to be disappointed.

But your strengths are often your weaknesses. McMullen would never, ever quit in the field, but occasionally his huge determination turned into a boneheaded stubbornness, an inability to know good advice when it was offered.

So he'd flounced out, in his mind making some kind of statement.

Almost immediately, he had regretted the move – no-one is irreplaceable, and the Squadron had just moved on without him, like the unstoppable train that it was – and he'd been too proud to ask to come back. He'd struggled with the transition to civvie street, and the money on offer for this job would make a massive difference to him and his family.

And Carr was very happy to have him along – Kevin was an exceptional patrol medic, and an equally good sniper, perhaps the best Carr had ever seen.

Back towards the end of his time leading the squadron, John Carr had led a team of blokes out near Sangin, the Afghan opium town in Helmand Province where his own younger brother had died with 3 Para in 2006.

Intelligence had come in which placed a key Taliban commander – a guy known as 'The Butcher' – in a compound deep in the green zone, near the river at the town's western extreme.

The source said The Butcher was planning to lead an assault

on the nearby FOB Wishtan, which was occupied at that time by an under-strength and battle-weary company of 1 SCOTS.

He had pulled together a major force, with heavy weapons, and his intention was to overrun the compound and slaughter every single man-jack inside.

Preferably in cold blood.

Under cover of darkness, the SAS patrol had got into the high ground across the river, and had watched the compound for near-on forty hours, as men drifted in from the surrounding area.

And then… Jackpot.

The Butcher himself had turned up towards the end of the second afternoon, on the back of a motorbike.

The Hereford team confirmed him inside the walls, and settled down to keep the bastard under observation, until the Squadron got there to kill or capture him.

But it rapidly became obvious that there wasn't the time for that.

Outside, in the shade of the twelve-foot mud walls, the guy at the handlebars of the little red Honda had turned the bike back the way it had come, and now he was sitting in front of the main gate, waiting.

Engine running.

Clearly, The Butcher wasn't planning to hang around to lead the assault.

After a few hugs and kisses, he quickly gathered around him a small group of men, most with AKs slung over their backs or in hand, and began using a long stick to draw in the sand.

Carr couldn't hear what was being said, but he'd delivered enough sets of orders to know that the bastard was running through the final plan with his senior guys, confirming their roles before he sent them on their merry way.

And the bike and the general air of urgency told him he had only a few minutes to act.

Carr had requested some air support to level the compound,

but the assets were all tied up with several major troops-in-contact across the AO.

No Apache could get to him within thirty minutes, and below him the briefing was already wrapping up.

The guy on the Honda revved his engine.

It had taken them months to get eyes-on The Butcher.

They might not get a second chance.

Carr made his decision.

Lying in the dust, he turned to Kevin McMullen, who was alongside him with his Accuracy International L96A1 rifle.

'Can you take that fucker out, Kev?' he asked.

McMullen never moved his eye from the scope.

He'd come out without his laser range finder – you can't carry everything – but he was a good judge of distance, and he knew the location of their op and of the compound from his map.

'It's a longish one, John,' he murmured, 'but, yeah, no problem.'

'You cannae miss, mate,' said Carr. 'You'll blow the whole fucking op, and we might never see the cunt again.'

'I won't miss,' said McMullen, quietly.

He saw some clothing hanging just outside the compound; it was flapping slightly in a gentle east-to-west breeze.

He adjusted for that wind, laid the centre of his cross-hairs on the Butcher's face, and then dropped his point of aim to the man's chest, to give himself some room for error.

Carr watched through his sniper spotting scope as McMullen slowed his breathing, the cross hairs lifting and falling slightly on the target.

Totally focused, the sniper then held his breath, keeping the rifle rock solid now, and gently squeezed the trigger.

The report was deafening, close-up, but The Butcher never heard it.

A 7.62mm Lapua round travels at a shade over 850 metres per second; sound itself lags far behind at a mere 343m/s.

The Taliban leader was halfway through a belly laugh when ten grams of lead collided with his forehead – McMullen had been slightly short in his range estimate – with a force of around 2,500 foot-pounds of energy.

The round took off the top third of his skull, and was deflected into the stomach of one of the onlookers.

The rest of them watched open-mouthed, and covered in blood and exploded brain, as their leader collapsed in a heap in his own sand drawing of FOB Wishtan.

'Fucking outstanding, Kev,' said Carr. 'Keep shooting, drop as many as you can.'

McMullen hadn't needed telling. The sound of the shot was only just arriving as he put down two more of the enemy fighters, each of them dying with an uncomprehending stare on his face.

The others finally reacted and scattered, the attack routed before it had even begun.

It was around that time that the Taliban had taken to calling McMullen 'The Silent Death' on the comms chatter.

A good man to have in Libya, Carr was sure.

Paul West – known as 'Fred', to the eternal amusement of the rest of the squadron, because he was a Gloucester lad from a building family – was the only member of the team who'd not come from the Paras.

Carr had always enjoyed pulling his leg by asking him, good-naturedly, which fish-and-chip outfit he'd served in before joining the Regiment; the answer was the Royal Electrical and Mechanical Engineers, and it wasn't always clear why he'd left his natural home.

Fred's abiding passion was engines, on trucks, cars, armoured vehicles, bikes, and anything else which you poured fuel into. He could have spent his whole career elbows-deep in grease and spanners, happy as a pig in shit, but he'd decided to go for Selection after a REME mate bet him he'd never get in.

As only happens in the SAS, he'd been put in Air Troop,

which was short of manpower, and not the Mobility Troop he'd requested and was best suited to, and he was famous for his fear of parachuting. He hated it with a vengeance – static line was bad enough, but HALO terrified him. Every time he stood on that tailgate of a C130, ready to jump, his legs shook, but it was testimony to the man that he'd never come close to backing out.

A decent amateur boxer and rugby player, with a nose that had been bust half a dozen times, it had taken him a while to develop his infantry skills, but he'd ended up doing fourteen years at Hereford, and had really come into his own as a demolitions instructor.

An exceptional demolitionist, there was nothing he couldn't do with explosives, and he was particularly known for his innovative and imaginative initiation methods.

On his dems course, the troopers had been tasked with making a victim-operated device.

West had handed in a motorcycle helmet.

'What the fuck's this?' the chief instructor had asked.

'It's a motorbike helmet,' Fred had replied.

'I can fucking see that,' had come the reply. 'What the fuck's it got to do with this course?'

'I hollowed it out inside here,' said Fred, pointing to the interior. 'Then I put a stick of C4 in. The initiation works via the visor. The cunt puts his helmet on and starts riding. As he builds up speed, visor down… Boom!'

'Not quite sure how you're going to get hold of your target's helmet,' laughed the chief instructor, who was not easy to impress, 'but I like the concept. Well done.'

These days Fred West was working security for an oil company in southern Iraq on a four-week rotation, and spent his off weeks chasing women and gambling in the casinos of London, Macau and Vegas. A poker fanatic, and a born optimist, he was convinced that one day the cards would make him rich.

Carr was happy with his team.

They just needed a plan.

# 62.

AT AROUND 4 P.M., some one hundred and fifty miles east-south-east of Skelton's house in Longtown, Zeff Mahsoud stood and watched with flat eyes and a blank expression as the woman in the latex gloves went painstakingly through the contents of his suitcase.

It had been brought to this room in the distant, empty parts of the airport, and was presently open on the floor to Mahsoud's right.

Across the table, the woman's colleague was flicking through his passport.

Both were wearing the uniforms of HM Customs – or the Borders Agency, or the UK Visas and Immigration Service, or whatever they were called this week – but if he'd been a betting man then Mahsoud would have put a significant amount of money on the pair of them being mid-level spooks.

'So tell me again the purpose of your visit to Tunis, sir?' said the male.

The female was looking quizzically at a black rucksack – a bag inside a bag? What was *that* about? – and shaking her head slightly. She put it down and picked up a training shoe, jamming her gloved hand down inside it, feeling for something.

*Anything.*

'I have many friends over there,' said Mahsoud. 'I do a lot of charitable work in the area and I have recently been unable to visit.' He smiled blandly. 'I am sure that you know why. But I have been cleared of any and all charges, and the judges were unambiguous: I have the absolute right to travel anywhere in the world that takes my fancy, the same as any other British citizen.'

'Yes, sir,' said the man, evenly. 'As I say, this is just a routine interview.' He looked away, back at the passport. 'You've mentioned this court case already. I have to say, I don't know anything about that. It's just pot luck, who gets pulled out. We talk to people randomly.'

'Of course it is,' said Mahsoud, his expression serene. 'Totally random.'

'And tell me who you'll be staying with?'

'I have already told you. I will be staying at the Golden Tulip hotel, on the Avenue Ouled Hafouz.'

'So who will you be meeting?'

'Friends.'

'Can you tell me their names?'

'Mohammed. Hassan. Roger.'

'*Roger*?'

'No, sorry. I forgot. Not Roger. Roger can't make it.'

The spook tried and just failed to hide his irritation.

Mahsoud beamed at him.

'Tell me about Mohammed,' said the spook, a little testily.

'I met him a few years ago. We are just friends.'

'You met him where?'

'I don't remember.'

'And you are travelling to see him *why*?'

'Do you not like to see *your* friends?'

'And Hassan?'

'The same.'

The spook sat back in his chair and looked at Mahsoud.

'Do you think we're stupid?' he said.

'I wouldn't go that far,' said Mahsoud, 'but I think you're going to have to let me go.' He looked up at the little white clock on the grey wall. 'My flight leaves in under an hour. Check it out. TU791. I would hate to miss it.'

'We can hold the flight. We also have the power to…'

'I know your powers as well as you do. Probably better. But why don't you look at the case of *Mahsoud v R*? I am sure you can google it. In particular, read the words of Sir David Herbert QC, the Appeal Court judge who handed down the decision. He was quite scathing of my treatment at the hands of the Security Service, and I don't think he would be happy to know that you are still harassing me.' He smiled. 'After all I've been through, I mean. It has been *terribly* stressful, and I am already planning to take legal action against the government, so…'

The male officer looked at the female, who shook her head.

'Wait here please, sir,' he said. 'My colleague and I just need to have a quick chat.'

They both left by a grey door, and Zeff Mahsoud sat back and looked around himself with detached amusement.

If there was a better place to get questioned by intelligence agents than the UK, he didn't know it; he'd be a lot less cocky once he got to Tunisia and beyond.

Not that he intended to be detained once he'd crossed the sea.

The door opened and the male spook walked back in.

'Right, sir,' he said. 'Thanks for your time. You're free to go.'

Mahsoud looked at the contents of his suitcase and carry-on luggage, strewn over the floor.

'What about my luggage?' he said.

'Oh, I'd like to help, sir,' said the spook, with a mirthless chuckle, 'but you know you're supposed to pack your cases yourself. Plus, I've a terrible bad back.'

'I meant getting it on the plane. I've checked it in once.'

'We'll make sure it gets loaded.'

Five minutes later, Zeff Mahsoud walked back out into the main airside shopping area at Heathrow.

All around him were young families heading off on their summer holidays – though bookings had already been hit by the recent incidents in Spain, and mums seemed to his eye to be keeping their children a little closer, dads to be a little more vigilant.

He could almost feel the CCTV cameras burning into him as he walked.

# 63.

AS MAHSOUD WALKED out of the room at Heathrow, Carr and the three members of his team were still sitting at Geordie Skelton's enormous kitchen table, drinking tea, and talking across a large scale military map of Libya.

Carr had laid out his thoughts, a few suggestions had been made, and it had been refined to the point where they all thought it was workable.

Essentially, it was as he had suggested to Justin Nicholls – fly to Tunisia, transport to the south of that country, tab across the border with small arms, collect vehicles and heavier weapons on the Libyan side, and then head across country to Sirte once MI6 had supplied the exact location of the hostages.

A lot would depend on the strength and disposition of the enemy forces, but they were confident that, with speed, aggression and surprise, they could overwhelm a reasonable number of men – many times in their Regiment careers, they had taken on forces ten times their strength and won.

And if they got there and found that the job was literally impossible, they would at least be able to act as eyes on the ground and report back.

As for extraction, Carr had planned for them to drive back out.

But Geordie Skelton had balked at that, on the basis that a

two-day drive across the Sahara, with two very valuable passengers, was too risky.

'We might have woken up half of fucking Libya, man,' he'd said. 'They could all be out looking for us. Sooner we're off the ground, the better.'

So, after some discussion, they had settled on a plan to head south of Sirte, out into the empty desert, before doubling back north to a point halfway to the coast, for extraction by air.

Given the UK government's difficulty in acting, this would have to be via a civilian helicopter, fitted with long range tanks, and flown by ex-RAF pilots.

But Carr knew a couple of men whom he thought would be up for the job, as long as the money was right. It all added significantly to the cost, but that wasn't his concern.

Finally, they started drawing up their kit list.

'Vehicles?' Carr said, turning to Fred West.

'Can't beat a Hilux, mate,' said West. 'There's a reason every fucker out there drives them. I'd go with twin cabs – three-litre diesels, manual gearbox, uprated suspensions, tuned engines. Full recovery kit, spare fuel, winches, two spare tyres each. Basically everything for a desert trip.'

'That's what I thought,' said Carr. 'What's the most popular colour? White? So we go with that. Way I see it, we're not going to sneak around, we'll hide in plain sight. Push out through the desert, and make good time. When we get to within a hundred K of the target area we can start to think about being more cautious. Until then, we don't want to be a needle in a haystack, we want to be a needle in a big, fuck-off pile of needles.'

'So not brand new, then,' said Skelton. 'Couple of years old, properly maintained, but roughed up if necessary.'

Carr nodded.

'Kit?' he said.

The shopping list took an hour to draw up.

They started with four Diemacos – C8s, all with standard ancillaries.

Four Sig Sauer P226s.

Two Minimis.

Four LAW anti-tank weapons, two for each vehicle.

One Barrett .50 calibre rifle.

And two 9mm Welrods – the genuinely silent pistol developed in World War Two for close quarter assassinations carried out by the SOE.

'No doubt we're going to get very up close and personal with some of these fuckers,' said Carr. 'If we can get in and out without going noisy, so much the better.'

'Make sure they're new ones,' said Kev McMullen. 'You know how the baffles deteriorate after you've put a few rounds through them.'

Ammunition – lots of it – for all of the above.

Grenades – frag and white phos.

Plastic explosive, bar mines, and claymores.

Medical kit.

Uniforms – American multicam.

Kevlar helmets with helmet-mounted night optics.

Kevlar body armour.

Encrypted UHF body comms – military standard – for intra-team communications.

Four Iridium Extreme satphones, all with unlimited air time and tracking capability.

'We can let them decide on the strategic comms they want to give us,' said Carr. 'But we'll need to send SITREPs and formalise the extraction.'

He sat back and drained his mug. 'What else?' he asked.

'We should get some money,' said Skelton. 'Just in case we need to buy ourselves out of the shit somewhere.'

'Good thinking,' said Carr. 'What do you reckon? Ten thousand

US dollars in hundreds, to keep the size down, and ten thousand dollars in gold coin, for each of us? And if we don't use it, we get to keep it as a little bonus.'

The other three men smiled.

'Sounds good,' said McMullen.

'Anything else?' said Carr, eventually.

A few other items were added, and then he looked at the list.

'They'd better have deep pockets,' he said.

'We'll need them to sort out a range somewhere in the UK,' said Skelton. 'So we can test-fire all the weapons, and get them zeroed, before they move everything out there.'

'Yeah,' said Carr. 'I'll make sure of that.'

He looked around the table.

'So it's shit or get off the pot time, guys,' he said. 'I've got to go back to my contact at Six tomorrow, so I need to know now if we're all signed up.'

'You know I am,' said Skelton.

Carr nodded: a man like Geordie, he couldn't turn down a job like this, not in a million years. In a professional career spent mixing with brave men, Carr had never met anyone braver than Geordie Skelton. It bordered on madness, or some sort of compulsion; when everyone else was ducking, he stood taller; when everyone else was thinking about an orderly retreat, Geordie was charging forwards. It was the only way he knew.

Fred West nodded. 'I'm in,' he said. 'I've got fuck all else do to except ponce about guarding oil wells and shagging tarts in Macau.'

Kevin McMullen ran a hand through his frizzy black bogbrush and exhaled, long and slow.

The truth – though he would never have admitted it to the others – was that he was unsure about the whole job.

Chatting it through in Geordie's kitchen was one thing; actually going out there and doing this insane thing was another.

Some nagging doubt, buried somewhere in the back of his mind, told him it was a bad idea.

But sometimes, like it or not, you just have to dance with the devil.

'That makes four of us, then,' he said, in his broad Cockney. 'The fucking missus'll kill me if she finds out. I told her I might have a bit of nice, easy security work with Fred.' He chuckled. 'Best thing is, she'll only be expecting me to earn a few grand, so I'll have a bit left over for a blow-out.'

Fred West and Geordie Skelton laughed, but Carr looked at him seriously.

'You sure you're okay to come, Kev?' he said. 'You need to be a hundred per cent comfortable with this. Us three, we've got no sprogs or basically grown-up sprogs. No women to worry about. It's different for you.'

'Nah, mate. I need the fucking money, it's as simple as that.'

Carr nodded. 'Okay,' he said. 'And, listen, when we get back I'll get you sorted for a job. You should have come to me in the first place. If I'd known you were struggling I'd have got you something.'

McMullen looked down, momentarily embarrassed.

'Mate, it's pride, isn't it?' he said. 'I've never had my begging bowl out. But I appreciate the offer, John. I'll take you up on it after this shit's done.'

Carr looked around the table.

'Last chance, boys,' he said, to the others. 'If you want to change your minds, I'm not going to think any less of you. It's not going to be like the Regiment. If we find ourselves in a situation, there's no cavalry.'

'They only spoil the fun, anyway,' said Fred.

'Okay,' said Carr. 'That's that, then.'

'When will we get a precise location?' said McMullen.

'My guy at Six is on it,' said Carr.

He yawned and stretched.

'Right, boys,' he said. 'That's me away back to London, to see the Six contact. Stay in comms. I'll update with intel as I get it, and with range details when I get them. Alright?'

With that, he was gone.

# 64.

JOHN CARR WALKED into the Savile Club in Brook Street at a shade after 21:00hrs, and jogged on up the grand staircase to the second floor.

He stopped by a door with a brass sign which said 'Flyfisher's Club' and grabbed a guy who was walking past.

'I'm here to see Justin Nicholls,' he said.

'Ah,' said the guy. 'I think Mr Nicholls is in the library. Would you mind waiting here, please sir?'

A moment later, he returned with Nicholls, who was wearing a dark grey pinstripe suit and a pale pink shirt.

Carr signed in and followed the MI6 man to a secluded pair of seats by the window, overlooking the Mayfair street below.

'Drink?' said Nicholls, adjusting his blue and red diagonal-striped tie slightly.

'Nah,' said Carr, looking at the tie. 'Guards, were you?'

Nicholls looked confused for a moment. Then he understood

'Oh, this,' he said. 'Yes, I commissioned into the Life Guards. Invalided out, unfortunately. Skydiving accident, on leave in Florida. Hospital for six months, and I couldn't really hack the physical side thereafter.'

Carr chuckled. 'I didnae know your mob of hats *had* a physical side,' he said, though inside he wondered whether Nicholls might be more than the buttoned-up suit that he appeared.

He looked around the otherwise empty room, which was full of books, pictures and other artefacts on the subject from which the club took its name.

'You fish, do you?' he said.

'No,' said Nicholls. 'Don't even eat the stuff. But it's a convenient and unobtrusive place for meetings like this. Less exposed than my other club.'

'Which is?' said Carr.

'Boodle's,' said Nicholls.

'Never heard of it,' said Carr, with a sniff.

'Ian Fleming was a member,' said Nicholls. He looked almost apologetic. 'And James Bond was a frequent guest at its fictional equivalent.'

Carr chuckled. 'James Bond, eh?' he said. 'And skydiving? Fancy yourself a bit, do you, Justin?'

'Shall we crack on?' said Nicholls.

Still grinning, Carr said, 'Any new int on their location?'

'Not yet,' said Nicholls. 'Our analysis has thrown up various places, but you know what that area's like. No shortage of hidey-holes all along that part of Libya. We need intelligence.'

Carr nodded. 'When do you think you'll get that?' he said.

'We're working on it, believe me,' said Nicholls. 'You know what it's like, but we have more people and money on this than anything I can remember since the Tube bombings. The one thing we can't risk is spooking them. So we're moving with extreme caution.'

'Understood,' said Carr.

He dug into his jacket pocket and pulled out several sheets of A4 paper.

'This is our shopping list,' he said. 'Details our infiltration and exfiltration plan, too. Anything you dinnae understand, call me or Mark Topham.'

Nicholls ran his eye down the first page, then the second.

He looked up at Carr.

'Christ,' he said. 'It's a hostage rescue you're working on, not World War Three.'

Carr looked at him, placidly.

'That's what we want,' he said. 'If it's one round short, one litre of drinking water down, we don't go.'

Nicholls nodded. 'Understood,' he said.

'Good,' said Carr.

'You have your team sorted?'

'Aye.'

'Can I ask who they are?'

'They're all good hands,' said Carr. 'Combat veterans, men who won't hesitate, don't worry about that. Names and essential details on the final sheet. For the payments, and the flights.'

'Excellent.'

'You'll also find the lat and long of the place where we want to get dropped in Tunisia, and the place we want the vehicles and weapons to be in Libya. Timings to be confirmed, but we'll want those in position, and watched, from two hours before we get dropped off.'

'Understood. Anything else?'

'Yes. The LAWs, explosives and all the other stuff can wait a day or two, but I want my hands on our personal weapons inside twenty-four hours, and a range where we can test and zero them.'

'I'm not sure I can manage that in that time frame,' said Nicholls.

Carr leaned forward. 'Listen,' he said. 'I got up at four this morning and drove to fucking Wales to brief the team. Then I turned round and come back down here to see you. I'm pretty fucking sure you can sort out four Diemacos, a few pistols and Minimis and a range between now and this time tomorrow. If you can't, then I don't think you have the capability to do this, full-stop.'

'Well…' said Nicholls.

'Let me tell you how these things go, Justin,' said Carr. 'I'm talking from experience, here. These kidnapping fuckers, they find a rathole and they go dark. But it only takes one little thing to spook them, and then they're in the fucking wind, and you might never find them again. As things stand, sounds to me like we had a lucky break with the intelligence pointing to Sirte. No guarantee we'll get another one. So my plan is to be in Tunisia as soon as possible, and ready to go the minute you nail their precise location. And for that to happen, we will need to be confident in our weapons systems.'

He stared hard at the MI6 man.

'We're not playing games, here, pal,' he said. 'You need to take this seriously, and pull your finger out.'

Nicholls almost blushed. 'I'm sorry,' he said. 'I am taking it seriously. I just don't have your experience of this. My skills are in other areas. I'll make some calls. I'm sure we can arrange your personal weapons and a range for tomorrow.'

'And I want something else, too.'

'Go on.'

'I want a guarantee,' said Carr. 'A guarantee that me and my team are not going to get extradited to Libya on murder charges at some future date. Because we *will* be killing people.'

'I give you my word.'

Carr held his gaze. 'With respect, Justin,' he said, 'it's going to take a bit more than a nod and a wink from a spook who's working off the books, however senior.'

'What would you need?'

'Something formal, agreed with my lawyer in advance, to cover us, in perpetuity. Who knows how long your bird's going to last at No. 10?'

Nicholls looked out of the window, into the late evening sunshine. In the street below, he watched a little girl snatch a teddy bear from her toddler brother, and the mother taking it from her and handing it back to the screaming boy. The incongruity between the normality down there and the conversation he was having up here was enormous.

'I'll get it done,' he said.

'That's us finished for now, then,' said Carr. He stood up. 'Just keep me in the loop re their location.'

'Okay.'

'You need to be a hundred per cent on all of this, Justin.'

'I will be.'

'I'll need to know where they are, who's guarding them, the works.'

'As soon as I know, you'll know.'

'No fuck-ups.'

'I guarantee it.'

'I've heard that before from you guys,' said Carr.

'You haven't heard it from me before,' said Nicholls, staring straight back at him. 'Guy de Vere will vouch for me, but I also have a personal stake in this. Penny Morgan is a childhood friend of mine, and an ex-girlfriend from my student days. I know Charlie, too. The thought of her…'

He tailed off.

Carr nodded. 'I will speak to Guy, by the way,' he said. 'Count on it.'

'Do,' said Nicholls.

Carr stood and stuck out his hand.

'That's me, then,' he said.

Nicholls shook his hand and Carr left.

As he took the stairs down, he pulled out his mobile and dialled a number.

It was answered by Oleg Kovalev, head of security for Konstantin Avilov, and therefore Carr's boss.

'Oleg,' said Carr. 'I need to take some leave.'

# 65.

TWELVE HUNDRED MILES south, Zeff Mahsoud stepped out of arrivals, underneath the blue lettering which read *Aeroport de Tunis-Carthage*, and into the stifling humidity of a North African night.

He crossed the road, and walked right, towards six flagpoles bearing the red Tunisian flag, where he stopped. There he made a big show of searching for something – a wallet, perhaps, or his passport – while checking to see if he'd been followed.

TU791 had landed at the fag end of the day, not long after the Madrid flight and half an hour before the scheduled arrival of the day's final inbound aircraft, the Paris-Orly service, so the place was relatively quiet by default. Even so, Mahsoud had waited in the airport lavatory for twenty minutes, to allow his fellow passengers time to disperse, and to give himself a better chance of seeing a tail.

Apart from a few policemen and the odd straggler, he could see no-one – certainly no-one to raise suspicions. Still, he walked on for another fifty yards, before turning left and walking back parallel to the terminal building, towards an identical set of six flags. Near there he halted again, and now he stood for ten minutes, back against the hard-ridged trunk of a palm tree which kept much of the orange overhead light off him, as though waiting for someone.

Finally, as satisfied as he could be, he walked back to the terminal building and got straight into the first in a line of yellow taxis at the rank, hefting his bag in alongside himself.

The driver, who was leaning on the bonnet of the Toyota and chatting to another cabbie, hopped behind the wheel and turned to Zeff.

'Where to, my friend?' he said.

'Café M'Rabet,' said Mahsoud, in passable *tounsi*, a local variant of Arabic. 'I'm meeting my friends there.'

'Down by Ez-Zitouna mosque?' said the driver, starting his engine and clicking on the meter. 'In Souk el Trouk, yes?'

'That's the one,' said Mahsoud.

The driver set off, and once he was clear of the airport, and out on the Boulevard Mohamed Bouazizi, he looked at Mahsoud in his mirror.

'You don't sound like you're from round here, boss?' he said.

'No,' said Mahsoud, watching the man's worry beads swinging. 'Waziristan. Originally, anyway, but now I live in England.'

As he said the word 'England', he allowed his lip to curl, and he saw the driver's face crease into a smile.

'You staying with these friends, or do you need taking to a hotel after?' said the driver.

'I'm staying at the Golden Tulip,' said Mahsoud. 'On the Avenue Ouled Hafouz. Is it far?'

'From M'Rabet?' said the driver. 'Maybe three kilometres.'

'I'll probably walk,' said Mahsoud. 'But give me your card anyway.'

He took the card and settled back into his seat, a satisfied smile playing on his face.

He had no intention of going anywhere near the Golden Tulip, but he wanted to plant the seed in the driver's head – just in case anyone asked him where the Waziristani with the British passport had been going.

'The Boulevard Mohamed Bouazizi,' said the driver, conversationally. He had come to a stop behind a bus. He gestured at the road outside. 'Named after the guy who set himself on fire. Did you hear about that in England?'

'Yes,' said Mahsoud. 'He started the Arab Spring, right?'

'That's him,' said the driver.

'And was that a good thing?' said Mahsoud.

The driver said nothing for a few moments, and Mahsoud wondered if he had not heard.

Then he looked over his shoulder and smiled.

'I wouldn't know, boss,' he said. 'I'm just a humble taxi driver.'

He didn't seem to want to add to that, so they drove on in silence for the next ten minutes, until they reached the Souk el Trouk, where Zeff Mahsoud handed over ten dinars and got out of the cab.

He waited for it to drive off, and then walked a couple of dozen paces down a nearby alley. There he knelt down, opened his suitcase, and pulled out a light blue T-shirt. He stepped into a doorway and quickly pulled the blue shirt on over the red one in which he'd flown. Then he jammed a faded green baseball cap onto his head. Finally, he transferred everything else inside the case into the black rucksack, which he hoisted onto his shoulders. Then he placed the empty suitcase in a large bin and strolled casually away, down into the souk.

He walked for half an hour, always alert for followers or strange eyes, doubling back, stopping suddenly, and turning this way and that, down meandering, narrow lanes. The whole of the medina was alive with people buying and selling almost everything under the sun – copper pots and leather goods and fine silks and jewellery – and it was impossible to be certain, but he felt reasonably happy.

In the Souk el Fekka, he lingered for a while over a display of nuts and raisins, weighing a bottle of *rouzata* pistachio syrup as though considering a purchase, while he had a final, careful look around.

Then he hurried on into the Souk el Attarine, the souk of the perfumers, a mere two or three hundred yards from where the taxi had left him. The oldest of the souks, it had been there since the thirteenth century, and the earliest Hafsids, and it announced its presence with the heady scents of sandalwood, jasmine and flower-of-the-night.

Half a minute later, Zeff Mahsoud stopped in front of a small shop, with an ornately-carved wooden frontage and an overhanging awning piled high with colourful cloth.

A quick look left, then right, and he walked inside.

The man behind the counter was old and grey, and his face was deeply lined.

He looked at Mahsoud with dead, bored eyes.

'Salaam,' he said.

'Salaam,' said Mahsoud. 'I wonder, do you have any rosewater from Kelaa M'Gouna? My wife is about to give birth to my third child, and she has requested it.'

The old man's eyes immediately came alive.

'If your third child is a boy, what will you call him?'

'Karim,' said Mahsoud. 'After my wife's father.'

'I have exactly what you are looking for in the back of the shop,' said the old man. 'Please, come this way.'

Mahsoud followed the shopkeeper through into a darkened storeroom.

The man took down a box from a shelf and unlocked it with a key on a thin leather cord around his neck.

He opened it.

'Mercedes,' he said, handing over a set of car keys and a small piece of paper. 'It's a little old, but a common model and it will run well. Parked at this address. No-one will bother you.'

'Thank you.'

'A Pakistani passport, as requested,' said the shopkeeper, handing over an envelope. 'And the money.'

'Thank you.'

'And this.'

The shopkeeper held out an automatic pistol, on a square of red silk, careful to keep his hands off it.

Zeff Mahsoud hesitated. 'I prefer to go unarmed,' he said. 'Allah will protect me, I'm sure of it.'

'Even so, it's very dangerous, the place you're going. And it never hurts to be prepared.'

Mahsoud paused for a moment.

'Perhaps it is wise,' he said.

# 66.

THE OLD MERCEDES smelled of sweat and vinyl seats, and it wallowed on the undulating asphalt like a foundering boat.

But the engine was sound and Zeff Mahsoud made good progress on the A1 coast road south.

He drove with a wary eye on his rear-view mirror, the ozone of the inky black sea to his left filling his nose through the lowered windows.

By dawn, he had covered well over five hundred kilometres, and was on the outskirts of the old Berber town of Medenine.

His eyes by now drooping with tiredness, he navigated his way through the slowly waking streets, following the route that he had memorised to the Hotel Jasmine on the southern outskirts.

He parked outside, and looked up at the sign, which claimed, optimistically Mahsoud thought, that the hotel was the 'Perle de Desert'.

It took him a while to rouse anyone, but eventually a young man with a bushy moustache and an attitude came through from the back.

'Yes?' he said.

'I would like a room, please,' said Zeff Mahsoud. 'I've been driving all night and I'm very tired. Do you have any available?'

'We have one,' said the young man, curtly. 'Forty dinars a night. How many nights?'

Mahsoud put his fake Pakistani passport and some notes on the counter.

'Just tonight,' he said, with a smile.

The young man plucked up the money with a sigh, scribbled down the passport number and showed Mahsoud to a room on the third floor.

Zeff Mahsoud shut the door behind him, switched on the air conditioning – it did not respond – and collapsed face down on the bed.

He was asleep within a matter of moments, but before he drifted off the image of a woman filled his mind's eye.

Charlotte Morgan, in her black gown and wig, at the Royal Courts of Justice.

# 67.

MAHSOUD WOKE in the early evening, still tired, his head thick, his mouth tasting foul.

He left the shabby hotel bedroom and drove out of Medenine, east, to the small town of Zarzis.

He kept his eye on his mirrors, and two or three times he pulled onto the side of the long, straight P1 highway, and then the smaller C118, and watched to make sure the cars behind him zoomed by.

In his line of work, there was no such thing as being too paranoid, but he was confident he had not been followed.

In sixty kilometres he made just one turn, a right onto the Avenue 20 Mars in Zarzis itself, and a few seconds after that he rolled to a stop outside the Publinet Fayez internet café.

He strolled inside, paid for an hour's access, and a coffee, and got down to surfing the net.

Mostly, he visited newspaper sports pages and dating sites, but at one minute past nine o'clock he logged onto his WhatsApp account.

There was one message, which he read quickly and deleted.

When his hour was up, he drove back to Medenine, and went to his hotel room.

He prayed for a while, and then climbed back into bed.

This time, sleep took a little longer to come, but come it did, and the next thing he knew he was being awakened by the dawn call to prayer from a mosque down the road.

He dozed for a little while, and eventually he pulled a book from his bag and read.

At eleven in the morning, the room hot and musty with the sun, he left the hotel and climbed into his Mercedes again.

This time, he drove first back into the centre of the town, where he found a dingy, smoke-filled backstreet café and ate a small lunch of barbecued chicken and *kaftaji*, washed down with Pepsi and a couple of Imodium – he hadn't got a local's stomach.

He ordered a second *kaftaji*, wrapped in aluminium foil, as a takeaway for later, and left, heading east towards Ras Ajdir, the northernmost border crossing into Libya, seventy-odd kilometres distant.

He had a feeling of great calmness upon him – the sense that what he was doing was pre-ordained, and that he was being watched over by a great benevolence.

Occasionally, fear did arise from the hidden depths of his subconscious, bringing with it the beautiful faces of Farzana and precious Aalia.

For him, death was never far away, and he had many times imagined his wife hearing the news, imagined her telling their daughter that daddy would not be coming home.

Unable to explain why.

No grave to visit.

No final call home.

Nothing but memories – memories which would fade until he was just a ghost.

Whenever he imagined that – and he tried hard to push it out of his mind – it brought a lump to his throat.

He feared for his wife and daughter, he had to admit that.

But, truly, he did not fear death itself.

He was a soldier, engaged in the greatest war of all, and if it was his time, then it was his time.

But Allah protected the righteous, and – though others would certainly have disagreed – Zeff Mahsoud firmly believed that he was among that number.

So he was able to harden his heart and push his wife and daughter away from his thoughts.

He was ready for a thorough interrogation at the Ben Gardane border post, but the Mercedes had several boxes of T-shirts in the boot, and he was hoping to pass as a day trader.

He was indeed pulled to one side by a couple of guards, who gave his passport a cursory examination and told him to get out of the vehicle.

'Why are you going over the border?' said one of the men, a beady-eyed character with acne scars and a thin moustache.

'I'm going to Zuwara,' said Mahsoud, in his halting *tounsi*. 'I have things to sell to the market stall holders.'

'Open up,' said the guard.

Mahsoud clicked the boot open.

The guard pulled his AK47 over his shoulder, reached in, and opened the boxes.

'Just T-shirts,' said Mahsoud.

The guard said nothing, but delved to the bottom of each box, feeling for any contraband.

Eventually, satisfied, he took a handful of the shirts, and spread them out on the bonnet.

'Tommy Hilfiger,' he said, approvingly. 'Genuine?'

'No,' said Mahsoud, with an apologetic smile. 'But they're the best copies you'll find. And the labels are real.'

'How much?' said the guard.

'Free of charge for you, my friend,' said Mahsoud. He dug into the front pocket of his jeans and pulled out two twenty dollar notes. 'Also,' he said, holding it out. 'For your families.'

The second guard took the money and a couple of the T-shirts, smiled, and slapped the roof of the car.

'You're good to go,' he said.

Mahsoud shut the boot, climbed back into the Mercedes, and drove on into Libya.

# 68.

ZEFF MAHSOUD'S local fixer, a fat young man called Tariq, had been waiting for him at a pre-arranged spot a few kilometres the other side of the border.

Mahsoud knew northern Africa well, having spent much of the last five years there – ostensibly on humanitarian aid work, in reality building his network of contacts among the jihadis who'd flocked to the region after the fall of Gaddafi – but it was a dangerous place to go wandering around alone, even for someone like him.

Tariq was monosyllabic, and he smelled strongly of sweat and onions, but the thousand US dollars it was costing Mahsoud to have him alongside for the journey to Sirte was money well spent: his father was a prominent local tribal leader, who also led a sizeable militia, and not much moved in this area without his knowledge.

Even the crazies would think twice about stirring up that hornet's nest.

As it was, the only dramas they encountered were at a couple of police or military checkpoints – on each occasion, Tariq had a few words, and they were waved through.

Mahsoud was almost grateful for the break in the monotony. The route to Sirte was six hundred kilometres of flat, empty, beige desert, pockmarked by low, green scrub, and interrupted only by the occasional scruffy town, and he had long since ceased to find it interesting.

They broke their mind-numbing journey at Misrata, stopping to eat and rest for a while at a large villa where Tariq was welcomed like a returning king.

The patriarch of the family, a man in his seventies, brought them through into a living room, where a large bowl of rice and goat meat was brought in and placed before them on a circular red carpet.

As Mahsoud sat and ate, he became aware that the man was regarding him with an undisguised suspicion.

The expression vanished as Tariq looked over.

'You can take that look off your face, you old fool,' he said, sharply. 'This is an honoured guest of mine, and my father's, and that's all you need to know.'

'Sorry, sir,' said the old man, looking away. 'Please, enjoy the food and ignore me. I get confused. It's my age.'

Tariq chuntered a little, but let it go.

Back in the Mercedes a couple of hours later, though, he turned to Mahsoud.

'So what *are* you here for, my friend?' he said, casually.

Mahsoud said nothing for some time, his mind turning.

He'd told the contacts with whom he'd originally negotiated that he simply needed safe passage to Sirte, a safe house in the city, and safe passage back to the Tunisian border when his work was done.

They'd asked no questions – the whole area was full of people doing things they did not wish to discuss, and discretion was always the order of the day – and Mahsoud had hoped that it could be allowed to rest there.

He should have known better.

And if Tariq and his tribe's protection could be bought for a mere thousand dollars, what might they do if they got wind that a prize as big as Charlotte Morgan was within their grasp?

He kept his eyes on the road, trying to think, trying to ignore the beady eyes boring into him from his right.

He was confident that Khasmohmad Kadyrov would have kept the circle of knowledge as small as possible – the property that the Chechen was using had been paid for with Saudi cash, via a third party in Balochistan, and then Egypt, and it was certain that the man who owned it did not even know himself what it was being used for.

Still, he couldn't just say nothing. Maybe he…

'Of course, we're not sophisticated city people from London, like you,' said Tariq, with a knowing smile. 'We're just poor people of the desert. But we're not stupid.'

Mahsoud turned to him, and tried to look sincere.

'Tariq, I would never think that of you or your people,' he said, earnestly. He pretended to hesitate, as though agonising over what to say next. Eventually, he said, 'Please do not be insulted, Tariq, but can I trust you?'

The Libyan laughed. 'I would die before I broke a confidence,' he said. 'You know this is true.'

Mahsoud knew nothing of the sort, but he nodded.

'Yes,' he said. 'Of course. I'm sorry.'

'So?' said Tariq.

'We have a plan to strike in Tripoli,' said Mahsoud, trying to make it look as though the information was being dragged out of him like a stubborn tooth. 'Some Americans, important people, they are coming over in two months for a meeting with the Army there. My contacts in Sirte and I, we are planning something.' He smiled. 'Something big. And, be assured, we will share the full knowledge with you and your father and your people when the time is right. If only to make sure you have no-one nearby.'

'The knowledge,' said Tariq, with a greedy smile, 'and some fruit, I hope?'

'That goes without saying,' said Mahsoud. He waved his hand expansively at the scrubland outside the window. 'Consider my thousand dollars for this trip but a grain of sand in the Sahara.'

Tariq chuckled, heartily. 'I don't like Americans, either,' he said.

# 69.

IT WAS ALMOST midnight when the plump young fixer leaned forward in the passenger seat of the Mercedes, squinted through the dusty windscreen, and turned to Zeff Mahsoud.

'Just up here,' he said. 'The compound on the left.'

A few moments later, Mahsoud pulled off the highway and onto the dusty, stony desert, and stopped outside a pair of wide, black gates set in a high, white wall.

'It's the home of one of my uncles,' said Tariq. 'Second man in our tribe, after my father.'

He got out and hammered on the gates with a small rock.

A moment or two later, a light appeared, and then the gates were slowly pulled open.

Mahsoud drove through, parked and got out, as they were closed behind him by a young man.

Tariq called to the man. 'You,' he said, imperiously. 'Take my friend's bag to his room, and get us some mint *chai*.'

The man nodded, careful not to make eye contact, and scurried inside with Mahsoud's bag.

'Houseboy,' said Tariq, by way of explanation. 'Follow me.'

Inside, the house was gaudily decorated, and lit by chandeliers, and it smelled of spiced food and vanilla.

Ceiling fans turned slowly, pushing the warm air around.

The only sounds were of chirping crickets and the low hum from a generator somewhere.

'Sit,' said Tariq. 'I'll go and fetch my uncle.'

Mahsoud sat, cross legged, on a large, heavily patterned rug, and took the *chai* brought by the houseboy.

He had almost finished it by the time Tariq returned.

'I have some bad news,' he said, sitting down opposite Mahsoud. 'My uncle is not here. He was called away on business. Back in a few days. So your stay will be a little longer. It might mean another thousand dollars.'

Mahsoud smiled inside – he'd been expecting the slippery bastard to try something to extend the job, and the payment.

But he was careful not to show it.

'I understand, Tariq,' he said. 'But I would like to liaise with my people. There's no reason why we need your uncle here for that, surely?'

Tariq drew in his breath, theatrically.

'It's not possible for us to leave this place without a letter from him,' he said, regretfully. 'He is a big man in this place, and he can guarantee our safety. But without that... Sirte is very dangerous right now. Very dangerous.'

*No more dangerous than the six hundred-odd kilometres we've just driven through, you fat fraud,* thought Zeff Mahsoud.

But he didn't say that.

Instead, he said, 'How long will he be away, Tariq?'

'I can't say,' said Tariq, with a shrug. 'Three days, maybe five. But you are quite safe here.'

# 70.

A FEW HOURS LATER, a vehicle carrying Charlotte Morgan and Martha Percival pulled up on a dusty track outside a compound somewhere in Libya.

It was pitch black, but Khasmohmad Kadyrov and Argun Shishani were wide awake and alert.

As the vehicle stopped, Shishani jumped out and limped over to the huge metal gates.

The man they had followed here – the eldest son of their contact in a Sirte, who was a gangster called Shaladi – put his shoulder to the gates, and Shishani helped.

Slowly, creaking and moaning, they swung open, and the Chechen's vehicle drove through.

'You should be fine here for a while,' said Shaladi Junior, handing over a set of keys. 'As you requested, it's out of the way. The owner died a year ago, and his family are all overseas. Nearest dwellings are half a kilometre. Farmers come twice a day to water the dates in the plantations, but they won't pay you any attention.'

'Good,' said Shishani. 'Food and water?'

'I brought stocks for you myself. Enough for two weeks.'

'Generator?'

Shaladi pointed to the left.

'Works fine,' he said. 'Oil tank is full.'

'Good,' said Shishani, again. 'But tell your father we will want a new place soon.'

Shaladi paused, and looked at the Chechen, his eyes narrowed. 'None of my business,' he said. 'But what exactly are you doing?'

'As you say,' said Shishani, 'it's none of your business.'

But then he thought again.

No point in antagonising this kid, or his father.

'We're not doing anything, yet, my friend,' he said, flashing a reassuring smile, and clapping the young man on the shoulder. 'We just need somewhere safe to hole up for a while.'

Shaladi nodded. 'You have our contact details,' he said. 'I'll be back in a week if I don't hear, just to check you're all okay.'

*You mean, to nose around and find out what we're up to*, thought Shishani, but he just smiled and nodded.

He followed the young Libyan back out through the gates and waved through his other two vehicles.

Once they had closed the gates, and they were certain that Shaladi had gone, his men removed the two women from their hiding places, and hustled them away.

Kadyrov came over.

'This is a good place,' he said, in a low voice. He nodded approvingly. 'A very good place. I prefer it to Sirte, in fact.' He looked up. 'Have one of the men take a machine gun up there. But tell him to be sure it is hidden from the skies.'

Shishani nodded. 'It's a big compound, though. Is nine men enough?'

'Eleven, counting ourselves,' said Kadyrov. 'But no, I think not. I don't want anyone from Sirte to come down here – that would just create a trail. Pay them off and send them home.' He chuckled. 'They will never know how lucky they are. I have spoken to my friend in Sinawin – he is sending a few more up to us.'

'Just in case,' said Shishani.

'Just in case.'

'Across the desert, even if they are seen no-one will make the connection.'

'Exactly, brother,' said Kadyrov. 'Now, time for some food.'

The giant Chechen turned and walked to the door of the main house.

Shishani himself walked around the side of the house, to a small building where the two women had been taken.

He pushed open the door and walked in.

Charlotte Morgan started as the door opened, and looked up.

She was lying on a rough mattress, dressed now in a black cloak, a cable tie around her left wrist holding her to the heavy steel bedframe. She flinched at the sight of the man with the dark eyes.

He stood looking at her for a few moments, a mocking smile playing on his lips.

'You are still a good-looking woman,' he said, in English. 'Even covered in dust and sweat and filth.' He looked at the two men in the room – both armed, one wearing a vest packed with explosives and ball-bearings. 'Perhaps I should send these guards away for a while so that we can get to know each other better. Your friend also.'

Charlotte coughed up what little saliva she could muster and spat it at him.

It fell well short, on the dusty floor.

He laughed, and she fought back tears of rage and frustration.

She tried to speak, but all that came forth was a croak.

What she wanted to say was: 'You can come and have a go, if you think you're hard enough.'

Because she had secreted the rusty nail from the fishing vessel inside herself, and if he got close enough she was going to drive it through this man's glittery black eyeball and into his evil, reptilian brain.

'I will leave you ladies to settle in,' said Argun Shishani. 'Good night.'

# 71.

IN THE MORNING, Mahsoud knelt alongside Tariq – who prayed ostentatiously and with too much pride, thought Mahsoud – and then the two men sat down to breakfast together.

The same houseboy from the previous evening brought out *bsisa*, an aromatic mixture of ground chickpeas and barley, coriander seeds, and fenugreek, mixed with honey and olive oil, a bowl of sweet Libyan dates, and glasses of hot, black tea.

'Is there any news of your uncle's return?' said Mahsoud, conversationally.

'No,' said Tariq, with a finality that suggested he did not want to discuss the matter further.

Mahsoud watched the fat young fixer spit a date pit onto the floor, and wondered idly whether he might not get up, go outside to the old Mercedes, recover the pistol from its hiding place under the back seat, and come back in and spread the fool's brains all over the wall.

He wouldn't, of course. Long ago he had been trained in the use of firearms, but his own forte was not in killing: killing was a job for others, his role was to pass through unseen, to observe the workings of the operation and report back.

And, unfortunately, he still required Tariq's assistance.

He still didn't yet know whether Kadyrov and Shishani were in Libya, much less had he seen them.

He needed Tariq, and his uncle, to help there – however unwittingly.

After breakfast, Mahsoud sat outside on a veranda which faced out to the beach and the turquoise Mediterranean a half-mile away.

It was cool in the shade, by the standards of the Libyan summer, with a gentle northerly breeze coming in off the sea; if you ignored the ugly towers of the chemical plant at Mosquée a few miles to the west, and the shell-pocked, bombed-out buildings visible on the outskirts of Sirte to the east, it was very beautiful.

His belly was full of nervous excitement, which had been bubbling under ever since the day of the operation on the beach. It had to be among the most ambitious actions ever planned by the forces of international jihad – perhaps exceeded only by 9/11, in terms of its execution and effect – and the sense that he was playing a significant role in the whole affair was almost overpowering.

As he stared out to the forever blueness of the Mediterranean Sea, he shivered; he was so close to Charlotte Morgan that he could almost feel her.

He went inside, to his room, and he stayed there until dusk.

# 72.

JOHN CARR AND his team had spent the day at Sennybridge Training Area, on a secluded range well away from prying eyes.

They had zeroed their personal weapons, and checked and re-checked the rest of the kit which had been sourced for them.

As he was climbing into his Range Rover for the drive back to London, Carr got a call from Justin Nicholls.

'They're in Libya,' he said. 'We've been watching the roads through Morocco and Tunisia, and all the time they were back on the bloody sea. The Italian navy found their boat last night – an abandoned fishing vessel drifting thirty miles offshore. Must have used another RIB to get inshore.'

'How do we know the boat's theirs?' said Carr.

'The crew had all been executed, for starters,' said Nicholls. 'That's a signature move – these people like tying up loose ends. Evidence of numerous passengers aboard the boat, too. But the clincher's that the Italians found a name in the hold. Scratched into the steel with a nail. "Charlotte M".'

'Smart girl,' said Carr. 'Why didn't they scuttle it?'

'Looks like they tried. But all the valves bar one were rusted shut, and the one they managed to open just let in enough water to heel it over on one side. Fortunately, the sea was calm. It's being towed back to the nearest port, and we're liaising with the Italians to get access for forensics. But it's them, John.'

'When did they go ashore?'

'From the state of the bodies they left behind, some time in the last thirty-six hours.'

'Any closer to identifying their safe house in Sirte?'

'Not yet. But we'll get there.'

'I think we should move,' said Carr.

'Are you sure you want to go before we're certain?'

'I want to be close enough to launch as soon as we get the location,' said Carr. 'We can stand off and stay hidden in the desert, fifty klicks to target, for as long as we have food and water. Then, you give us the word and *bang*. Better that than sitting on my arse in Primrose Hill, Justin. If it's on, it's fucking on.'

'Your call,' said Nicholls.

'We're happy with the weapons and other shit,' said Carr. 'You can have it collected and transported whenever you like. What about vehicles?'

'Already sourced and serviced,' said Nicholls. 'I've got trusted people in-country waiting to move you.'

'Book our flights,' said Carr.

# 73.

FOR ZEFF MAHSOUD, the following morning began much as the first had, with breakfast followed by a lazy hour on the veranda.

But as he sat watching the Mediterranean, day-dreaming of the Phoenician and Greek and Roman galleys that would have plied their trade up and down this stretch of water in ancient times, there was the noise of a flyscreen door opening behind him.

He turned.

It was Tariq.

'I need to go into town,' said the young Libyan, tersely. 'It's okay for me, but not for you, not without my uncle's permission. I'll take your car. I'll be back before dusk.'

Mahsoud nodded.

The flyscreen door banged shut again, and he listened carefully for the sound of the Mercedes starting up on the other side of the house, and then the noise of the steel gates clanging shut.

He waited for half an hour, and then he went back inside, took his encrypted satellite phone from his bag, and walked back onto the veranda.

He was followed by the houseboy and another man.

The man said, 'Mr Tariq says we must keep you safe, and watch over you.'

Mahsoud smiled. 'Of course,' he said, calmly. The man had a handgun tucked into his waistband, badly hidden beneath a flowing white shirt. 'I need to make a call. It's private, so don't get too close.'

He walked out into the sandy garden area, and stood under the shade of a large pink bougainvillea.

He turned, breathing in the scent of the flowers, and watched the two men watching him from the veranda.

He dialled a number and put the satphone to his ear.

It rang out for a while, and when it was answered, he covered his mouth with his hand and spoke quietly.

He went through the usual coded identification protocols that his trade demanded, and then said, 'I can't speak freely, and I can't leave. The uncle is away.' He smiled, for the benefit of the men watching him. 'He's trying to find out what is going on, just as I expected.'

He listened for a moment, and then said, 'I don't think I'm in any serious danger, but these people – it's all about money for them. They'd turn me over in a heartbeat.'

He listened to the reply.

'Not yet,' he said. 'But I'm confident. As soon as I see Kadyrov and confirm everything, you'll be the first to know.'

He pressed the red button, deleted the record of the call, and looked at the phone, his thoughts suddenly miles away.

His mind had turned once again to his beloved wife, Farzana, and their cherished Aalia: he had no way of knowing when he would be with them again – truth be told, *if* he would be with them again – and he had to fight the urge to call home.

To hear Farzana's voice, the giggles of his daughter – it would be beyond price.

But to do so would leave a trace right back to his family, and that was something he could not risk.

He turned his mind to Khasmohmad Kadyrov, and Argun Shishani.

They had done an amazing job – he had to admit it.

All the planning, the danger, the dedication.

And now they were within grasp of getting away with it.

But he wouldn't allow himself to believe it until he had seen them – and preferably her – with his own eyes.

'Come on, Khasmohmad,' he breathed to himself. 'Come to me, my friend.'

# PART THREE

# 74.

JOHN CARR AND his team flew in that day on the lunchtime TunisAir flight from Gatwick.

As Carr cleared immigration and walked out into the arrivals hall, he scanned the multitude of men holding up boards.

At the far left, standing quietly at the back, was a local guy – swarthy and thick-set, and wearing shades and jeans and a plain T-shirt – holding up a plain piece of paper with 'Mister Carr' written on it in thick marker pen.

Carr walked over.

'John Carr,' he said, holding out a hand.

The man shook it. 'Firas,' he said. 'Follow me, please.'

Firas led them outside to a white VW Transporter minibus.

It was mid-afternoon, and the sun was high, and the humidity was punishing: in the minute-and-a-half it took them to clear the airport and get into the vehicle, Carr's T-shirt was stuck to his back.

'Fucking hell,' said Geordie Skelton, as he climbed in alongside him. 'I knew there was a reason I didn't like Africa.'

'You going to moan the whole of the trip?' said Carr.

'Probably,' said Geordie.

Firas eased them through the traffic south, then east, and in ten minutes or so he pulled into an underground garage.

'Safe house,' he said, over his shoulder. 'Offices below, apartments upstairs.'

They followed him to a lift, and up three floors to a stark, white-tiled corridor, with half a dozen doors.

'All are empty,' he said. 'So no-one will bother you.'

He opened the nearest door and led them inside. The flat had a small kitchen, a bathroom, and two other rooms. It was unfurnished apart from a table and chairs and four mattresses on the floor in what would have been the living room, and a fridge humming quietly in the kitchen.

'Coke and water in the fridge,' said Firas, with an open smile. 'Food also. At six o'clock will come your contacts.'

'Thanks, pal,' said Carr, shaking his hand.

The Tunisian left, and the four men dumped their bags.

Kevin McMullen went for a piss, and Geordie and Fred West lay down on the nearest mattresses.

'Wake me at six,' said Fred, a man who could sleep anywhere, anytime.

The far wall of the apartment had sliding doors which looked out onto a balcony with a view of the Lac de Tunis.

Carr walked over, closed the curtains most of the way, stood in the remaining gap, a foot or two back to stay in shadow, and looked out at the city below.

He stood there for some time, running through the plan in his head, going through his mental checklist.

Eventually, he turned and lay down on the remaining mattress, closing his eyes, trying to clear his mind.

At a quarter to six, he opened his eyes again and stood up.

'Look lively,' he said, prodding Fred West with his boot.

There was a knock at the apartment door just before the hour.

Geordie Skelton opened it. Two people – a dark-haired, bearded man in his late forties, who was carrying a small sports bag, and a brunette in her thirties.

'John Carr?' said the woman, in a voice out of Home Counties central casting.

'No,' said Geordie. He pointed with a thumb. 'That's him.'

Carr stepped forward and shook the woman's hand.

She held it for a beat longer than strictly necessary, her eyes on Carr's.

Then she turned to the bearded man.

'Would you mind waiting outside, Peter?' she said. 'Leave the bag.'

She waited until he'd left, closing the door behind him, and then turned back to Carr.

'I'm Arabella Barnes,' she said, with a smile. 'I'm from Six at the embassy. Justin Nicholls in London sent me to meet you.'

Her hair was scraped back in a tight ponytail, and she wore a loose black business suit, but Carr had the feeling that underneath the modest exterior was a tidy rig.

'Is that so?' he said. 'I was expecting a guy. Don't know why.'

'Old-fashioned sexism?' said Arabella, with a mischievous grin. 'I'm sorry to disappoint.'

'I'm not disappointed,' said Carr.

'Good.' She had big brown eyes, and they flashed as she spoke. 'I'm to make sure that you hand over any personal effects which might link you back to the UK, give you a last briefing, and help you with anything else you need.'

'Anything?' said Carr, with a grin. 'That sounds promising.'

'Howay, man,' said Geordie, under his breath. 'For fuck's sake.'

Arabella turned to look at him, eyebrow raised.

'He's just bitter because he never gets the girl,' said Carr.

'And you do?' said Arabella.

'Depends.'

'On what?'

'On whether I like her or not,' said Carr. He nodded at Geordie. 'I rely on my good looks and effortless charm, whereas he relies on his money. Have you met multi-millionaire Geordie Skelton?'

She chuckled. 'So,' she said, lifting a small attaché case onto the table. 'You need this from me.'

She handed over four small packages, which were surprisingly heavy.

'Your gold and US dollars,' she said, when she saw Kev McMullen raise his eyebrows at the weight. 'And I'll take your passports.'

Carr hesitated. 'It occurred to me,' he said. 'What if we get a tug on the way down, with no ID on us?'

'The Tunisian police are not particularly dedicated,' said Arabella, 'and they are most certainly not incorruptible. You'll be unlucky to get stopped, and if you are then Firas will be able to sort it.'

'Okay,' said Carr. He leaned forward, removed his wallet and passport from his back pocket, and handed them over.

The others followed suit.

'You'll need to get your mate outside to take our bags, too,' said Carr. 'We had to make it look like we were here for a fortnight's holiday.'

Arabella nodded. 'Now, there's a change to your RVs,' she said. 'Latest intelligence has various Islamic groups active in the area where you intended to cross, so we've moved you a little further north.'

'Same distance, though, pet?' said Geordie Skelton. His one concern about this job was the tab across the border – he was fit and strong, but his right femur was held together with a titanium plate and screws.

'Because of the lie of the land, it does add about three kilometres to your route, I'm afraid,' said Arabella.

'Okay,' said Geordie, with a nod. 'That's fine.'

'What are they up to?' said Carr.

'We think it's foreign fighters moving into Libya,' said Arabella. 'They used to push in through Ras Ajdir and then strike out east for Tripoli and beyond, but they were upsetting too many of the tribal militias in that area so the crossing's been tightened up.'

'Foreign from where?'

'Morocco, Algeria, Tunisia, obviously,' said Arabella. 'Europeans and others among them, too, heading down through Spain since Egypt got tougher for them.'

'Interesting,' said Carr. 'So they're pretty much using the same route as us to go east?'

'It's not easy to get the intelligence, but yes, we think so.'

'What groups?'

'Al Qaeda, Islamic State remnants, Ansar Al-Sharia. The usual.'

Carr looked at the others.

'Doesn't really change anything else apart from the RVs, does it?' he said.

'No,' said Geordie. 'You'd expect the place to be crawling with the fuckers anyway.'

Fred and Kevin nodded.

'We'll have to keep our eyes peeled,' said McMullen, with a grin, 'but I was planning to do that anyway.'

'So that Firas guy is taking us down there?' said Carr.

'Yes,' said Arabella. 'He'll pick you up here tomorrow morning at nine.'

'Reliable?' said Carr.

'Of course,' said Arabella. 'He's a hundred per cent trustworthy. He's been trained by us.'

'With respect, Arabella,' said Carr, 'that doesn't fill me with confidence.'

She said nothing, and Carr shrugged. At the end of the day, it was a drive south from Tunis to the first RV. He had no real choice but to trust Nicholls and this girl and Firas.

'And what's our story?'

'Story is, he's your tour guide, taking you down to Ksar Ouled Soltane, to see the granary there.'

'Why would four blokes be going to see a fucking granary, pet?' said Geordie.

'You're *Star Wars* nerds,' said Arabella, with a grin. 'They filmed bits of *The Phantom Menace* there. It's supposed to be the slave quarters of Mos Espa, where Anakin Skywalker lived as a boy.'

'I actually wouldn't mind seeing that,' said Kevin McMullen. 'My kids have watched all them films a million times. Picture of me in the ruins would go down well.'

Carr looked at him and shook his head.

'Fuck me,' he said.

Arabella picked up the sports bag that the bearded guy had left and slid it across the table to Carr.

He opened it and pulled out four faded T-shirts from the *Star Wars* franchise and four small digital cameras.

'The cameras are preloaded with tourist shots of Tunis,' said Arabella. She grinned. 'And the T-shirts have been washed repeatedly to make it look like you've all worn them for many years.'

Carr picked up one of them, a black thing with a white stormtrooper's head motif, and looked at it.

'I get the cover story,' he said. 'But do we look like fucking geeks to you?'

He stood up, peeled off his own T-shirt, and pulled the stormtrooper on.

He looked at her. 'I mean, for fuck's sake,' he said.

Arabella's eyes drifted over his biceps, and lingered on his shoulders and chest.

'Hmmm,' she said. 'Well, I think it looks pretty good on you.'

'Aye, well you can store that one in your memory bank,' said Carr, with a grin. He peeled it off again and dropped it on the floor. 'I won't be wearing it again. It might work if we were a group of pencil necks from your outfit, but otherwise, no. We'll rely on Firas to talk us out of any shit.' He laughed. 'I'm surprised you're not asking us to wear *shemaghs* and false beards.'

Arabella watched him put his own T-shirt back on, and then looked away.

'Up to you,' she said. 'Now, Ksar is just south of Tataouine.

That's five hundred kilometres from here, maybe five-fifty. It will be dark by the time you get there. You're crossing near Wazin, which is a little further south.'

She sat back.

'I think that covers everything,' she said. 'Unless you have any questions?'

'I've got one,' said Geordie Skelton. 'Where can I get some proper scran, like?'

'There are several very good hotels around this area,' said Arabella. 'The big embassies are all clustered around the lake, so the security is good and the food won't give you any stomach problems. The Hotel L'Acropole is good. So are the Paris Concorde and the Berges du Lac.'

'Which is nearest?'

'L'Acropole.'

'That's me, then. Boys?'

Fred West and Kevin McMullen nodded, but Carr shook his head.

'Nah,' he said. 'You fellas knock yourselves out. No drinking, though. We want to be on it tomorrow morning.'

'What are you doing, then?' said Geordie, standing up.

'I'm going to have a mooch around the old town,' said Carr.

Arabella looked at him. 'Have you been to Tunis before, John?'

'Aye,' he said. 'But not as a tourist.'

'Would you like me to give you a guided tour?' she said. 'There are some stunning sights.'

Behind her, Geordie Skelton mimicked pushing two fingers down his throat.

Carr winked at him.

'That sounds great,' he said, with a smile.

# 75.

JOHN CARR'S MIND was turning at a thousand miles an hour.

He was swimming in the sea – hidden deep under the surface, the daylight above no more than a faint glow.

He was moving relentlessly forwards, like a shark, towards unseen and unknown prey.

His mind focused, his muscles taut and coiled, he rose slowly through the cool water.

And then he broke the surface and saw himself, as though from above.

He was carrying a weapon, and wearing body armour, and wading ashore, towards that mysterious target.

Next to him was a man he didn't recognise at first.

Then he realised it was a young Trooper, 'Wayne' Rooney, who had died in a house assault back in Baghdad, during the days of Task Force Dagger.

And then the dream dissolved, and he woke.

It took him a moment to find himself, lying slick with sweat, in this hot Tunis bedroom.

It was just before dawn, and the sounds of the call to prayer and a little light traffic were filtering in through the flyscreen covering the open window of Arabella Barnes' apartment, a few blocks from the Embassy.

The ceiling fan was turning slowly and almost noiselessly overhead, but he'd told her to leave the aircon off – he wanted to acclimatise as much as he could – so he was lying naked on the bed, the covers in a pile on the floor.

He turned to his right.

The girl from MI6 was nude next to him, lying on her front, her face turned to look at him.

Her eyes were wide.

'Everything alright?' she said. 'You were twisting and turning like a mad thing.'

'Just a dream,' said Carr.

'Oh?' she said.

'Someone was about to get clipped,' he said, with a yawn. 'Fucked if I know who.'

Arabella Barnes said nothing.

Carr put a hand out and slapped her bottom, watching it wobble slightly.

'Ouch, you cheeky so-and-so,' she said, with a grin. 'Didn't you get enough of that last night?'

'This might be the last arse I see,' said Carr.

'Really?'

'Last I see *today*, anyway.'

She lifted herself up onto her elbows and looked at him through half-closed eyes. 'Well, I hope it's satisfactory.'

'It's more than satisfactory.'

'What are you actually here for?' she said.

'London didn't tell you?'

'They told me the basics – the stuff I had to know. But the mission itself… No.'

Carr just looked at the curve of her hip.

'I mean, I assume you're SAS?' said Arabella.

'It must be those ruggedly handsome good looks and charm I was talking about,' said Carr. 'Though that doesn't explain Geordie.'

'No,' she said. 'You're just the four scariest bastards I've seen since I joined the service. And you're covered in Parachute Regiment tattoos and obviously dreaming about killing people.'

Carr looked at her for a moment.

Then he said, 'You're young, but you've been around long enough to know what you don't need to know. Loose lips sink ships, and all that bollocks.'

'Yes,' said Arabella. 'I suppose so.'

She turned her head away to face the wall.

'Be careful, won't you?' she said. 'I'd like to give you your passport back in person, not send it home in a brown envelope to your wife.'

Carr smiled at her blatant fishing.

'I'm a hard man to kill,' he said. 'Plenty have tried, but they only got one go. Plus, I havenae got a wife. And I'm not looking for one.'

She said nothing.

'Anyway,' he said, 'I'm not coming back out through Tunis. You'll have to post it back via your people at Six.'

She turned back to look at him.

'Or I could deliver it in person,' she said. 'Next time I'm in London. I have some leave due.'

He smiled, and looked at his watch.

Five-thirty.

He reached out and gently slapped her backside again.

'You'll get more out of me if you stroke it,' she said.

Later, after she'd gone off to work, he showered and dried himself thoroughly, and then sat on the bed, almost meditating.

Thinking about the job ahead.

At just after 8 a.m., he left, carrying nothing except for two hundred US dollars in the pocket of his trousers, and leaving nothing behind.

It was a fifteen-minute walk back to the underground garage, and he enjoyed the feel of the morning sunshine on his face, and even the smell of the traffic fumes.

He was starting to get that tingling feeling, that feeling of being just a little more alive.

At 8.15 a.m. he was outside the door to the apartment.

He knocked, and Geordie opened it.

'You bastard,' he said, shaking his head.

Carr followed him inside.

'Just the way it is,' he said. 'I had Arabella, you had Mrs Palm and her five sisters.'

'I'm just too fucking professional to spend time mincing around with some posh tart,' said Geordie, witheringly. 'I got me head down ready for the job.'

Carr just grinned.

'Fuck off,' said Skelton.

The other two were up and ready, and pulling on their well-worn boots: no-one wanted to be breaking in new footwear.

'Alright, guys?' said Carr. 'Any chance of a brew?'

'Bob Hope and no hope,' said Fred West. 'No teabags, no kettle. It's fucking ridiculous.'

'Better be some in the rations on the fucking wagons,' said Kev McMullen. 'I kid you not.'

'Aye, fucking right man,' said Geordie. 'We need a brew on ops, John.'

'Don't panic,' said Carr. 'It's all sorted. Once we're on those vehicles it'll be like Iraq and Afghan all over again.'

He got himself a Coke and a protein bar from the fridge – he didn't want either, but he needed something – and went again to the window, to look out at the lake.

At just before nine, there was a gentle knock at the door.

Fred West opened it, and Firas walked in.

'Morning, gentlemens,' he said. 'All is good?'

'All good,' said Carr.

They followed him down to the garage and into the VW Transporter.

With a final look over his shoulder, Firas pulled away and drove smoothly up the ramp from the carpark and away.

The traffic was surprisingly heavy, and typically Tunisian, so he drove in silent concentration until he was out of the narrower city streets and onto the wide, flat Sortie Ouest.

Then, over his shoulder, he said, 'We drive now for eight hours. There is food and water in the cool box. Or you can sleep if you wish.'

West and McMullen had already spread themselves out into comfortable positions on the rearmost seats.

Geordie Skelton turned to Carr. 'That pair'll be gone in a minute,' he said. 'I reckon one of us two should keep his wits about us, eh, mucker?'

'Aye,' said Carr. 'That lassie kept me up half the night, so you can stag on. Being as how you were so professional, and got your head down, and all that.'

'You're a lucky bastard,' said Skelton, bitterly. 'What the fuck do they see in you?'

Carr just closed his eyes, a contented smile on his face, and drifted off, to the sounds of Skelton's muttered curses.

# 76.

JOHN CARR WAS jolted awake by an elbow to the ribs and Geordie Skelton telling everyone to wake up.

He glanced at his watch: gone two.

'Checkpoint, mate,' said Geordie, out of the corner of his mouth.

Carr was instantly wide awake and alert, and feeling suddenly very vulnerable without a weapon.

Up ahead, he could see a pickup parked next to a bi-lingual sign which read 'Mareth'.

A guy in dark clothing was standing in the middle of the road, an AK47 over his right shoulder and his left hand signalling them to stop.

Three others were leaning against the vehicle, smoking and holding their weapons casually.

'This looks dodgy,' he said.

He glanced out of the side window: through the darkened glass, under a blue sky that stretched forever, he could see a flat expanse of desert, picked out with regimented rows of palm trees fed by some unseen oasis, and then the beginnings of the small town.

'Everything okay, mate?' said Geordie, to the driver. 'Not fucking militia, are they?'

'No,' said Firas, over his shoulder. 'Army border patrol.'

'Are we not a bit far from the border yet for that, man?' said Geordie.

'They operate all the way up and down this road,' said Firas. 'It should be okay. Everybody be cool.'

'Who's he think he is?' said Fred West, under his breath. 'George fucking Clooney?'

The VW Transporter was slowing, and it rolled to a stop ten feet or so short of the guy in the road.

That forced him to walk towards the vehicle, creating a little separation between him and his oppos.

*Good drills*, thought Carr.

Maybe Firas had been trained better than he'd thought.

The guy with the AK was spinning his hand, indicating that the window should be lowered.

Firas complied.

'Good afternoon, sir,' he said, in Arabic, with a genial smile.

'Where you going?' said the guy.

Carr saw now that he was wearing a dusty uniform shirt with a name tag which said 'el Jaziri'.

'Down to Ksar,' said Firas, with a shrug, and a weary shake of the head. 'These people. Their movies.'

'You've left it late. It'll be dark before you get there.'

'We got caught behind a big pile-up by Haffuz,' said Firas. 'We were there a couple of hours. I told them we should try again tomorrow, but…' He tailed off.

El Jaziri poked his head in and looked at the four men. He had a hooked nose and piercing eyes, which ran quickly over them all.

'*Star Wars*?' he said, dismissively. 'It's for kids, isn't it? These are grown men.'

'Westerners,' said Firas, with another shrug. 'You know what they're like.'

'Show me their passports,' said el Jaziri.

'They left them back at their hotel,' said Firas. 'Only their second day here. They don't know the rules.'

El Jaziri stood back.

'Get out of the vehicle,' he snapped.

Firas did as he was told, and Carr took the opportunity to slide back his door, too.

He made it look casual, yawning as he did so, but this el Jaziri was a wrongun if ever he'd seen one, and he wanted to minimise the time it would take to get to him if it all went south.

'Maybe I should arrest them and take them into town for the night?' said el Jaziri.

'Do what you want,' said Firas. 'It makes no difference to me, I still get paid. But I think it would be a waste of your time.'

El Jaziri slapped him across the face.

'Do not disrespect me,' he said, his voice laced with menace.

Over his shoulder, Carr saw the other three border guards stop talking and look over for a moment.

One of them lifted his AK for a second, and then spat on the floor and turned back to carry on the conversation.

'I am sorry, sir,' said Firas. 'I am a poor man. Please, sir, I am sorry.'

'So you should be,' said el Jaziri, with a cruel smile. 'But I need fifty dollars apiece to forgive you.' He looked briefly at Carr. 'Or things might get a lot worse.'

'What do you mean, sir?' said Firas.

'Plenty of people around here looking to buy Westerners,' said el Jaziri. 'What are they? Americans?'

'Irish, sir.'

The policeman tried to hide his disappointment.

'Same thing,' he said. 'Still worth a few thousand dollars each.'

Carr nudged Geordie, who nudged him back.

Both men trying to look casual, but completely wired.

In the back seats, Kevin McMullen and Fred West leaned forward, sensing the danger.

Carr tensed his body and moved his left foot towards the open door. Much more talk of selling Westerners, and he was going out of it and straight for Mr el Jaziri.

Drop him, get his AK, hose down the other three before they had time to turn the minibus into a cheese grater.

Of course, if the weapon was in bad order – and judging by the state of these dickheads it might well be – then they were fucked.

But they were fucked anyway if things took that turn.

'You wouldn't sell them, sir,' said Firas. 'Surely not?'

Just then, one of the other border patrol men leaned into the cab of their pickup and spoke into the radio.

He pulled his head back out, shouted something, and climbed into his car.

El Jaziri glanced at the four white men.

'I'm a merciful guy,' he said, holding out his hand. 'But it was fifty dollars apiece, and now it's a hundred. Quickly. And don't let me catch them on the way back.'

'Four hundred dollars, sir?' said Firas. 'Please. I don't have any money. Four hundred dollars? Are you joking?'

Outside, the driver of the pickup was pumping his horn and waving frantically through his windscreen.

'Ask them for it,' said el Jaziri, nodding at Carr and Skelton.

But before Firas had the chance, the pickup accelerated towards them and skidded to a halt.

'Leave them alone and get in the fucking car, Yussef,' said the driver, through his window. 'There's a problem on the other side of town.'

'Ah, *shit*,' said el Jaziri. He looked malevolently at Firas. 'This is your lucky day,' he said. 'If I catch you on the way back…'

Cursing, he ran to the vehicle and jumped into the passenger seat.

Carr watched as it performed a screeching U-turn and sped off south in a cloud of dust.

'*His* lucky day,' said Carr, as Firas climbed back into the minibus. 'He was one wrong word from me getting out and fucking him up.'

'You speak Arabic, John?' said Firas. He pronounced it *Chan*. 'It's unusual.'

'Useful in my line of work,' said Carr. 'You okay?'

Firas grinned at him.

'Ha,' he said. 'Sure. He slaps like a girl. A fool with a gun, all talk and no balls. But if the other men don't call him, we have to pay. It's a game, yes?'

'So what was he saying?' said Geordie.

'He was talking about selling us to AQ,' said Carr.

'Fucking hell,' said Geordie.

'Aye,' said Carr. 'Your turn to get some kip, anyway. I'll stag on for the rest of the journey.'

'There is zero fucking chance of me going to sleep now,' said Skelton, 'and you fucking know it.'

Outside, the desert flashed by, as the minibus ate up the miles.

# 77.

AT EIGHT O'CLOCK, an hour after the sun set, they drove through Tataouine.

An hour after that, Firas turned off the blacktop onto a desert track, stopped and switched off the headlights, and looked over his shoulder.

'The rendezvous is about fifteen minutes from here, John,' he said.

He took a small radio from the glovebox, checked the channel, and pressed the talk button.

There was a brief exchange, and Firas turned to Carr.

'They're waiting,' he said.

Carr turned to the team. 'Fifteen minutes, guys,' he said.

The Libyan restarted the VW and sent it bouncing along the uneven track, skittering stones, navigating by the light of the half-moon.

Carr's own night vision was good, and he could see the way ahead reasonably clearly.

But to the sides, all was black.

After a short time, Firas pulled off the track and down into a shallow wadi, touching the brakes now and then to slow the vehicle.

The red brake lights repeatedly illuminated the area, and Carr chuckled to himself, reviewing his take on the efficiency of the MI6 training.

'Where d'you learn your drills?' he said.

'Old Libyan Army,' said Firas, proudly. 'Khamis Brigade. Like special forces.'

'Oh, aye?' said Carr.

By now they were near the bottom of the wadi. In the low light, he could just make out the shape of a vehicle, and two men standing next to it.

One was smoking, the red glow from the cigarette illuminating his face every time he took a drag.

Firas rolled to a stop.

'Look at them,' he said, waving a palm in irritation. 'My brother and his half-witted son, smoking. He will give us away.'

He opened the window.

'Put that cigarette out, you fool!' he yelled.

Carr smiled at the irony: they'd just lit up the whole area with their brakes, and now anyone within five hundred metres would have heard Firas shouting.

But there was no point worrying about it now.

He slid open his door and got out, taking a moment to stretch and to sniff the air.

It was damp and warm, and it smelled faintly of sulphur.

On the other side of the VW, Geordie and Kevin McMullen were doing the same; Fred West was standing off to the rear, having a piss.

Firas brought the two men over.

'My brother Hassan, John,' he said, 'and his fool of a son, Mehdi.'

John Carr shook Hassan's hand; Mehdi had turned away, looking sheepish.

'Okay, Firas,' said Carr. 'Time's pressing. Let's get the gear.' He looked over his shoulder. 'Guys, let's go.'

They walked round to the rear of Hassan's vehicle, and Mehdi pulled aside the tarpaulin, revealing four numbered bags and four numbered Peli cases, into which each man had placed his zeroed weapons after the range day at Sennybridge.

'Check your weapons and get changed,' said Carr, though the instruction was superfluous.

He opened his own Peli, to reveal his Diemaco, the night sight already fitted and five thirty-round magazines lying at the side.

He picked the weapon up, and cleared it from years of habit. Satisfied, he inserted a magazine into the housing, pointed the rifle away and cocked it.

It felt good in his hands.

He switched on the night-sight, the green glow inside illuminating his eye as he scanned the area.

No-one in sight.

Happy, he switched off the sight, and went through the same drills with the Sig Sauer pistol.

Next, he dropped his jeans and climbed into his US pattern multicam, which had been given a dozen washes to remove its new stiffness. He pulled on his equipment carrier, holstered the pistol and picked up the Diemaco.

He did a quick check of his carrier to make sure it had everything he needed at hand – ammunition, twenty-four-hour emergency rations, water, med kit, radio, and a metal mug for cooking and making brews.

The lifesaving basics which he'd carried with him for two decades.

They were travelling light scales: the heavier weapons systems and the remainder of the kit from his list would be aboard the two other vehicles waiting for them on the Libyan side.

But at least now if they bumped into the likes of el Jaziri the odds were back in their favour.

He took out a Garmin GPS, fired it up, waited for it to locate him, and punched in the coordinates for the first route RV.

The device confirmed the route, which was roughly due east.

He switched it off – it was purely for backup – and set a bearing on his compass.

Then he knelt down, produced his map, and illuminated it

with a small torch, shielding the light as he did so. He'd broken the route down into ten legs, each ending at an RV sited at a distinctive topographical feature – a river bed junction, say, or a saddle between two peaks.

If anything went wrong *en route* from one RV to the next, or they somehow got split up, this allowed them to move back to the previous RV, and regroup.

RV1 to RV5 was eight kilometres, and took them to the border crossing; from RV6 it was six kilometres to the final RV, 10, which was just short of the place where they would pick up their vehicles.

The route was testing in places – the ground was rough, and they'd have to make a few gentle climbs – but they were travelling light and they were all fit, even Geordie. The man from Newcastle liked to whine about his leg, but he was as strong as an ox and as stubborn as a mule, and Carr had no concerns about him.

Five hours of steady pace patrolling – no dramas.

He looked at his watch – a nice, robust Casio G-Shock.

A shade before 22:00hrs.

A five-hour tab meant they'd be at the RV well before dawn, but they needed to get cracking.

'Gather round, guys,' said Carr. 'Come on – *jildy, jildy*.'

He pointed to the map and showed them their route again.

'Everyone happy?' he said.

Three nods.

'Happy, John,' said Fred West.

Carr turned to Firas, who had gathered up their discarded civvies.

'Firas,' he said, in Arabic. 'Thanks for your help. Your brother and his son, too. We owe you one, okay?'

The Libyan shook his hand.

'Whatever you are here for, may God protect you, my friend,' he said. 'Maybe one day I will see you back in Tunis.'

With that, the three Tunisians were gone.

The four men watched them drive off, and waited on for another twenty minutes, enough time for them to be on the road and away.

Then Carr said, 'Okay, guys, listen in. As discussed, from this point on I'm in charge. Just like back in the Regiment, yes? Geordie's 2 I/C. And we treat this like any op, okay?'

Three nods.

'Order of march will be Kev at the front, then me, then Fred. Geordie will bring up the rear.'

More nods.

'We'll just test-fire, and then we're off.'

All four men turned south, looked through their sights, and fired off a couple of rounds into the emptiness.

It sounded deafening in the still night.

Carr turned to Geordie. 'I fucking love that sound,' he said, with a smile.

'You always were frigging mad,' said Skelton, with a shake of the head.

Carr laughed. 'Right, guys,' he said. 'Let's go.'

The four of them knelt in a straight line, Kevin McMullen scanning the ground to his front with his night-sight.

He looked back over his shoulder to Carr and gave the thumbs-up.

Carr returned the signal, and the Londoner stood up and started heading east.

Carr let him get five metres ahead, passed the signal to Fred West, and followed.

His Diemaco was carried casually across his body, horizontal to the ground, his safety catch was off, and the barrel followed the movement of his head.

Everywhere that Carr looked, the muzzle followed.

His pulse was slightly elevated, his mouth slightly dry, and his head buzzing with excitement.

He felt utterly alive.

# 78.

JUST SHY OF THREE hours later, the four men moved cautiously towards the fifth RV.

The going had been good so far – the desert night was cool, and the rocky terrain easy underfoot – though the final climb to this point had been a little more testing.

Fit as they were, they'd not tabbed across hills like this, carrying equipment, even light scales, for several years.

Carr felt his chest thumping as he arrived at the crest, just behind Kev McMullen.

McMullen had already gone to ground on one knee, and was facing forwards, towards twelve o'clock, scanning the eerie green landscape to the east through his night-sight.

One by one, the others followed suit, until each was covering his area of responsibility in an all-round defence.

Geordie was the last man up, and he was feeling good about himself. He'd never have admitted it to Carr – he didn't want to jeopardise his position on the job – but privately he'd been worried about his leg. After eight kilometres, it was no more than a niggle. He was confident he'd be fine.

He took up position, grinning, and faced back west to their six.

They knelt there in silence for several minutes, watching, listening, and taking a breather.

Then Carr tapped Skelton on the shoulder.

'Have a drink, Geordie,' he whispered. 'I'm going to do a quick map-check. Pass it on.'

Geordie took out his water-bottle and passed the message on. Once he'd finished, and secured his water, Fred West had a drink. They were working on the tried-and-tested buddy-buddy system – Kev and Carr, Geordie and Fred. Whenever one performed any basic task, the other was alert.

Carr got out his map. He was confident that he knew exactly where they were, but there was no point in compounding any error if there was one, so he switched on his GPS and used it to confirm the lat and long.

He smiled to himself: they were within five metres of where the map said they were.

He took a map bearing to the next RV, and whispered it to Geordie who set it on his compass and passed the message around the team.

South-east 1.5km – a pleasant stroll, though a psychologically-important one. Halfway between here and RV6 was the Tunisia-Libya border, which meant they'd be crossing from what was, at least in theory, a safe country into a very dangerous one.

He turned the GPS off, and replaced his map.

'All downhill from here until a small climb to the FRV,' he whispered. 'Should be there by 03:00hrs – 03:30hrs at the latest.'

Geordie Skelton grunted. 'Be glad to get in them fucking vehicles,' he said, quietly.

Carr nodded: moving across open terrain like this in the dark was one thing, but on foot, in the blinding daylight of the North African desert, they'd stick out like a bulldog's bollocks unless they could find good cover. They needed the sanctuary of the trucks.

'Okay,' he said. 'Let's go. Stay switched on.'

Kev stood up and the team followed him, picking their way slowly south-east.

They made excellent time, and were at the final FRV by 02:45hrs, a good two hours before first light.

It was a few hundred metres short of the actual vehicle handover point, to allow them to overwatch the area.

John Carr and Kevin McMullen left Skelton and West behind and moved cautiously forward from the FRV to get eyes-on the vehicles.

They were back a few minutes later.

'Nothing there,' said Carr, quietly.

'Definitely the right spot, John?' said Fred West.

'Hundred per cent,' said Carr.

'Fucking raghead cunts,' hissed Geordie. 'Where the fuck are they?'

Carr looked at him. 'Stop flapping,' he said. 'They'll be here. We'll just have to wait.'

'Don't call me a flapper, John,' said Geordie. Feeling slightly embarrassed, he turned his back and checked their six.

Carr shook his head. 'Okay, guys,' he said. 'Let's take this opportunity to grab an hour's kip till the vehicles show. Two on, two off, and everyone awake at 05:00. Kev, Fred, you get your heads down first.'

He waited until McMullen and West had gone – it only took a minute, maybe two – and tapped Geordie on the shoulder.

'Stay positive, mate,' he whispered. 'Don't let me hear any more negativity from you. We've been in worse situations than this, and we aren't even *in* a situation yet.'

'Sorry, John,' whispered the big northerner, over his shoulder. 'Just the thought of going back over that route if the vehicles don't turn up…'

'I know. But they *will* turn up. Listen, I need to let spooks know we're at the FRV.'

He took out a satellite phone and watched the screen search for satellites.

When it locked on, he sent a pre-set SMS message reading 'ARNHEM' to a phone in an office in Vauxhall.

The reply came back almost instantly: 'Confirm ARNHEM.'

Carr powered it back down and placed it back in its pouch.

It was a lifeline, but he would be happier once they had the military satellite radio on the vehicles for comms: this whole area was covered with friendly and unfriendly communications surveillance, and, while that very brief burst of SMS data was safe enough, he didn't want to risk the satphone for voice calls unless he had to.

Back in London, the phone on Justin Nicholls' bedside table bleeped, waking him.

'They're across the border,' said a voice.

Five minutes after that, the Prime Minister replaced her own mobile on the bedside table in the master bedroom at Chequers and lay there, staring at the ceiling.

She was still staring at it as the grey light turned pale blue in the early morning dawn: sleep had not come easily to her since her daughter had been taken, and she could not stop thinking about the four men on hostile ground, risking everything for Charlotte.

At just after 5:30 a.m., she gave up the battle and slipped wearily out of bed and down the grand staircase to her study.

She watched a pair of blackbirds squabbling on the lawn, until they flew off as two armed police officers patrolled slowly past.

When this was all over, thought Penelope Morgan, she would like to meet those four men.

At that precise moment, the men in question were sitting in a shallow depression on a Saharan hillside, a few miles from the Libyan border settlement of Wazin.

The first fingers of the sun were just starting to lift over the eastern horizon, and they were already feeling very exposed.

John Carr had just come back from another look at the vehicle handover location.

Still nothing.

'I'm confident they'll be here, boys,' he said. 'You know how these things go. There's always some fuck-up. We'll take turns stagging-on and watching the area of the meet, and just take it from there. Okay?'

Three nods.

'Geordie, you're on stag first. Thirty minutes apiece.'

'Okay, mate,' said Geordie. 'No probs.'

Taking his Diemaco in one hand and a set of binos in the other, he moved forwards in a crouch to a position which gave him a good view.

'Might as well get a brew on, then,' said Fred West.

'Fucking right, Fred,' said Kev. 'Good man.'

Carr smiled: just like the old days, Fred and his brews.

West took out a small gas cooker and teabags from his ration pack, and filled his metal mug with water.

Five minutes later, they were all sharing a hot brew.

'Fucking excellent,' said Kevin McMullen. 'What a morale booster, eh.'

Carr drank his share, and then looked east. 'I'll take this last bit to Geordie,' he said.

He moved over to where Geordie lay in the sand, scanning the area.

'Here you go, mate,' he said, handing over the brew.

'Cheers, John,' said Skelton, swigging back the remnants. 'Just what I needed.' He went back to his binoculars. 'Not being negative,' he said, 'but what do you reckon if…' Then he stopped. 'Wait one,' he said. 'We've got company.'

Carr took his own binos and followed Geordie's gaze.

Four or five klicks south he could see a column of dust, picked out against the pale blue early dawn sky.

'Take Fred back his mug and tell the guys to stand-to,' said Carr.

Geordie quickly moved back and Carr kept his binos trained on the dust column.

It grew slowly, until at about two kilometres he could make out four vehicles, moving across the open plain.

At a thousand metres, he saw that they were pickups: Toyota Hiluxes, two camouflaged, two white.

He relaxed slightly.

*About fucking time*, he thought.

# 79.

THE VEHICLE HANDOVER went smoothly, and they left the RV at a little after 07:00hrs, driving in the direction of a small desert settlement called Tabaqah.

A one-horse town where the horse was a long-dead bag of bones buried in a fifty-foot sand dune, it lay alongside a dry wadi roughly halfway to their target, though well to the south and away from populated areas.

The days of navigating using time and distance bearings had long gone, but it made a useful reference point on the map – not that John Carr was going anywhere near the place. He would turn north and skirt round it thirty kilometres out.

Their route took them across country, just under the Jebel Nafusa mountains, and over the Al-Hamada al-Hamra plateau, a wide, elevated stretch of stony emptiness, blackish with desert varnish on the lower reaches and turning red-brown as they climbed.

It was a barren and unpopulated place, and the latest intelligence they had received from Justin Nicholls helped them to avoid suspect locations.

Still, several times they saw fast-moving vehicles in the distance. They might have been Islamists, or tribal militia, or people traffickers – or they might have been innocent traders, themselves desperate to avoid all three – but Carr worked on the basis that every other living soul out here was a bad guy; each time, Kev changed his direction and moved away.

Fred maintained a distance of some 150 metres, slightly offset, so as to avoid the inevitable dust cloud thrown up on the desert tracks.

The vehicles were laden high and the cab rear-view was useless, so Carr glanced at his wing-mirror regularly, making sure that Fred was still there. If something happened to Geordie's Hilux at 45kph and Carr wasn't concentrating, it would be easy to be a couple of klicks separated, maybe a lot more.

Behind him, Geordie Skelton was doing the same, to make sure that nothing was coming up to the rear, and, every now and then they had a quick comms check, just for confidence, and always initiated by Carr.

To minimise the time on air, they had agreed that Geordie would only come up if absolutely necessary; it was unlikely that they would be intercepted over UHF, but being cautious kept you alive.

Being armed to the fucking teeth did the same thing.

Carr had his pistol on his waist, his Diemaco – 40mm grenade launcher attached – between his legs, and a small bag over his shoulder containing an extra four magazines and half-a-dozen 40mm HE.

The remainder of his kit – and the day's water and food – was neatly placed on the rear seat behind him, next to Kev's.

In the rear footwell lay a Minimi, fully loaded and ready to go, with a belt of 200 7.62mm rounds, a mix of ball, tracer and AP, and a couple of 66mm LAWs.

Carr was confident that they could deal with most threats, but hoping that they didn't have to find out.

It was monotonous, mind-numbing work driving through this empty, beige land, so they broke it up every hour with a stop, to stretch their legs, have a chat and a piss – and a fag, in the case of Kev McMullen – and do a map check.

At mid-morning, the sun high and bright and roasting overhead, they stopped for breakfast in the bottom of a wadi, in the shade of a rare wild pistachio tree.

Fred made the brews and handed them over.

'Weird, ain't it?' he said quietly, as he sipped his own. 'It must be near enough forty degrees out here, and I'd still rather drink this than anything.'

'What's that cider shit you like?' said Kev, with a grin. 'Cornish Rattler? How about a pint of that?'

Fred smiled. 'Ice cold in Alex? Yeah, fair one.'

Carr smiled, went to dunk a biscuit into his tea – and then stopped, his hand in mid-air.

A few metres away, on stag in a slightly elevated position, Geordie Skelton had raised his own hand.

'What's that?' he hissed.

All four of them held their breath and cocked their heads.

'I can't hear fuck all,' whispered Carr.

'Someone coming,' said Geordie.

Carr crammed the rest of the biscuit into his mouth, and grabbed his weapon.

In a matter of seconds, each man was facing towards the threat.

And then Carr heard it: an almost musical jingling noise, carried on the southern breeze.

A moment later, an old man came into view out of a depression, two hundred metres or so away, slowly leading a handful of moth-eaten camels.

'Bedou,' said Carr.

'Jesus,' said Fred West, turning south and looking through his scope. 'He must be about a hundred and twenty.'

'Probably half that,' said Carr, watching the man approaching slowly. 'Sun dries you up like a prune. Ask Geordie's ex-missus.'

West chuckled.

'Can't see anyone else,' said Skelton, scanning north.

'Maybe he'll miss us,' said Kevin McMullen, hoping that he was right: being compromised out here, only three or four hours into the job, was definitely not in their plan.

'Nah,' said Carr. 'He's not seen us yet, but he's walking straight into the wadi.'

'Fuck,' spat McMullen.

'Want me to put him away, John?' said West, his sights on the centre mass of the old boy.

Carr turned to look at his friend.

Fred's finger was on the trigger, and the barrel of his rifle was steady as a rock.

He turned back to look at the bedouin herdsman, weighing the guy's life in the balance.

And made his decision.

'No,' he said. 'We aren't here to kill old men.' A half-minute later, the man wandered into their little camp.

Carr had no option but to stand up and confront him.

'As salaam aleikum,' he said, rifle pointing down, a smile on his face.

The man stopped in his tracks, a look of surprise on his face.

'Wa aleikum as salaam,' he said, quietly.

'Are you well?' said Carr, in Arabic. 'May I ask, what is your name?'

'Qamar,' said the man, his voice and expression wary.

'I invite you to sit with us, Qamar. Would you like some water? Some tea?'

The old man spoke a western desert dialect, but he understood fine, despite Carr's accent.

Fred West made the man a hot, sweet, black tea, and he sat cross-legged in the sand to drink it.

As he sipped, he said nothing, but just observed the four white men through eyes as black as the night sea.

When he had finished the brew, he carefully handed the mug back to Fred, and nodded his thanks.

Then he turned to Carr.

'Scottish?' he said, in English.

Carr was by nature ready for most things life could throw at him, but this knocked him back a little.

'What?' he said, his eyebrows raised. 'Did you say "Scottish"?'

'Yes,' said Qamar, back to Arabic. 'You look Scottish. Good men. I remember them from many years ago. The fighting in the north, against the men with yellow hair.'

'The Germans?' said Carr.

'Yes, Germans. And the others. Italians. I was a young boy. They were good men, the Scottish. Kind men.'

Carr nodded. 'Do you need anything from us?' he said.

Qamar looked at his small group of mangy camels, and then back at Carr.

'My life,' he said, simply.

Carr was suddenly guilty, and ashamed that he hadn't seen the fear in the old man's eyes.

He leaned forward and gripped his shoulder. 'You have nothing to fear from us, Qamar,' he said, with an open smile. 'There is no harm here.'

'You look like men who would do harm.'

Carr shook his head. 'Only to our enemies,' he said. 'And you are a friend.' He looked at Kev McMullen. 'Kev, get this old boy a bottle of water and a packet of biscuits.'

McMullen was back in a moment or two, and handed them to Qamar.

The old man took them, uttered a low *shukran*, and stared at Carr for some time.

Then he looked around the other men, nodding his head slowly.

Then he stood up, in an easy motion which belied his years, and started walking away.

A few paces off, he turned and looked at Carr.

'I see many things in the desert, Scottish man,' he said. 'I do not speak of them. Peace be upon you, my brother.'

'And upon you,' said Carr.

Geordie broke the silence as the old man disappeared on up the wadi with his camels.

'Hard bugger, man,' he said. 'Fancy spending your life tabbing across this bastard.'

'You reckon he'll tell anyone he saw us?' said Kev McMullen. 'It's bad news if he does.'

'I doubt it,' said Carr – though he was wondering, as he spoke, if he was correct. 'But if he does, he does. Let's mount up and get out of here.'

They got into the vehicles and continued on their way.

# 80.

TWO KILOMETRES ON, Carr reached into the back and grabbed a fresh litre of water, glancing to his left as he did so.

Kev McMullen was scanning the horizon methodically, his jaw tightly clenched.

He looked to be concentrating *too* much, his thumb drumming out a staccato rhythm on the steering wheel.

'You okay, pal?' said Carr, casually, taking a long swig of water and grimacing at the heat of it.

In fact, Kevin McMullen wasn't okay: he was worried. He'd always been a superstitious sort of bloke – probably a relic of his Roman Catholic upbringing – despite the fact he'd survived fourteen years on ops with the SAS. He had hidden it during that time behind the black humour that soldiers often use as a defence mechanism.

But he'd had a bad feeling about this job, right from that day at Geordie Skelton's place when they'd all met up to talk the whole thing through.

He couldn't explain it, or even name it – it was just a sense of unease, over and beyond that which you'd expect to feel, deep into a desert teeming with ten different sorts of maniac.

And now the old Bedouin… That was a bad fucking omen, thought McMullen. He knew that John Carr was right, as he usually was – shooting the old geezer would have been wrong – but it was still major bad karma that someone knew they were here.

An image kept intruding into his mind: himself, lying bleeding out in the sand.

He knew he was being irrational; but he also knew that if he hadn't needed the money he would have fucked this one off.

Not that he was going to admit any of this to John Carr, a man in whose eyes he had never seen so much as a hint of fear.

'Yeah, I'm good, mate,' he said, glancing over, with a smile that he was sure looked strained. 'Never better.'

'We're all thinking the same thing, Kev,' said Carr. 'But worrying's for women and children. You were at the top of my list. You wouldn't have been if I didn't think you were a good hand.'

He meant it, too: Kevin McMullen was a warrior of the highest order, brave to a fault, and as game as they came.

'We'll be in and out,' said Carr, 'and they'll never see us coming or going.'

McMullen nodded and grinned, but, not for the first time, he wondered at his old squadron sergeant major's apparent ability to read minds.

If anything, it spooked him even further.

'I'm okay, John,' he said, more firmly. 'Seriously. I'm fine.'

Carr slapped an insect on his arm and dropped it out of the window.

'How's the family?' he said. 'Must be about time you knocked the missus up again?'

'Four's plenty,' said McMullen. 'Trish would have liked more, but we can't fucking afford it, so I had the snip.' He laughed. 'She'll be on at me to have a reversal when I bank the cash from this.'

'Is your oldest still going in the Mob?'

'He's talking about it,' said McMullen, staring out to his left. 'His mum's against it, obviously. Says if he's going to join up, he needs to go to uni first, then Sandhurst, and go in as a rupert.'

'Fuck me,' said Carr, shaking his head.

'I know. I've told him, Para Reg as a Tom, or he can fucking forget it. But I don't know if he's got it in him.'

'Of course he's fucking got it in him,' said Carr. 'He's got Trish's genes.'

Kevin McMullen chuckled, but a mental picture of Richard – at sixteen already three or four inches taller than his old man, a good-looking boy who'd got straight As in his GCSEs, and had the world at his feet – slipped into his brain.

He had a sudden feeling that he'd never see him again – nor Hope, nor Emily, nor little Georgia.

Nor Trish.

He felt a sudden wave of emotion come over him, and coughed to hide it.

*Get a fucking grip.*

'How about your lot?' he said. 'Did I hear George was thinking about Selection?'

'Aye,' said Carr. 'Next course.'

'Will he do it?'

'Good a chance as anyone.'

'And your little girl? After that shit on the beach with these cunts?'

'She'll be okay,' said Carr. 'Saw shit she shouldn't have seen, but she'll get over it.'

'Fucking lucky,' said McMullen. Then he brightened. 'How's your love life?'

'Complicated,' said Carr. Then it suddenly occurred to him – a juicy bit of gossip to take McMullen's agitated mind off things. 'I've not told anyone this,' he said, 'and it's between me and you, yes? It goes no fucking further.'

McMullen looked sideways at him, intrigued. 'Go on,' he said.

'Guy de Vere's daughter.'

McMullen looked at him, eyes wide.

'*What*?' he said.

Lieutenant-General Guy de Vere had served with both of them, first as a young officer in 3 Para and then as he rose through the ranks of the SAS and beyond. He was currently a very big noise indeed – Commander Field Army, the British Army's second-in-command.

'I know,' said Carr, wincing. 'Met her at a party in Fulham. I had no idea who she was. Must have seen her at Regiment family days over the years, but she's certainly grown up since then.'

'Does Guy know?'

Carr glanced at him. 'Well, *I'm* not going to tell him,' he said.

McMullen cackled. 'Fucking hell,' he said. 'He'll go fucking mental if he finds out. I heard she was getting engaged to some duke. What was she thinking, knocking you off?'

Carr grinned. 'She's only human,' he said.

McMullen smiled and turned his eyes front.

Carr watched him for a few moments. He didn't believe in premonition, but he'd known a number of men who had somehow got it into their heads that their numbers were up, and it had turned out that they were.

Something about Kevin McMullen put him in mind of those men.

They rumbled on in silence for a kilometre or so, and then Carr said, 'Mileage?'

McMullen glanced at the odometer.

'Just under 150 klicks inside the Libyan border,' he said.

'Okay,' said Carr. 'I think we should…'

But then there was a clunk, and the front end of the Hilux dropped.

'Flat,' said McMullen, through gritted teeth. He shook his head, the nerves reappearing in his belly, the sense that this whole thing was jinxed. 'Shit. Brand new fucking tyres.'

He slowed to a bumpy, rumbling stop.

Fred West, at the wheel of the second Hilux, pulled up behind them.

All four men dismounted, Diemacos in hand.

'Problem?' said Geordie, as he swept the terrain to their rear through his scope.

'Nearside front's gone,' said Carr.

He took his binos and climbed up onto the top of the cab, scanning the whole area.

A man of average height on flat ground can see roughly five kilometres to the horizon. The atmospheric refraction generated by the midday late summer heat made it tricky to gauge, but Carr estimated that, from his elevated position of around twelve feet, and given the topography, he had maybe nine kilometres of visibility.

A vehicle doing 60km/h – top end for this terrain – would obviously cover that distance in nine minutes, though the dust of any approaching traffic would show up from further than that.

Carr wiped salty, stinging sweat from his eyes and turned through 360 degrees.

The shimmering desert – the desert fought over by his forefathers in Ralph Bagnold's LRDG, and then Stirling's SAS originals – was empty.

He hopped down and beckoned Geordie over.

'All clear at the minute,' he said. 'Me and Kev will get this wheel changed.' He pointed at a stony ridge, maybe two metres high, fifty or sixty metres off to the east. 'Get Fred up on that bit of high ground with his binos and your Minimi. You back your vehicle down there, take our gun and keep an eye out as well.'

Geordie reached in and picked up the light machine gun.

'Crack on then, mate,' he said.

While Kev McMullen removed one of the two spares that each vehicle was carrying, and rolled it to the front, Carr started working the jack on its square desert plate, grunting and sweating with the effort in the blistering heat.

One by one, the nuts came off, burning to the touch, until Carr was able to remove the wheel with the shredded tyre.

He pushed it a few metres out into the desert and watched it fall on its side.

'We'll leave that there,' he said, half to himself. 'I dinnae think the local Kwik Fit will value our custom.'

He wiped more sweat out of his eyes, and looked up at Kevin McMullen.

'Fuck me, it's hot, mate,' he said.

But McMullen didn't reply: he was staring over Carr's shoulder at Fred West, who was looking back at him intensely, giving the thumbs-down signal – enemy – and indicating roughly south.

'Everything alright, Kev?' said Carr.

'Fred,' said McMullen. 'He just shouted something. His comms must be down, but it looks like we've got more company.'

Carr followed his gaze and dropped the wheelbrace.

# 81.

JOHN CARR REACHED into the rear of the vehicle cab for his body armour and equipment carrier and looked down the track to Geordie Skelton, fifty metres back by the second Hilux.

Skelton had just seen the signal and was turning his weapon to face the threat.

'Get your kit on, Kev,' said Carr. 'And prepare the LAWs. I'll be back in a minute.'

'Roger,' said McMullen, his nerves tingling.

He reached for the first anti-tank tube and removed the end caps, as Carr sprinted up the rise to Fred.

'What we got, mate?' said Carr, looking towards a column of dust some six or seven kilometres distant.

'Two vehicles, possibly three. Look like technicals. Heading straight for us. Five minutes away, maybe a bit more.'

'Shit,' said Carr. He raised his own binoculars. Fred was right: they were at ninety degrees to his route and pointing his way. 'Definitely three,' he said. 'The last one's got some sort of vehicle-mounted gun. Can't see what.'

'Fuck,' said Fred. 'The old boy?'

'Nah, he's way over there,' said Carr. 'They must just have seen our dust.'

He took the binoculars down and looked at West.

'Not enough time to get the new wheel on,' he said. 'So this is where we start earning the big bucks. Whatever happens, you concentrate on that last vehicle. And you don't open fire until I do, or they do. Okay?'

Fred West nodded, placed some spare ammunition at hand, and got down behind the gun in a good firing position. He cocked it, and began the waiting game.

'Good luck, mate,' said Carr. Then he turned and ran, crouching, down the lip and across to Geordie, shouting, 'Standby for contact, standby for contact!' so that both he and Kev knew what was coming.

'What's the plan, John?' said Geordie.

'It's on, mate,' said Carr. 'Three technicals. A dozen or so blokes. Three or four minutes.'

'Ah, fuck. I wish it was dark, man.'

'Me too, but it's not. And it gets worse.'

'Aye?'

'The one at the back's got some sort of rear-mounted weapon system.'

'Ah, shit,' said Geordie. Even with an ad hoc fit on the back of a technical, a .50 cal would outrange them by a good kilometre. 'I hope the fuckers don't stand off with that,' he said. 'They'll smash us.'

'We need to lure them right in close,' said Carr. 'Make sure they don't see us as a threat.'

'How?'

'I've got an idea.'

'That's always a bonus,' said Geordie.

'Fred's on that rear wagon,' said Carr. 'You concentrate on the second, and me and Kev will sort out the front. Don't fire until I do.'

'Roger,' said Geordie.

'You okay?' said Carr, patting him on the shoulder and flashing him a wicked grin. 'Bet that comfy bed in that big house of yours is a lot more appealing now, eh?'

'Fuck off, man.'

'You can't take it with you, Geordie,' said Carr.

Cackling, he ran back down to Kevin McMullen.

Skelton watched him go, shaking his head.

Back down by the stricken Hilux, Carr gripped McMullen.

'Get yourself out of sight with the LAWs,' he said, 'and get ready to take that first vehicle out.'

As Kev moved around to the front of their vehicle and hid himself, Carr looked over at the approaching men.

Three minutes away now, tops.

No deviation, still heading straight for them.

He reached into the back of the pickup, and pulled out a white dishdash and a red shemagh.

Quickly, he pulled them on.

Then, one last look.

He lifted his binos.

At least two of the vehicles were flying black flags.

'Fucking *Muj*, guys,' he shouted. 'All or nothing, here they come.'

'Let's light the fuckers up,' roared back Geordie.

Carr had a final look around.

If these bastards suspected anything, saw any threat, then all bets were off.

But Geordie and Kev were hidden on the blindsides of their vehicles.

Fred was hard to spot up on that little ridge, lying down and camouflaged in the thin salt bush and esparto grass.

So if Carr could look as unthreatening as possible…

He leaned his Diemaco against the side of his Hilux, strolled out into the open, and put a hand up to wave.

Saying, quietly, 'Come on, you wankers. I'm just a guy who's got bogged down in the desert and thinks you might give me a tow.'

Up to his left, Fred West rocked his Minimi back and forth, took a bead on the rear vehicle, and started tracking it.

Almost within range now, and no sign of them standing off; he pulled the butt of the machine gun tight into his shoulder, and breathed slowly, closing his mind off to everything but the target.

Down below, a few metres behind Carr, Kev McMullen lay prone, his heart pounding against the hot, baked earth, his mouth full of the taste of salt and adrenalin.

He pulled the cocking lever forward on his 66, gave the Diemaco lying next to him a gentle tap, and crossed himself.

Carr glanced back and saw him do it.

'God might help out later, Kev,' he said. 'I'd put more faith in yourself and the weapons at the moment.'

McMullen said nothing, a sheepish look on his face.

Carr turned back to face the oncoming vehicles.

'Four hundred metres,' he shouted, with a slight smile. 'Stupid fuckers are planning to rob me and chop my head off if they don't like the cut of my jib.'

'None of us like the fucking cut of your jib,' shouted Geordie, and then all four men went silent and readied themselves.

Carr took the pistol from his robe pocket, and stood with it behind his back, in his right hand. He raised his left again, this time in a show of acknowledgment to the approaching vehicles.

Now they were close he could see that the rear two were driving directly behind the point man.

*Clowns*, he thought. When it went noisy they were going to be too busy trying to get the shit out of their eyes to see what was killing them.

The first vehicle came to a stop about forty metres from Carr, and the others stopped behind, virtually blind in all that dust.

The vehicle commander, sitting in the front passenger seat, leaned over and said something to the driver.

Then both men got out.

# 82.

THE COMMANDER – A TALL, skinny man in a yellow T-shirt and a chest rig – stayed where he was, watching carefully, while the driver started towards Carr.

All show and bravado.

Holding an AK, but it was slack in his hand, he was that cocky.

Big bloke, big beard.

Big mistake.

He realised just how big when he got within ten metres of Carr and saw first the camouflage trousers and boots below the white robe, and then Carr's grin, and then the 9mm Sig.

That was the last thing he ever saw.

Carr put four rounds into the centre of the guy's chest and ran for his Diemaco as Fred West and Geordie Skelton both opened up with their belt-fed Minimis.

The commander in the yellow T-shirt took off back around his vehicle, running and shouting.

That saved his life, for the moment: almost before the big guy had even hit the deck, Kevin McMullen stood up and fired the 66mm straight into the engine block of the first pickup.

As it exploded in a ball of fire, he dropped the empty tube, picked up his Diemaco and started putting rounds down.

'With me, Kev,' shouted Carr, and he and Kevin McMullen

punched forwards, moving quickly and aggressively, not giving those men who had survived the machine guns and the LAW the chance to get their heads up and react.

Carr shot one guy in the face, Kev put another down with three gut-shots and finished him off with one to the head, and then it was all over.

Just two men were left, lying curled up in the dirt on the far side of the middle pickup, unarmed, fingers in their ears, terrified.

One was the tall skinny guy in the yellow T-shirt, who had been blown backwards by the blast from the LAW, but was unhurt.

The other was another big fucker with another big beard.

'Cease fire,' shouted Carr. 'Cease fire.'

The gunfire still ringing in his ears, he stepped over one of the dead men and walked carefully to the pair of them.

He pointed his weapon at them and, in Arabic, told them to put their hands behind their heads.

'What?' said the guy in yellow, looking at him with staring eyes. 'I don't fucking speak Arabic.'

The man's accent was unmistakeable.

'You're a *Brummie*?' said Carr, incredulously. 'Hands behind your heads.'

Both men complied immediately.

'Who are you, bro?' said the guy with the beard.

'Shut the fuck up,' barked Carr. 'Do not speak unless I speak to you. And I'm not your fucking bro, you cunt.'

He turned to his left. 'Kev,' he said, 'get back to the vehicle and get that fucking wheel changed. We need to be moving ASAP.'

The Londoner nodded, and ran off.

'Geordie,' shouted Carr. 'Over here. Fred, keep your eye out, mate.'

Fred threw him a thumbs-up as Skelton hefted the Minimi and ran to Carr's position.

'They're British,' said Carr, shaking his head. 'Pair of fucking Brummies. Search them.'

Geordie Skelton quickly searched both men, and stood up holding two mobile phones.

'Clean apart from these,' he said. He looked down at the two men. 'Should have picked your weapons up, you soft twats, man.'

'Okay,' said Carr. 'Get up, and sit with your backs to the vehicle.'

Both men scrambled to do as they were told.

Carr looked down at them in the deafening silence.

The smell of diesel smoke and burning rubber from the front vehicle's tyres filled the air.

'So what the fuck are you doing all this way from sunny Birmingham?' he said, eventually.

'We're… hostages,' said the guy in the yellow T-shirt. 'We came out here on a religious visit, and they forced us to fight.'

'Fucking hell,' said Carr, with a grin. 'You must think I come up the Clyde in a banana boat, pal. You were commanding that front truck. I'd say you're in charge of the whole thing.'

'We just want to go home,' said the second man, the guy with the beard.

'Aye, I bet you do,' said Carr. 'I bet you'd give anything to be mooching round the old Bull Ring now, eh?'

'What group are you with, marra?' said Geordie.

'They'll kill us if we say,' said Beard.

'*We'll* kill you if you don't,' said Carr.

'You wouldn't kill us,' said Yellow T-shirt, a trace of defiance entering his voice. 'We're unarmed. We're British citizens, and you're British Army. It'd be murder. We've got human rights.'

'Is that so?' said Carr, with a chuckle. 'Have a shufti round, pal. I look to you like I give a fuck about your human rights?'

Yellow T-shirt leaned in towards Beard and said something under his breath.

'We'll not have any of that,' said Geordie, leaning down and dragging the bearded guy away by his collar, and pushing him face down into the sand.

'I'll ask you again,' said Carr.

'We're with some people,' said Yellow T-shirt, his chin trembling. 'But I swear, we were forced…'

'What's your code?' said Geordie.

He was standing with a foot on the back of the neck of the bearded guy, and holding up the iPhone he'd taken from the other man.

'I…'

Skelton stepped over and placed the muzzle of his Minimi against the guy's groin.

'Go on,' he said. 'Give me a fucking excuse.'

'Zero-one-two-one,' said Yellow T-shirt, his voice resigned.

'Jesus, man,' said Skelton, shaking his head, and grinning. 'What kind of a dickhead uses his own area code to unlock his phone?'

But the grin dropped from his face as he began scrolling through the phone's contents.

'Jesus, John,' he said, his eyes blazing. 'Have a look at this.'

As Carr took the phone, the skinny guy in the yellow T-shirt started crying.

The first video showed the guy with the beard cutting the throat of a young man whose hands were tied behind his back, while a group of others – including the skinny guy – laughed.

The second showed the stoning of two women, who were buried up to their waists, in some village somewhere.

Carr scrolled no further.

Geordie lowered his weapon and put three rounds straight into the back of Beard's head.

It exploded like an overripe melon.

Yellow T-shirt vomited through his crying.

Carr gave him a moment, and then said, 'Do you want to talk now, Brummie?'

'Yes. But please...'

'What's your name and address?' He nodded to the lifeless Beard. 'And his?'

Geordie pulled out a notebook and wrote them down.

'Who were your UK contacts? How did you get here?'

Geordie's pen moved across the page.

'And are you the only Brits in this little party?' said Carr.

'Yes,' said the man. 'There's one Australian and five Chechens as well. The other four were locals.'

Geordie looked at Carr, eyebrows raised.

'Five Chechens, eh?' he said. 'And how about back at base?'

'Three or four more Chechens. A few other Westerners. The others are mostly from Pakistan.'

'Names of the Chechens and all the Westerners,' said Carr. 'Quick, I havenae time to fuck about.'

Yellow T-Shirt gave them up, as far as he knew them.

'And how far away are these men?'

'Twenty miles. Maybe thirty.'

Carr looked at Geordie. 'Could be the group our friend at Six warned us about down near Sinawin,' he said.

'Yes, mate,' said the man, nodding frantically, trying to build a rapport. 'Sinawin. That's where they are.'

'Any of them following you up?'

'No. We were... We were just out looking for people we could tax.'

Carr scratched his chin and looked over at Kev McMullen.

'Nearly there, Kev?' he shouted.

'Sixty seconds, John.'

'This lot's last vehicle's a Hilux,' said Carr, over his shoulder. 'When you've finished, take their spare to replace that one of ours. Then chuck all their weapons and kit in the back and set the fucker on fire.'

'Roger.'

Carr focused back on Yellow T-shirt.

'What can you tell me about Argun Shishani?' he said.

'Nothing.'

The guy looked genuinely mystified.

'Khasmohmad Kadyrov?'

A momentary look of recognition shot across his face.

'I'm getting tired of playing games,' said Carr, testily. 'You are thirty seconds from me turning you into dinner for them fuckers.'

He pointed upwards, and the man's eyes followed: far overhead, three Eurasian black vultures were circling lazily in the deep blue sky.

'They'll kill me. A hundred per cent.'

Carr levelled his Diemaco at the guy's forehead.

'Wait, wait,' said the guy. 'Please, wait.'

'Ten seconds,' said Carr. 'And believe me, I know when men are lying to me.'

'I don't know him, personally,' said Yellow T-shirt, gabbling now. 'I only know he's a great leader. He was doing something up on the coast, somewhere near Sirte.'

'What?' said Carr.

'I don't know, I swear. Some sort of big project.'

'Where in Sirte?'

'I don't know. I promise I don't. Last I heard was they might be moving elsewhere, anyway. Somewhere south.'

Carr looked at Geordie.

He looked back at Yellow T-shirt.

'Where?' he said. 'Where south?'

'I don't know. I can't remember.'

Carr raised his weapon again, and started to take up the pressure on the trigger.

'You'd better remember,' he said.

'Fuck,' said the man in the yellow T-shirt, tears streaming down his face. 'Fuck. My head's cabbaged. I can't fucking remember.

Maybe I've got it wrong and they're still in Sirte. I only heard a rumour. If you give me a minute to think…'

'Time is short, pal,' said Carr.

'Oh, fucking hell. Our leader was going to send men if they were needed. I heard him say they'd be paying us two hundred dollars per day each, and more for the leader.'

'And has he sent men?'

The guy hesitated for a moment.

'Were *you* those men?'

'No,' said the guy.

He looked away as he said it, and Carr narrowed his eyes.

'You're fucking bullshitting me, pal,' he said.

'No, I promise.'

'How many men does he have?'

The skinny Brummie in the yellow T-shirt was refusing to look at him, now.

'I don't know,' he said.

Carr stabbed him hard in the mouth with the barrel of his weapon, opening his upper lip and knocking out his front two teeth.

'How many?' he said.

'I don't know,' said the guy, spitting blood and teeth into the sand. 'About ten or twelve, I think.'

'That's all you know?'

'I swear.'

Carr looked at him in silence for a few moments.

He was sure the guy was hiding something, but he didn't have the time to force it out of him.

'I swear,' said Yellow T-shirt, again.

'Well, then,' said Carr. 'That's us finished.'

He looked down at the man.

Fifty metres away, the rear truck burst into flames as Kevin

McMullen threw a burning rag into the diesel running from its severed fuel pipe.

'If I let you live, and you can somehow get out of here, what will you do?' said Carr. 'Go back to the UK?'

Yellow T-shirt said nothing.

'Because I'm afraid I can't allow that,' said Carr.

He stood up and levelled his rifle at him.

'Please,' said the guy, holding up his hands in a futile defence. 'No.'

'I bet that's what those two wee girls said before you stoned them to death,' said Carr.

He put two rounds into the guy's heart and walked away.

They took two or three minutes to photograph the corpses, and take whatever they could that might be of use to Justin Nicholls and MI6, and then Carr looked up at Fred West over on the ridge.

'Fred, down here, mate,' he shouted.

He turned to Kevin McMullen.

'Burn that last vehicle, Kev,' he said. 'Then let's mount up and go.'

As McMullen went about the task, Carr looked at Skelton.

'What do you reckon to that?' he said. 'Are they in Sirte, or have they fucking flown already?'

'I dunno what to make of it, mate,' said Skelton. 'He obviously knows the main man. But he was fucking terrified. If he'd known, he'd have told you.'

Carr nodded.

He thought for a moment.

Then he said, 'I'll notify Nicholls at my next SITREP. See if he's got anything new. Until then, we'll just carry on as planned.'

A few minutes later they were moving east again.

Behind them, three columns of dirty, oily smoke rose into the late afternoon sky, and the first vulture landed a few feet from a shape on the ground.

So much sudden death in this part of the world: even the wildlife knew the signs.

The bird cocked its head on one side, and then cautiously approached.

It flew off, croaking in alarm, as the first few rounds started cooking off in the back of one of the trucks.

But it circled round and soon landed again, at a safe distance.

And there it stood, watching through cruel eyes, waiting for the fires to die out.

# 83.

IT WAS NEAR DUSK and a hundred klicks from the contact before Carr stopped, so that they could get some food, stretch their legs, and battle-clean their weapons.

While Fred West got the brews on, and Geordie busied himself with his Minimi, Carr sent his SITREP to Nicholls.

He detailed their present location, and passed on the identities and photographs of the dead Brummies and their comrades, and the intelligence he had gained from them – all information which would be shared with the Met's Counter Terrorist Command and MI5 within half an hour.

He finished by highlighting the possibility that the Chechens might already have moved on from Sirte.

It was acknowledged, with a brief note of thanks, but no new information came back.

Then Carr stood to their rear, staring back the way they'd come.

The fires might well have attracted interest, but the desert was empty, as far as he could see through his night vision. Visibility was down to one or two kilometres, thanks to a moderate summer *ghibli* – the local variant of the sirocco – which had started up behind them not long after they'd left the location of the firefight, and was still blowing dust up from the south.

Kev McMullen appeared at his side, and passed him a US Army MRE.

'Think we'll get followed up?' he said, scratching his thick, black hair to get the grit out of it.

'Not unless they've got fucking Tonto with them,' said Carr. 'Stop flapping.'

'I'm not flapping,' said McMullen, defensively. 'Doesn't hurt to think about it.'

Carr decided to go easy on him. 'Aye, fair enough,' he said, swallowing a mouthful of beef stew and suddenly realising how hungry he was. 'But it's not a drama. Anyone who comes across that shit is going to think twice about coming after us. And if they do, which way do they go? This wind will have blown our tracks away.'

McMullen nodded. 'So what's the plan?' he said. 'When we stopping for some proper rest?'

Carr looked at his watch.

He'd identified a final LUP in a small cluster of mountains on the far side of another small town, Ash Shwayrif.

That was some two hundred kilometres from Sirte, and still a good eight hours away.

By the time they got there they'd have been on the go for something like forty-five hours, bar the two or three hours' kip they'd grabbed in the minibus on the way down from Tunis.

Adrenalin would keep them going for a while yet, but tiredness was the enemy, and it led to mistakes, and mistakes got you killed.

Against that, he was sure of one thing: he didn't want to get bounced again. He'd been planning to move by day as much as by night, but the contact had made him think. They'd won it easily enough, but if the technical with the .50 cal had stood off while the other two vehicles had come in to recce, the outcome might have been very different.

He felt like he'd used up the trip's ration of luck; next time they might bump into men who knew what they were doing.

'We'll keep going for now, and lie-up during daylight,' he said. 'Safer that way.'

'Good,' said McMullen, turning away.

Carr watched him walk back to pick up a mug of tea from Fred.

He finished his MRE, turned back to the wagons, took a now-lukewarm brew of his own from Fred, and gulped it down.

'Right, lads,' he said. 'Ten minutes, then we move out.'

# 84.

TARIQ'S UNCLE FINALLY came back three days after Zeff Mahsoud had arrived in Sirte.

It was gone 2 a.m., but Mahsoud was sent for.

He found the old man sitting cross-legged on a rich-red and gold carpet in the middle of the largest room in the house.

Next to him was an ornate coffee pot, on a highly decorated silver tray.

He was alone, and he smiled up at Mahsoud as he stood opposite him.

He was clearly not a man who smiled much; rather than put Mahsoud at his ease, it looked sinister.

'Tariq, leave us alone, would you?' said the uncle. 'I would like to speak to our guest alone. Just for a few moments.'

Tariq's face fell, and it looked for a moment as if he was about to protest.

But he thought better of it, bowed slightly, and left the room without speaking.

When he had gone, the old man gestured to the carpet in front of him.

'Sit with me,' he said. 'Please.'

Mahsoud sat.

'Coffee?' said the old man, pouring out a small cup without waiting for a reply, and handing it over.

'Thank you,' said Mahsoud.

As he took the small cup, he saw that the old man had only one eye, and that the empty socket was heavily scarred.

He sipped the coffee: it was black and bitter and very sweet.

The old man looked at him, through his one eye, and said nothing.

Mahsoud had the feeling that his mind was being read, but he had many years' experience of hiding his thoughts and emotions – had his religious beliefs allowed gambling, he would have made an excellent poker player.

He knew that the old man would see nothing.

'I am sorry I was not here when you arrived,' said the old man, eventually. 'I am a bad host.'

As he spoke, he tried to smile again.

'Please do not be sorry, *sayidi*,' said Mahsoud. 'I have enjoyed Tariq's hospitality.'

The old man laughed, mirthlessly. 'My brother's son is a half-wit,' he said. 'But we're not supposed to notice.'

He took a sip of his own coffee.

'I know a little about you,' he said. 'When my brother called me to ask me to give you shelter, he told me all about your recent trouble with the British government. It must have been a terrible ordeal.'

'British jails are not like Libyan jails,' said Mahsoud.

'Quite so,' said the old man, with a chuckle. 'But still.'

Mahsoud inclined his head, slightly.

'I know you are waging the jihad,' said the old man. 'My time has gone, but if I were young again…'

*If you were young again, you would only be interested in the money you could make off the back of chaos*, thought Mahsoud. *No different to now.*

But he said nothing.

'When I was away, it was because I wanted to find the man who was providing your Chechen friends with their safe house here,' said the old man. 'Took me two days, but I found him.'

Mahsoud felt his heartbeat rising, and the acid bubbling in his stomach.

'That does not surprise me, *sayidi*,' he said. 'You are a man of great power and influence, second only to your brother in your tribe. Your standing is unquestionable. No-one moves through this area without you knowing about it, I'm sure of that.'

*And I'm damned sure you want a piece of the action, too.*

If he was flattered, the uncle didn't show it.

'Fellow called Shaladi,' he said. 'He should have involved me from the start.' Then he added, almost as an aside, 'He won't make that mistake again.'

Again, that mirthless chuckle.

Mahsoud nodded. Something in the way the old man spoke made him glad that he wasn't Shaladi.

'But that's my problem,' said the old man. 'The strange thing is, Shaladi says the Chechens told him the safe house was a base for an attack on Benghazi. They want to stop the new government from getting established there. But you…' He paused. '*You* tell my nephew Tariq something entirely different, about an attack in *Tripoli*. I must confess, I am confused.'

The old man spread his hands, in a gesture of openness.

'My friend, you are an honoured guest,' he said. 'But this is my town. If you are honest with me, I can help you. But if not…'

Mahsoud's heart rate increased, but he said nothing as he wrestled with how to answer this question.

Give the wrong answer, and things might go very badly for him.

But he certainly couldn't tell the old man the truth.

'*Sayidi*,' he said, at length. 'I am humbled to share your home, and will be forever in your debt. It is my dearest wish that I might one day be able to call you a friend. But, respectfully, there are many reasons why I cannot tell you everything.' He paused. 'Forgive me, but you have heard of the cell structure, yes?'

The other man raised his eyebrows. 'I think so…' he said.

'It's designed to make it harder for the enemy to penetrate our ranks and uncover our plans,' said Mahsoud. 'In any operation, the commanders limit each individual's knowledge of the other participants, and even of the operation itself, to the barest basics that each man needs to do his job.'

The old man nodded, thoughtfully.

'The idea,' said Mahsoud, 'is that, if one man is captured, he cannot give away everything.' He paused. 'Because the Americans, they have ways of making anyone talk.'

'So I am told,' said the Libyan.

'And what you don't know, you cannot tell.' Mahsoud smiled, apologetically. 'So, yes, I was not entirely truthful with Tariq, but then it's also entirely possible that my superiors did not tell me the truth. As for Shaladi – I have never heard of him.'

The old man said nothing.

'Now,' said Mahsoud. 'Because you are who you are, and out of respect for you, I will tell you what I know for sure, and what I do not know. But I implore you – it must go no further than this room. Not even your brother.' He raised his eyes. 'The drones, the satellites, they are always up there. It is for your safety, and the safety of your family, as well as for the success of the operation. The Americans, the British… they are not playing games.'

'I understand,' said the man. 'It goes no further.'

Mahsoud inclined his head, slowly and gravely.

'Thank you,' he said. He cleared his throat, and lowered his voice. 'The truth – as far as I know it – is that the operation is an attack in Cairo,' he said. 'I don't know what or where – maybe the US embassy, maybe some visit by someone important, it's not my job to know. It was conceived in Saudi Arabia some time ago, and has been financed by a very rich man from that country, via another man in Balochistan, via a man in Cairo itself. The Chechens who will lead the attack need a safe house. I assume your friend, Mr Shaladi, agreed to provide one.'

The old man nodded.

'By the way,' said Mahsoud. 'Not only do I not know Shaladi, I do not know the man in Saudi, nor the man in Balochistan, nor the man in Cairo.' He paused. 'The cell structure, you see? If I am captured, I cannot give anyone, or any target, away.'

'So who are you working for?'

'My instructions come direct from a representative of the financier in Saudi. It's a lot of money. My job is to be the Saudi's representative on the ground, to ensure the money is spent correctly, and to help the Chechens achieve their goal in any way I can.'

'Who are the Chechens? Shaladi didn't know their names.'

'I don't know, either,' said Mahsoud, comfortable that this lie would remain undiscovered. 'It's all done through intermediaries. I only know that their leader is a respected *emir.* Truthfully, I doubt he is even aware of my existence. Of course, I'm sure he is expecting *someone* to be in the vicinity on behalf of the financier, but I am nothing but a minnow. I am still waiting for my Saudi contact to give me the address of the safe house, so that I can go and make myself known.' He paused. 'I'm surprised that the information hasn't come yet. Maybe…'

The old man held up a hand.

'I can tell you why that is,' he said.

'Oh?' said Mahsoud.

'Something has happened,' said the old man, his ego loosening his lips, 'and the Chechens are no longer coming to Sirte. Shaladi was asked to find them a new place. Just temporary – they want to keep on the move. Something has worried them.'

He looked expectantly at Mahsoud, a crafty expression on his face.

Mahsoud kept his own face impassive.

'For people like us it pays to be cautious,' he said. 'I'm sure that's all it is. But I am grateful to you, *sayidi.* That explains why I have not yet been informed. I expect I shall get a call tomorrow from the Saudis.'

'Ah,' said the old man, his tone suddenly less genial, and his gaze harder. 'I'm afraid you have a problem, there. I understand from one of my men that your satellite telephone isn't working. He has just gone to your room and taken it away for repair. I hope it will be okay, but one never knows.'

Mahsoud smiled, faintly, waiting for the follow-up.

Once again, he felt as though that one good eye was trying to break into his mind.

'We are both men of the world,' said the old man. 'Is it not so? I do not know what your mission is, and I do not want to know. Tripoli, Benghazi, Cairo, the moon… who cares? I wish you success. But you will need our assistance.'

'Go on,' said Mahsoud.

'If your satellite telephone is beyond repair, and your Saudi friends cannot contact you, you will need someone to give you the new location, yes?'

'Yes, *sayidi*,' said Mahsoud.

'And I think that information would be worth quite a lot more than one thousand dollars.'

Mahsoud said nothing, just waited for the inevitable.

'I can tell you the new location myself,' said the old man, 'because Shaladi told me.'

Zeff Mahsoud cleared his throat and stared at the old man's one eye for a few moments.

'We are both men of the world, as you say,' said Mahsoud. 'So let us – what do the Americans say? Let us cut to the chase. How much?'

'Twenty-five thousand dollars,' said the old man. 'And another twenty-five thousand to send Tariq with you. My word doesn't run so strong in the new place, but you will be safe with him along.'

Mahsoud stood up, walked to the window, and stared out into the night, thinking.

Fact was, he had no way of knowing if this old man was trustworthy – assuming the information he had was correct, he could easily be playing more than one side, and Mahsoud might find himself walking into a very difficult situation.

But the guy had him over a barrel, and they both knew it.

He had no choice.

He turned back to the old man.

'Fifty thousand dollars?' he said. 'I can arrange this via the tribal bank, and my people in England. But no more surprises. And you stay out of everything. And I will need my satellite phone to come back in working order.'

'Pah,' said the old man, with a wave of his hand and a smile. 'I think the problem with the phone was very small. A loose screw, I believe.'

'We have a deal, then,' said Mahsoud. 'So where is the new location?'

'It's a place in Houn,' said the other. 'Down in the Fezzan, at Al Jufra. Two hundred kilometres, maybe three. Half a day.'

# 85.

JOHN CARR AND his team had made excellent time, averaging forty klicks an hour – mostly on ancient camel-train tracks, but on metalled roads when Carr thought it safe.

He'd weighed the risk of compromise against the need to get to their lying-up point and get heads down.

'We're just two pickups,' he'd told Kev McMullen, when the latter had queried him. 'It's dark, and we're miles from habitation. If we see anyone up ahead, we'll just go off-road.'

As a result, they reached the LUP at a little after 03:00hrs, just as Zeff Mahsoud and the one-eyed man were wrapping up their conversation.

They'd found a long, deep wadi, with a re-entrant that curved round to the left, and into which McMullen and Fred West had reversed their wagons – allowing for the quickest possible exit should it be necessary.

Carr had scrambled back up the scree and was scanning the area with his night-sight as Geordie Skelton arrived at his side.

'What d'you reckon, John?' whispered the big northerner.

'About as good as we're going to find,' said Carr.

A moment later, the other two men joined them, weapons in hand.

The night air was still, and for a moment all they heard was the ticking of two cooling engines below them, and the scuttering of some small creature nearby.

'Okay, guys, listen in,' said Carr, quietly. 'Situation is we don't know if the target is still in the Sirte area, or if they've moved somewhere. Hopefully we'll find out soon enough, but until we do this is home. Clear?'

Three nods.

'Normal routine. One on stag, one awake by the vehicles sorting out his admin – scoff, weapons, usual shit. The other two sleeping, and we rotate through every hour. Agreed?'

Three thumbs-up.

'Geordie, you're on stag first. I'll send the SITREP, and see about any update. Kev, Fred – fuel up the vehicles, get some scoff and a brew down you, and then get your heads down. And well done, the pair of you. That was a long drive – you must be fucked.'

'Nah, I'm raring to go,' said McMullen.

West chuckled at the sarcasm.

'We've got plenty of time, we'll all get plenty of kip,' said Carr. 'Last light is 20:00hrs, so tomorrow we'll all stand-to at 18:00 hours for a last bit of scoff and a brief, in case Six have pulled their fingers out and got us some targeting intelligence. Any questions?'

Three shakes of the head.

'Crack on, then.'

Geordie Skelton slid down the side of the wadi to get one of the Minimis, and then moved back up the bank, looking for a good stag position. He found one among a collection of boulders just below its crest: from there he could hunker down out of sight, but with a decent view up and down the dried-up bed, and out into the desert in all directions.

He keyed the pressel on his radio.

'John,' he said. 'In position. Radio check.'

'Strength five,' said Carr.

'Likewise. Out.'

Geordie got comfortable, and began watching and listening.

Back down below, Kev and Fred quickly refuelled the vehicles, and then cleared areas for their roll mats and lightweight maggots.

Exhausted, they each wolfed down some unheated food and water, and then lay down, webbing for pillows, Diemacos by their sides. In a matter of minutes, both men were asleep.

A few metres away, Carr had set up the VSAT dish, and had sent a brief SITREP with their present location, confirming that their LUP was secure, and that the likelihood of compromise was low.

Then he pulled out his stove and mess tin and set about boiling water for a cup of tea and something to eat.

Fifty minutes later, he relieved Geordie Skelton on stag.

The sun was just starting to light up the eastern sky, and the desert was cool and empty.

Carr settled down, scope to his eye, and began sweeping the horizon.

# 86.

THE FOLLOWING DAY passed slowly.

Dawn came and went, and the sun rose high overhead, the temperature soaring into the late thirties.

For a long time, the four men's sheer exhaustion defeated the punishing heat, and they alternately slept and watched, and slept and watched.

But by the back end of the afternoon, even those who were supposed to be sleeping were just lying in what shade there was, resting up.

Carr had been in similar positions many times during his years in the Regiment, and he wasn't fazed.

There was no threat of discovery from the air – it was surprisingly hard to locate vehicles in the desert from aircraft even when you were actually looking for them, and nobody was – and they were invisible on the ground, unless someone drove into the wadi and turned into the re-entrant.

That was so unlikely it was like winning the world's biggest shit lottery, and if it happened they would deal with it.

The main enemy they faced, actually, was themselves. If you weren't careful, an LUP could start to feel like a little safe zone, where the world outside did not exist; over long periods, he'd seen men get too relaxed, and too comfortable, and start arguing and bickering over fuck all as the boredom got to them.

But he wasn't worried about that here. They all knew only too well that the world outside this shallow, dried-up riverbed was very real, and full of men who would love to kill them, and that did help to focus the mind.

And they were all highly experienced hands, and very good friends, and they weren't going to be here long enough to start getting on each other's nerves.

So it was simply a question of stag on, or kip, or eat, and wait.

At around 17:00hrs, Kevin McMullen wandered off to the far end of the wadi, where they had designated a rudimentary latrine.

His nerves were ramping up slightly, but he took control of his breathing, determined not to show it.

Over the past few hours he had reached a settlement with fate: if he died out here, he died. His wife and family would be taken care of in a way that he could never have managed while alive, and they'd know that he had perished in a noble cause. Coming out here to rescue two girls stolen away by these barbarians… If that wasn't a job worth risking your life for, what was?

He finished urinating, put himself away, and stared down at the patch of damp sand.

One thing still bothered him, though.

If he…

Then he heard a sound, and turned to his left.

It was Fred West.

'What's up, boy?' said West, in his Gloucestershire drawl. 'You alright?'

'Yep,' said McMullen, with a grin. 'Why?'

'Dunno,' said Fred. He took off his desert hat and inspected the sweat-soaked interior, before rubbing his blond hair and replacing it. 'You were standing here staring into space, is all.'

'Ah, I was just thinking about them fucking vultures,' said McMullen. 'If… you know.'

He shivered slightly, despite the temperature.

Fred West clapped Kevin McMullen on the shoulder.

'Fucking hell, boy, you think too much,' he said, with a grin. 'We're all dead – it's just a question of when. You know that. The whole of life's a roll of the dice, but John ain't dying, because he's John. Geordie'll never die, he's too miserable. As for you, I've heard you say this bollocks a thousand times. Week from now, we'll all be on the piss somewhere, and you'll be worrying about your missus finding out about all this shit.'

'Yeah, you're probably right,' said McMullen.

He turned and walked back to his vehicle.

Fred West watched him go, thoughtfully.

It was true, what he'd said: Kev was one of those blokes who'd thought his number was up every time he left camp.

Fred understood the psychology – it was all about not tempting fate – but not the logic.

McMullen was one of the best men he'd ever worked with.

He'd been in dozens – probably *hundreds* – of very sticky situations, in the Middle East, the Balkans, Africa, South Armagh…

And he'd come through them all without a scratch.

A memory came to West: pitch-black, January 2003, driving like hell down a main road in Iraq, near some town the name of which was long gone.

Five hundred klicks behind enemy lines, before the air war was even launched.

They'd been in one of four pinkies sent to recce some defensive positions – Kev McMullen at the wheel of the lead vehicle, Jock Lawlor in the commander's seat, himself at the gun.

Suddenly, tracer had erupted all around them, and the vehicle behind them had been hit.

They'd all shaken out and started putting fire down, as the damaged vehicle extracted itself.

It had seemed like an eternity, swapping rounds with a massively superior enemy force, all sorts of munitions flying towards them – S60, .50 cal, 7.62mm, the sky lit up like a firework display.

But they'd stood firm, and had eventually withdrawn in good order.

Amazingly, no-one had been hit.

They found out later that they'd driven into an air defence battery and its supporting infantry, including some armour – about four hundred blokes, the intelligence suggested.

Fred West smiled to himself as he remembered that night: the Iraqis were brave men, and they were always up for the fight, but their accuracy was shit.

Sure, the job they were on now was dicey, no doubt about it.

But compared to *that*? Piece of piss.

John Carr had proved often enough that he was a hard man to kill, and he generally kept his blokes alive, too.

Just then, Carr walked over.

'Not moving tonight,' he said. 'No word from Six on the 18:00 about the new location.'

# 87.

AT 06:00HRS THE following morning, Carr set up the comms laptop once again.

He was prepared for the long haul, but the morning's message from MI6 changed all that.

'Intelligence confirms information gained via your tactical questioning sent on earlier SITREP,' it said. 'Targets have moved away from Sirte. Believe new safe house located approx 100km south-east of your current position. Stand by for more 18:00hrs. Note: intelligence suggests targets may move again soon.'

Carr acknowledged, closed the laptop, and walked over to where Geordie Skelton was lying, right next to one of their wagons.

He tapped the big northerner's foot with his boot.

'Fuck off, man,' said Skelton, quietly. 'I'm asleep.'

'Wake up, then, you lazy fucker,' said Carr, with a grin. 'It's not Sirte. That Brummie cunt was right. The Chechens were spooked by something and they've done a runner. But Six think they've found them. They're trying to confirm. Tell Fred. I'll tell Kev.'

He clambered up the steep side of the wadi and walked along the lip to where Kev McMullen was on stag.

He squatted down next to the Londoner and told him what he'd told Geordie.

'We might be moving tonight,' he said.

McMullen nodded, his eyes sweeping the horizon behind a pair of matt black Oakleys.

Carr patted him on the shoulder.

'It's going to be good, mate,' he said.

The confirmation arrived in the 18:00hrs report from the SIS.

Nicholls himself had sent the information – the exact co-ordinates for the target compound, which was down at the extreme southern edge of the town of Houn, a hundred kilometres south-east from Carr's current position.

He included some detail about the area, and a series of photographs of the compound, taken from close up, and reiterated that the intelligence suggested that this new location was itself temporary.

Carr looked at the pictures. They were at a strange angle, and slightly blurred – probably stills from a video filmed from a moving vehicle – but he was impressed: Nicholls clearly had people on the ground who were actually coming across with the intel he needed.

'That's a first,' he said to himself, quietly.

He saved the images, took the dish down and stowed it, and looked to his left.

Fred West was out of sight, on stag.

Kev McMullen was cleaning his weapon and smoking.

Geordie Skelton was sitting with a brew, reading a battered Bernard Cornwell paperback.

Carr wandered over to him, carrying the laptop under his arm.

'Reading without moving your lips, mate?' he said, with a smirk. 'Any good pictures in it?'

'Fuck off,' said Skelton, never taking his eyes from the page.

Carr squatted down next to the man from Newcastle and bent his neck to look at the front cover.

'*The Pale Horseman*,' he said. 'One of his early Saxon series? That's a good read, mate. Uhtred dies at the end, though.'

Geordie looked at him.

'You wanker,' he said. 'I was fucking getting into it.'

Carr chuckled quietly and looked over at McMullen.

'Kev,' he hissed. 'Over here.'

The Londoner came over and Carr opened the laptop.

'Phots,' said Carr. 'And the location.'

The three men looked at the compound – it stood some ten metres off a wideish track, with sizeable date palm plantations to either side. It was surrounded by a wall, which was estimated at 2.5 metres high and laid out in a rough square, each side approximately fifty metres in length.

There were two gates, both solid plate steel, and both a dusty, rusty blue – a double at the front, wide enough for vehicles and with a judas gate built in, and a single at the rear, which led out into barren wastelands.

An overhead, probably shot from a satellite, showed the layout.

There was a large central house – white, two-storey, with a balcony to the front and a flat roof with a waist-high wall around it.

Skelton pointed to something on the roof.

'Gun position,' he said.

'Could be,' said Carr.

Behind and to the left of the main villa, against the wall, was a darker square, marked on the image as '*Generator and fuel tank*'.

That made sense, Carr thought: Libya's electricity grid had been bombed back to the Middle Ages, but even at its best you'd want a back-up down there in the back of beyond.

On the opposite side of the compound, tucked away near the rear of the compound, was a small building, marked '*Servants' quarters*'.

'Looks good for a prison cell,' said Carr. 'Single door, one room, easier to watch them and easier to guard than the main house.'

Three vehicles were parked nearby, along the rear wall, and two men were visible, one inside and one outside the perimeter wall.

'Sentries?' said McMullen.

'Aye,' said Carr. 'I don't suppose they'll all be inside watching telly.'

'Any idea on their strength?' said Skelton.

'It's out of the way,' said Carr, 'so Six haven't been able to get too close. But they think ten or twelve.'

'That's light,' said Skelton. 'That Brummie twat said they had Chechens with them. Reckon they *were* the reinforcements he was on about?'

'Maybe,' said Carr. 'And when they didn't show...'

'You think they know we're on our way?'

Carr thought for a moment, and then shook his head.

'Nah,' he said. 'If they thought for one second that their guys had been clipped, and that the people who did it were inbound, they'd already have fucked off.'

'But the int says their current position is only temporary?' said McMullen.

'Makes sense,' said Carr. 'It's what we'd do ourselves, isn't it? Something goes wrong, you assume the enemy knows your plan. They can't move every day, that would be logistically impossible, but if it was me I'd be there for three or four days, a week max, and then I'm moving again.'

'Fair one,' said Skelton.

'So what do we do?' said Kev McMullen.

'Let's have a look at the map,' said Carr.

He spread it out on the bonnet of his Hilux, and they spent a few minutes studying it in the dusk.

Houn was a small town halfway between the similar-sized settlements of Sawknah and Waddan. All three had grown up over centuries because of the existence of the Jufra oasis, whose underground sweetwater springs bubbled up into the sands and turned this tiny sliver of the vast, barren Sahara green with olive and palm trees.

The target compound was at the very south of the town, just north of a sprawling range of ancient black basalt mountains.

Carr pointed at the highway which led straight down to Houn from Misrata on the coast.

'Given the urgency and our location, this is the obvious way in,' he said. 'Join it fifteen klicks north, down into the top of town, skirt round on the ring road.'

'Fucking hell, John,' said Kev McMullen, his heart pumping a little harder. 'Through Houn itself? That's a big old gaff – twenty thousand people, lot of fucking eyes, and trigger fingers.' He pointed at the mountain range. 'I'd rather cut down across country round here and come back in from the south.'

'That'd add twelve hours to the drive,' said Carr. 'They could be gone by then, and we don't have the fuel or resources to play catch-up. It's now or never. We've got to hit them tonight.'

Skelton looked at Carr. 'Fucking dicey, John,' he said.

'Who Dares Wins,' said Carr, with a grin. 'No-one said it was going to be easy.'

'Bound to be checkpoints on that road as well.'

'Ad hoc, according to Six,' said Carr. 'We see something we don't like, we just fuck off into the darkness.'

Skelton said nothing for a moment, but stood staring at the map and scratching his beard.

'It's the only way, Geordie,' said Carr, quietly. 'They aren't paying us what they are because it's a vicarage tea party.'

The giant northerner grinned. 'Yeah, you're right,' he said. 'Great risk produces great rewards.'

'I dunno, John,' said McMullen, shaking his head. 'I'm not happy about this. If we get seen, we're fucked. I still say we bypass the town, come round under the mountains and…'

Carr cut him short. 'I'm not saying you have to be fucking happy about it,' he said. 'That route isn't workable. It would take all night and we'd have to lie-up tomorrow.'

'Yeah, but…'

Carr put his hand on McMullen's shoulder and looked him straight in the eyes.

'Listen, Kev,' he said. 'The Chinese parliament's over, understood? They move those girls again, we're fucked and so are they.' He released McMullen's shoulder. 'You signed up for this. And I'm glad you're here. You're one of the bravest and best operators I've ever had the privilege to work with, but whatever the fuck's got into you, you fucking get rid of it. Yes?'

McMullen said nothing.

Geordie Skelton stepped in.

'Easy, boys,' he said. He looked at Kevin McMullen. 'John's right, mate,' he said. 'Is the plan perfect? No. But it's the one we have. We took the shilling. Now it's time to earn it.'

Kevin McMullen nodded.

'I'm okay, John,' he said. 'I told you that. I'm prepared for anything, including dying out here. I've made my peace with that. I'm just… I'd rather not take any unnecessary risks, that's all. But if you say this is necessary, that's good enough for me.'

'It *is* necessary,' said Carr. 'And I'm not planning on dying out here myself.'

'Too fucking right,' said Skelton. 'I still haven't got round to changing my will, so if I peg it out here my ex-missus gets the house. And I'd rather die than see that happen. Not that that makes any fucking sense, like.'

They all laughed, and that broke the tension.

McMullen stuck out a hand, and Carr shook it.

'Good man, Kev,' he said. 'It's forgotten about. Now, I'm going up to brief Fred, and work up the route, and let's get this fucking show on the road.'

By the time that was done, it was well after dark.

Carr gave the order to load everything back into the wagons, and stand-to, ready to move.

At 19:45hrs they rolled out of the wadi and turned south.

# 88.

AS THE FOUR men began their journey, Charlotte Morgan was forcing down some bread and water which had been handed to her by one of their guards.

It was hard work – her mouth was ridden with ulcers, the bread somehow managed to be both greasy and stale at the same time, and the water was warm and brackish.

But she was determined not to give in.

Against the far wall, Martha Percival's own bowl and cup were untouched. Charlotte could see her friend's hip bones, angular through the loose fitting black *abaya*.

She was no expert on starvation, but it looked to her as though Martha was a week, or perhaps ten days, away from death.

On the dusty floor between their two beds sat two guards.

There was always a pair of them in the room, and, each time they changed over, a waistcoat was passed by one of the old guard to one of the new.

It had taken Charlotte a while to work out what it was, but over time its bulky form had slowly revealed itself to her.

It was a suicide vest, and it terrified her.

One of the guards – a handsome young Eastern European, who had just come on duty for the night – seemed particularly pleased by the fear it inspired.

He had taken delight in showing her the wires, and the battery, and the blocks of plastic explosive, and finally the clacker, the handheld metal device which he would use to detonate the bomb.

He would hold up this switch, and make a squeezing motion with his other hand.

Then he would shout 'Boom!' in her face, his spittle and bad breath all over her, and start laughing.

He seemed to speak no English, but the message was very clear: even if your people find you, they won't take you from us alive.

*Abandon hope, all ye who enter here.*

She finished the bread, and washed it down with a swallow of the unpleasant water.

'Martha,' she said, quietly. 'You need to eat.'

But her friend made no reply.

One of the guards stood and walked over to Charlotte.

He leaned over her, raising his hand as though to slap her across the face, and said something to her in a foreign tongue that she didn't understand.

But she understood his message, and was silent.

# 89.

ALL BANTER HAD ceased in both vehicles now.

No-one gave the order; it didn't need giving.

Fifty klicks from Houn, an hour after dark, Carr had pulled them over for a final brew and to get kitted up.

Few words were spoken as they stood in the evening humidity to put on their body armour and equipment carriers. As they climbed back into the vehicles, they pushed their seats all the way back to give them as much room as possible. It was still tight – the Hiluxes were not designed for this – but they barely noticed the discomfort.

They were almost within touching distance of the enemy, and they had to be ready for anything.

They moved closer to Houn, travelling more slowly now, and very alert.

At just before 23:00hrs, they reached the metalled Houn-Misrata highway, and went firm in a slight dip a hundred metres shy of it, lights and engines off.

Carr got out of his vehicle, and scanned north and south with his night-sight.

The road was long and straight, and the terrain flat, so he could see for miles in either direction.

It was all quiet.

After ten minutes, when not a single vehicle had passed, he got back into his seat and turned to McMullen.

'Crack on, Kev,' he said.

McMullen nodded, started the engine, and drove slowly onto the tarmac, turning south, and picking up speed, driving with lights off.

Five or six kilometres out from Houn, the road undulated slightly as it dropped into a large wadi, and as they climbed out on the other side they entered an area thick with vegetation, which suddenly sprouted out of the otherwise arid earth on either side.

And there, on the right, fifty metres ahead and backed into the undergrowth, was a vehicle.

Several men stood alongside it, well-positioned to catch anyone coming unawares out of the climb.

As long as they were alert.

Luckily for Carr and his team, the men had relaxed, with the road empty, and were clearly not expecting any traffic. And while they must have heard the two vehicles coming at speed, they had been thrown by the fact that they were unlit.

As his Hilux drew level, Carr could see the men – three of them, all armed – reacting, heads swivelling, weapons being raised.

He keyed his pressel.

'Geordie,' he said. 'Company on the right, mate.'

Next to him, Kev McMullen reacted instantly himself, gunning the accelerator.

The pickup surged forwards, picking up more speed, and they were through and beyond the group in the trees, and charging onwards.

Behind them, Fred West was also stamping on the pedal, as the first flashes from the weapons lit up the night to his right.

The sound of the gunfire was quickly left behind, the three men firing blind into the darkness.

'Break left, break left,' said Carr, to Kevin McMullen. 'Get us off this fucking road.'

McMullen immediately slowed and moved off the highway and back out into the inky desert.

Behind him, Fred West followed.

'Geordie, you guys okay?' said Carr, over the net.

'All good, man,' came Geordie's voice. 'Missed us by fucking miles. But… Wait one. Right, that's lights on the main road behind us now, just seen them. They're trying to follow us up.'

'Yeah, seen,' said Carr. 'Stop here, Kev. Engine off. Stay in the wagon.'

McMullen did as instructed, and Carr climbed out just as Fred West coasted to a stop behind them.

He met Geordie Skelton between the two vehicles, and they stood looking back towards the highway.

They watched as, a kilometre or so away, the lone vehicle passed in line with their position and headed south, its engine screaming.

Carr reached into his equipment carrier and took out his radio. Although it was encrypted for traffic between members of his team, it was in other respects a standard walkie-talkie, with the usual pre-set frequencies.

He started clicking through these.

The first three or four buzzed with empty static, but he hit the jackpot on the fifth.

'I've got them,' he said, to Geordie. 'Local militia. They were pickets for a VCP a few kilometres further on. They're currently getting a massive bollocking from their boss for firing at us. He's calling them all the cunts under the sun for not just radioing him to say we were inbound. They think we're smugglers, and they want our cargo.'

Skelton chuckled and started to say something, but Carr held up a hand to silence him, listening to more excited Arabic chatter.

'Right,' he said, more urgently. 'The boss is telling them to turn round, and he and the rest of his blokes at the VCP are sweeping up the road, hoping to intercept us. If we get a shift on, we can get back onto the main drag below them and get through the checkpoint while it's unmanned.'

Thirty seconds later, both Hiluxes were bouncing along parallel to the road, a thousand metres out into the desert.

Almost immediately, headlights appeared, coming north – miles in the distance at first, but rapidly drawing closer.

Eventually, they drew parallel.

Carr counted three technicals as they steamed past.

'Fucking Keystone jihadis,' said Kevin McMullen, shaking his head.

'Aye,' said Carr. 'But it won't be long before they realise what's happened.' He keyed his radio, speaking to both McMullen and the other vehicle. 'Let's get a fucking wriggle on.'

Kev McMullen nodded, and the pickup surged forwards.

By the time he bounced back onto the tarmac he was already doing 80kph, and, with his foot to the floor, the tuned, three-litre turbo had them three kilometres down the road in no time.

Up ahead, in the distance, Carr saw that the road was partially blocked.

Kevin McMullen had seen it, too, and was slowing.

As they got closer, Carr saw a dozen oil barrels, painted red-and-white, and doubtless half-full of rubble and concrete, arranged across the tarmac in a rough chicane.

'VCP two hundred metres ahead,' he said, to Skelton and West. 'Unmanned.'

'Clowns,' said Geordie. 'Good for us, mind.'

'Lights on,' said Carr, as they drove through the checkpoint.

He wanted to look as normal as possible, now.

A minute later, they reached the outskirts of Houn.

There was a lot of people and traffic out and about in the town itself – North African countries tending to avoid the heat of the day and come alive after sundown – and Carr felt the hair on the back of his neck stand up.

Almost all of the streetlights were out, but still, he squeezed the pistol grip of the Diemaco across his legs, and moved the safety catch to fire.

Up ahead of them, the cars slowed to a stop at a large traffic island, with some bombed-out office buildings to its right.

Through a gap in the taller buildings, they could see a tower and several white domes, lit up and rising into the sky.

'There's the old mosque,' said Carr.

'Seen,' said McMullen.

To Carr's right, a group of young men were sitting outside a run-down villa, passing round a hubble bubble.

One of them, a tall, thin guy in a Barcelona soccer shirt, was bouncing a football on the pavement.

He said something to the bloke next to him, and they both laughed.

The man with the pipe inhaled deeply, blew out some smoke and idly turned his head.

And looked straight at John Carr, who was faintly illuminated by a light outside the villa.

'Is it on?' said Kevin McMullen, straining with every fibre of his being to work his drills: look relaxed, don't make eye contact, yawn, smile, scratch your arse – do anything, as long as you look like a man without a care in the world.

'Nah, he's just having a bit of a nose,' said Carr. He smiled at the guy through the passenger window, and raised a hand in casual acknowledgment. 'It's dark, Kev, we've got beards and tans. We're fine.'

And, sure enough, the guy smiled back at Carr, nodded politely, and turned to pass the pipe to the man next to him.

The traffic freed, and McMullen turned right, checking to make sure that Geordie and Fred were still there.

All four of them had memorised the route, which, fortunately, was simple.

'One kilometre down here,' said Carr. 'Old town on the left.'

'Roger,' said McMullen.

'Five hundred metres.'

'Five hundred metres.'

A minute later, McMullen swung south.

Behind him, Fred West did the same.

'Old police HQ on the left,' said Carr. 'Going right after this olive farm.'

'Seen,' said McMullen. 'Next right.'

He started to make the turn, and then had to stop sharp for a man who was crossing with a donkey pulling a small water bowser.

Behind him, Fred McMullen jammed on the anchors, and behind Fred a local was forced into the same manoeuvre.

The donkey was going nowhere, because of traffic on the opposite side of the road.

Three vehicles back, the local driver started blowing his horn, and waving his fist out of the window.

The old man sat on the water bowser, oblivious, and waiting for a truck to lumber past.

'Fucking hell,' said Kev McMullen. 'Why the fuck would you cross this road here?'

Carr leaned forward and looked into his wing mirror.

'He's just an old boy,' he murmured. 'Chilled as fuck.'

'Unlike the cunt behind us.'

The man was now leaning on the horn, so that it made one long, continuous noise.

'Aye.'

In the other vehicle, Geordie Skelton was watching the scene unfold in his own wing mirror.

'Twat's getting out, man,' he said, to Fred West. 'Coming your side.'

Fred put his hand on the Sig Sauer on his hip.

'Steady,' said Geordie. 'He's just late home from the camel farm.'

The guy drew level, but now he could see that the problem was not of Fred West's making, so the anger went out of him; he shouted a few things at the old man with the donkey, threw Fred a shrug, and returned to his car.

'Jesus,' said Fred.

Ahead of them, the old man and his donkey finally crossed, and Carr and McMullen started off.

'Three klicks,' said Carr, looking at his handheld GPS.

'Three klicks,' said McMullen.

A kilometre on, they had left the built-up area behind and were heading into the outskirts of the town.

On either side were walled-off compounds, and squares of palms, all laden with the dates that the region was famous for. As they got further from the centre of Houn, the groves became more spread out, and the compounds, too.

An old Mercedes passed them going the other way, but apart from that they saw not a soul.

'Kilometre to go,' said Carr.

'Roger,' said McMullen.

He stopped and killed the lights. Each man put on his helmet, pulled down his HMNOs, and the night turned green.

Kev waited five minutes before rolling forwards again, in as high a gear as the heavily laden Hilux would take, and keeping his revs low, until he was five hundred metres away – sound travels further in still, humid air, and they were now at the absolute limit of vehicle noise from the target.

McMullen pulled off the road and round the back of a broken down old stone hut, perfectly placed to give them some cover from view.

As they got out, Geordie and Fred rolled silently to a stop behind them.

# 90.

ALL FOUR MEN, fully alert now, got out and took up positions in all-round defence.

There they sat and waited for some time, scanning the area for signs of life.

There were none.

The plan called for Carr and McMullen to go forward and recce the target, while Skelton kept watch and West prepared some demolition charges.

Carr looked at Geordie.

'Okay, mate,' he whispered. 'Me and Kev will crack on. Make sure you monitor the VSAT.'

Geordie Skelton and Fred West both gave him the thumbs-up.

'Roger, John,' said Skelton. 'Look after yourself, pal.'

Carr turned away and started moving.

Between his position and the compound were several palm groves, each marked off by stone walls about four feet tall.

As McMullen covered him, Carr put his left hand on top of the first wall and his right firmly on the pistol grip of his Diemaco. With the weapon pointing towards the threat, ready to fire, he was over the first wall in a single, smooth movement, dropping soundlessly into the sandy earth on the other side.

He immediately took up a firing position and waited for McMullen to follow him.

And then both men went firm for a few minutes, looking for any movement among the bristly trunks of the trees, listening intently for any sound that might betray a presence to their front.

This – the quiet before the storm – was always the moment that Carr felt most.

He'd done this kind of thing a thousand times before, and he was at exactly the right balance between relaxed and alert.

He was not a man who felt fear, but it was the unknown that got you, and he could taste that familiar adrenalin in his mouth. This was the enemy's backyard, and he had no idea how good they were. Kneeling here, his back to the small wall, it was easy to imagine some bad guy taking aim, right now, through a night-sight centred on his chest.

And, of course, these cunts were experts at the use of IEDs. Could they have laid them out in the surrounding area, to give them warning of an approach? He couldn't discount it, even though logic said they wouldn't want to blow a date farmer to pieces and turn the locals against them.

Carr banished these thoughts and, satisfied that the way ahead was clear, stood up.

Slowly, silently, he began moving forward, his cautious steps mirrored by McMullen, some five metres to his rear.

He carried his Diemaco across the centre of his body, horizontal to the ground, sweeping the way ahead with the barrel. It looked almost casual, but everywhere the barrel went his eyes went too, and he was ready to engage without thought if necessary. The secret in any chance encounter was to be the man who initiated the contact, not the one reacting to it. If the enemy appeared, he intended to hit him hard and quick, to give himself and Kev the initiative while the targets were reeling from the weight of fire.

Every now and then, he stopped, raised the weapon to his shoulder, and looked through his night-sight.

Then, satisfied that all was clear, he moved forward again.

It took them twenty minutes to cover the five hundred metres to the target.

Once there, they took a knee and went firm again.

McMullen watched their rear, looking for anyone who might be following them up from behind.

Carr concentrated on the compound to their front.

He could see the top half of the main villa, which was in darkness. He kept his eye on the south-facing balcony and the flat roof in particular – he would certainly have put men up there – but he saw no-one in the green light of the night-sight.

He settled down to wait, and watch.

He had to consider the possibility that the quarry had already gone, but something – some indefinable feeling – told him that they had not.

Sure enough, a few minutes later, he heard the clang of metal, loud in the still night, as a bolt was pulled back to open the judas gate within the main steel gates to the compound.

Carr raised his weapon and put his eye to the scope, the darkness again turning to eerie light.

He watched as the gate opened inwards, and a man carrying an AK stepped out.

Instinctively, Carr laid the inverted yellow V of his sight on the centre of the man's mass. He could just make out the dark shape of another man just beyond the gate, his left arm high and no doubt holding the bolt that had just been pulled back.

A few quiet words were exchanged, a laugh, and the gate was shut with an audible clang.

The guy on the outside looked right and then left, as though deciding which way to go, and then began walking along the perimeter wall towards Carr.

He looked fit and strong – a professional, if you could call him that – and he held his AK at the ready, and was wearing an equipment carrier loaded with what looked like spare magazines and a radio.

But there was something about the way he moved that told its own story to Carr's experienced eye. The guy was well-trained, that was obvious, but he was going through the motions. That meant that they were reasonably comfortable here, and it also suggested that there was no imminent move.

Just in front of Carr's position, a few metres away at the corner, the man paused, slung the AK over his shoulder, dug into his pocket, and pulled out a packet of cigarettes and a lighter.

Carr smiled to himself – just like any young Tom, even jihadi fanatics were jack bastards when they got out of sight of the boss – and took a good look at the man's face in the flare of the flame.

He was young, bearded, and Eastern European in appearance.

Looked hard and capable.

Then the lighter was away and the guy was strolling on, completely unaware that he was being watched.

Carr's eyes followed him as he turned right, down the gap between the wall and the palm plantation, and then right again so that he disappeared around the back of the compound.

He switched his gaze to the far end of the front wall again.

Sure enough, a few minutes later, the sentry reappeared at that corner and walked up to the gate.

He stopped to flick away another cigarette butt – Carr watched it describe a lazy, glowing arc in his night sight – and then he banged on the gate twice with the flat of his palm.

There was the sound of the bolts being shot, and a creak as it opened.

There was an audible chuckle, and the sentry vanished inside.

As the gate clanged shut, Carr looked at his watch: 01:00hrs.

He dropped his head below the plantation wall, and nudged McMullen.

'This is them, mate,' he whispered. 'One sentry. Another guy on the gate. Shit drills, casual as fuck. Got radios, but no NVGs. Looks like it's an occasional round – probably on the hour, something like that.'

McMullen nodded. 'Lazy wankers,' he said quietly, over his shoulder. 'That's our way in, then.'

'That's what I was thinking,' said Carr. 'I'll just brief the boys. Then let's withdraw, come back in to the rear from the top end of these palms, and have a shufti up there.'

McMullen gave him the thumbs-up. Carr called up Geordie and Fred West on the net.

'Definitely the place,' he said, quietly. 'They're chucking a sentry out to patrol now and then, and there's another guy on the gate. We need to recce the northern and eastern perimeters. I'll see if we can get a look over the wall, but I don't want to push it.'

'Roger,' said Skelton.

Carr checked his watch again: 01:21hrs.

'See you in about an hour,' he said.

He and McMullen carried out the same painstaking reconnaissance on the other walls of the compound, using the dead ground and the darkness to move, quietly and unseen, around the rear perimeter.

Twice, they had to pause and go to ground, as the same guy made his rounds – on the half-hour, as it happened.

Carr shook his head as he watched him go: the stupid bastard was way too relaxed, and way too comfortable, and it was going to cost him dear.

When he disappeared inside for the third time it was 02:06hrs, and Carr and McMullen began to move back round so that they could get a good look at the front elevation.

But as they started to move, two things happened.

The first was that a door opened onto the flat roof of the villa, and a man came out on to it – temporarily framed by lighting from the internal stairwell.

The second was an urgent message in Carr's earpiece – a call of 'Standby, standby!' from Skelton.

Carr and McMullen immediately went to ground, listening for the next transmission.

# 91.

CARR WAITED, STILL watching the villa through his night sight.

A moment later, Skelton transmitted again.

'That's one Bravo on a motorcycle, towards the compound,' he said.

'Roger,' whispered Carr, just as he heard the hairdryer whine of a small-engined motorbike.

He watched as it appeared on the road out front, its headlight glowing weakly, and then disappeared out of sight to the front of the compound.

'Stop, stop, stop,' said Skelton.

'Roger,' said Carr. 'What's happening?'

'Wait one,' transmitted Skelton. Then: 'I can tell it's stopped near the compound, John, but I'm too far away to get any detail. Sorry, mate.'

Carr cursed quietly.

He turned to McMullen.

'You hear that, Kev?' he whispered.

McMullen nodded.

'I need to find out what's going on,' said Carr. 'Stay here and cover my arse, okay?'

Before McMullen could even respond, Carr was moving. He

went as quickly as he could, using the darkness and cover to get into a position from where he could observe.

Half a minute later, he was lying prone behind a small scrub bush, watching the motorcycle rider resting casually against his bike, forty or so metres away.

The Judas gate was open, and the guy who had been walking around the compound was standing outside, leaning against the wall, smoking, saying nothing.

Clearly, they were waiting for someone.

And then another man appeared at the gate and stepped through.

A man Carr had seen once before, on a beach in Marbella.

A man with dark eyes, and a limp, and the blood of many men, women and children on his hands.

Argun Shishani.

Carr was a hundred per cent certain.

It was that unmistakable gait that gave him away, the rolling limp as much a positive ID as if Carr had been staring directly into his face.

'You fucking cunt,' he breathed, the anger welling up from deep in his soul.

He was momentarily transported back to that beach in Marbella… his son and daughter next to him, the sea, the little children playing in the sand – and the man with the dark eyes and the hole in his leg looking casually at Carr and then beyond, at his targets.

It was all Carr could do to stop himself from dropping the bastard there and then.

But he gritted his teeth and watched on.

Clipping the Chechen now would blow everything, and they'd come too far to let emotion get in the way.

Carr was going to kill this man, he'd never been more sure of anything.

Just not now.

Shishani turned towards his guy and shouted something angry.

Carr didn't need to hear what was said: it was obvious, as the guy threw away his cigarette, took the AK off his shoulder, and immediately tried to look a little more like a man ready to respond to a threat.

The guy on the motorbike was digging his hand into a bag slung over his shoulder, and handing something over.

Shishani said something, the guy said something back, and that was it.

Then the Chechen limped back inside the compound, followed by his footsoldier, and the gate clanged shut once more.

As the bolts were slammed home, the guy on the bike revved the engine slightly, turned in a lazy semi-circle and started back the way he'd come.

The guy on the roof, who had clearly been in some sort of overwatch role, disappeared down below again.

'That's the motorcyclist heading your way, Geordie,' said Carr.

'Roger,' said Skelton.

Carr moved quickly back round to McMullen.

'What happened, John?' said the Londoner.

'Just saw Shishani, Kev,' said Carr, his eyes blazing. 'The girls are there, for definite. I'd bet my life on it. No way he'd let them out of his sight. Too valuable.'

'Fucking hell,' breathed McMullen. 'And the bike?'

'Guy handed something over.'

'What?'

'Fuck knows,' said Carr. 'Winning lottery ticket, a takeaway, a secret message. Whatever it was, it's irrelevant. The int says they're going to move, and it looks to me like it might be tonight.'

'That's the bike past me and gone,' said Geordie, over the net.

'I just saw Shishani,' said Carr.

'Say again,' said Skelton.

'That's a confirmed Shishani, on target.'

‘Fuck me,’ said Skelton. ‘Jackpot.’

‘Exactly,’ said Carr. ‘Get your shit together and come to us. RV in the palm grove west of target. I’ll guide you in. We’re going now. It’s on.’

# 92.

HALF A KLICK AWAY, back at the vehicles, Geordie Skelton felt a surge of excitement, and an irrepressible grin swept onto his face.

A metre or two away, Fred West was already pulling on a daysack containing several demolition charges, a bar mine strapped to its side just visible in silhouette.

Neither man spoke.

Neither needed to.

They were going through a well-practised drill – a thing almost of instinct, borne of years on operations. It took a matter of moments to make their final equipment checks, the last being to ensure that the ammunition belt of each Minimi was across its feed tray, the working parts pulled to the rear, safety catches on.

Their senses, fuelled by a controlled excitement, were operating at a level far above the normal, but their pulse rates were only slightly elevated, and their minds icy calm.

Every fibre of them both was itching for action.

'Once more unto the breach, Frederick,' said Skelton quietly. 'Time for some vengeance and retribution.'

# 93.

INSIDE THE LARGE villa on the other side of the wall, Argun Shishani was knocking softly on Khasmohmad Kadyrov's bedroom door.

He heard a muffled response from within, and depressed the handle.

Kadyrov had just turned on the lamp next to his mattress, and was sitting up and rubbing his eyes.

'My apologies, Khasmohmad,' said Shishani, quietly. 'I know you need sleep.'

'It's fine, it's fine,' said Kadyrov, beckoning him inside. 'What time is it?'

'A little after two o'clock.'

'The whores?'

'All quiet.'

Kadyrov yawned. 'Good,' he said. 'So is there a problem?'

'The courier just delivered the address,' said Shishani. 'I was wondering if…'

'Where is it?'

'Place called Qatrun.'

'I don't know it.'

'Neither do I,' said Shishani. 'It's a good distance further south.

About five hundred kilometres, apparently. The helicopter will need to change its route, but it's not a problem.'

'Just what I need,' said Kadyrov, with a chuckle. 'Another long drive.'

He had been suffering from mild dysentery for a couple of days, though it was starting to pass.

'It will be worth it in the end,' said Shishani. 'And you were right – it makes sense. There's no way of knowing what happened to the men coming up from the south, but why take the risk? And after the arrest of your friend in Balochistan...'

'You let the courier go?'

'I did, for now. No point in causing trouble while we are still here. Shaladi vouched for him, and he will deal with him later.'

'It's crucial that we close every door that we can,' said Kadyrov, suddenly serious. 'I still wonder if we should not kill Shaladi and his brother in Cairo, also.'

'Don't worry about them, Khasmohmad,' said Shishani, his voice reassuring. 'They have as much to lose as we do. And the money will buy their silence. That's all the greedy bastards care about.'

'What's that expression the English have?' said Kadyrov, a twinkle in his eye. 'The pot and the black kettle?'

'Something like that.'

Kadyrov stood up, stretched and scratched his belly. 'You still think the British will pay up? Their responses have been evasive.'

'They may not have received our proof of life film yet, brother,' said Shishani. 'And even so, they have to play it carefully. They have laws against paying ransoms and it would look bad for them. But I am certain that they will pay. Her father is very rich. The delay is probably due to them trying to decide how to put the money together and transmit it to us, without their voters and their newspapers finding out.'

'Her daddy won't be happy when we send her back in pieces.'

‘No. But by then we will be a long way away.’

‘Our new identities are finalised?’

‘Yes. Passports, ID cards, bank accounts, everything. We will have to be very careful, but one day…’

Kadyrov nodded. ‘So you said you were wondering if… what?’

Shishani hesitated. ‘I was wondering if perhaps we should move tonight?’ he said. ‘Now.’

Kadyrov looked at him, carefully. ‘Only Shaladi and his courier know our location?’ he said.

‘Yes.’

‘And you’ve just said that neither of them will talk.’

‘Yes, but…’

‘You are unusually nervous, Argun,’ said Kadyrov, with a smile. ‘Are we timid women, who flinch when the wind blows, or are we men? It is right that we should move, but there is no immediate rush. Better to let the men who are sleeping have a night’s rest, and the guards sleep tomorrow, and then move in an orderly fashion tomorrow evening.’

‘I suppose that way we would avoid travelling by day,’ said Shishani, rubbing his chin, thoughtfully.

‘Exactly,’ said Kadyrov. He reached out and clapped the other man on the shoulder. ‘Go back to bed. Preserve your strength. Who knows when it will be needed?’

# 94.

GEORDIE AND FRED arrived ten minutes after John Carr's last radio message.

The four men formed a small huddle in the dark date palm plantation, and listened in while Carr outlined the plan that they were about to execute.

When he'd finished, he looked round them.

'Any questions?' he whispered.

No-one spoke. Each knew his part, and each knew, too, that this was either the ballsiest or the stupidest thing he'd ever done, and probably both.

The plan was sketchy, and full of what-ifs and other unknowns, and they were outnumbered and had no support.

A few minutes from action, each man's life now hung in the balance, suspended by the thinnest thread.

And they loved it – even Kevin McMullen's dark thoughts were long behind him.

This was what it was all about.

They'd signed up for the money, but the truth was the money meant nothing.

Every man jack of them had really come for the chance to feel like this: alive, focused on what was ahead, exhilarated at the prospect, about to test themselves in the greatest arena of all and risk their lives to give two young women, whom they did not know, the chance to live theirs.

Carr grinned to himself.

Geordie Skelton must have read his mind.

'We must be proper fucking daft, man,' he said, chuckling softly. 'But let's be fucking at it.'

Suppressing all thoughts of his family, McMullen crossed himself, though it was out of habit as much as anything, the battlefield being the only place he prayed.

Skelton hefted a Minimi in his hands, enjoying the extra weight, anticipating the awesome firepower it would bring at close range.

Fred West did what he'd done since his first patrol in Northern Ireland, and momentarily visualised a winning hand of cards – a Royal Flush of spades. Nodding happily, he adjusted his daysack slightly.

John Carr's own mind was empty of everything except the information he needed to perform his task.

As long as he did his job, and his mates did theirs, they stood a good chance.

Though fate had a way of fucking up the very best of men.

He looked at his watch.

'We've got ten minutes to be in position for our first chance on the perimeter guard,' he said. 'If we miss him we'll we have to wait forty minutes, and that's not an option. You all know what you're doing. See you at the main gate when phase one's done.'

With that Carr stood up and started moving towards the north-western corner of the compound, followed closely by McMullen.

Geordie took up position so that he had the trigger on the main gate, and the western aspect. Fred covered rearwards, back in the direction he had come.

Eight minutes later, Carr was in position, standing up, back flat against the wall, just around the corner.

His Diemaco was slung across his front, the barrel pointing at the ground. In his right fist, down by his side, was a Welrod.

Kev McMullen was beyond him, about ten metres out from the wall, and covering back towards the north-east, just in case.

Carr pressed his transmit button. 'Geordie, we're in position,' he said.

'Roger, mate.'

Carr looked at his watch: half-past the hour.

He felt the tension beginning to build.

Fifty metres away, Skelton heard the scrape of the metal bolt from the gate – bang on time.

If nothing, they were punctual.

He watched the gate through his night-sight, waiting for the man to show.

'Standby, standby,' he said. 'That's him, one Bravo, Foxtrot out the gate, turning right, right, towards the first corner.'

'Roger,' said Carr.

'He's stopped. He's lighting a fag.'

'Roger.'

A creature of habit.

'He's at the first corner, and towards you,' said Geordie.

'Roger,' said Carr, turning so that his stomach and body were flat against the wall, his right arm now closest to the corner. This would reduce his silhouette to the sentry when he made his turn.

'Halfway.'

'Roger.'

In Carr's mind's eye, he pictured the target's location.

Any moment now, Geordie would begin to count the guy down in five metre increments, to the corner where death waited for him.

And now he made the call.

'Fifteen metres.'

No response from Carr.

He repeated the call.

Nothing. His comms had failed.

*Shit. Battery fucked.*

No time to mess around replacing it.

Carr had lifted his weapon now, so that the barrel was parallel with the ground and the muzzle was about five inches back from the corner of the wall.

But he heard nothing from Skelton.

*Come on, Geordie*, he thought. *What the fuck's happening?*

He felt blind, and vulnerable, and had an almost overwhelming urge to look around the corner, and to look back over his shoulder to see what was behind him, but he stayed firmly in position, trusting Kev to watch his back.

Skelton could only watch helplessly as the guard approached the corner.

For a moment, he aimed at the centre of the guy's back, debating whether to take the shot, but he knew that a burst from the Minimi would compromise them, and blow the whole job.

He took his finger off the trigger, trusting Carr.

The sentry turned the corner, taking a big drag on his cigarette as he did so.

Smoking wasn't going to kill him, but it helped: he was more interested in his fag than his patrolling, and was completely unprepared for what happened next.

He walked blindly around the corner, sucking on his fake Marlboro, and straight into the barrel of John Carrs's Welrod.

Carr pushed the barrel forwards and squeezed the trigger.

A fraction of a second after that, the 9mm round should have left the muzzle with the merest 'pop' and entered the man's head through the right side of his temple, just above the eye, smashing its way into his brain and out the back, taking half of his skull with it.

But what actually happened was nothing.

A faulty percussion cap had prevented the bullet from firing.

The Welrod was a single-shot weapon, which required a manual reload.

And there was no time for that.

Carr reacted instantly, hurling the pistol straight into the still-reeling sentry's face and simultaneously reaching with his left hand for the handle of the Damascus steel fighting knife and drawing it quickly from its sheath.

He punched the blade directly into the man's chest, and felt the impact as the blade stopped on one of the magazines on his chest rig.

That half-second was all it took for the guy to recover his wits.

As Carr's knife glanced off the mag, the sentry reached for the cocking lever on his AK.

But the safety was on, and the lever stayed in place.

Frantically, too shocked to cry out, he raised the barrel of the rifle and stabbed it forwards at Carr, catching him on the right side of his collarbone.

The impact split the skin, pushing him back momentarily, but he caught himself, and surged towards the Chechen, ignoring the flare of pain in his shoulder, driven by the need to finish this quickly.

Free hand grabbing at his opponent's throat, the knife hand drawn back, he pushed the man back and down onto the soft earth.

Closing his eyes to protect them against the desperate fingers which were now clawing and scrabbling at his face, Carr moved his hand over the guy's mouth and rapidly punched his blade four, five, six times into the exposed rib cage at the side.

For a moment, the mortally wounded man's strength seemed to increase, but then his hands fell from Carr's face and he went limp.

He was still breathing, but it was laboured, frothy blood from his ruptured lung spilling from his mouth.

Then he gave a kind of resigned sigh and was silent.

Carr wiped the knife and his bloodied gloves on the dead man's tunic, recovered the Welrod, and stood up.

As he re-sheathed the knife, Kev McMullen appeared at his

elbow. 'What the fuck happened?' he whispered. 'I'm watching our six and then I turn round and you're rolling around on the floor with the cunt.'

'Fucking Welrod didn't fire,' said Carr, under his breath. 'Had to use the knife.'

'You okay?'

'He fucked my shoulder up a bit,' said Carr. 'But I'm fine.'

He looked at the pistol.

'Need to know this bastard works,' he said. 'Wait one.'

He twisted the cocking mechanism at the rear of the weapon to expel the dud round from the chamber, and then pushed it forward to reload the weapon.

He put the barrel to the head of the man at his feet and pulled the trigger.

This time, the weapon gave its characteristic near-silent pop, and a neat entry hole appeared in the guy's forehead.

Shaking his head and muttering to himself, Carr reloaded it and replaced it in its holster.

A few metres away, Geordie Skelton breathed a sigh of relief and quickly replaced his dead battery.

Carr dragged the body fully around the corner, and keyed his mike.

'All call-signs, phase one complete,' he whispered. 'Move to the gate.'

'Me and Fred moving, John,' said Skelton. 'Fucking battery died. Sorry, mate.'

'Doesn't matter, Geordie,' said Carr. 'Least of our worries.'

Carr threw a quick look to make sure Kev was following, and they quickly moved along the wall towards the main gate, the shapes of Geordie and Kev approaching from the south-west, moving purposefully towards the judas gate, and their entry point, and phase two.

After that it was all into the unknown.

# 95.

THE FOUR MEN were stacked up outside the judas gate.

John Carr was at the front, on the hinged side to the right, Kevin McMullen behind him.

They were the entry men, first through the breach.

Each carried a suppressed Diemaco: they had no idea how many fighters were on the other side of the wall, and that ruled out the single-shot Welrod.

Of course, this increased the chance that they would be heard going in.

But Carr was confident that the hum of the generator, and the noise from the multiple aircon units protruding from the walls of the villa, would mask the crack of his shots to anyone who wasn't close.

Anyone who *was* close would see him coming anyway.

It would be the last thing they *did* see.

Facing them were Fred and Geordie, the method-of-entry team.

They were armed with Minimis – more cumbersome, true, but they would need that sheer firepower once they were inside the confines of the walls. Room clearances would be down to Carr and McMullen.

Skelton was at the back, watching their rear.

Fred West was at the front – he would create the breach, provide the entry point.

There are many ways to effect entry. Sometimes you blow a man-sized hole in a wall. Sometimes you smash down the door with a sledgehammer, or take off the hinges with a shotgun, or just turn the handle. In this case, West would simply knock on the door.

Once the guy on the other side started to open it, Fred would lean forward, give it a push, and stand back as the entry men went through and started their killing.

Just to his left, placed against the wall, was an explosive entry charge which he had constructed.

This was a highly unpredictable moment, and you always want an alternative in case something goes wrong. If the man at the gate somehow got wind of them, and refused to open up, they would quickly reconfigure and use the charge to blow the whole of the main gates off.

And now Carr watched as the man from the West Country did a final check to make sure that he could see the connector for the M57 initiation device – or 'clacker' – which was attached to his left leg.

When activated, it would send an electrical impulse to the detonator, causing a small explosion which would, in turn, activate the main plastic explosive charge.

If the initial entry plan did fail, then it would take Fred mere moments to connect the initiator and detonate the explosives.

Carr hefted his Diemaco in his hands, and checked that the safety was off.

He took a long, slow breath, and aimed the muzzle at the gate.

Behind him, Kevin McMullen reached forward and pushed his left hand beyond Carr's shoulder, giving him a clear thumbs-up to signal that he was ready to go, before gripping his own Diemaco and following his leader's aim.

Carr glanced down at his watch.

Seven minutes since the guard had exited to conduct his perimeter check, and now Carr heard movement from inside the compound.

Obviously his mate, coming back to get ready to open the judas gate on the signal.

It was time.

He looked directly at Geordie and Fred, nodding once he had made eye contact.

A few seconds, now.

Carr steeled himself, preparing mentally for what was to come, running through the drill.

It was like a well-practised dance routine, and it needed to be fast and fluid.

As soon as that gate opened he was going to kill the man on the other side, and then he was going to step straight through to confront whatever threat lay beyond.

He would go left or right, making an instantaneous decision based purely on what he saw in front of him, and he would then take responsibility for a ninety-degree arc starting from the wall behind him.

McMullen, a half-second afterwards, would be responsible for the opposite ninety degrees.

You were committed, then – right or wrong, you went with it and you trusted your partner.

Fred West looked across at him, nodded, and gave two rapid bangs on the steel.

Close up, the scraping, ringing sound of the bolt being slid back was loud.

The judas gate started to swing slowly inwards on the hinges beside Carr, who was now getting his first glimpse into the inner compound.

West stepped forward and, using all his weight, gave an almighty push.

As the gate was propelled rapidly inwards, he moved smoothly out the way, and took control of his Minimi.

Carr stepped into the breach as it expanded.

The gate man was exactly where Carr had expected him to be, slightly to the right and off-balance, surprised at the sudden violence of the opening.

His brain didn't have time to tell his body what to do about the strange man who had burst through: before he knew what was happening, two 5.56mm rounds from Carr's Diemaco smashed into his chest.

The first hit a rib and split into four fragments which chopped his left lung to pieces. The second glanced off his sternum, and exited out of his side, taking a tennis ball-sized lump of his liver with it.

He dropped where he stood and Carr moved past him, kicking away the AK that he'd been holding, and quickly clearing his arcs.

To his left, McMullen was doing the same.

The compound was clear.

Carr took a second to orientate himself, scanning the windows of the villa for any motherfucker reacting to his shots.

So far, nothing.

To his front, the main house was all in darkness.

To his left, against the wall at that side, the generator – louder now, its noise contained with the walls – and its oil tank.

Further into the compound, around the right hand side of the house, he could see about a third of the servants' quarters, a faint sliver of golden light glowing under a window shutter.

He was praying that that was indeed where the women would be: if it came to fighting their way through the main building it was going to be very unpleasant.

Geordie and Fred came through the gate, Fred pausing to activate the radio control receiver on his explosive charge.

That would allow him to blow it remotely, now, which might

be very useful if they found themselves having to leave in a hurry, or wanted to add to the confusion and chaos that they were about to unleash.

As Geordie closed the gate behind him, sliding the bolt back into place, Fred quickly dragged the body of the guard a few metres away, into the darker shadow at the base of the wall. To a casual observer, there would be nothing untoward at the front gate: everything now was about buying a few seconds before the inevitable happened.

If they could, they'd get in and out without firing another shot, but they all knew that life wasn't like that.

They were about to have a fight on their hands.

All four men now went to ground, scanning their arcs, ready to start that fight.

It seemed like an eternity since the gate man had unwittingly allowed his killers entry, but in fact no more than a minute had elapsed.

And now, above the sound of the generator, Carr suddenly caught the sound of the guy's laboured breathing from a few feet away where he lay, his blood staining the sand black.

Then he groaned, softly.

'Fuck,' Carr said to himself.

He stepped across, placed the barrel of the Diemaco against the man's forehead, and put him out of his misery.

*I bet you didn't think you'd end up like that sixty seconds ago, pal*, he thought. *Funny how life turns out, eh?*

He turned to Fred West and gave him the thumbs-up.

West moved forward and around to the left of the villa. There he went down on one knee, placed his Minimi down close at hand, and removed the bar mine from his pack. He placed it alongside the wall of the villa, opposite the generator and its fuel tank, grinning to himself as he activated the RC receiver for the detonator.

Second device activated and in place, and that one would be awesome when he detonated it – the walls would contain the fearsome blast of the 8.4 kilograms of RDX/TNT, designed to take out a main battle tank, and kill or seriously fuck up anyone inside the villa on that side.

As an added bonus, it would set the generator fuel tank on fire, and generate a massive fireball which would create further pandemonium.

West almost chuckled.

Finally, he checked his transmitter – full charge.

Happy, he doubled back, crouching in front of the villa.

He removed a Claymore from his pack and set it down five metres from the front door, at an angle of forty-five degrees.

He'd thought about a tripwire, here – catch any bastard who came running out looking for trouble – but, as Carr had pointed out, they couldn't rule out the possibility that the women were inside, and that the wankers would hustle them out that way.

Be a shame to come all this way and reduce the hostages to mince.

So device three was also on RC.

The moment West activated it, anyone who came out of that door was going to be shredded by 700 3.2mm steel ball-bearings, propelled outwards at 1,200 metres per second by 680g of C4.

That part of his job done, Fred quickly moved back to the team, gave Carr the thumbs-up, and took up position facing the villa.

Carr turned back to the servants' quarters.

He moved slightly right, to get a better angle, and raised his Diemaco, looking at the small outbuilding through the scope.

To its right were three vehicles – a Hilux and a couple of Land Cruisers.

But what really caught his attention was the guard sitting outside the door on a chair, an AK47 held slack across his lap.

Completely oblivious – he looked like he was dozing.

Certainly hadn't reacted to the shots.

So far, so lucky.

And that had to be where the girls were, thought Carr. No way they were guarding it for any other reason.

He looked over his left shoulder.

'Psst,' he said.

Kev McMullen looked at him.

Carr made a thumbs-down sign.

*Enemy.*

Then he indicated towards the servants' quarters, and pointed first to himself and then to McMullen.

*We're going over there.*

McMullen gave a thumbs-up.

*Roger.*

He passed the signal on to the others, and then the four of them were off and moving, as a group, staying close to the wall, using the extra darkness it created and the sound of the generator to move as stealthily and as quickly as they could.

*En route*, Carr placed Fred and Geordie down with their two Minimis, their role being to cover the main villa and the gate.

Both men lay prone, a few metres apart, weapons into their shoulders, 200-round drums fixed with others at their side, ready for a quick change.

The two weapons systems would be devastating at close range: 800rpm of 7.62mm flying around at 3,000 feet per second would really ruin anyone's day.

Cautiously, as quietly as possible, Carr and McMullen moved behind the three vehicles and close to the far wall.

Phase 2 was over: they were inside the compound, with everyone in position.

Now to start Phase 3.

Find the women, and get out alive.

# 96.

INSIDE THE SERVANTS' quarters, Charlotte Morgan lay on a thin, grey mattress against one wall.

She was still secured to the bedframe by a cable tie around one wrist, but her legs were free; early on, both women had been chained round the ankle, but the ball-ache of taking the chains on and off so that they could use the bucket toilet in the corner of the room had worn the guards down.

Charlotte stank of urine and sweat and filth, and her body was sore and emaciated from days of gastroenteritis, but she was in better condition than Martha Percival.

While Charlotte was consumed with thoughts of escape, and revenge, she knew that her friend had long since given up.

Martha had said barely a word since they had been taken from the beach – the sight of her husband being gunned down in front of her eyes had clearly been too much for her – and all of Charlotte's efforts to raise her spirits had come to nothing.

Charlotte looked over at her, in the glow from a single, low-wattage bulb in a cheap, bare table lamp which stood in the dust in one corner.

She was lying on a similar mattress twenty feet away on the other side of the room, her back turned and facing the wall.

She'd been like that almost permanently since they had been moved to this location a few days earlier.

Martha had slimmed down for the holiday – Charlotte remembered her complaining good-naturedly, on the flight out to Málaga, that it had taken her eight weeks to lose three kilograms – but now she looked a bag of bones.

Somewhere in her rational, detached, lawyer's mind, Charlotte Morgan noted, to her surprise, that it was amazing how quickly you lost weight in the right circumstances.

And the weight was only part of it: Martha was a striking woman, but now her face was covered in lesions and cold sores, and her hair was thinning and full of flaking skin.

Charlotte hadn't seen her own face in a mirror for many days, but she had to imagine that she herself looked no better.

And she was glad: there had been a time when the man with dark eyes, the man called Argun, had looked at her in a way which made her feel frightened.

But he'd never taken his opportunity, and now he no longer looked at her in the same way.

On the same side of the room as Martha were two guards.

The older of the two was leaning against the wall and losing the fight to stay awake; his head kept dropping and then coming back up, and each time his eyes opened wide, and a startled expression crossed his face.

The younger, the good-looking Eastern European in his early twenties who liked to frighten Charlotte with that horrible, fearful suicide vest, was sitting cross-legged on the floor, cleaning the stripped-down parts of an AK47 with an oily rag.

Every now and then, he looked up and over at Charlotte, and when he did that it sent a shudder through her: his eyes were merciless and cold and empty, like those of a shark.

To his left, lying in the far corner, was the vest.

Lately, perhaps because of the heat, or because of complacency, the young guard had not bothered to put it on whenever he came in to take over the watch.

But it was close enough at hand, and Charlotte could still see the detonator, and the wire.

Mesmerised, she looked at it, and only tore her gaze away as she saw the man's eyes turning towards her.

For the thousandth time, she tried to work out what her chances of survival were.

She had had no contact with the outside world from the moment she'd been seized in Marbella, and her captors had said very little to her. The fact that she was still alive meant that she had some value to them – whether as a bargaining tool for some prisoner release, or a political goal of some sort, or as a mere commodity to be traded for a sum of money, she didn't know.

She hoped it was the latter: she knew that her father could raise almost whatever capital sum was needed, but that there was no way that her mother would be able to make significant and overt changes to British government policy just for her own daughter. Charlotte had listened to enough dinner table talk to know that.

Though it was probably a moot point, anyway. Even if it *was* just a financial thing, she had very little confidence that the people who were holding her would keep their side of any deal.

So, as it did dozens of times each day, her mind turned again to the question of whether there was a way – any way, however impractical or risky – that she could get herself and Martha out of here.

Several times, the guards – clearly comfortable that she was no kind of a threat – had left one of their weapons close to her.

An AK47 – everyone knew that was what they were called, and everyone knew where the trigger was, too.

She'd thought about grabbing for it – dreamed about shooting these two, blowing their brains out, consumed by a pure, furious hatred that she didn't recognise in herself.

But she knew that there was more to it than just pulling the trigger. She'd fired shotguns, and they had safety catches, and so must AK47s. She imagined them laughing at her as she held it, not knowing what to do: more than anything, the horror and shame of trying and failing in front of them was what stopped her trying.

That, and the realisation that she had no idea what was on the other side of the door. She didn't even know which town, or which country, she was in.

It was all…

And then she heard the gunshots.

# 97.

JOHN CARR AND Kevin McMullen were fifteen or twenty metres away, in the shadows.

It was McMullen's turn to be No. 1 – first man through the breach.

The breach was to be created by Carr, using a strip-charge made up of three 6ft sections of detonating cord applied to double-sided tape, which could be quickly unrolled down the hinge side of the door.

Once placed, he would initiate the detonator with his own clacker, the charge would cut straight through the wood, and Kev would step in.

The shockwave and noise from the blast would disorientate any guards before they had a chance to react.

That, at least, was the plan.

But their first challenge was to get to the door.

Through his night-sight, Carr could see the exterior guard, dozing on his chair, AK across his lap.

If they approached him they risked waking him – and being compromised – so they'd have to take him out before they crossed the open ground.

Over on this side of the compound, the helpful rumble of the genny was less intrusive, and Carr knew that it was likely that someone would hear the shot, even with the suppressor fitted.

But sometimes caution is advised, and sometimes you just have to go for it.

Carr keyed his pressel.

He was about to do something that was unprofessional – he didn't need to send anything, because they'd be going noisy with the door charge in a matter of seconds, and that would be all the notice Geordie and Fred needed – but he had the urge to say something.

To let them know the cards were about to be thrown in the air.

A big grin spreading over his face, he simply transmitted, 'Who Dares Wins.'

Away to the rear, both men on the Minimis heard the call, and smiled.

Next to Carr, Kev McMullen heard the transmission and turned his eyes.

Carr gave him the thumbs-up, and McMullen took aim on the centre of the guard's face.

The *crack* from his weapon sounded fucking loud to Carr, but the shot was a beauty: the 5.56mm round hit the sleeping man just above the top of his nose, the pressure blowing the top of his skull clean off, taking half his brain with it, and punching him off the chair and into the dust.

And that's when their luck ran out.

The sloppy bastard had been holding the weapon with his finger on the trigger, and the safety off, and, although the bullet had stopped his brain immediately, a complex combination of chemical interactions in his spinal nervous system had caused a cadaveric spasm, a reflex electrical action which had closed his hands.

Half-a-dozen 7.62mm rounds smacked into the far wall, but the noise of the discharge, deafening and unmistakeable in the night air, blew away all hope of their remaining covert.

'Fuck,' hissed Carr, moving immediately and rapidly across the open ground towards the door.

Surprise was gone, now it was all about speed and aggression.

A second and a half, maybe two seconds after the shots, he was at the left-hand side of the door, and – ensuring that he kept his body well away from the doorway itself – was rolling the door charge down the inside edge of the flaking, white-painted wood.

A second later, he stepped back along the wall, flattened himself, and looked across at Kev, who had his weapon up and was ready to go.

There was no time for niceties.

Carr connected the end of the wire to his clacker, flicked the safety off with his thumb, gripped the device in his hand, and began to squeeze it shut.

# 98.

INSIDE THE ROOM, things had happened very quickly as soon as the gunfire sounded.

The older guard had woken up, and was looking, groggily, at the door, and reaching for his weapon.

The younger guard was frantically trying to fit his oily AK back together, and shouting, 'Adlan! Adlan! What's happening out there?'

Charlotte Morgan's heart felt as though it was about to burst from her chest – even Martha was sitting up, eyes wide, her mouth moving, but no sound coming from it.

The younger man, his hands shaking, finally managed to replace the bolt carrier and piston, and now he pushed them all the way forward.

Cursing under his breath, he picked up the carrier spring and inserted it, under tension, into the rear of the bolt carrier.

He thought he had it aligned, but as he took his hand away the spring shot back out and down onto the dusty floor.

Scrabbling for the spring, he heard movement at the door.

'Adlan?' he shouted. '*Adlan?*'

But still there was no reply, and now he felt cold terror grip his heart.

He dropped the AK and turned towards the older man.

'What do we do?' he shouted. 'Adlan isn't replying.'

The older man looked at him. He was a Libyan, a former sergeant in Gaddafi's Revolutionary Guard Corps special forces unit, and he was tired of the young Chechen blowhard's casual lack of respect.

The Chechens – they all thought they were better.

'Adlan's dead,' he said, flatly. 'Put your vest on. This is our time.'

The younger man just stared at him, his brain scrambled by fatigue and shock.

The old man raised his own AK.

'I said, put the fucking vest on, you young fool,' he spat.

With that, he fired a burst through the door – fourteen rounds, in a little over a second.

The noise was deafening, but the effect zero: Carr and McMullen had trained for this, and were expecting it, so they were standing well to the sides.

Five seconds after the outside guard had died, with the panicked shouting of men coming from inside the servants' quarters, Carr depressed his clacker.

The remnants of the door blew inwards, showering those inside with bits of wood and dust, and momentarily stupefying them.

McMullen pushed straight through the opening, moving to his left, weapon into his shoulder.

His mind was working at light-speed, fired by a potent cocktail of adrenalin, cortisol, and testosterone.

He took in and processed his arc in half a second or so.

Standing not three metres away was a man – an AK47 raised and pointing towards the doorway.

The man pulled his trigger a second time, but he had been blinded and disoriented by the flash from the explosion and his wild, unaimed burst rattled harmlessly high into the wall above the door.

And then his magazine was empty.

McMullen fired rapidly into the centre of the shooter, knocking him backwards and down, large chunks of meat and bone exploding from the exit holes in his back.

At the same time, McMullen saw something move, near the wall to the left of the man, and realised it was a girl.

Dressed in shapeless black.

She started to scream.

*Six seconds.*

Room combat is all about speed, aggression and surprise: you trust your partner to cover his arc, you kill everyone who needs killing in yours, and you live or die by how well you execute these skills.

Carr had punched through the murder hole immediately after McMullen, going right and clearing the opening.

As he'd gone through, he'd first heard the AK, and the rounds smacking into the plasterwork above his head, and then the reply from Kev's weapon.

He resisted the urge to turn and help, and instead searched for targets of his own.

In the choking dust and darkness, he picked out a woman, curled up on a bed, hands over her head, and the shape of a man, moving purposefully from left to right.

Instantly, John Carr fired two shots.

The first clipped the guy in the right elbow, deflecting the bullet down and out of his arm at the wrist, taking out both of those joints, along with the controlling tendons and most of the muscle, and rendering his arm useless.

The second round took the man in the hip, ripped onwards through his stomach, and dropped him, blood spraying and pumping, to the floor.

Somewhere in the back of his mind, Carr congratulated himself: not bad shooting, when you've just had a dozen 7.62mm rounds fired six inches over your head.

The target was screaming and writhing in pain, but he was also trying to drag himself into the corner of the room, his good arm stretching out for something.

Carr fired a single shot into the crawling man's head.

The round smashed his skull open, painting the floor and wall with brain and other tissue, and the overpressure forced his eyes from their sockets.

He flopped to the floor, blood pulsing from his shattered body and quickly beginning to pool around him.

*Eight seconds.*

'Clear the room, Kev,' shouted Carr.

He maintained a firing position, half-turned to watch McMullen, but keeping his weapon aimed at the girl sitting on the mattress in front of him.

From outside, came the heavy, percussive rattle of several AK47s, and responding bursts of fire – controlled, deliberate, aimed – from the Minimis of Geordie Skelton and Fred West.

Behind him, McMullen moved towards the man he'd shot, who was thrashing noiselessly around on the ground, and placed the barrel of his Diemaco to the man's forehead. The guy actually pressed upwards against the hot steel, almost gratefully, embracing his end as Kev pulled the trigger.

McMullen patted the two women down, looking for weapons in their shapeless clothing. Once he was happy that they posed no threat, he quickly cleared the rest of the room.

When he got to the corner near Carr, he turned.

'Suicide vest,' he said.

*Twelve seconds.*

'Aye,' said Carr. 'They…'

But just then, the girl sat up, and pointed at the man he'd shot.

'Shoot that bastard!' she yelled. 'Shoot him! Shoot him!'

'Stay down,' shouted Carr, holding out his hand, palm up. 'He's already dead. Stay the fuck down, and shut up.'

But the girl ignored him, and stood up.

McMullen turned, hand to her chest, and pushed her firmly back onto the bed.

'Stay down,' he barked. 'And be fucking quiet.'

'Shoot him,' she said, more quietly.

'He's fucking dead,' said Carr.

Behind him, he became aware of the sound of the other woman, wailing.

Over his shoulder, Carr said, 'For fuck's sake, Kev, shut her up, will you?'

But McMullen, on that side of the room, was already grabbing her by the shoulders.

'You're okay,' he said, staring into her eyes. 'We're here to help, but you've got to be quiet.'

The screaming continued, so McMullen slapped her hard across the face.

She shut up.

For the first time since they had entered the room there was silence.

Apart from the cacophony of the firefight going on outside.

'Which one of you is Charlotte Morgan?' said Carr.

No reply.

He looked at the nearest of them.

'Which one's Charlotte?' he said, louder.

'I am,' she said. 'It's me.'

'And that's Martha?' said Carr.

'Yes. Did he have to slap her?'

Carr looked down at her.

It was too dark – and she was too skinny and dirty and bedraggled – for him to positively identify her, but he'd heard her voice and knew that it was her.

*Tough little fucker, worrying about her mate, with all this shit going on around her, and after all they'd been through.*

'He did,' he said. 'We need to get out of here, and you girls need to listen in. It's not over yet.'

As he spoke, there was a loud bang outside – the sound of Fred West setting off the Claymore positioned outside the front door to the main building.

That meant men had been coming through.

And he could hear the distinctive sound of the Minimis, and the duration of the bursts was increasing, as Geordie and Fred attempted to gain the upper hand and win the firefight.

But there was a lot of AK flying back the other way: they were in a major contact, clearly, and time was pressing.

Carr turned, keying his pressel, trying to get some situational awareness out of the empty doorway.

A few rounds punched into the outside wall.

He looked at his watch.

Less than a minute since they'd entered.

He transmitted blind, not expecting the guys to answer.

'Jackpot, Jackpot, Jackpot,' he said.

*We've got them both.*

'Who are you?' said Charlotte Morgan. 'SAS?'

'Close,' said Carr. 'All you need to know is we're the good guys and we're going to get you out of here. But it's not going to be easy. Can you run?'

'Out of *here*?' said Charlotte. 'Of course I can bloody run.'

*Good girl*, thought Carr, again. *Ballsy as fuck.*

'Her?' he said, nodding at Martha.

Martha Percival was lying back on her bed, staring wide-eyed at them, making a low, croaky moan through her filthy, skeletal fingers.

'I don't know,' said Charlotte.

'Can you help her? We need to be able to use our weapons.'

'Yes,' said Charlotte. 'Of course.'

'Quick,' said Carr, using his knife to slice through the plastic tie holding her to the bed. 'And keep your head down.'

Charlotte Morgan got off her bed and ran across the room to Martha.

Carr cut her tie, too, and then knelt by the two women, as Kev McMullen – standing back in the dark shadows of the room – fired a couple of shots at fleeting targets.

'Listen,' he said. 'Stick with us and just do as we say, yes?'

Charlotte nodded. Martha did not respond.

'Get her up,' said Carr.

Charlotte tried to pull her friend upright, but she was a dead weight.

'Please, Martha,' she said. 'Stand. Come on, you need to.'

But the other woman just sat there, eyes vacant.

'Fuck,' said Carr. 'Okay, change of plan. Kev, you're going to have to carry her, mate.'

McMullen put a thumb up.

Carr turned to Charlotte. 'Right, listen,' he said, speaking slowly and clearly. 'You hear all that shit going on out there? That's where we're going, okay? You need to get your head round that.'

Charlotte nodded, trying to ignore the terrifying noise.

'I know it's scary,' said Carr, 'but you'll be fine if you do as I say. I'll lead, you follow. And stay close. Kev will bring up the rear with Martha. Do not stop for *anything.* Understand? Doesn't matter what happens, you keep moving. You stop moving, it's game over.'

'Yes,' said Charlotte. 'Yes, yes, I understand. Keep moving, never stop. I understand.'

She realised that she was gabbling, but in her defence she was terrified. The shooting outside was unbelievable – she could hear bullets smacking into the walls, and the ricochets pinging off into the night.

Suddenly, she didn't want to leave.

She felt safe inside this building, behind the block walls, and the dirty-white plaster.

But she knew that that feeling was an illusion.

She didn't want to leave, but she had to.

She looked up at Carr – marvelling at how calm, and assured, and in control he looked.

'What's your name?' she said.

'What?' said Carr.

'What's your name? If I'm going to die here, I'd like to know the name of the man who tried to save me.'

'You're not going to die as long as you do as I say,' said Carr. 'Then again, I have been known to be wrong. So I'm John. That's Kev, and outside are Geordie and Fred.'

'Is that it?' she said.

'That's your lot, darling,' said Carr. 'But we don't need any more than that.'

He bent his head and spoke into his mike.

'Geordie, Fred,' he said. 'Stand by to give rapid fire and blow the gates on my call. We're about to come out.'

Carr looked at McMullen. 'You ready, mate?' he said.

'Yep,' replied McMullen. 'I'm fucking ready, John.'

# 99.

OUTSIDE, GEORDIE SKELTON and Fred West had taken up supporting positions a few metres apart, behind what cover they could find.

Each man had a belt of 200 rounds fed into his Minimi, and ready to go, and a further 600 alongside him, with more stowed in his pack.

They'd heard Carr's 'Who Dares Wins' call, and then the burst of fire from inside the servants' quarters.

A few seconds later, Carr's door charge had gone off, and all hell had broken loose.

They heard more shooting – clearly AK – from inside the small outbuilding, and glanced over at each other.

But they were committed, and there was nothing they could do to help – they were about to have their own hands very full indeed.

If it was all going south then they'd deal with it, as and when they could.

For now, they waited, weapons into their shoulders, focused on the main villa – where the reaction would surely come from.

And come it did.

From an upstairs window, a man opened up on the servant's quarters with an AK.

Immediately, Geordie Skelton put a burst of a dozen rounds into the room and the guy vanished.

Whether he'd been dropped or had just taken cover, Skelton couldn't tell, but his fire had the effect of drawing the attention of the fighters inside the villa to his position.

Several weapons opened up from various points inside the building, and both Skelton and Fred West replied – relying on their better accuracy and discipline, and the far greater weight of fire that their Minimis could supply, compared with the assault rifles being used against them, to keep them on top.

Suddenly, the front door of the villa opened, and three men emerged.

They started to move towards the corner of the building which would lead them around to the servants' quarters, but they'd taken only a few steps when West detonated his Claymore, showering them in a lethal hail of molten steel.

Two were killed instantly, eviscerated by the fragmentation, but the third, almost unbelievably, was left unscathed. Skelton tracked the man with his muzzle as he turned and ran back into the building, but he was unable to catch up with him before he vanished.

'Lucky fucking bastard,' breathed Geordie.

Both he and Fred – moving to whatever new cover they could find – began to fire deliberate, aimed bursts through the windows, trying to keep the men inside on the back foot.

It seemed to be working – the incoming was patchy and sporadic – until they were lit up by a long burst from an automatic weapon coming from the villa.

It was inaccurate, but it was close enough.

'Where the fuck's that come from?' shouted Skelton.

'I didn't...' said West.

But then there was a second burst, closer this time, and he saw a hint of muzzle flash from one of the upper floor windows.

The fucker was keeping his weapon in the room, and firing

from depth – he knew what he was doing, but it also made it difficult for him to locate Skelton and West, and so he was firing blind.

Fred West put a long burst into the room, and the shooter quietened down.

And then the weight of the enemy fire dramatically increased again.

It was coming from several of the ground and upper floor windows, and was clearly concentrated and controlled by someone who was giving commands, and was no fool.

It was inaccurate, mostly smacking into the wall high behind them, but both Geordie and Fred recognised it immediately for what it was – an attempt at suppressive fire, intended to force their heads down.

That could only mean that other fighters were going to try and flank them.

Geordie heard Carr's 'Jackpot, Jackpot, Jackpot' call over the net at exactly the same moment that he saw movement at the left-hand corner of the building in front of him.

As the tempo of fire from the building increased again, two men stepped out from the corner.

One began firing at Geordie Skelton, close enough that he heard the whine of the rounds passing his head.

The other had something long over his shoulder, and now he levelled it at the two Britons.

'RPG!' shouted Geordie, firing a sustained burst at the men.

He hit them both, but not before the RPG man pulled the trigger on his weapon.

Geordie saw the blazing, firework trail of the warhead as it left the tube and started towards him, almost in slow motion at first, until the warhead suddenly seemed to accelerate.

It disappeared harmlessly over the wall and out into the desert; Skelton just had time to confirm that both shooters were dead where they'd stood before he was back on his gun and trying to kill a man who was firing two- and three-round bursts from an upper window.

Just as he thought he'd got the guy, his weapon stopped firing.

'Stoppage!' he shouted, cursing.

At that exact moment, Fred West yelled the same thing from his position a few metres away, down behind a short, fat date palm.

There was a split second's silence, as both men realised that they'd run out at the same time.

'Change your belt, Kev, change your belt,' shouted Skelton. With that, he stood up and reached for the 66mm LAW he was carrying on his back.

'Motherfucker,' he said, feeling for the pin holding the rear cap in place and pulled it out, the sling taking the front cap away too.

As he extended the weapon, he felt the rounds from multiple firing points passing him – standing there like this, big bastard target that he was, was truly shit without covering fire.

For a fleeting moment, his courage almost failed him, the desire to take cover all but overwhelming.

But it passed in a heartbeat: he had to do this, or they were fucked.

Geordie fully extended the weapon, pulled the arming lever forward, and quickly aligned the sight with the upper window where most of the fire was coming from.

As he located the target, something punched him in the chest and rocked him back a little – a single round had hit him straight over the heart, but his body armour had done its job.

Taking a breath, he realigned the sight and depressed the firing mechanism.

The flaming trail of the rocket flew straight into the blockwork just to the side of the window, spewing white-hot shrapnel and heavy chunks of masonry into the room.

He had no way of knowing it, but the shot had killed two of the shooters and mortally wounded a third.

He threw the empty tube away and dived back behind his Minimi, feeding a new belt into it as Fred's weapon banged away to his right.

'They fucking shot me, Fred,' he shouted.

'You mental bastard,' shouted West, not moving his eye from his gunsight. 'That was fucking crazy.'

Over to his right, near the servants' quarters, he saw a figure, crouching low, holding a long weapon, run from behind the house and get down behind the three vehicles which were parked there.

Moving the muzzle, West fired a long burst into the area around the vehicles.

A moment later, and to his irritation, he saw the figure run back for the safety of the building.

'You okay, you daft cunt?' he yelled.

'Think so,' shouted back Skelton. 'Thank fuck for Kevlar.'

It seemed like an eternity they'd been out here, but it had in reality been no more than two minutes.

And they were starting to win the firefight.

They'd never know how many men they had killed, and how many had been wounded or had just lost their nerve, but the weight of fire coming back at them was definitely dropping.

But it was not finished.

'We need to get the fuck out of here,' shouted Geordie Skelton.

'No fucking shit,' said Fred.

*Come on, John*, thought Geordie. *Our luck won't last forever.*

And just then he heard Carr's voice in his earpiece.

*'Geordie, Fred. Stand by to give rapid fire and blow the gates on my call. We're getting ready to come out.'*

'Roger,' said Geordie.

Over to his right, Fred West was already reaching for his detonator.

Skelton resumed a steady rate of fire into the building.

# 100.

KHASMOHMAD KADYROV and Argun Shishani had barely lain back down on their mattresses when the first shots rang out.

Shishani sprang up, heart beating hard, and hurried down the corridor to Kadyrov's room.

This time, he barged in without knocking.

'They found us, brother,' he said, his voice high with an unexpected panic.

Outside, there was the sound of an explosion.

'Calm yourself, Argun,' said Kadyrov, reaching for his AKS-74U Krinkov. 'Who has found us?'

'I don't know,' said Shishani. 'The shooting… I just thought…'

Kadyrov cut him off, irritably.

'Fear is for women, and stories are for children,' he said, clapping the younger man on the shoulder. 'I need to know what *is* happening, not what you *think* is happening. Go and find out.'

As Shishani left the room, he almost collided with a tall, well-built man.

It was Ayub – head of the military side of the operation, and a man who had been fighting almost constantly, and fearlessly, since Podrinje in 1992.

He was shouting, 'To arms, brothers. Prepare yourselves. To your fighting positions, quickly, quickly.'

As he spoke, he shook his head: he'd warned Kadyrov that the whores should be inside the main building, where they could be guarded more closely, but the great emir had refused to sleep under the same roof as them.

He'd asked also for more battle-hardened Chechens like himself, but had been given only four. The rest were a rag-tag group of assorted Libyans and Egyptians – men who could barely shoot straight, despite his drilling, and had been chosen only because they could be liquidated when all of this was over.

He'd been promised reinforcements from the south, but they had never shown up.

Well, now perhaps his warnings were coming home.

'Ayub,' said Shishani. 'What's going on?'

Ayub stopped. He had little time for Shishani, sensing a weakness behind his bravado; while he was in theory answerable to the other man, he respected only Kadyrov, and regularly went to him over Shishani's head.

'I know as much as you do,' he said, curtly. 'Something's happening outside. I've sent my best men to see.'

'The guards at the gate?'

'I can't raise them. Nor the ones with the whores.'

Shishani nodded, trying to maintain some sense of authority.

'Very well,' he said. 'Report back to me when you know...'

But as he spoke there was a loud *crump* from the front of the villa – Fred West's Claymore being detonated – and the flash from the explosion lit up the house and corridor, followed a millisecond later by the sound of every window on the front elevation shattering, and then the rattle of automatic gunfire, incoming and outgoing.

Shishani had dropped to the floor, but Ayub had remained standing, and now he looked down at his dark-eyed comrade.

'Well,' he said, a mocking smile on his lips. 'I think that answers our questions. We're under attack, and someone has come for the women. Maybe you should go and get your weapon, and come with me.'

With that, he turned on his heel and stepped into the nearest room.

'Kill them, kill them!' he shouted, as he went. 'Allahu akbar, Allahu akbar!'

The intensity of the firefight increased, rounds bouncing off the walls and occasionally ricocheting into the corridor, as Shishani began crawling back towards his room.

Through the open doorway, he heard Ayub shout, 'Heavy fire, brothers, heavy fire! Ibrahim and another are moving around. Heavy fire!'

The tempo increased further still, as Ayub and the three men with him blazed away at the two shooters down below, emptying magazine after magazine.

Ayub was just starting to move forwards – he would have to risk showing himself to get a better shot – when he heard Ibrahim's RPG7 fire.

But there was no explosion from the warhead – he must have missed – and now Ayub was a few feet from the shattered glass, and he saw the RPG detonate far off in the desert on the other side of the wall.

And then, down below, he saw a dark shadow rise.

'Him!' he shouted. 'Shoot him!'

The figure below stood there, like a rock in a raging sea, rounds missing him by a few feet at most, and lifted a tube onto his shoulder.

Ayub had time to marvel at his enemy's courage, and the time to recognise that he was carrying some sort of missile launcher, and the time to take careful aim at the man with his own AK.

He fired one shot at the man, aiming for his chest.

He was an excellent marksman, and he clearly saw the target stagger back slightly from the impact, but when he pulled the trigger again he heard the dead man's click.

He pressed the magazine release catch out, and the empty mag clattered onto the floor. He was feeling for its replacement when he saw the flash as the 66mm rocket left the launcher.

Ayub's remaining sensations were confused and brief and unpleasant.

There was a bright flash a metre to his left, and then he was picked up and thrown across the room, as though by a giant hand.

He was knocked unconscious, but he came round after a few seconds, puzzled as to why he was on his back, on the floor.

A moment later, the pain hit – the fireball from the 66mm HEAT explosion had roasted the entire front left side of his body.

He couldn't see anything – his eyeballs had both been cooked to opacity – and he couldn't hear anything, either. The initial blast wave had been followed immediately by a rapid and transient depressurisation, and this sudden double change in the local air pressure had destroyed his inner ears.

It had also ruptured his lungs and his gastro-intestinal tract, and he would probably have died of these injuries in a matter of hours.

But what was actually going to kill him, much more quickly, were the devastating injuries caused by the fragmentation from the warhead and scabbing from the wall which had hit him at colossal speed, ripping open the front of his body.

He made to stand up, but found that he couldn't, and when he reached down he found that his legs were gone from the thigh down.

He lay there for a few moments, his lifeblood spreading across the marble tiles of the floor, encircling empty cartridge cases and chunks of masonry and jagged lumps of steel.

He was confused but just before he slipped away he smiled through cracked, blackened lips: he was on his way to paradise, sent there by a brave warrior who had stood like a rock in the sea.

In the hallway outside, Shishani had hit the ground again at the sound of this second, bigger blast.

And now he watched in horror as a wounded fighter – he

couldn't recognise his burned, bloodied face – stumbled from the room, blood pumping from multiple holes in his body.

'Ayub is dead,' choked the man, whom Shishani now saw was one of the Egyptian mercenaries. 'Ayub is dead. They're all dead.'

With that, the man collapsed onto his knees, and died where he knelt.

Shishani closed his eyes and looked deep into his own soul.

He could still hear the sound of automatic fire, though most of it seemed to be incoming now.

He could also hear men screaming and wailing.

Whoever was outside, they were good.

There must be many of them.

All those years earlier, fighting with Basayev and the 055 at Mazar-e Sharif in Afghanistan, that shell splinter which had ripped away half of his calf – even as he'd lain there, bleeding and waiting for help, he'd known that this was a lucky wound.

A wound that would get him out of there, with his head held high.

He was recovering in a makeshift field hospital even as his comrades were butchered.

He'd tried to convince himself that he'd been saved for a greater day – but now that that greater day seemed upon him it occurred to him that he didn't really want to die.

Not yet.

All around him was the sound of automatic gunfire.

Another fighter appeared – a young Libyan, unscathed, wide-eyed.

'Argun,' said the fighter. 'Almost everyone is dead or wounded. What do we do?'

Shishani opened his eyes and looked at him.

'You and me, Jalal,' he said. 'We're going out of the back gate. They must have vehicles here somewhere nearby. We can hit them as they load up.'

The man nodded.

'Good idea, Argun,' said a voice behind him.

Shishani turned to see the towering figure of Kadyrov looming over him.

'I will come with you,' said the older man.

'Maybe you should keep them occupied at the front?' said Shishani.

'No,' said Kadyrov, a strange look entering his eyes. 'We'll fight together, and die together if necessary.'

'Inshallah, brother,' said Shishani. 'Let me get my weapon.'

He ran back into the room in which he'd been sleeping, picked up his own Krinkov, and threw his magazine carrier over his shoulder.

Then, an eye on the door, he opened a bag at the foot of his bed. He pulled out two passports and a wallet stuffed with hundreds of US dollars and credit cards in four names, lifted the front of his shirt, and pushed it into his underpants.

Steeling himself, he strode from the room.

# 101.

JOHN CARR HEARD the brief lull in the fire from outside, followed by the boom of the 66mm rocket hitting the building.

A moment later, both Minimis resumed firing.

He pressed his mike.

'Rapid fire,' he said. 'Rapid fire.'

He went straight out of the doorway.

Over to his front left, he saw the muzzle flash from Geordie Skelton's gun, as the big northerner put down a withering burst of sustained fire.

A second later, Fred West blew the charge at the gates – there was a huge bang, and they were smashed inwards, twisted and ruined, taking a metre of wall with them on either side.

Almost instantly, Carr heard Fred's Minimi join Geordie's.

Carr went left, weapon up at the ready, moving fast and smooth.

Behind him, Charlotte Morgan had hesitated, frightened by the explosion and the suppressive fire, not understanding that it was for her own benefit.

Kev McMullen pushed her in the small of the back.

'Go,' he shouted. 'Fucking go!'

And she was off and running, following Carr.

Kev was a step behind, Martha Percival thrown over his left shoulder, his Diemaco held in his right hand, ready if needed.

Martha was light, but it made running awkward, and he had to fight to keep up with the others.

He was focused on that, and on getting to Geordie and Fred, and then moving beyond them and through the gaping, smoking hole where the gates had been, and he almost missed the silhouette which appeared from the corner of the building.

But he didn't miss the muzzle flash, and he heard the crack and whine of the rounds as they passed over and behind him.

Still on the run, he pulled the butt of his weapon into his side, giving him a stable position, and began firing one-handed towards the shooter.

The fourth round found the man in the groin, and he fell to the ground, out of the game.

Up ahead, Carr was ten metres out from Fred.

'Coming in from the right, coming in from the right,' he shouted, knowing that Fred would be aware of the movement coming from the servants' quarters, needing him to know that it was friendlies.

A moment later, Carr dropped down, just to the right and rear of Fred, who was continuing to put rounds into the villa.

'Get down, get down,' shouted Carr, at Charlotte.

She did as instructed, just as Kev McMullen appeared and unceremoniously dropped Martha on the ground.

'Magazine!' he shouted, quickly changing his magazine for a full one, and beginning to fire at the building to support Fred and Geordie.

'You okay, guys?' Carr shouted, over the noise.

'Aye, man,' shouted Geordie. 'But less fucking chatter, and let's get the fuck out of here.'

'Nearly there,' said Carr. 'Just a bit longer. I need to take their vehicles out. Put some fire down.'

With that he stood up and started running back towards the three pickups.

Charlotte went to rise with him, but Fred West grabbed her arm.

'Stay where you are,' he yelled. 'He'll be back.'

Carr ran to the middle vehicle, blew out the side window with three rounds, and removed the pin on a phosphorous grenade.

'Fire in the hole,' he shouted, dropping the grenade into the cab and sprinting back towards the team.

In a matter of seconds, the enormous heat from the phosphorous was igniting the vehicle, and those next to it.

Back with the team, Carr took a knee.

'Geordie, Fred,' he shouted. 'See you on the other side of the gate.'

Neither responded – they were concentrating on getting as many rounds down as possible to keep any remaining fighters on the back foot.

Carr grabbed Charlotte Morgan by the wrist and led the way.

He could hear the odd round being fired from the villa, but it was half-hearted and ineffective.

He struggled to keep a grin off his face: it was over in there, he knew it.

They had fucking done it.

They were not quite home and dry, yet, but they had *fucking done it*.

Seconds later, all four were outside the gate.

'Kev,' said Carr. 'You take the girls and fuck off into the palm trees. Go firm just inside.'

As McMullen ran off, Martha back over his shoulder, Carr turned and began to put fire back into the compound, to allow Geordie and Fred to withdraw.

He moved to get into a better position, and almost tripped over Charlotte Morgan, who was kneeling on the ground and had clearly not run with Kev.

'Get out the fucking way, Charlotte,' he said.

She moved to the side, and lay flat.

'Geordie, move now, Geordie, move now,' shouted Carr.

Inside the compound walls, Skelton heard the call.

'Time to fucking go, Fred,' he said. 'You move first.'

He fired a long burst through the area of the front door and the windows either side.

'Moving,' shouted Fred West, getting up and sprinting a short bound beyond Geordie, in the direction of the gate.

There he stopped, down on one knee, and began firing towards the building.

'Move, Geordie,' he shouted.

'Moving,' said Skelton.

They pepper-potted back like that for thirty seconds until both were clear of the gateway and alongside John Carr.

He took a final look inside the compound, through the night sight on his Diemaco.

It looked like hell on earth in there: the villa itself was alight where Geordie's 66 had hit it, and the three vehicles were well ablaze. Every window was shattered, every square metre of wall pock-marked with bullet-strikes or Claymore ball-bearings.

He could see at least five bodies.

There was no fire coming back at them, now.

'Geordie,' he said. 'Cover me towards the plantation.'

'Aye, man,' said Skelton. 'Get fucking going.'

Carr bent, grabbed Charlotte Morgan under the arm, and dragged her to her feet.

'Come on, sweetheart,' he said. 'Time to move. You're doing well. Nearly there.'

Half a minute later, they were with Kev and Martha.

Charlotte Morgan put her arms protectively around her friend and held her tight, as the two men took up positions covering back towards Geordie and Fred.

They had both ceased firing, had put a new 200-round box on their weapons, and were scanning for movement.

There was none.

'Move, Geordie,' said Fred. 'Move now.'

They repeated their withdrawal drill, but this time they were silent, their weapons ready but unused, their instructions and acknowledgments to each other hissed, not shouted.

They quickly crossed the open ground towards the plantation, where Geordie slumped down beside Carr.

'How the fuck did we get away with that?' he whispered, hoarsely. 'The bastards shot me. I always get fucking shot when I'm with you.'

Carr looked over, concerned.

'You okay?' he said.

Geordie chuckled, quietly. 'Don't worry about me, mam,' he said. 'I'm fine.'

'Fuck off,' hissed Carr. 'I just don't want to have to carry you, you fat bastard.'

He glanced at his watch.

Seven minutes since he'd stepped through the gate and killed the guard.

'And it's not over yet, mate,' he whispered.

He looked at Charlotte.

'You okay?' he said.

'I will be when I've had a fag and a stiff gin-and-tonic,' she said.

'First drink's on me,' said Carr, with a grin.

'And it's not often you hear that,' said Geordie.

But just as he spoke a new burst of automatic fire came from the compound and shredded the leaves above their heads.

Whoever was firing was guessing, but it was a reminder.

'Geordie, Kev,' said Carr. 'Take the girls and get back to the vehicles as quick as you can. Me and Fred will RV there with you in ten minutes.'

'But John...' said McMullen.

'Don't make me grip you again, you daft fucker. Just go.'

Charlotte Morgan grabbed John Carr's arm – befuddled by the dark and the noise and drama.

'What's happening?' she said.

'We've got vehicles waiting half a kilometre that way,' said Carr. 'Kev and Geordie are going to get you there. Me and Fred are just going to make sure that no one follows us up. Don't worry, we're not planning on dying. I want to get back to my kids, and Fred's got his stamp collection.'

'I'd rather stay with you,' she said, anxiously. 'I don't think...'

'Oh, for fuck's sake,' said Carr. 'Not you as well. Kev, take her and get the fuck out of here.'

'Come on, Charlotte,' said McMullen. 'There's no point fucking arguing with him.'

Carr watched them go, Skelton just behind them, and then turned back to Fred West.

'Right, mate,' he said. 'Let's blow that generator fuel tank, now, and give the bastards something else to think about.'

West grinned. 'This should be fucking exciting,' he said.

There was another wild, unaimed burst of fire from the villa.

A moment later, Fred pressed his transmit button, and there was an instant bang, and then a secondary flash and a *whoof*, as first the plastic explosive detonated and then three thousand litres of kerosene went up.

The resultant fireball went hundreds of feet into the air, turning night into day, and Carr felt the heat even at this distance. It also blew into the main building through every available aperture, sending flame and death through the rooms and hallways, incinerating several wounded fighters.

'Good work, mate,' said Carr, clapping West on the shoulder, and standing up. 'Let's go.'

Both men got up and began to run.

# 102.

KHASMOHMAD KADYROV had looked out of the upper floor of the villa, just in time to see figures moving into the plantation that lay to the side of the compound.

He assumed that they had vehicles in that direction – they had to be close, too, because they weren't going to get far on foot.

His plan – the only possible plan, now – was to pursue them and kill them.

Most of all, he wanted to kill the women.

There would be no ransom paid, but all thought of that was gone anyway.

In its place was a cold, murderous rage, born of his failure and humiliation.

He would kill those whores, or die trying.

He led the young Libyan fighter, Jalal, and Argun Shishani quickly downstairs and out of the rear door.

Kadyrov was first out of the back gate, followed by Jalal, but, in the darkness, neither man noticed Shishani hesitate behind them, and then strike off alone into the flat stretch of desert between the compound and a disused farm building three or four hundred metres north.

Because of the dark, Kadyrov waited for a moment, to allow his eyes to adjust.

As his pupils drank in the faint available light, the darkness lifted, and on the ground, a few metres on, he saw the body of the first man John Carr had killed.

His anger rose further: they had been fools, too complacent, too weak, and they had paid the price.

He began to make out the desert contours off to the right, and the shapes of the trees to his front.

He hefted his Krinkov in one big paw and turned.

'Ready?' he said.

Jalal, an RPG-7 over one shoulder, said, 'Yes, sir.'

'Argun?' said Kadyrov.

Then, more urgently, hissing, '*Argun*?'

'I think he went ahead, sir.'

'Went ahead *where*?' said Kadyrov.

Jalal said nothing, but felt himself flush in the dark.

'Doubtless he is trying to outflank them,' said Kadyrov, but in his black heart he knew the truth, and was cursing the other man. Ayub had warned him about Shishani, and he should have listened, but it was too late for that now. 'Come on.'

Hugging the wall as a guide, and hurrying as much as he reasonably could, the huge Chechen began to go forward, the shadows of the wall providing cover from view.

And then… He stopped dead, holding up a hand.

Halfway along the wall, he saw the shape of a big man enter the plantation, at the double, carrying what looked like a light machine gun.

He raised the Krinkov to his shoulder, and began to apply pressure to the trigger.

But then he thought better of it.

The chances of hitting even that one man were slight, and he would give away his own position.

He wanted them *all* dead, the women especially, and he needed to see them, not as shadows in the night.

He stood still, straining his eyes to see where the big man had gone to, readying himself for the pursuit.

As he stood there, he heard a burst of fire from above and behind him in the building.

Someone was still in there, still trying to kill the infidels: maybe all was not lost, after all.

He turned to his rear.

'Jalal,' he whispered. 'Did you see that? One of them just moved into the plantation. Quickly, quickly, come with me.'

Jalal opened his mouth to reply, but before he could speak Kadyrov felt an enormous pressure wave, and sensed rather than saw a giant fireball erupt a few metres away inside the compound.

The heat singed most of the hair and beard off that side of him, and instantly blistered his face; the pressure blew him and Jalal off their feet, and left them winded on the ground, and showered in rubble from the collapsed wall.

A sizeable chunk of the generator had landed a few metres from them, but the blockwork had taken most the force of Fred West's bar mine, and apart from his burns Kadyrov was unharmed. Thanks to the strange physics of explosions, Jalal was not hurt at all.

Gritting his teeth against the pain, Kadyrov clambered back to his feet.

And in the glow from the dying fireball, he saw two men kneeling in the palms.

Now his rage was all-consuming, and all thoughts about the women, and any careful, tactical pursuit, had vanished from his mind.

Now he just wanted to kill anyone.

He was raising the Krinkov to his shoulder when he heard the RPG-7 firing behind him – Jalal, reacting with impressive speed.

The rocket-propelled grenade exited its launcher at 117 metres-per-second, and armed itself five metres into its flight.

At eleven metres, the piezoelectric fuze activated the grenade's rocket motor and it began to accelerate.

It would eventually have reached almost 300m/s, but it was halted by the trunk of a date palm, which it struck two metres to John Carr's right, and three metres above his head.

The HEAT round was loaded with 730g of OKFOL high-explosive, enough to send its molten copper warhead knifing through armoured steel, and the blast took off the top of the tree and punched it ten metres on.

The design of the weapon meant that much of the force and the molten metal splashed harmlessly onwards and outwards, too, but some of it did not.

The blast knocked John Carr off his feet, and blew the Diemaco out of his hand.

As he lay in the dirt, gasping for air, temporarily confused, his ears ringing, he saw Fred West climb groggily onto one knee, and take aim and fire a long burst at the RPG shooter.

As the shooter went down, West turned to Carr.

'Fuck it, John,' he said. 'I'm hit.'

And, with that, he pitched, face down, into the earth.

Carr looked around himself for his weapon.

It was lying some five or six metres away.

'Wait one, Fred,' he said, as though West had any choice. He started trying to stand up. 'I'm just…'

But as he spoke, an AK started firing, the shots ripping into the trees around him at just above head height.

Carr hit the deck, and rolled away, scrabbling frantically for some sort of cover, trying to get eyes-on whoever was shooting.

He saw a huge, bearded man, not far from where the RPG firer lay.

The big, ugly fucker was coming towards him, silhouetted in the flames, firing a weapon in short, controlled bursts from the hip, like the Angel of Death, walking from the pits of hell.

Twenty-five metres away, now.

Throwing away his empty magazine.

Striding closer, a fresh mag in his hand.

Twenty metres.

Reloading the weapon, he was close enough that Carr could hear the weapon being cocked and the bolt carrier slamming forward, putting a round into the chamber.

Carr looked at his Diemaco.

No fucking chance.

He grabbed for his Sig Sauer, rolling onto his front as he did so, but the big man with the beard was only fifteen metres away, and raising the weapon, and firing.

At this distance, on a clear day, chilled and relaxed on a range, Khasmohmad Kadyrov would have grouped the contents of his magazine into a target the size of John Carr's head with ease.

But his veins were full of fire, not ice, and this was not a clear day on a range, so the next burst of four shots he fired landed just short of Carr.

They buried themselves harmlessly in the soft ground, but they threw dirt and detritus into the Scot's eyes, blinding him temporarily.

He drew his pistol and fired a desperate, wild shot of his own, which passed harmlessly wide of the target.

Kadyrov didn't even flinch: he could see that his target was struggling to clear his eyes.

Smiling savagely, his teeth bared like those of a wolf, he took aim at the prone figure and took up pressure on his trigger.

But then someone – a man, way off to his left, in the haze of smoke and darkness – shouted something, and opened up with a pistol.

The shooter was inexperienced, and too far away to make the rounds count, but one of them at least cracked off near enough to the big Chechen's head to make him flinch, and the burst of

7.62mm which should have turned John Carr inside out instead screamed off into the night.

With a howl of fury, Kadyrov swung around towards the new threat and fired at the man, who was standing a dozen metres way in a weak combat shooting stance.

The first round went low as the Krinkov came up in the turn, and the second took some of the flesh of his thigh away. But it was the third which did the damage, hitting the shooter in the hip, smashing through bone and rupturing the femoral artery, and spinning him off his feet and out of the fight.

The big, bearded terrorist turned back to deal with John Carr, but that half-second interruption had given Carr all the time he needed.

From fifteen metres, even under these conditions, there was no way in the world that he could miss.

Four shots, two double-taps fired in less than a second, hit Khasmohmad Kadyrov in the chest, pushing him backwards and then over onto his arse as he stumbled, dropping his carbine.

Sighing, he fell back into the sandy earth.

Carr scrambled to his feet, holstered the pistol, and picked up his Diemaco.

He walked purposefully towards the man, who was struggling to push himself up with his left hand, and stretching towards the Krinkov.

His chest was covered in blood, and his breathing laboured, but there was a determination to him which Carr recognised, even admired.

He knew he was dead, but he was not giving up.

As his fingers scrabbled around the pistol grip, Carr stood on the weapon.

He looked down at the man.

'You must be Kadyrov,' he said.

Kadyrov looked back up at him.

Carr could almost feel the hate in his eyes.

'Infidel,' wheezed Kadyrov.

'I may be an infidel, pal,' said Carr, placing his barrel against the big Chechen's forehead, 'but I'm a fucking winner.'

He pulled the trigger.

# 103.

THE MAN WHO had fired the pistol shots lay on the ground, looking up at Carr.

Carr fought the urge to check on Fred – he needed to establish who the fuck this new guy was, and that he posed no threat.

Kicking away the guy's pistol, he trained his Diemaco on his face.

Pakistani, he thought, or Afghan, maybe.

Even in the strange light from the fuel fire, he could see the death pallor settling on the man.

He was holding his thigh with both hands, and blood was pumping out between his fingers, glistening thick and black in the flames.

His eyes were wide and vacant, and his breathing rapid and shallow.

Carr had seen the signs too often – unless this man got help, and quickly, he was dead.

Whether he got that help or not would depend on how the next few seconds went.

'Who are you?' said Carr.

The man whispered something.

'What?' said Carr, bending his head.

The man tried again, a little louder this time.

'Zeff Mahsoud,' he said. 'SIS.'

'What the fuck did you say?' said Carr. '*SIS?*'

But the man had lapsed into unconsciousness.

The name he'd given sounded familiar, but Carr couldn't put his finger on it, and as soon as the thought entered his head it was gone.

He laid down his Diemaco and quickly searched the man.

He was clean.

He picked up his wrist and felt for a radial pulse.

It was there – not as strong as it might have been, but it was there.

Carr stood up, picked up his weapon, and moved over to Fred.

He was lying face down, the sand wet with his blood.

Carr gently turned him over.

Fred's eyes were open but empty, and his mouth slightly parted in what looked like surprise.

A shard of RPG steel had sliced open his neck – how the hell he'd managed to get off the shots he had Carr couldn't work out, but thank God he had.

'Shit, mate,' he said, closing his friend's eyes.

He got back to his feet, and, as he did so, he felt a sharp pain in his right buttock.

He knew instantly that a sliver of shrapnel from the RPG that had taken Fred out had hit him, too.

He pulled off a glove and felt round. His combat trousers were damp with blood, but it felt like a flesh wound.

It could wait.

He got on the net.

'Kev,' he said, 'I need help. Fred's down.'

'How bad?' said McMullen.

'Bad.'

'Roger. On my way.'

Back at the vehicles, Kev McMullen turned to Geordie Skelton.

'Hear that?' he said.

Skelton nodded.

'Watch your back,' said McMullen.

Slinging a trauma pack over his shoulder, he set off back into the palms.

Carr had moved back towards Zeff Mahsoud, and now he was kneeling beside him and feeling the wound on his leg.

Kev McMullen came running in and quickly took in the scene – Fred West lying on his back, some big Chechen dead a short distance away, and Carr leaning over a third man off to the right.

He spent a few moments with Fred, but it was clear that there was nothing he could do.

He went over to Carr, who was pulling a tourniquet tight on the third man's upper thigh.

'Fred's gone, mate,' he said.

'I know,' said Carr.

'Who the fuck's that?' said McMullen, nodding at Mahsoud.

'I don't know.'

'Fuck him,' said McMullen. 'Leave him and let's go. Won't be long before people start showing up here.'

'I'm not leaving him,' said Carr. 'He saved my life. Get Fred and start moving back towards the vehicles.'

'Okay,' said McMullen. 'But we need to fucking go, John. *Now.*'

Carr hefted Mahsoud onto his shoulder, McMullen did the same with Fred's body, and the two men began moving back toward the vehicles as quickly as they could.

Geordie Skelton watched them come in through his night-sight.

Once there, Carr took out a set of plasticuffs and bound the injured man's hands – there was no point in taking any chances, no matter how out of it he looked.

When that was done, he turned to Skelton.

'Help me get this guy in the back of my vehicle,' said Carr. 'We'll have a proper look at him once we get clear.'

'Who is he?' said Skelton.

'Tell you later,' said Carr.

They slid the injured man into the back seat of Carr's Hilux, as McMullen placed Fred in the front seat of the second truck and belted him in.

Charlotte – sitting in the rear – leaned forward.

'He's dead because of us, isn't he?' she said, her voice trembling.

'No,' said McMullen, firmly. 'It's because of the people who took you. Fred knew the score, and accepted the risk. He died knowing we'd succeeded. That's good enough.'

Outside, Carr closed the rear door of his truck and looked at Geordie.

'Start your engine, mate,' he said. 'Me and Kev'll lead.'

He walked over to McMullen. 'You okay?' he said.

'Yeah, sure,' said McMullen. 'Gutted about Fred, but we can worry about that later. You?'

'I've taken a bit of shrapnel to the arse,' said Carr, with a grin. 'It's going to make driving through the desert very fucking enjoyable, but I'll live.'

'Want me to have a butcher's at it?'

'Any excuse mate, eh?'

McMullen chuckled. 'Suit yourself.'

'Maybe when we get clear,' said Carr. 'I want to get at least ten klicks south. If there's no follow-up we can stop for a minute, and you can treat yourself to a look at my arse, and see if there's anything more we can do for your man in there.'

'He might not make it ten klicks.'

'Shit happens,' said Carr. 'But we're going to give him a chance.'

They set off into the stony desert, heading due south.

Seven or eight minutes and ten kilometres later, with no sign of any pursuit, Carr instructed Kevin McMullen to pull into the bottom of a small wadi and stop.

McMullen was quickly out and examining Mahsoud.

The seat and his trousers were both wet with blood, and his radial pulse was very weak.

'I reckon he's still fucking bleeding,' said McMullen. 'What was his pulse like before?'

Carr leaned in and grabbed Mahsoud's wrist.

'Not great,' he said. 'But it was stronger than that.' He paused for a moment, still feeling the wrist. 'Hold on,' he said. 'I've lost it altogether, now.'

McMullen pushed his hand away and took hold of Mahsoud's wrist himself.

He couldn't find a pulse, either.

'Shit,' he said. 'The artery must be damaged. Help me get him out so I can have a look.'

The two men laid Zeff Mahsoud out on the ground, and Kevin McMullen knelt over him.

'Give me some light,' he said.

Skelton shone a torch onto Mahsoud's upper leg.

Despite the tourniquet, arterial blood was still oozing from the wound.

'Bang some fluids into him,' said Skelton.

'Nah,' said McMullen. 'Not till I sort out the artery. If I give him any fluid before that it'll just piss straight out of him. I need to get inside the leg and clamp it first.'

He took his knife and cut away the top of Mahsoud's trousers, exposing the bloody entry hole.

He took out his water bottle and poured it over the wound. His hands were filthy, but he had no choice. He pushed two fingers and a thumb into the wound.

Mahsoud didn't respond.

McMullen located the artery, which was clearly still intact.

Hooking his two fingers underneath it, he slowly pulled it from the wound and got down closer to look at it.

There was a tiny nick – caused by a bone splinter, or a fragment of Kadyrov's bullet – and blood was slowly oozing from it.

McMullen turned slightly. 'Geordie,' he said. 'Clamp this fucker off just above where my finger is.'

Skelton reached into the med pack, took out the forceps and clamped the artery above the wound.

McMullen taped the forceps flat to the leg and applied a first field dressing.

Then he got into the crook of Mahsoud's elbow, found a vein – not easy, his blood pressure was low, now – and inserted a large-bore cannula.

'Drip,' he said.

Skelton handed down a bag of saline. McMullen attached it to the giving set, then held the drip up and watched as the saline flowed down the tube and out the end. Satisfied it was free of air bubbles, he attached the end to the cannula, and passed the bag back to Skelton.

'Hold this up, mate,' he said.

Under gravity, the fluid began to flow into the vein.

McMullen maintained his hold on the injured man's wrist.

'Come on, you fucker,' he said, under his breath. And then, when almost half the bag was exhausted, he felt a faint spark of life return. 'Got it,' he said. He took a quick blood pressure reading, and then turned to the other men.

'Okay,' he said. 'Get him back in.'

Carr and Skelton carefully lifted the unconscious Mahsoud back into the vehicle, McMullen hooked the remains of the bag above him, set the drip to a slow rate and allowed gravity to do its work.

'What do you reckon?' said Carr.

'Out of my hands, now,' said Kev, wiping his bloodied hands on his trousers. 'The pulse is back, and he's got some blood pressure. But he needs proper medical attention soon, or he's dead.'

He looked at Carr.

'Right, drop your kecks.'

'There's no time for that, boys,' said Skelton.

Carr did as he was told, and McMullen crouched down to look at the injury.

'In and out,' he said. 'I'll just clean it and dress it, but you'll be fine.'

As the Londoner quickly worked on Carr's wound, Skelton – his eye to his sight, sweeping through 360 degrees – said, 'So who is he, John?'

'Says he's SIS,' said Carr. 'I havenae a fucking clue if he's telling the truth, but I do know he saved my life back there.'

McMullen applied a field dressing, and Carr pulled his combats back up.

'Right,' he said. 'We need to get moving again. South, for now.'

With that he got back into the vehicle, looked across at McMullen in the driver's seat.

'Let's go, Kev,' he said.

# 104.

THEY DROVE ON, due south, McMullen concentrating hard on driving, Carr still looking for that possible follow-up.

And thinking.

He was working on a new exfil plan. It was going to have to be dynamic, and Nicholls probably wouldn't like it, but the more he looked at it the more he realised they had no choice.

The original plan had called for the four men and the two rescued women to strike out north towards the coast and to lie up in the desert.

A privately owned heli, fitted with long range tanks, and flown by two ex-military pilots from a naval asset out in the Med, was then to come in under cover of darkness and take them out.

As plans go it had always been dicey, but there was no easy way of getting out of Libya, and it was a quicker and better and safer option than retracing their steps all the way back to the Tunisian border.

But now – with only three fighting hands instead of four, with the checkpoints and roving militia to the north, and with Houn almost certainly turning into a hornets' nest… Now, dicey had become near-suicidal.

He finally directed McMullen to stop after another hour, fifty kilometres on.

The truck rolled into a deep depression which would give them cover from view to anyone who didn't stumble right into them.

Carr got out, carrying his Diemaco, and climbed to the lip.

A moment later Geordie Skelton joined him with a Minimi, and together the two men scanned the dark desert through their night-sights.

The first fingers of pink dawn were appearing in the east, and they had excellent visibility over the flat, open terrain out to the horizon.

There was no-one in sight.

'How they doing?' said Carr.

'The main bird's fine,' said Geordie. 'The other's away with the fucking fairies.'

Carr grimaced. 'Poor little sod,' he said. 'She saw her husband shot on that beach.'

'Aye,' said Skelton. 'I'd like to kill them wankers all over again.' He turned south, scanning the horizon. 'So what we doing?' he said. 'Losing Fred and having them fuckers to the north make it a bit complicated, eh?'

'I'm not going north,' said Carr.

'I was hoping you'd say that, man,' said Geordie.

'That means the heli's out,' said Carr. 'Too far, even with extra tanks.'

'You're not thinking of driving back to the border?'

'No. I'm going to get us a plane.'

Skelton raised his eyebrows.

Carr had to be talking about an Airbus A400M 'Atlas', the recent replacement for the old C130 fleet. 'Think they'll risk one?'

It was a fair question: a special forces Atlas was a significant strategic asset. Throwing something like that onto the table was a big call.

'Depends how badly the Prime Minister wants her daughter back,' said Carr. He scratched his chin, and suddenly realised how tired, hungry and thirsty he was. 'Listen, you stag on here. I'll let them know the state of play, and me and Kev will sort Fred and get a brew on. Keep your eyes peeled.'

'Aye, man.'

Carr returned to his Hilux.

Kevin McMullen was crouched inside, checking on Zeff Mahsoud.

'How's he doing?' said Carr.

'Same as,' said McMullen. 'Still got a pulse, but it's weak.'

'Had a look at the girls?'

'Yeah. I gave them some water and Imodium to help with the shits, and some sweets for a bit of energy. I've put a couple of roll mats down for them, and got them in their maggots.'

Carr nodded. 'Give me a hand with Fred, eh?'

'Yep.'

The two men walked to Geordie Skelton's vehicle.

Fred West was slumped in the front seat, his shirt stained with dried blood.

Kev McMullen lifted his friend's head to look at the wound that had taken his life.

There was an almost invisible entry hole in the left-hand side of his neck, where a minute sliver of steel from the RPG had hit him.

It would have been no bigger than a fingernail, but that was all it took. Both McMullen and Carr had known men who had survived multiple gunshot wounds, traumatic amputations, horrendous burns, and others who had been killed by a single tiny piece of shrapnel just like this.

It was the luck of the draw, and Fred – the happy gambler – had finally been dealt a shit hand.

Carr unclipped him, and the two men lifted his body from the Hilux and laid him gently down into a body bag.

They zipped it closed, and then stood looking at it for a moment.

McMullen glanced at Carr.

'I was convinced it was going to be me,' he said.

Carr smiled. 'You don't say?' he said. 'You hid it well.'

McMullen did not return the smile. 'Fucking Fred,' he said. 'I passed Selection with him. He saved my life in Afghan. He was my best man. Fuck *me*.'

'Could have been any of us,' said Carr. 'He knew it could happen.'

McMullen looked over, longer this time. 'Christ, John,' he said. 'He was a friend. He was *your* friend.'

'We've all lost friends, Kev,' said Carr. 'We aren't pressed men, are we? We all volunteered for this.'

'You're a hard bastard,' said McMullen, shaking his head.

Carr didn't speak for a while.

Then he said, 'Want to know what I'm *really* thinking? I'm thinking if it had to be any of us I'm glad it was Fred. I didn't want it to be Geordie, and I certainly didn't want it to be me. But, most of all, I didn't want it to be you. Fred was divorced. No kids, that he knew of. I can live with breaking the news to his mum, but I didnae want to have to break the news to your missus, and your children.'

McMullen looked away, momentarily embarrassed.

'It's been some fucking night, eh?' said Carr. 'And we're not clear yet, mate. So stay focused, else there might be more of us in bags before the day's out.'

'Yeah,' said McMullen, suddenly sparking into life. 'Fair one.'

'We need a brew and some scoff,' said Carr. 'You sort some out for us two, and relieve Geordie when you're finished. He can sort himself and the birds out. I'm going to send a SITREP, and see about getting us a taxi.'

As McMullen moved away and started busying himself with the stove, Carr began setting up the VSAT and connecting the laptop.

While the dish was locating its satellite, he typed out his encrypted message.

He kept it brief.

*'JACKPOT,'* he wrote. *'Current location Lat: 28°26'09.6"N Long: 15°58'21.1"E. Successful rescue of both hostages. Safe and well good physical condition. Contact broken. Multiple enemy forces KIA. 1 x friendly force KIA Paul West. 1 x friendly WIA – unknown male claims SIS source require confirmation. Will not be able to action original exfil plan. Must speak to Justin Nicholls urgently. Have alternative exfil plan will require clearance at highest level. Will open voice comms in figures 30 from this transmission.'*

He sent the message, and looked at his watch.

Just before 05:30hrs local, so 04:30hrs in London.

Somewhere, probably on the third floor of the MI6 building at Vauxhall, he knew some geek would be sitting glued to a screen, waiting for exactly this message.

The geek replied in a little under three minutes.

*'Confirm receipt of transmission. Voice communication schedule confirmed for 06:00hrs local time Libya. Please confirm all possible details claimed SIS source.'*

Carr scratched his head.

He took out the satphone, checked the power and the signal – both were good – and placed it on the bonnet of his vehicle, the antenna vertical.

What name had the guy given to him, back there in the palm plantation?

He had an excellent memory for that sort of thing – honed by undercover work with the Det and the Regiment, in Northern Ireland and elsewhere – and he'd thought he recognised the name as soon as the guy had said it.

But in the heat of battle, there hadn't been time to think about it further, and he'd moved on to the next job.

Now he sat back in his pickup seat, searching his memory.

He knew that it would come to him if he stopped feeling for it, so he got out and turned to look up to Geordie Skelton, down behind his Minimi, on the lip of the depression.

No, still not coming to him.

He climbed back into the truck, pulled the laptop over and began to hit the keys again.

*'Asian male,'* he wrote. *'Mid 40s, approx 1.7m and 80kg. No other details kn—'*

But before he could finish the word 'known', it came to him.

*Zeff Mahsoud.*

He finished his message, taking a guess at the spelling: *'Asian male. Mid 40s, approx 1.7m and 80kg. Self ID ZEF MASOOD.'*

It was as he pressed 'send' that he suddenly realised why the name had sounded so familiar earlier on.

'Shit,' he said to himself, standing up and turning. 'That fucker's not SIS, he's fucking *Muj.*'

McMullen was back by his truck, kneeling over the prone figure of Mahsoud, checking the tourniquet on his thigh as he waited for the stove to boil.

'Stop that,' said Carr, curtly.

'Why?' said McMullen.

'He's a fucking Islamist,' said Carr. 'He was all over the news earlier this year... Jailed for aiding terrorists in Libya, then they let him go. He must have been in on the whole thing.'

As he stood looking down at the unconscious man, Charlotte Morgan wandered over, unsteady on her feet.

'I wondered if I could get that fag now?' she said to Carr.

Without speaking, McMullen dug into his combats and pulled out a battered pack of Camels and a plastic lighter.

'Thanks,' said Charlotte.

She lit the cigarette, her hands shaking, and inhaled deeply, holding the smoke in for as long as she could.

She exhaled, coughing slightly, and looked down at the man on the roll mat.

'This is our MI6 chap, is it?' she said.

'He's a fucking terrorist,' said Carr. 'His name's Zeff Mahsoud.'

'Fucking *who*?' said Charlotte, dropping the cigarette in her surprise. She picked it back up, came closer and leaned in. 'Jesus *Christ*,' she said. 'He looks different like that, but you're right. It's Zeff.'

'You know the bastard?' said Carr.

'He was my client,' said Charlotte Morgan, her mind spinning to make sense of this. 'I got him off on appeal earlier this year. He was…' And then she stopped, and put her hand to her throat. 'Oh my God,' she said, quietly. 'He asked me where I was going on holiday. And I told him.'

# 105.

JOHN CARR LOOKED at Charlotte Morgan.

'What do you mean?' he said.

'A few months back,' she said. 'He was in prison, and appealing against conviction. I was the junior barrister. After we were successful, we were in a conference room at the High Court and he… He asked me about my summer holidays. Started talking about Spain, about how great Barcelona was. I said I was going to Marbella.'

'Did you tell him the date?' said Carr.

'No,' said Morgan. 'But he could have found that out easily enough from Chambers.'

'Jesus,' said Kevin McMullen.

He turned to John Carr. 'So what do we do with him? Shoot the cunt?'

Charlotte Morgan stepped forwards. 'You can't do that,' she said. 'It would be murder.'

'See that body bag over there?' said McMullen, stabbing with a finger. 'One of *his* mates put *my* mate inside it. Never mind the rest of it.'

'And he should answer for that,' said Morgan, shakily. 'That's exactly why we need to get him back to the UK. So that he can stand trial, and be punished for whatever crimes he's committed.'

'Fucking lawyers,' spat McMullen. 'Punished for his crimes? A hundred and fifty people murdered, and he gets a comfy cell and three squares a day, for the rest of his life? You're fucking joking.'

'If you shoot him, I'll inform the police,' said Charlotte Morgan, defiantly, hands on her wasted hips. 'Kevin, please. I'll forever be grateful to you for what you've done for me and for Martha – *forever.* I'm so sorry about your friend. But I can't stand by and watch you murder a helpless man. I'm sorry, but I just can't.'

McMullen stared at her, his face angry.

'Shut up and listen in, the pair of you,' snapped Carr. 'Depending what comes back from London, *I'll* decide what we do with him.' He turned to Charlotte. 'And believe me, it won't be good for Mr Mahsoud if it turns out he's bullshitting us.'

'But…'

'I said *listen*, not talk,' said Carr. 'You've got your morals, I get it. But there's a time and a place for morals. We're a long way from home, now. We're a long way from fucking civilisation. And whatever happens here, stays here. Unless you want your mum standing in the dock alongside us. Is that clear?'

Charlotte took a moment, and then nodded.

She didn't look happy about it, but Carr didn't much care about that. It wasn't his job to make people happy.

'We've risked our lives for you, and Fred's *given* his. Don't you ever threaten us again. Okay?'

He looked down at the unconscious Mahsoud.

'Mind, this doesn't make fucking sense,' he said. 'He saved my life. That fat, bearded cunt was a millisecond away from brassing me up. Why would he do that if he's one of them?'

Morgan and McMullen were silent.

'Ah, who gives a shit?' said Carr, eventually. 'There's fuck all he can do to us now. Kev, get that brew and scoff sorted.'

He turned and walked back to the laptop.

A message was waiting for him.

It said, '*MAHSOUD: treat as team member, include in any extraction plan.*'

Well. Maybe he was telling the truth?

Carr sent an acknowledgment, and Kevin McMullen appeared at his elbow.

'John, here you go, mate,' said McMullen, handing him a hot brew, and a boil-in-the-bag sausage and beans. 'Heard back from London?'

'Yeah,' said Carr. 'Whoever the fuck he is, they want him back in one piece.'

'You trust them?'

Carr's mind travelled back a few months, to Justin Nicholls sitting in his flat in Primrose Hill.

Guy de Vere – one of Carr's oldest friends, from way back in 3 Para – alongside him.

Nicholls knowing full well the vengeance and mayhem that Carr had recently wreaked across the Irish Sea.

And protecting him from any fall-out.

'Aye,' he said. 'I do.'

He took a sip of the scalding tea. 'Fuck me, that tastes good,' he said. 'You squared away?'

'Yep.'

'Okay,' said Carr, ripping open the steaming food bag. 'Go and relieve Geordie. Tell him to come straight in. Don't be chatting up there.'

As McMullen grabbed his kit and headed up towards Skelton, Carr walked back over to Charlotte Morgan.

She was back in her sleeping bag, huddled close to Martha Percival.

Martha seemed to be asleep, but Charlotte Morgan watched him coming.

Carr looked down at her. 'Mahsoud lives,' he said. 'So you can stop worrying.'

She relaxed, visibly. 'I'm sorry,' she said. 'It was a silly thing to say. I'd never have done it.'

'We all say stupid things now and then,' said Carr. 'Want a drink?'

He held out his mug.

'What is it?'

'Tea.'

She took it, and sipped at it, before pulling a face and handing it back.

'Horrible,' she said. 'How much sugar's in that?'

'Three,' said Carr, with a laugh. 'Geordie will make you one without in a minute.'

'How long will we be here for?' she said.

Her eyes were wide and, with the adrenalin gone, she looked exhausted. For the first time, in the early dawn light, Carr thought he could see fear on her grimy, sweat-streaked face.

'We need to lie-up here for a bit and call in our extraction,' he said. 'Don't worry, you'll be home soon. How you feeling?'

'Not great,' said Charlotte. 'And I smell like a farmyard. But I'm more worried about Martha.'

'Let her sleep,' said Carr. 'When she wakes up, keep talking to her. Let her know she's safe. She'll get taken care of as soon as we get back.'

The young woman nodded.

There was a noise behind Carr, and he turned to see Geordie Skelton jogging down from his stag position.

'How, man,' said Skelton. 'Give us a swig of that brew. I'm fucking gagging.'

Carr tipped the rest of the tea down his throat, and smacked his lips.

'Make your own, you lazy fucker,' he said, with a chuckle. 'Make one for the girls, and another for me while you're at it.'

'Fuck me, Carr,' said Skelton. 'All these years and I'm still your brew bitch.'

Charlotte watched them bantering, confused. She couldn't understand how they could joke with each other like this – after what they'd just done, with their friend dead a few feet away, and while they were still out here, exposed and alone.

Weren't they scared?

She knew *she* was. She'd managed to build up a façade, a mechanism to protect herself, but it was slipping, and she knew it.

But their relaxed confidence and easy manner reassured her a little, too.

John Carr turned to her. 'Geordie will make you something to eat, as well,' he said.

'I feel sick,' she said.

'Just nerves,' said Carr. 'You need to get something inside you, and we don't know when the next chance will be. Okay?'

'Okay,' she said.

Carr looked at his watch.

Five minutes to his call.

He turned away to his own vehicle, and then he heard Charlotte Morgan call his name, softly.

'John,' she said. 'We *are* going to get out of here, aren't we? Promise me we are.'

'I don't make promises I've no control over, Charlotte,' he said.

'Please,' she said. 'Please just say we will.'

'I'll promise you this,' said Carr, looking her straight in the eyes. 'We'll get you out of here, or die trying. Our lives for yours, if it comes to it.'

'Fuck that,' said Geordie Skelton. 'Speak for yourself.'

Carr shot him a glance, and Skelton nodded, feeling suddenly foolish.

Carr was right: they needed Charlotte Morgan to keep control of herself, and for that she needed hope.

'Only joking, pet,' he said. 'We get you out, or we die trying, like John says. But let's hope it doesn't come to that, eh?'

# 106.

JUSTIN NICHOLLS HAD been dozing on the sofa in his office – he'd slept at work for three nights, now, much to his wife's annoyance – when his phone buzzed.

'Message in from John Carr, Justin,' said the voice on the other end. 'He's transmitted JACKPOT. But he needs a voice call with you at five a.m. our time. He says it's urgent.'

'Okay,' said Nicholls, instantly wide awake. He stood up. 'Confirm that call for me, please.'

'Will do. Also, they've picked someone up. A man, claiming to work for us.'

'Name?' said Nicholls. 'Description?'

'Carr didn't say.'

'Ask him for all possible details,' said Nicholls. 'And I'll take it on from there.'

'Right you are.'

Nicholls bent over the terminal on his desk, entered the confidential feed set up for the operation, and read John Carr's first message.

He picked up his phone, and dialled.

Across the River Thames, a mile or so due north, a secure line rang next to Prime Minister Penelope Morgan's bed.

She answered immediately.

'Hello?' she said.

Nicholls could hear the fear in her voice.

'They've got her, Penny,' he said. 'She's safe.'

There was the muffled sound of uncontrollable sobbing, and Nicholls heard a man's voice.

A moment later, Paddy Morgan came on the line.

'Justin?' he said, his voice high and trembling. 'Tell me.'

'John Carr and his team have recovered Charlotte and the other girl,' said Nicholls. 'They're…'

'Are they in the air?'

'No, but they're some distance from where they were being held, with no sign of any pursuit.'

'When will you… When will they…?'

'We're working on that now,' said Nicholls. 'I need to speak to Penelope, Paddy.'

'Of course,' said Paddy Morgan, his voice thick with emotion. 'I'll put her back on.'

There was the sound of whispering, and then the Prime Minister came back on the line.

'I'm sorry, Justin,' she said, clearing her throat. 'It's been a terribly stressful time.'

'Of course,' said Nicholls. 'Listen, Penelope. She's safe and well, but Carr's original extraction plan is blown. I have a voice call with him in twenty minutes. I'll know more then.'

'Oh my God.'

'Don't worry,' said Nicholls. 'We'll get her out. I promise.' He paused. 'Look, I have to go. I'll keep you updated.'

He replaced the receiver, just in time to see Carr's second message come across.

'Jesus,' breathed Nicholls.

He typed a reply – *MAHSOUD: treat as team member, include in any extraction plan* – and then got up from his desk.

Time for a coffee and to splash some water on his face before he called Carr.

# 107.

THE SAT PHONE on the bonnet of John Carr's vehicle bleeped quietly as the second hand on his watch swept up to the vertical.

He picked it up.

'Carr,' he said.

'John, it's Justin,' said the voice on the other end. 'Congratulations. And I'm sorry about your KIA.'

'Congratulate me when we get out,' said Carr.

'Yes,' said Nicholls. 'About that. You can't extract by the planned route?'

'No,' said Carr. 'It got very noisy, and every man and his camel in Houn will be out and about by now. Plus the north was already crawling with fuckers in technicals. We nearly got bumped coming in, and with a man down it's not an option.'

'I see. So what are you suggesting?'

'We need an aircraft,' said Carr. 'A400M.'

'Landing where?' said Nicholls.

'There's no shortage of flat desert out here,' said Carr. 'So we can create a TLZ, if necessary. But I've checked my maps and there's a long, straight stretch of newish road around sixty klicks south of my position, on the run-in to a place called Al Fuqaha. It's a ghost town. Night strip – we can mark it, and we'll clear it. I'm sure you can get all the info from satellite anyway.'

'An A400's a big call, John,' said Nicholls. 'It's a strategic…'

'I know what it is, Justin,' said Carr, cutting him off. 'Do you want the Prime Minister's daughter home, or not?'

There was a brief silence, apart from the quiet buzz of static as the signal bounced off a satellite a hundred miles above him, in the frozen vacuum of space.

'I'll get it approved,' said Nicholls.

'Good,' said Carr. 'And give Mark Topham a bell. If he hasn't made a contingency plan for this, I'll be fucking amazed and he shouldn't be DSF.'

'Give me ten minutes,' said Nicholls.

'Ten minutes,' said Carr.

He ended the call.

In London, Justin Nicholls dialled another secure number.

It was answered by Major General Mark Topham, Director Special Forces, who was standing in the kitchen of his house in Putney.

He'd been there for several hours, expecting just this call to come in at any moment.

Nerves ticking.

'Yes?' he said, his hand wrapped around a mug of tea.

'Mark, it's Justin,' said Nicholls. 'I've just spoken to John Carr. He's pulled it off.'

'Bloody hell,' said Topham, his shoulders sagging slightly with relief. He shook his head and chuckled. 'The mad bastard,' he said. 'No duress code?'

'No, it's genuine. They have the two hostages, and are presently sitting out in the Sahara, miles from anywhere.'

Topham took a swig of tea. 'I can hear a "but", Justin,' he said, with a smile.

'The original exfil plan is no longer viable,' said Nicholls. 'Carr wants an aircraft. Is it doable?'

'Of course it's doable,' said Topham. 'I always thought he might struggle with his heli, so I've already had a preliminary plan drawn up. Where's he want it?'

'He's suggesting landing on the main drag near a small town called Al Fuqaha.'

'Send me the lat and long,' said Topham. 'I'll need to get Air Ops to confirm its viability, but Carr knows what he's doing. Wouldn't be the first Tactical Landing Zone he's marked. Of course, it will need authorising by No. 10. An A400, not to mention the aircrew and a dozen SAS men… That's a very big hole to fill indeed. She needs to be aware of that.'

'Yes,' said Nicholls. 'I'm going to call the Prime Minister after this. She's bound to ask about the risks.'

Mark Topham finished his tea and put his mug in the kitchen sink.

'Well, they're basically as discussed before,' he said. 'It could be shot down. It's unlikely, but it's possible.'

'What sort of percentage are we talking?'

Topham stared out of his window at the small garden, and the grey dawn.

How many times had he been asked this question, or considered it himself, over the last couple of decades?

'Never say never,' he said. 'But we fly in and out of these places all the time, and we've not lost an aircraft in years.'

'When was the last time?'

'Only happened once. We lost a C130 to ground fire in Iraq, back in 2005. But that was in daylight. Chances of it getting shot out of the air over the Sahara, under cover of darkness, are slim. Getting compromised? Bit higher, but that's a matter for the politicians to consider. The main vulnerability is when it's on the ground.'

'What can we do about that?'

'Trust John Carr to secure the area as best he can.'

'And you're willing to take the risk?' said Nicholls.

'Taking risks is what we do, Justin. Get me that lat and long and the PM's approval, and we can crack on.'

'Understood,' said Nicholls. He hesitated a moment. 'Listen, Mark, one of Carr's men was killed, I'm sorry to say.'

'Ah, shit,' said Topham. 'Who?'

'Paul West,' said Nicholls.

It was Mark Topham's turn to pause.

He sighed. 'That's a real shame,' he said. 'He was a good man, Fred.' He shook his head, ruefully. 'Mind you, it could have been worse. I'll be honest, Justin, I was quite prepared for you to be ringing to tell me they were *all* dead. One thing's for sure – I'm going to want a full debrief with Carr and the others when they get back. There'll be lessons here we can learn.'

# 108.

INSIDE THE NEXT half-hour, Justin Nicholls had received authorisation from the Prime Minister for the use of an aircraft, and had relayed Carr's current position, and his intended landing location, to Mark Topham.

In turn, Topham had been on to the CO of 22 SAS up in Hereford, giving him the green light.

Two weeks earlier, before Carr and his team had even left the UK, Topham had tasked the CO with preparing for just this eventuality – though he had kept the circle of knowledge very tight. Only the commanding officer, elements of Regimental Headquarters and the D Squadron HQ had known why they were drawing up the plan.

A dozen men from the Squadron had been put on thirty minutes' notice to move, and well inside an hour after Topham and Nicholls had ended their call they were sitting in a briefing room at their Hereford camp, waiting to be told what the task was.

At the front of the room, a map of Libya was projected onto a large screen.

There was a buzz of excitement in the air, and it heightened when Squadron Sergeant Major Rich Arnold walked in with the OC.

Arnold wasted no time.

'Alright guys,' he said, in his deep Scouse voice. 'Listen in. Time's pressing, there's a CH47 inbound to fly us to Brize and onto an A400, so alls I'm gonna do is outline this for you now. We all know the PM's daughter was kidnapped a fortnight ago.'

There were a few nods and glances: there'd been a lot of speculation as to why they'd been placed in a state of readiness, and high up the list of possibilities had been that it was to rescue Charlotte Morgan and her friend.

'The good news is she's free,' said SSM Arnold. 'The bad news is she's stuck in the middle of the Libyan desert.'

There was a slight murmur of surprise – after all, the only people who got involved in this sort of thing were the people sitting in the room.

And if *they* didn't know anything about it…

'How the fuck did she get free, Rich?' asked the Troop Staff Sergeant, a short, stocky guy called Simon Pearce, who headed up the team.

'It's sensitive, Si,' said Arnold. 'But since most of you know him… John Carr got her out.'

The buzz in the room intensified at that. The bulk of the team had served under Carr and those who hadn't certainly knew 'Mad John' by reputation.

But he'd left the Regiment a few years earlier for a cushy job in private security.

What was he doing cutting about the Sahara?

The question was voiced by the troop staffie.

'*John*?' he said, his face puzzled. 'What the fuck's that about?'

'Mate, I don't know,' said SSM Arnold, 'and we don't need to. Explains why the fucker wasn't up from London for Nick's birthday do last week, though.'

There was a burst of laughter, and more chatter.

'Okay, guys, settle down,' said Arnold, raising his voice to silence the room. 'This is the concept of operations. Move from here to Brize by CH47. We land next to an A400 which is already on the pan and waiting to go. Fly straight down to Sicily, courtesy of the Yanks and the Eyeties.'

He used a laser pointer to illuminate Naval Air Station Sigonella, on the eastern edge of the Italian island.

'From Sig, it's low-level, straight in, over *here*.'

The laser showed a point on the north Libyan coast, near to the Tunisian border crossing point at Ras Ajdir.

'From there, straight on down to a TLZ somewhere around *here*, outside the town of Al Fuqaha, which John will mark and secure. We land, we secure the area around the plane, we get the ground team on board, and then we fuck off back to Sicily. Simple as.'

He looked around the room.

'We'll be launching around 01:00 tomorrow, so we'll have time to refine the plan and have a full brief reference roles, responsibilities *et cetera*, once we get to Sigonella. In the meantime, any questions?'

'Who's the pilot?' said Simon Pearce.

'Stretch Armstrong.'

Pearce nodded his approval. Armstrong was a good pilot, and a man he knew from many a trip.

'Enemy dispositions, Rich?' said another older hand.

'Hopefully, zero,' said Arnold. 'As I say, this is outline only. Al Fuqaha's a ghost town, and there's no recent reports of any major concentrations of bad guys operating in that area. Doesn't mean they aren't around, obviously, and we'll need it all firming up. But Int are working on it.'

'What about ROE?'

'Ideally we get in and out without firing a shot, and no fucker ever knows we were there. But usual rules apply if it goes tits up. I'd rather we were judged by twelve than carried by six.'

Lawrence Jones cleared his throat. The young Welshman was the new Troop officer, fresh from Selection.

'What's the air threat like around that area?' he said.

'Pass,' said SSM Arnold, without bothering to look at him. 'We'll let the RAF worry about that one.'

Jones' face reddened, and he piped down.

A few other questions were asked and quickly answered, and then Si Pearce spoke up again.

'Rich,' he said, 'you keep saying "*We'll* do this" and "*We'll* do that". You're not thinking of fucking tagging along, are you?'

'Too fucking right I am,' said Rich Arnold, with a chuckle. 'Sorry, mate, but I'm heading this one up. There's no way I'm not going to be there to step off that plane and find out what the fuck Carr's been up to.'

Slightly behind and to his left, the OC looked at Arnold and shook his head. He'd tried to talk the SSM out of going – it wasn't a big enough op to warrant his leading it – but Arnold was as stubborn as a mule and some battles aren't worth fighting.

'Right, fellas,' said Arnold. 'Let's get moving.'

An hour later, thirteen men stepped off the back of a CH47 and started moving to the rear of the A400 which was already turning and burning on the pan at Brize.

Rich Arnold watched his men walk up the rear ramp, and then followed them, giving the loadmaster the thumbs-up to confirm all were on board.

The tailgate started to rise and the plane lurched forward.

As the team started to stretch out on the seats, Arnold made his way forward and said his hellos to the crew – all experienced men he knew and respected.

The navigator handed him a headset which he put on.

'Alright, Rich?' said Stretch.

'Good, mate,' said Arnold. 'You?'

'Had a nice bird lined up for tonight,' said the pilot, 'but she'll keep.'

Arnold grinned, as he accepted a brew from the loadmaster and sat down on the jumpseat behind the pilots.

In a matter of moments, the four 11,000 horsepower Europrop engines had lifted the huge aircraft off the runway and it was leaving the green Oxfordshire countryside behind, and heading south.

Arnold settled back, enjoying the familiar buzz and hum of the Atlas, and sipping his tea.

*John Carr, you mad bastard*, he thought to himself, with a smile. *How the fuck did you get yourself on this one?*

Three hours later, the A400 landed at NAS Sigonella in Sicily, taxied into a secure hanger, and the team disembarked and started to sort their equipment out.

'Guys, listen in,' shouted Arnold. 'Everyone including aircrew in the briefing room in sixty minutes.'

It was just after 14:00hrs local time – a little under eleven hours until they launched.

# 109.

AT THAT MOMENT, John Carr was relieving Geordie Skelton on stag in the depression in the desert, sixty kilometres south of Houn.

It had been a tough, wearing few hours since he had received confirmation from Justin Nicholls that the aircraft would be coming in at 03:00hrs the following morning, and his eyes were sore with sweat and grit from a light sandstorm which had hit them a little earlier.

The temperature in the silent, exposed bowl had touched the early nineties in the midday sun. They'd erected some overhead protection to create some shade, but the heat was still punishing and exhausting.

The two women had slept fitfully, often crying out in their sleep, and Geordie Skelton and McMullen had managed to grab an hour's kip here and there.

But Carr himself could not – would not – close his eyes.

He was now as confident as he could be that there'd be no follow-up, but he couldn't rule out the possibility that any survivors had put out a message offering a reward for the return of the two Western girls, and the heads of their rescuers. The place might be crawling with search parties, for all he knew.

Human instinct was to move, to get further south, to put

as many miles as possible between him and the carnage to the north.

But he knew that wasn't a good option – he didn't know what lay beyond the horizon, and moving in daylight was too risky, a man down and light on ammo.

Hunkered down in this bowl, they'd have to be fucking unlucky for someone to stumble on them.

So the best thing to do was to sit tight, watch the shimmering horizon, and wait for the sun to sink in the western sky.

At least the summer days were reasonably short at this latitude, and the twilight brief. The light would start to fade at 18:20hrs, and full darkness would envelop them not long after that. Then they would move south.

It was only a relatively short journey – sixty or so kilometres – to the RV, a stretch of road leading into the tiny Berber settlement of Al Fuqaha.

It wasn't his first preference. The A400M, like the C130 it had replaced, could land pretty much anywhere, as long as the ground was hard enough, and anything that might fuck up the aircraft was cleared – last thing you needed was a stray rock bursting a tyre or two. Ideally, he'd have found a stretch of desert well away from any habitation, and marked out a proper TLZ. But it took time and manpower to mark and clear a TLZ, and time and manpower wasn't something he had. So the road it was: it would still need clearing, and any debris removing, but at least it was relatively new and likely to be in good nick. He smiled at the irony: the roads were in better order out here than the patched-up, pothole-ridden crap around Hereford. All he needed was a thousand metres – enough for the A400 to land, turn, and take off again. The turn might be awkward, but better that than trying to clear, mark and secure a strip twice as long.

He felt a bead of sweat drip off the end of his nose, and took a quick drink of warm water from his bottle.

Through his scope, the desert was empty all the way to the horizon, which was lost in the haze.

Squinting in the white glare of the sun, he ran through his plan.

Leave at 19:00hrs, arrive at 22:00 at the latest.

Check that the area was clear.

Then – and this was where they'd have to chance their arm – drive up the centre of the road, lights on, and move any shit out the way. Not ideal, but it had to be done to avoid fucking up the plane, and walking it in the dark would be too slow.

That should take them close to midnight.

They'd use subdued lighting to mark the runway, elevating it about three feet off the ground to give the pilot the best acquisition. In an ideal world, he'd talk to the guy on approach, but this world was far from ideal and he had no ground-to-air comms.

They'd be exposed while they worked, but the road was historically quiet and once they'd finished they could sit off and wait until it was time to light up the strip, at minus-ten minutes to landing, which was set for 03:00.

Nicholls had said that the pilot was the best the RAF had, and thus probably the best there was, and Carr believed him – from personal experience, all the guys from the Special Forces flight were phenomenal.

Still, it was going to be ballsy as fuck, bringing a bird in, in the pitch black, on a hasty landing strip marked out by a guy with an O level in geography, and secured by a mere three blokes.

It was like sitting in a car, lights out, 100mph, and driving at a narrow gap between two points, all on the say-so of some guy you didn't know, who told you it was clear all the way. Total trust was required – there was no recovering the aircraft if you came in at 200 knots and the guys on the ground had fucked it up.

Carr tried to game the possible issues.

They ranged from a casual compromise – some local stumbling

into them – to a serious contact initiated by an aggressive enemy force, and everything in between.

In his next sched to Nicholls, he'd confirm the final co-ordinates of the strip and would also lay down the abort protocols.

A green flare on approach meant it was safe to land.

A red flare, and the pilot was to pull out of the landing, go into a holding pattern and re-approach after ten minutes.

No flares at all…

Well, that meant they were deep in the shit.

The aircraft was to RTB, and Carr and his team would have to take their chances fighting their way out and extracting in the vehicles.

There was no way he was going to bring the plane in to a bad situation. No doubt there'd be men on it whom he knew, and he wasn't going to be responsible for any more deaths if he could help it.

That thought turned his mind back to Fred West, lying dead a couple of dozen metres away. Just as quickly, he turned his mind away again. There'd be plenty of time for memories and mourning in the coming days and weeks, but first they had to get home.

He glanced at his watch. Another ten minutes, and Kev would be up to replace him, and he could get a brew on.

He looked back out at the harsh desert.

He wanted to get those girls back home, more than anything.

The plan wasn't perfect, but few are.

He'd have liked more men and more time, but they had what they had.

And he was confident it would be enough.

Some might say they'd been lucky so far, but Carr didn't believe in luck.

He believed in speed, aggression and surprise: their plan, their courage and their skill had got them to this point, and it would get them home,

Any cunt got in the way, they paid the price.

He looked at his watch again.

'Come on, Kev,' he murmured to himself. 'I need that fucking brew.'

# 110.

CARR HAD EVERYONE up and standing-to, watered and fed and ready to go, with the vehicles fuelled, an hour before they were due to leave.

He'd run through the plan one final time with Skelton and McMullen, and the three men had cleaned their weapons, checked their ammo scales, and loaded themselves down with every round they had left. They'd run through a lot of ammunition the previous night, and another firefight like that would leave them perilously short.

It was to be avoided at all costs.

He glanced at the rear truck. Mahsoud was unchanged, and Carr would not have bet a great deal on his seeing home again. The two women had crashed completely, now – the exhaustion and relief had overwhelmed them, and both had surrendered their lives to fate.

Just before the sun sank over the horizon, he sent the sched to Nicholls.

And then, as the pale blue sky darkened and turned deep orange in the west, they mounted up and started south.

Twice, they saw the lights of vehicles moving some way off to their flank, but they were not close enough to warrant stopping and Carr just pushed on.

In the event, they reached the target area without encountering anyone.

There they halted, a hundred metres short of the road.

It was just after 10:00hrs.

Over to the east, they could just see the dark mass of the small town of Al Fuqaha. There was one light on in the whole place, and it was extinguished not long after they arrived.

Ahead of them, a wide, flat, straight strip of asphalt stretching left and right for several klicks.

If Carr had had time on his side, he'd have watched the highway and tried to establish something close to a pattern of life, but with three guys and a kilometre of road to clear, and only four or five hours to play with, he didn't have that luxury.

So, after a quick scan of the area, they moved straight to the place on the ground where the lat and long marked the start of the strip, a couple of hundred metres before the point where the pilot would actually touch down, and began putting out the markers on either side of the road.

A couple of times, they removed debris – some unidentifiable strip of aluminium, a sizeable chunk of rock that had somehow found its way into the road – but, other than that, it was perfect for the job.

'This is fucking ideal, man,' said Skelton, over the comms, as they reached the end. 'They've got better roads than ours.'

Carr smiled, and indicated to Kev McMullen that he should pull off into the desert.

The A400 was going to have to turn, and that would mean leaving the asphalt. He'd have liked to use a penetrometer to test the ground, but he didn't have one, so the best they could do was to drive the vehicle out on the northern side and see what happened.

It wasn't an ideal test, but Carr had marked out enough strips and the ground seemed firm enough.

Satisfied, they all pushed out to an area about 300 metres south and parked up.

It was now midnight.

Carr stepped out of his vehicle and took out his satphone.

After a couple of rings the phone was answered.

'John,' said Justin Nicholls, his voice full of tension. 'How is it?'

'Good to go,' whispered Carr.

'How are the girls?' said Nicholls.

'Bearing up. But it's fucking tough for both of them.'

'And Mahsoud?'

'Still in the land of the living, just.'

'You guys okay?'

'Fuck me, Justin,' said Carr, with a grin. 'You'll be asking me what the weather's like next, and what my plans are for the weekend. The strip's good to go, we'll be in place at H hour minus ten, and the area is quiet. Tell the blokes in the back that we're two vehicles to the south. I don't want some new guy lighting us up as they come off.'

There was a momentary static hiss as Nicholls made a careful note.

Then he said, 'Okay, John, understood. Great job, the PM is ecstatic.'

'Let's get us out of here, first,' said Carr. 'We can worry about my bonus later.'

'Bonus?'

'I'm fucking joking. Let's get the bird warned off, see you in the morning.'

'Okay, mate,' said Nicholls, some of the tension gone from his voice. 'Take care.'

'*Mate*?' said Carr, to himself, as he closed down the satphone.

He stowed it in his truck, walked to the other vehicle, and leaned in to look at Charlotte Morgan.

She was awake, and staring into space. 'Three hours, darlin',' he said. 'Your transport home is arranged, and will be taking off shortly.'

'Thank you,' she said, in a small voice.

Carr had a quick glance at Zeff Mahsoud – he was motionless, and his breathing was raspy and shallow – and then walked over to McMullen and Skelton, who were scanning the surrounding land through their sights.

'Geordie, keep watch,' he said. 'Kev, me and you are going to sanitise the vehicles and bag up everything that needs to go home – weapons, comms, *et cetera.* We'll stick the bags in my wagon and get the spare fuel ready. Soon as the bird lands and turns, we torch the vehicles.'

'Roger,' said McMullen.

The two men set to work. It took them an hour, working slowly and methodically in the dark, and when it was done they sat back and waited.

From time to time, Carr glanced at his Casio, but he knew that patience was key. Watching the minutes tick by wasn't going to add fifty knots to the A400's airspeed.

Slowly, slowly, time moved on.

At 02:40, he turned to the other two men.

'Right, guys,' he said. 'Aircraft here in twenty. Kev, you know what to do. Up to the landing end, take the vehicle with Mahsoud in it, and let's get this strip lit up. We'll take the girls with us. At H minus one you drive back down to us, just south of the pick-up point. If you need us give us a shout on the radio and we'll be straight up there, mate.'

McMullen nodded, stepped into his vehicle and drove off towards the first two lights, which would be used by the pilot to line up his landing.

Carr and Geordie got into the other vehicle, and drove down towards the lights which marked the far end of the strip, and the pick-up point.

As he drove, Carr spoke over his shoulder.

'Not long now, ladies,' he said. 'Plane's on the way. Twenty-five minutes, and this will all be behind you.'

At the end, Carr pulled off into the desert, dismounted, and looked at his watch, for what felt like the hundredth time that night.

'He'll be here in eight minutes, Geordie,' he said. 'Let's…'

But Skelton held up a hand. 'Wait one, John,' he said, nodding in the direction of Al Fuqaha.

Carr turned and raised his weapon.

'Fuck it,' he said, softly. 'I thought it was all going too well.'

# III.

SIX HUNDRED METRES away, and closing quickly, he saw a pickup truck, driving on one solitary sidelight.

Skelton trained his Minimi in the direction of the oncoming vehicle, and rested his finger lightly on the trigger.

'Say the word, mate,' he said.

Carr was silent, just watching the approaching pickup.

At 400 metres, he began to make it out better.

'Geordie,' he said. 'Turn our vehicle lights on quickly.'

The big northerner ran to the Hilux and leaned in.

'What's happening, Geordie?' said Charlotte Morgan, trying and failing to hide the anxiety she felt.

'Company,' said Skelton. 'Don't worry, pet, it's all good.'

As the lights came on, Carr stepped into the middle of the road, confidently, and held up his hand.

He was working on the basis that the driver would be used to random checkpoints, and he was right.

Almost immediately, the vehicle began to slow.

It rolled to a stop a few metres from John Carr, and the driver's door opened.

As Skelton killed the lights, out stepped a man.

He was unarmed, and his body language unaggressive.

He said something, in Berber.

'What's he say, mate?' said Skelton, the muzzle of his machine-gun covering the cab.

'Dunno,' said Carr. 'I don't speak the lingo. Watch my back.'

He walked forwards, Diemaco ready but lowered, and looked into the vehicle.

He could see a woman, and two young children.

'Hello, my friend,' he said, in Arabic. 'Can I ask where you're going? It's very late.'

Taken aback by the strange accent, the man said nothing for a moment.

There were a lot of foreigners in Libya now – dogs who had shamed the name of Islam.

He hated them, and the trouble they had brought, but this man did not look like one of them, nor a militia man, nor a smuggler.

Carr asked him again, and the man, this time speaking Arabic himself, said, guardedly, 'We're going to the market at Sawknah. I want to be there before daybreak, for my prayers and to get a good stall.' He paused. 'Why do you ask? Who are you? Americans?'

'No, my friend,' said Carr. 'We're British, and everything is fine. I promise you, we mean you and your family no harm. We are here for a few minutes only, and then we are gone.' He gestured to the bed of the truck. 'What are you selling?'

'Dates,' said the man, almost defiantly. 'So you don't need any help?'

'No,' said Carr. 'But thank you.'

The man nodded. 'Then I will be on my way,' he said, and started to turn.

'I'm sorry,' said Carr. 'But I can't allow you to leave. You must stay with us, until we're gone. Only a few minutes, I promise.'

Behind him, Geordie Skelton spoke.

'Five minutes, John,' he said. 'We need to move this fucker on, or flatpack him.'

Carr spoke into his radio.

'Got a family stopped here, Kev,' he said. 'Shit timing, but there it is. We're sorting it, but I don't want to rush things, so Geordie's going to send up the red flare and give us ten minutes.'

Behind him, he heard Geordie Skelton mutter something in exasperation.

In front of him, the man had begun to look angry.

'You can't hold me,' he said. 'I need to go.'

Carr grinned in appreciation of the guy's courage – stopped in the pitch dark, by armed men, and here he was, laying down the law.

'My friend,' said Carr, firmly. 'We have an aircraft coming in to land on this road in a few minutes. I can't let you stay here, but I also can't let you drive on. If you were to tell somebody about us…' He shrugged. 'So I ask you a small favour. If you follow me a little way, and wait with us until our aircraft arrives, I will pay you two hundred US dollars for your time. And then you can be on your way.'

As he spoke, he raised the Diemaco slightly, but enough to send a message.

*I'm calling this a favour, pal, to save your face.*

*And I'm offering to wedge you up, into the bargain.*

*But make no mistake: it's an offer you can't refuse.*

A few feet away, Skelton had taken out a mini-flare, already prepared.

He looked towards the heading on which the aircraft would come, and lifted his night-sight and started to scan the low horizon.

Any moment now.

He cursed this fucker, and his family, and their shitty pickup, and gritted his teeth.

Keyed his radio. 'See or hear anything, Kev?' he said.

A kilometre down the road, McMullen spoke into his own set.

'Wait one, Geordie,' he said. 'Yes, I think…'

Skelton heard the drone of the engines himself almost at that moment, well before he could pick up the blacked-out plane in his night-sight.

'Inbound, John,' he said.

'In a few moments,' said Carr, never taking his eye off the man to his front, 'a red light will go up, yes? Then we will have ten minutes before our plane arrives. Ten more minutes, and we're gone. Two hundred dollars. Yes? Do we have a deal, my friend?'

The man looked at him, directly in the eye.

Tough bastards, the Berber, and this one had the balls of his ancestors.

But he had no personal issues with the British, and the man in front of him wasn't threatening him.

And two hundred dollars, for twenty minutes…

Behind them both, there was a whoosh, as Skelton fired the flare vertically.

The area was momentarily lit by a bright redness, as the flare exploded at 1,000 feet, and Carr saw through the windscreen into the cab of the truck.

A woman, her face covered, sat on the passenger seat.

Next to her a small boy, craning his neck to see what was going on outside.

On her lap, two more kids, toddlers.

Just a family, trying to eke out a living.

# 112.

THE HUGE A400M was on its final approach when the flare went up.

Stretch Armstrong had picked up the strip miles out, bright in his goggles in the green-coloured night below, and was thirty seconds from wheels down.

The engine note was dropping off as he and his co-pilot went through the landing procedure and the Airbus slowed.

In the back, the team had been counted down at sixty seconds, and then thirty, and were all standing up, holding onto the netting on the fuselage, lit dimly by the red interior night lighting.

Final weapons checks had been completed ten minutes ago, and all the banter had long ceased.

Each man was focused and running mentally through his role: as soon as the bird stopped, they would be out, and pushing into the inky blackness, providing 360-degree protection.

Rich Arnold looked at Lawrence Jones, the new Troop Rupert.

He looked a tad white, and was clearly trying to hide his nerves.

Arnold grinned. It had been a long time since he'd felt that kind of anxiety himself, but he understood it.

He punched the young officer playfully on the shoulder, and winked at him.

Leaning in, and shouting to be heard over the noise of the four engines, he said, 'Might be earn-your-money-time tonight, or it might just be a day trip. Let's see, eh?'

No sooner were the words out of his mouth, than the engine note screamed suddenly louder, and the aircraft banked aggressively to the port side.

Up and down the length of the interior, men stumbled into each other and battled to stay upright.

Arnold, the netting wrapped tightly round his left his wrist, looked immediately towards the cockpit, as the loadmaster shouted over the roaring turboprops.

'Sit down, sit down, everyone get your belts on!'

The team were quickly into their seats, and Arnold was moving as quickly as he could to the front of the aircraft, struggling against the angle.

He pulled his way inside as the aircraft levelled out, and put on a headset and pressed the talk switch.

'What's up, Stretch?' he said.

'Abort signal,' said the pilot, his eyes fixed ahead but his voice calm.

'See anything on the ground? Any tracer?'

'Nope, but I'm not fucking landing until I get a green, now.'

# 113.

ON THE DESERT floor below, John Carr heard the sound of the aircraft's engines grow suddenly much louder, as the pilots threw the throttles forward a second after Geordie's flare exploded.

He sensed the giant Airbus banking left, and roaring off into the empty desert to its holding pattern.

The man in front of him ducked in confusion, looking upwards for the aircraft, blinded by red light.

Then the initial brightness died away, and the glowing flare started drifting slowly back to earth on its parachute.

'You won't harm my family?' said the man, now looking a good deal more nervous.

'I give you my word,' said Carr. 'But please, you must do as I ask.'

'Okay,' said the man.

'Follow us,' said Carr. Over his shoulder, he spoke to Skelton. 'Geordie,' he said. 'Get in the back of the truck and be ready to light this guy up if he looks like doing anything silly.'

Skelton clambered up into the flatbed of the Hilux and trained the Minimi on the Berber's pickup.

Carr climbed into the driver's seat, and slowly led the man away and up to their other vehicle.

When they arrived, he dismounted and walked back to the Berber's truck.

It had to be thirty years old, and was covered in rust and bodged repairs.

It was driving on one sidelight because the other lights were fucked.

Which gave Carr an idea.

'Forgive me,' he said, leaning in next to the man, and shining a torch into the cab.

He saw an elderly AK47 propped up next to the woman.

Nothing sinister in that: everyone carried some form of protection out here.

'I must take your gun away for a few moments,' said Carr. 'And also the keys to your vehicle.'

The man began to protest, but Carr patted him on the shoulder.

'I will put them both in the cab of my own truck,' he said. 'The truck will be just down there. And when I leave it will be *your* truck.'

'My truck?' said the man, surprised.

'Yes,' said Carr. 'We have two. We will burn one, but the second we will leave for you. So you get two hundred dollars and a brand-new double-cab pickup, for this inconvenience. Yes?'

The man turned to his right and gabbled something to his wife in their own language.

With a grunt, she hefted the AK up and over to him.

'Jesus,' said Carr. 'I hope the fucking safety's...'

But before he finished the sentence the man was pushing the weapon – barrel-first – out of the open window, and handing over his ignition keys.

'Whooah!' said Carr, pushing the barrel to one side, and grasping it. 'It's okay, Geordie.' He shook his head as he pulled the AK clear. 'Fuck's sake,' he said. 'Okay. Thank you.'

He leaned back into the truck, and handed back a fistful of notes – probably closer to three hundred dollars than two.

'So this is where we say goodbye, my friend. You will not see our aircraft until it lands, but you will hear it. When it lands it will turn, and we will climb aboard. Then it will leave. After it has left, you can go down and collect your new truck, and your weapon. Okay?'

The man nodded.

'One final thing,' said Carr. 'You must stay in your vehicle until our aircraft has departed. If you do that, you're safe. But if you move, it will go very badly for you all. Understood?'

The man nodded, again.

Carr reached in and offered the man his hand.

'Good luck, and thank you, my friend,' he said. 'May God bring blessings to you and your family.'

# 114.

THE RAF AIRBUS had moved out north-west to its holding area, and several minutes had elapsed by the time it got there.

'We'll start the new run-in in ninety seconds, Rich,' said Armstrong, his voice clipped and calm.

'Roger,' said Arnold, removing the headset and heading back to the rear of the aircraft.

Quickly, he briefed the guys on what had happened, and was back in position when the loadmaster held up his hand and showed him five fingers.

Five minutes.

The team were back up and in position, but there was an undeniable tension in the air now.

On the ground, the guys would take on anything: sitting in an aircraft, your destiny in another man's hands, was a different thing altogether.

Arnold stole a quick look at Lawrence Jones, and was pleased to see that the officer was doing his best to look unconcerned.

And then the loadmaster held up his fist.

The green flare had gone up, and the run-in was beginning, for the second time that night.

Sixty seconds.

*Here we go again*, thought Arnold. *Hope you're okay down there, John.*

# 115.

AT 03:07 HRS, Carr called Kev McMullen down from the far end of the runway.

They were now all together, some two hundred metres due south of the pick-up point, and Carr was scanning the western skyline.

A minute later, he picked out the dark shape of the A400 at the same moment that the distant hum of its engines reached his ears.

'Geordie,' he said. 'Green flare, pal.'

Skelton fired off the flare, and a matter of seconds later, getting bigger and louder at an astonishing rate, the giant aircraft kissed the tarmac a kilometre away.

The sound was deafening, as the giant turboprops were reversed, and then the air was filled with dust and grit, and avgas fumes, and the smell of burning rubber from where the huge tyres had bit into the road.

The Airbus rolled to a stop bang on the markers, the rear bay door already descending.

A moment later, a dozen men disembarked the massive aircraft, quickly fanning out into defensive positions.

Carr walked forward with Skelton, stopping short as the pilot began his turn, in preparation for take-off.

Once that was done, a figure stepped off the tailgate as Carr approached, hand out.

'Welcome to Libya, Rich,' said Carr, with a grin. 'How's life?'

Rich Arnold looked at Geordie Skelton and shook his head in mock disgust.

'Fuck me,' he said. 'Not you as well.'

'Some cunt's got to look after this mad bastard, Richard,' said Skelton, with a laugh.

'So what the fuck are you doing out here?' said Arnold.

'Job was too tough for the Regiment,' said Carr, deadpan. 'So they called in a few experts instead.'

Arnold laughed, and turned to his left.

'Liam, Scotty,' he said. 'Help the two ladies aboard, please.'

He saw McMullen and rolled his eyes.

'Jesus,' he said. 'Any fucking more of yous?'

'Fred West, Rich,' said Carr. 'But he's in a body bag, unfortunately.'

Suddenly, all the levity went from Arnold's face.

'Fuck me, poor bastard,' he said. 'Fred was a good hand.'

'Aye,' said Carr. 'We've got one injured as well, mate.' He pointed to his truck. 'In the back, over there, with Fred.'

Arnold turned away again.

'Jordan, Ryan – casualty and a body bag over there, lads,' he said.

As the pair of troopers ran to the pickup, McMullen and Skelton began to load on the bags containing the weapons and ammo, laptop and comms equipment.

Carr turned to Arnold.

'Give me a sec,' he said. 'Got to deny one of the vehicles.'

'Only one? And how comes there's three?'

'We got some visitors,' said Carr. 'Didn't have time to tell you.'

'Who are they?'

'Don't ask.'

'Well, it's a good job you marked them, else the boys would have brassed them up.'

Carr jumped into the cab of his vehicle and drove it a few hundred metres away from the aircraft. Then he took a jerry can of fuel from the back and splashed it liberally over the interior, threw a phosphorous grenade into the cab, and turned away.

As it exploded and illuminated him, he raised a hand to the distant Berber family and started running back towards the aircraft.

'Good luck explaining your new wheels, pal,' he said to himself.

# 116.

CARR SAW THE Hilux fuel tank go up as the A400's ramp was closing.

The pitch of the engines increased, as the pilot pushed the throttles forward.

A hundred tonnes of airframe, fuel and human cargo strained against the brakes, and suddenly they were released, and the aircraft lurched forward.

Its acceleration was impressive, and its take-off seemingly vertical.

Within a matter of moments they were airborne, and banking savagely, and heading north, foot to the floor.

They lost Zeff Mahsoud to a cardiac arrest just as they crossed the coastline and headed out over the dark sea.

Kev McMullen and a patrol medic whom Carr didn't know battled hard to save him, and managed to restart his heart once, but he didn't have the strength to fight on.

Justin Nicholls was waiting there for them at Sigonella, having flown over at the express instruction of the Prime Minister, to meet Carr, and to be a friendly face for her daughter.

As they were waiting for the Airbus to be refuelled for the direct flight back to Brize, Carr took Nicholls to one side.

'Your man, Mahsoud,' he said, quietly. 'What was his story?'

'Between me and you?' said Nicholls.

Carr just looked at him.

'Alright, alright,' said Nicholls, hastily. 'His real name was Rasool Mehsud. Born near Wana in South Waziristan around 1970. They came to England in '74 after his father came off worst in some sort of tribal dispute. Ended up in Bradford. Father drove a taxi, mother eventually became a social worker. Rasool himself did well at school, joined the Green Howards in '93. He transferred to the Intelligence Corps as a corporal after 9/11, and started talking to us in 2003. Officially, he was kicked out of the Army for theft, but that was to give him the cover to work for us. We thought we could get more out of him that way, and he agreed.'

'So he was gen, then?'

'Very much so. Full-time agent ever since.'

'The court case?'

'We needed to get him inside Belmarsh to infiltrate an Islamist cell operating out of there. He hated them for what they were doing in the name of his religion, and he did an outstanding job.'

'And the attack at Marbella?'

'We had nothing on that, but he had the perfect credibility – and the balls, frankly – to follow it up, and help us track them down. Zeff insisted on getting involved – felt a personal connection to Charlotte and the Souster girl. We got a stroke of luck when a chap was lifted in Balochistan by Pakistani intelligence. That tipped us off to the Sirte connection. We got another when our friend Shishani inadvertently mentioned Kadyrov's first name on the video they shot. Those clues got us so far, but Zeff…'

He stopped, noticing that Carr's face had darkened.

'What?' he said.

'Fucking Shishani,' said Carr. 'I dunno. We might have got him, but I never saw his body. I wanted to kill that cunt and see him die with my own eyes.'

'We'll keep looking.'

'If you find him…'

'We'll *keep* looking.'

Carr nodded. 'So the footage of the target building, the intel about them bugging out?'

'All from Zeff. The only thing he couldn't do was actually get inside the compound and get eyes-on – that would obviously have blown him. But the rest of it – his backstory gave him some freedom of movement down there. He used their cell structure against them, knowing that one side of their op wouldn't talk to the other, and he used the greed of the Sirte tribes to find their local connection. Wangled himself a stay with a local bigwig, knowing that the bigwig would immediately go off and make enquiries. Took a few days, but the guy came back with the exact location.'

'What was he doing there on the night we went in?'

'His job was to be my eyes and ears on the ground, and he was a man who did his job to the *nth* degree,' said Nicholls. 'So I imagine he was being my eyes and ears on the ground.'

'Lucky for me that he was,' said Carr.

'Indeed.'

'Brave guy,' said Carr.

'Great Britain was his country, and he wanted to serve it,' said Nicholls. 'Beyond that, he believed that God had a plan for him and he was happy to commit his life into the hands of the Almighty. Not sure it would work for me, but it takes all sorts.'

Carr was silent for a moment. Then he said, 'Family?'

'Wife and a toddler daughter.'

'They'll be looked after? Properly, I mean?'

'I would be very surprised if they were not.'

'When you see her, tell his wife that her husband was a brave man,' said Carr. 'No shit, I owe him my life.'

'I will be sure to.'

Stretch Armstrong walked past, looking like business.

Carr saw him flash his hands twice at Rich Arnold.

*Twenty minutes, and we're on the way home*, thought Carr.

A beer would be nice, and a decent bed. Maybe he'd give Antonia de Vere a bell, see if she was in town and fancied dinner. He knew he shouldn't but…

A thought struck him.

'Justin,' he said, looking at the MI6 man. 'If Zeff didn't tell the Chechens where Charlotte Morgan was going to be on holiday, who did?'

# 117.

ALMOST AS JOHN CARR said that, officers from the Metropolitan Police's Counter Terrorism Command, accompanied by several MI5 operatives, were removing the last computers and paper files from the Luton town centre offices of the law firm Spicer, McGraw and Hill.

The partners and senior staff had all been arrested, and were currently dispersed around various police stations in the south-east of England.

The senior partner, Paul Spicer, had been detained in the early hours at his eighteenth century former rectory home in a village near Luton, and was currently refusing to answer questions in an interview room at Paddington Green.

Spicer was unhappy and bewildered – unhappy, because he hadn't had his usual hearty breakfast, just a stale Met Police cheese roll and a cup of weak tea, and bewildered because he had no idea what was going on.

They kept talking about his relationship with Emily Souster – poor, beautiful Emily, the true believer, campaigner for Palestine, well-bred champion of the poor and downtrodden, and scourge of American imperialists – who had been murdered on that beach in Morocco not three weeks before.

And for the life of him he couldn't understand why.

In time, the police would come to realise that his bewilderment was genuine – though their investigations would uncover serious legal aid frauds and offences of incitement to commit perjury which would finish Spicer's legal career and see him receive a long jail sentence a year from now.

What they were trying to establish was not so much the relationship between Spicer and Emily Souster as the relationship between Emily Souster and one Argun Shishani, a Chechen jihadist who was suspected of involvement in the Marbella and Málaga outrages, and the kidnapping of Charlotte Morgan, Martha Percival, and Emily Souster herself.

And of complicity in Souster's murder.

Souster's grieving parents had gone to clear out her flat, and had discovered certain items, including an iPad in a locked box at the back of her underwear drawer.

Her father had broken open the box and cracked the code on the iPad – she always used some combination of family birth years.

On it he found hundreds of WhatsApp messages between his daughter and a man calling himself 'Hamid'.

Hamid was a man with dark eyes and a cruel mouth, and it soon became clear that he and Emily had begun a relationship. His messages had started out innocently enough, but had soon descended into the gutter, so much so that Mr Souster felt terrible for prying.

Still, he read on.

He stopped when he came to a message which read: 'So, where is Charlotte Morgan going on holiday this summer?'

At that, Mr Souster had telephoned the police.

# 118.

BACK IN THE UK, Carr had a minor op to tidy up the shrapnel wound to his buttock, and then spent a couple of days unwinding with Skelton and Kev McMullen, and a few Regiment and ex-Regiment guys who'd known Fred West, and were not deployed or otherwise out of the country.

On the Thursday, he visited West's mum at her small, neat home in Gloucester, to tell her that her son had died doing what he'd loved, and in a noble cause.

He explained that, as Fred's only surviving relative, she was owed her son's share of the money – his £300k fee, and the million for his death.

Mrs West, a stoical, resolute woman, thought for a few moments, and smiled sadly.

'That's alright, my dear,' she said. 'What would I do with that kind of money, at my age? I've got my memories, and I'm proud of my boy, and that's enough. There's worthier causes.'

'Such as?' said Carr.

'Give half to the charity at the camp,' she'd said. 'The Clocktower Fund, is it? For the families of the lads who've died. Give the other half to Leukaemia Research, would you? Paul had an older sister, you know. He was only five when she died. But he never forgot her.'

'That's very generous of you, Mrs West,' said John Carr.

'It's what he would have wanted,' she said.

And then, dignified and polite, she showed Carr to the door.

The following day, he was collected at his flat in Primrose Hill in a black Jaguar and driven to 10 Downing Street, and then shown up to the Prime Minister's flat on the third floor.

The door was opened by a man – late fifties, greying, expensively dressed – who held out his hand.

'Mr Carr?' he said. 'I'm Paddy Morgan. Please come in.'

Carr followed him through to the living room, where Penelope Morgan and Justin Nicholls were sitting on beige sofas.

'My wife,' said Morgan. 'And I think you know Justin?'

'Aye,' said Carr, shaking hands with the Prime Minister, and nodding at Nicholls.

'Please,' said Penelope Morgan. 'Sit.'

Carr sat in the armchair she had indicated.

'Mr Carr,' said Paddy Morgan, sitting down next to his wife. 'Look, I… We can never thank you enough for what you and your colleagues did for us. There aren't the words.'

Carr nodded. 'John's fine,' he said. 'How is she?'

'She's doing surprisingly well… John,' said Penelope Morgan. 'She's lost a lot of weight, but she was otherwise unharmed.'

'Psychologically?' said Carr.

'That's going to be a longer process,' said Paddy. 'She's already setting up a charitable foundation in her boyfriend's name, and I expect she will throw a lot of time and energy into that.'

'She's a tough cookie,' said Carr. 'You should be proud of her.'

'We are.'

'The other girl?'

'Martha's a different story,' said Penelope. 'She's currently in the Maudsley. They're making some small progress, but they think it's going to be a long haul.'

'Poor lassie,' said Carr.

'At least she's alive,' said Penelope Morgan. 'You lost a friend yourself. I'm very sorry about that.'

An image came to Carr: Fred, on his back in that palm grove, eyes staring emptily into the night.

'He knew the risks,' said Carr. 'He was a gambling man. Once the cards are in the air you don't know how they're going to fall.'

There was a pause, and Paddy Morgan filled it by leaping to his feet.

'I'm so sorry,' he said. 'Can I offer you a drink?'

Carr winced. 'I've spent the last two days on it,' he said. 'I wouldnae mind a brew, though. Milk, three sugars.'

'Right you are.'

As her husband disappeared into the kitchen, the Prime Minister leaned forwards.

'The Spanish would like to award you and your son the Real y Distinguida Orden Española de Carlos III,' she said. 'For your actions on the beach.'

Carr looked blank.

'Their equivalent of the George Cross,' said Penelope Morgan.

'Very decent of them,' said Carr.

She smiled. 'I've spoken to Guy de Vere and Mark Topham,' she said. 'Based on the debrief you gave them, and the known facts, I'd also like to recommend you for some sort of award. All of you.'

Carr chuckled. 'We didnae do it for the medals,' he said. 'Not when we were in, and not now.'

'Are you sure?'

He wrinkled his nose. 'I'd take a peerage, I suppose,' he said. 'Lord Carr of Niddrie's got a nice ring to it.'

Penelope Morgan leaned back, and looked at Justin Nicholls for support.

'Er...' she said.

'I think John's joking,' said Nicholls, 'though it's not always easy to tell.'

Carr chuckled. 'You're learning, Justin,' he said. He turned back to Morgan. 'Forget me and Geordie, not interested. If you give one to Kev McMullen he'll only flog it.'

'Mr West?'

Carr thought for a moment.

'Aye,' he said. 'A posthumous award for Fred would be a nice touch. If it could be arranged.'

'I'd like to do the same for Zeff Mahsoud, but unfortunately that would blow his cover. The intelligence he provided from inside Belmarsh and in a number of other areas…' She glanced at Justin Nicholls. 'Well,' she said. 'Let's just say that it was invaluable, and it's supporting ongoing operations.'

'You're making sure his wife and daughter are looked after?' said Carr.

'We are, through our private funds,' said Penelope. 'Neither of them will ever want for anything.'

Paddy Morgan reappeared with a cup of tea on an exquisite china saucer.

'From Palmerston's own tea service,' he said.

'Is that so?' said Carr, looking at the pale, insipid brew. 'You could have left the bag in a bit longer, Patrick.'

'Oh dear,' said Morgan. 'Would you like me to make another?'

'Nah,' said Carr, with a grin. 'It's fine. Thank you.'

'Paddy, darling,' said Penelope Morgan. 'Justin and I have some official business to talk to John about. Would you mind…?'

'No, no, of course,' said Paddy Morgan. 'I was going to nip out to meet Giles at White's anyway. He's going to head up Charlotte's charity.' He turned to Carr. 'John, once again – I'm indebted to you and your colleagues. If you ever need anything…'

He tailed off, bent to kiss his wife on the cheek, and then left.

'Now, John,' said Penelope Morgan, as the door closed. 'Paddy never could make a decent cup of tea, so put that down and have a drink.' She looked at Justin Nicholls, and smiled conspiratorially. 'Because I don't trust a man who won't drink with me.'

Carr grinned again. 'Okay,' he said. 'If you insist. I'll have a Scotch. Something old. Single malt. Not too peaty. One ice cube.'

'I'm sure I have just the thing.'

She was back in a moment, with a silver tray bearing three crystal lowball glasses, each half-full.

Carr took it, and sipped his whiskey.

It was good.

'So, John,' said Penelope Morgan, raising her own glass to him. 'You obviously have a very particular set of skills, and you enjoy employing them. So Justin and I were wondering if you might be interested in other challenges?'

# EPILOGUE I

SIX HOURS AFTER John Carr left 10 Downing Street, a General Atomics MQ-9 Reaper drone, on station 25,000ft above the Libyan city of Sirte, described yet another lazy, left-hand turn.

Far below, no-one noticed; at that altitude, the aircraft was invisible to the naked eye even in daylight, and the sound of its rear-mounted, 950-horsepower turboprop was washed away long before it could have interrupted the ambient street noise of the night.

The UAV had been loitering overhead since before dusk, when its camera had followed a silver BMW 535 saloon to the target location, a large villa on the left of the main highway, surrounded by a high, white wall in an unusual hexagonal shape.

The car had contained two men – neither of them the primary target – and had been parked up at the villa ever since.

The Reaper, its Raytheon EWS countermeasures scanning restlessly for hostile radar and any other threat, was being operated remotely by a XIII Squadron flight lieutenant, sitting in front of a bank of screens in a control room almost two thousand miles away at RAF Waddington in the flat, green countryside of Lincolnshire.

And now he picked up his mug of PG Tips and polished off the dregs, never taking his eyes from the screen.

Just as he replaced his mug on its Yorkshire County Cricket Club coaster, he saw movement on his main screen.

'Stand by,' he said.

The WHOT picture he was looking at showed the brilliant white figure of a man, stark against the cool black of the compound, leaving the main entrance to the villa and walking silently towards the parked BMW.

Behind the pilot, a female squadron leader leaned forward to take a better look.

Several other people in the room pushed back in their chairs and turned to a large wall monitor which was showing the same images.

The man got into the car, and a moment later there was a white puff from the rear of the vehicle, the exhaust fumes giving away their heat signature as the engine was turned on.

Ten or fifteen seconds later, three more men left the villa and walked towards the waiting BMW.

There was a slight delay while one of them opened and closed the gates, and then the car moved off, heading south-east.

The female squadron leader, pressing her headset to her ears, leaned forward again.

'Maintain control of that vehicle,' she said.

*What the fuck do you think I'm going to do?* thought the pilot, but he merely nodded his head.

The BMW moved steadily through the built-up area, the crosshairs on the screen never wavering from its roof, as the flight lieutenant waited for confirmation on what his next action would be.

He had no idea as to the identity of the men in the car: if the job tonight involved taking out a proper High Value Target then it was just possible he might find out who it was on the news in a couple of weeks' time.

Otherwise he would never know.

As it happened, in the rear of the vehicle was a fat young fixer called Tariq.

Sitting next to him was an older man – a tribal patriarch, with a wizened face and only one eye.

Tariq's uncle, in fact.

The driver and the other passenger were henchmen of the uncle, whose job it was to frighten Tariq into frankness.

And then to dispose of him.

Blood he might be, but the uncle had grown tired of his brother's oafish son.

He looked out of his tinted window.

They were heading out of the city, and the traffic was getting sparse.

In the Reaper control room in Lincolnshire, the squadron leader got the message she was waiting for, via her headset: confirmation that the primary target was indeed inside the BMW.

She offered up a silent prayer of thanks: by now, the vehicle was almost out of the city and into the desert, and that greatly minimised the risk of collateral damage.

She leaned forward once again and spoke to the pilot.

'Clear hot,' she said.

'Confirm clear hot,' he replied.

As he spoke, he flicked the safety cover from the firing mechanism, and pressed the button.

Immediately, one of the aircraft's Brimstone 2 missiles was released, its solid-fuel rocket propelling it forward and down.

'Twenty seconds to impact,' said the pilot, maintaining the cross hairs on the moving vehicle.

In the car below, Tariq looked at his uncle, nervously.

'Where are we going, sir?' he said.

But the uncle made no reply.

He wanted to get to the bottom of what had gone on a few days ago in the villa down in Houn – the new safe house that that fool Shaladi had arranged for those damned Chechens.

He couldn't shake the nagging feeling that the events of that night were connected in some way to the man whom the imbecilic Tariq had brought to his door – the fellow from England who had said that he was the link-man between the Saudi money and the Chechens.

Something very bad had happened to the Chechens and their hired hands, and the uncle was concerned that it might end up back at his door.

They were unforgiving people, Chechens, and if their friends somehow found out that he himself had given the accursed fellow the address, just before the villa was hit…

He looked through the window again.

The lights of Sirte were falling behind.

They had reached the open country, and in a few minutes they would be at the abandoned oil storage depot, where he was going to make Tariq talk, and then beg, and finally squeal.

He shook his head, bitterly.

The mysterious man from England had insisted on going down to Houn alone, even though he'd willingly paid the extra $25,000 for Tariq to go along – which, now you thought about it, made no real sense.

And he had not been heard from since.

The more the uncle pondered it all, the less he liked it.

Partly, privately, he was cursing himself for being blinded by the dollars the man had handed over.

But mostly he was blaming Tariq.

He turned to his left, and looked at his fat, sweating nephew.

In the glow of the dash, he saw that Tariq's lower lip was trembling, and he smiled.

He opened his mouth to speak, but he never got to speak the words, and Tariq never got to hear them, nor to give his answer, and he was never tortured and taken out and shot in the desert to the south.

Instead, there was a huge noise and a flash, and all four men and the silver BMW were blown into thousands of tiny fragments by fourteen pounds of high explosive, delivered on the tip of a missile designed to take out a main battle tank.

High above, the RAF drone circled for a few moments, as the pilot assessed the damage, and then it turned north and began flying unhurriedly home.

Thousands of miles away, in the control room at RAF Waddington, the squadron leader got up and patted the pilot on the shoulder.

'Another brew, Steve?' she said.

Steve stretched, and hid a yawn behind his hand.

'Yeah,' he said. 'Go on then, ma'am.'

# EPILOGUE 2

## NINE MONTHS LATER

THE MAN WITH the dark eyes had taken to eating every Friday evening at L'anciüa, a small, family run seafood restaurant in the narrow Via Angelo Custode, in the north-west quarter of the old city of Lucca.

He knew it was against all the rules to set a routine, but he'd grown comfortable in this area, where he was anonymous, just another face among faces.

Not to mention, it amused him greatly to while away an hour or two in a street named for Guardian Angels, a slaughterman strolling among the unsuspecting *kuffar* sheep, who thought they were safe from men like him.

And the €20 set menu was very good.

Tonight he'd had *cigales de mer* and *spaghetti alle vongole*, served by a pretty young waitress who had flirted with him shamelessly.

Next week he would get her mobile phone number: a man had to have some entertainments, and it was permitted to misbehave in service of the greater cause. He hated these filthy Western whores, and taking them and ruining them was one of life's great joys.

As he left the restaurant, and headed out into the narrow streets of the medieval Tuscan town, his mind was on a meeting he was due to have in Paris some time in the next month.

Three brothers from Syria were due to arrive, to plan and carry out an attack on the Louvre, and the tourists who filled it to gawp at its unholy pictures, and he was to serve as their armourer.

He had the contacts in Eastern Europe, so getting the weapons would be easy.

What had happened in Libya all those months ago had been unfortunate, but – what was the phrase the British used?

It was time to get back on the horse.

He paused at the junction with Via Sant'Andrea, lit a Marlboro Light, and watched two young women in short skirts and tight silk blouses wiggle towards him.

The taller of the two smiled at him, and he smiled back.

He felt nothing in his heart for her but hatred.

He pulled deep on the cigarette and turned down Via Sant'Andrea.

He walked slowly on into Via Buia, hemmed in by fading plaster walls dotted with jewellery stores, boutiques and opticians' shops with windows full of €300 frames by Gucci and Ted Baker.

Limping slightly, he felt the familiar ache in his leg, where that shell fragment had taken a chunk out of his calf and broken his tibia and fibula at Mazar-e Sharif.

It was a wound from many years ago which served both to remind him of the past and to strengthen his commitment to the future.

He had driven all thought of his ignominious escape from the compound at Houn from his mind.

On still, into Piazza del Salvatore, where young drinkers sat under red parasols and stared at the marble statue of a bare-breasted woman, standing over a stone bathtub into which water spouted from a lion's mouth.

Near the second table of drinkers, he finished his Marlboro Light.

'Scusami,' he said, flashing them his most charming smile, and leaning over to grind the butt out in an ashtray.

‘Prego,’ said one of them, a young woman.

He smiled again, and moved on, enjoying the warm evening air, down into Via Santa Giustina, where he had rented an apartment in an old townhouse.

Two policemen were wandering idly in the opposite direction, deep in conversation.

The dolts ignored him as he passed them, the wolf moving unseen amongst their flock.

A few steps on, he stopped, in front of a large brown door.

From habit more than anything, he paused and looked around himself, for signs that he had been noticed – men standing in the shadows, cars parked in odd places.

But he saw none of this, and he smiled to himself.

He took a small set of keys out of the pocket of his white Armani jeans, turned one of them in the lock, and pushed the door open.

Inside, the cool hallway smelled musty.

He climbed the grey marble steps to the first floor and unlocked the door to his apartment.

Whistling tunelessly to himself, he pushed open the door and paused for a moment.

He listened for any noise from within and then, happy that all was as it should be, he walked inside.

He walked to the little desk against one wall of the yellow-painted living room, put his iPhone and keys on the wooden top, and draped his burgundy Ermenegildo Zegna leather jacket over the back of the old chair.

Sat at the desk, flipped open his laptop, and entered his lengthy password.

And then…

*Was that a noise?*

He stopped, hands poised over the keyboard, head cocked to one side.

Listening.

No, nothing.

He turned.

No-one there.

*Getting paranoid, Argun.*

He opened an encrypted email account.

*Just check for any update from the Syrians.*

As he waited for the email to load, he walked into the kitchen for a drink of water.

The glass chinked, the tap hissed.

He raised it to his mouth, and then he froze.

Something, some ancient animal instinct, told him that he was not alone.

The hairs on the back of his neck vibrating, he turned.

In the doorway stood a man in dark clothes.

Big man, strongly built, scar on his chin.

Scar like an inverted crescent moon.

Latex gloves on his hands.

*Pointing something at him.*

*Smiling.*

Shishani realised what it was only as the 9mm round from the Welrod took him in the Adam's apple.

The glass shattered as he fell to the floor, clutching his ruptured throat and drowning in his own hot blood.

He began thrashing around on the floor, his eyes wide and terrified.

John Carr closed the distance quickly, rechambering a round as he moved.

For a moment, he considered putting the Chechen down like an injured dog, but then an image came to him: children, murdered on a Spanish beach, on the orders of this fucker.

So instead he held the Welrod by his side and stood on the dying man's ankles, to stop him kicking around and making a noise.

It took Argun Shishani ninety seconds to lapse into unconsciousness, and all the time he stared up in horror at John Carr, who smiled back down at him.

When the light had gone from the terrorist's eyes, Carr recovered his daysack, took the Welrod apart and placed it inside.

Then he began what would, in his old life, have been called a Sensitive Site Exploitation, to provide Justin Nicholls with as much information as possible from the flat.

He quickly searched the bedside table and removed the three passports – British, French and Italian – and put them in the daysack.

In a bag under the bed he found two tight bundles of US dollars – twenty grand, easy, and all used notes.

Those went straight into his inside pocket: fuck handing that over, just so that the government could piss it up the wall.

Then he went back to the living room and looked at the laptop.

Standard Dell running MS Windows, which surprised him.

Still on, still connected.

The penny-sized black disc which he'd applied to the underside of the laptop earlier – a combined microprocessor and sensor – would have sucked up all Shishani's keystrokes, so that his password was now known.

But to be on the safe side, he inserted a USB stick into one of the ports and followed Nicholls' directions.

While he was downloading the contents of the computer, he opened up the Control Panel and – as a further countermeasure – switched the 'Sleep' option to 'Never'.

The download finished, he ejected the USB stick and slipped it into the inside pocket of his black leather bomber jacket.

Then he placed the laptop in the daysack, fully opened out.

He spent the next ten minutes making as thorough a search of the apartment as he could, locating and bagging the router, a couple of other mobile phones, and numerous documents.

He couldn't believe how sloppy the bastard had been.

'All out in the open,' he murmured, to the unhearing Shishani, as he went through the kitchen cupboards. 'Too fucking comfortable, mate, and now look at you.' He shook his head. 'Let that be a lesson, you soft twat.'

Next he searched the dead man, and removed his wallet.

It contained cash, credit cards and receipts.

'Excellent,' said Carr.

He took a small vial from his pocket, and opened it. The cap had an integral swab-stick, which he used to collect a decent amount of Shishani's blood, for DNA analysis.

He screwed the lid back on and chucked the vial into the daysack.

Then he took out the device Nicholls had given him and placed the Chechen's fingers onto the screen, scanning them in turn.

Finally, Carr picked up Shishani's iPhone.

It was locked, so he knelt down next to the dead man and pressed the lifeless, still-warm thumb of his left hand onto the unlock button.

It was a long-shot, but any man stupid – or arrogant – enough to eat in the same place every Friday night thought that he was bulletproof, metaphorically-speaking, so…

Nothing.

Carr did the same with the right thumb.

The phone woke up.

Carr chuckled and shook his head.

'Seriously?' he said, under his breath.

He checked the iPhone's battery – 92%, more than enough that it wouldn't die on the journey ahead of him – and went into Settings, where he switched the 'Auto lock' setting to 'Never', and pocketed it.

Carr took a final look around, his eyes sweeping everywhere, in every room.

Nothing.

It was a while since he'd performed an SSE, but he was confident he'd got everything there was to get.

Satisfied, he zipped up the bag, picked it up and walked to the flat door.

The spyhole told him that the hallway was empty, so he pulled on the motorcycle helmet, hefted the daysack onto his back, and left, unhurriedly, pulling his bike gloves on over the latex ones as he went.

In the street below, the warm night air on his face, he smiled.

'We have your man with the dark eyes at an address in Tuscany,' Nicholls had told him, twenty-four hours earlier. 'Do you fancy it?'

There was only one answer to that question.

Carr was in deep now, deeper than he'd ever though he'd be.

But bringing men like Argun Shishani before the courts, so that expensive lawyers could argue about his punishment before the British taxpayer paid for a bed and three square meals a day for the rest of his life – the time for messing around with shit like that was over.

Carr turned left out of the exterior door, and walked along the centuries-old blue-grey cobbles, careful to keep his pace measured and his demeanour relaxed. There was almost no CCTV coverage in the old part of town – which was obviously why Shishani himself had chosen the location – but there was no sense in attracting any undue attention.

At the end of Via Santa Giustina he turned left into Via Burlamacchi, and twenty yards further on he came to his motorcycle, a red, five-year-old Honda CBR600RR, chosen because it was the most common colour of the most common bike in Italy.

Casually, like a guy heading home after a day at work, he swung a denim-clad leg over the seat, and fired it up.

Carefully sticking to the speed limit, he pottered his way out of Lucca, never looking back.

Even when he hit the *Strada Statale* 12, he fought the desire to open the throttle, and instead kept to a steady 130kph.

As he rode, he examined himself mentally: he felt cool, and good, and his heartbeat was only slightly elevated.

Less than forty-five minutes after he had put Argun Shishani out of the world's misery, he arrived in the outskirts of Pisa.

Almost immediately, he turned left off the SS12 onto Via A. Paparelli.

He pulled off the road into a car-park and parked the Honda in the same motorcycle bay from which he had collected it earlier that day.

He'd been told to clip the helmet and gloves to the bike, but leaving his DNA attached to his getaway vehicle seemed to him like a very fucking stupid idea, however remote the chances of the Italian police putting two and two together, so he ignored that instruction and walked away from the bike without a backward glance.

A mile on, he stuffed the motorcycle helmet deep down under the garbage in a communal dumpster. A mile further, and he hit the Arno.

He walked onto the Ponte della Fortezza, and, halfway across he stopped, leaned on the railings, and admired the view for a moment or two.

Then, very casually, he dropped the bike gloves into the river.

It was flowing quickly, after a couple of days of unseasonal rain over the Apennines to the east, and they slid straight under the bubbling surface.

Without looking back, he walked on, turned right on the far bank, and strolled on for a few hundred yards, before crossing back over on the Ponte di Mezzo.

A minute or so later, he reached a restaurant with a red awning and a sign which said *Il Dado del Lumière*.

There were three grey-green tables outside. Two were occupied by young couples and singles. At the third, two men were drinking coffee – a stocky blond guy in his late twenties, and an older man, who had greying, thinning hair cropped very close, and a pair of Bollé shades pushed up over his forehead.

Carr pulled off the daysack and put it on the ground next to the only empty chair.

He unzipped his leather jacket, and sat down.

The guy with the cropped hair leaned forwards.

'That seat is taken, I'm afraid,' he said, in an upper-class English drawl that irritated Carr immediately.

'Aye,' said Carr. 'By me, pal.'

The man smiled. 'May I ask your name?'

'You can ask it,' said Carr, 'but if you don't know it already, you don't need to know it. And, by the way, do Six deliberately train you fuckers to stand out like tits on a bull?'

'You seem very much as described,' said the man, with a faint smile. 'My name is Miles Hanson. I'm based in Rome, but Justin Nicholls asked me to pop down here and see a man about a dog.'

'Right,' said Carr.

'Job done?' said Hanson. 'Whatever it was.'

'Job done,' said Carr.

'My instructions are to take that bag and get it back to the UK ASAP, so, if you don't mind, my young colleague here…?'

'Be my guest,' said Carr. 'You'll want these, too.'

He took the USB stick and iPhone from the pocket of his jacket, and put them on the table.

'Excellent,' said Hanson.

The blond guy next to him immediately picked up the bag, the phone, and the memory stick, and walked away without speaking.

Miles Hanson finished his coffee.

‘Well,’ he said, ‘much as I’d like to sit here and chew the fat, my secondary instructions are to get you up to Rome, so that you can catch the first flight home tomorrow morning for a debrief.’

‘Is that so?’ said Carr.

He rubbed his scarred chin and smiled at a girl at the table behind Hanson’s head.

She was dark-haired, with full lips and a fuller figure, which was barely contained in a low-cut black dress, and now she smiled at him briefly before looking shyly away.

He turned to Miles Hanson.

‘Nah,’ he said. ‘I’m in no rush. You toddle off, pal. I’m going to stick around, have something to eat, and see the sights.’

# ACKNOWLEDGEMENTS

Thanks to my wife who keeps me on the straight and narrow, your counsel is invaluable.

Thanks also to my agent Jonathan Lloyd and all the team at Curtis Brown for their support and guidance, and to all at HarperCollins for their hard work and dedication.

Finally thanks to my friends and former comrades from the Parachute Regiment and 22nd Special Air Service who have helped me along the way, no names but you all know who you are. It's not the critic who counts…

ONE PLACE. MANY STORIES

Bold, innovative and
empowering publishing.

FOLLOW US ON:

@HQStories